PRAISE FOR *THE PATTERN ARTIST*

"*The Pattern Artist* is a compelling story of the human spirit's longings and dreams, written with Nancy's usual excellence that I've enjoyed in her other books. The character travels from potential to purpose as she journeys through uncertainty, courage, and faith. . . . Nancy never disappoints with her stories. She's an excellent storyteller whose intriguing characters delight, teach, and entertain."

—Yvonne Lehman, author of 57 novels
including *Hearts that Survive—A Novel of the Titanic*

"*The Pattern Artist* kept me reading long into the night. When I should have been sleeping I couldn't resist turning the next page to see what would happen next. This book is filled with fascinating twists that intersect with actual historical events of the time. Altogether one of the best books I've read this year!"

—Hannah Alexander, author of The Healing Touch series

"Rich in historical detail and compelling characters, Nancy Moser's *The Pattern Artist* takes readers into the fascinating life of a young immigrant woman who attempts to find love as she forges a new life in the world of fashion and design. It's a sweeping, strong story that you won't put down until you've read the final page."

—Judith Miller, award-winning author of the Refined by Love series

"Delightful! *The Pattern Artist* is a story of determination through adversity, a plucky heroine with an expert eye for New York fashion, and an inspiring message that it's never too late to get out there and chase a dream."

—Kristy Cambron, award-winning author of
The Illusionist's Apprentice and the Hidden Masterpiece series

"The romance, intrigue, and rich historical detail of *The Pattern Artist* create a mesmerizing novel that grabbed me from the first page and never let go. Moser's storytelling ability is second to none, and her novels are on my must-read l̶ Hi̶

…rary ueberry Barrens
ope Beach series
2017.

THE
PATTERN
ARTIST

NANCY MOSER

SHILOH RUN  PRESS

An Imprint of Barbour Publishing, Inc.

Print ISBN 978-1-63409-792-5

eBook Editions:
Adobe Digital Edition (.epub) 978-1-63409-794-9
Kindle and MobiPocket Edition (.prc) 978-1-63409-793-2

All scripture quotations are taken from the King James Version of the Bible.

This book is a work of fiction. Names, characters, places, and incidents are either products of the author's imagination or used fictitiously. Any similarity to actual people, organizations, and/or events is purely coincidental.

Cover design: Faceout Studio, www.faceoutstudio.com

Published in association with the Books & Such Literary Management, Janet Kobobel Grant, 52 Mission Circle, Suite 122, PMB 170, Santa Rosa, California 95409-5370, www.booksandsuch.com

Published by Shiloh Run Press, an imprint of Barbour Publishing, Inc., P.O. Box 719, Uhrichsville, Ohio 44683, www.barbourbooks.com

Our mission is to publish and distribute inspirational products offering exceptional value and biblical encouragement to the masses.

ecpa Member of the
Evangelical Christian
Publishers Association

Printed in the United States of America.

To my mother, Marge Young
Thank you for teaching me how to sew
and be creative.

CHAPTER ONE

1911
New York City

A nnie Wood! I demand you wipe that ridiculous smile off your face. Immediately."

Annie yanked her gaze away from the view out of the carriage and pressed a hand across her mouth to erase the offending smile.

But as soon as the attempt was made, she knew it was impossible. The grin returned, as did her gumption. She addressed her accuser sitting across from her. "But Miss Miller, how can any of you *not* smile? We are in New York City! We are in America!"

The lady's maid sighed with her entire body, the shoulders of her black coat rising and falling with the dramatic disdain she seemed to save for Annie. She granted the street a patronizing glance. "It's a big city. Nothing more, nothing less."

"Looks like London," said the younger lady's maid, Miss Dougard.

Miss Miller allowed herself two glances. "A city's a city."

If Annie could have done so without consequence, she would have made them suffer her own disdain by rolling her eyes. Instead she said, "If you'll pardon my directness, how can you be so indifferent? We've just crossed an ocean. We're in a foreign land, another country."

"Hmm," Miss Dougard said. "I much prefer France."

"Italy is the country of true enlightenment," Miss Miller added.

Show-offs. For they *had* traveled with the Kidds to many far-off places.

But Annie could play this game. "I happen to prefer China."

She earned their attention. "When have you—?"

"I haven't, in body. But I *have* visited China in my mind. Multiple times. Multitudious times."

"Multitudious is not a word."

Annie rearranged her drawstring purse on her lap. "I am excited to be here because I've never traveled five miles beyond the village. Even when the Kidds travel to London for the social season I'm left behind at Crompton Hall."

Miss Miller smoothed a gloved hand against her skirt. "You wouldn't be along on this trip, excepting I knew her ladyship would get seasick."

What?

Miss Miller's left eyebrow rose. "Don't look surprised, girl. Even though you're traveling with the two of us, you are still just a housemaid, here to do our bidding as much as the family's."

Annie was tempted to let loose with an indignant *"I am not 'just' anything."* What about all the special sewing and handwork she did for the viscountess and her daughter? She had assumed *they* wanted her along because of her talent.

"Pouting does not become you," Miss Miller said.

Annie pulled her lower lip back where it belonged, hating that they'd witnessed her pain. Searching for a comeback, she bought time by yawning as if their assessment of her position meant little. Then she had it: "Considering her ladyship kept the contents of her stomach contained on the voyage, is it fair to assume my duties are now over? Am I free to enjoy myself at the Friesens'?"

"Don't be daft," Miss Dougard said.

"Or impertinent," Miss Miller added. She flashed a look at Annie over her spectacles. "There will be chamber pots aplenty wherever you go, Annie Wood."

Annie felt her cheeks grow hot. *Under* housemaids had the burden of emptying chamber pots. As an upper housemaid Annie claimed cleaner duties that involved changing the linens and dusting the fine bric-a-brac that couldn't be entrusted to lower maids.

Except on the ship, when she *had* endured the wretched pot duty.

She drew in a deep breath, willing her anger to dissipate. As it waned, her determination grew deeper roots. Someday she'd rise high enough in the household that the Misses wouldn't dare make such a comment.

Someday she'd be their equal.

Until that day. . . Annie revived her smile and returned her attention to the city passing by. She was in America, and she was not going to let anyone dampen her pleasure. No one in her family had ever even hoped to travel so far. When she'd told her parents about her opportunity, they'd scoffed. *"Who would want to go there?"* She should have anticipated their reaction but refused to let their naysaying ruin the adventure. *She* wanted to go to America. She wanted to experience *everything.* If they were content to live in the cottage where Ma was born, taking in laundry or doing odd jobs to get by, let them. Annie had dreams.

The progress of the carriage was slow amid the teeming streets. On the ship, Annie had been astounded at the number of people gathered in one place. That number was a mere handful compared to the throngs capturing the streets of New York City. Everyone was going somewhere, in the midst of amazing missions. "They're so alive," Annie said, mostly to herself.

Miss Miller allowed herself a quick glance. "They look like ants rushing about, dizzy over a bread crumb. They don't realize life is ready to squash them. Like this. . ." She pressed her thumb against her knee and gave it a maniacal twist.

"Excuse me, ma'am, but if not for those busy ants, who would have built these enormous buildings? Who would grow the food that will be in abundance at dinner tonight? Who would do *all* the work a day requires? And if the truth be told, are *we* not ants, doing our work for the Kidds?"

The wrinkles in Miss Miller's face deepened. "I am not an ant!"

"Nor am I." Miss Dougard flipped a hand at the window. "If you can't see the difference between those of us who serve with dignity and those. . . those. . ."

"People who also work very hard?" Annie offered.

Miss Miller hovered a finger in the air between them. "Never group the two of us with laborers who toil."

Two of us. Not three.

"*We* do not toil," Miss Miller said.

"Never toil," Miss Dougard said.

Although Annie knew she should nod and let it go, she heard herself say, "I agree."

The women blinked, and Annie changed the subject before they could dissect her full meaning. "Do you think the Friesen home is much farther?"

As those who did *not* toil discussed the correct answer, Annie let herself enjoy the sight of others like herself who did.

⌒⌒

The two carriages—the one carrying the servants and the lead one transporting Lady Newley and her daughter, Miss Henrietta—parted ways when they reached the Friesen mansion as if a line of demarcation was drawn on the cobblestones dividing "them" and "us." The mistress waiting at the front entry for "them" was a distant cousin of Lady Newley's husband who'd married an American. Annie wasn't sure how Mr. Friesen had obtained his money but had overheard gossip back home that he *and* his wealth were uncouth and *nouveau riche*. Apparently new money was vulgar. Annie didn't see it. Didn't new money spend the same as old? From what she'd seen back home, old money had a hard time sustaining itself century after century. New was good. New was exhilarating. New was very American.

Annie set thoughts of the family aside when the servants' carriage stopped at the destination for "us." They were greeted by the mansion's staff, who offered a quick hello before everyone focused on the unloading and dispersing of the multitudious—she still enjoyed the word—Kidd family luggage. The two Misses did the pointing, and soon there were two stacks of large trunks and satchels, and one lesser one comprising the luggage of the three servants. The Friesen staff were swiftly organized and so began the hauling from the basement to the floor that held the family's bedrooms.

Annie waited for her traveling companions to assist with their personal luggage, but they made a quick escape into the house, chatting with the housekeeper, the butler, and various others who were their equals.

"They abandoned you," said a lad of twelve or thirteen who had helped with the unloading.

"They do that. I believe *I* am but baggage to them."

He laughed. "A steamer trunk or a carpetbag?"

"Definitely a carpetbag in hopes of becoming a grand trunk with brass fittings."

The boy swept a hand through a thick shock of wheat-colored hair. "I'm Danny. I'm the hall boy and do-whatever-they-don't-want-to-do boy."

She admired his pluck. "I'm Annie, an upper housemaid and do-whatever-they-don't-want-to-do girl."

"No one can call us lazy."

"But they might call us crazy."

He made his eyes grow too large and wiggled his hands by his face. "I won't tell if you won't."

She raised her right hand. "It will be our secret."

He nodded toward the luggage. "It's time to do whatever they didn't want to do. Tell me whose bag is whose."

Annie did so and was about to take charge of her own small satchel when Miss Miller appeared at the door leading inside. "Annie! Get in here. There's unpacking to be done."

"Coming." She gave the boy her thanks and rushed inside.

"See you at dinner, Whatever-girl," Danny called after her.

How unexpected that her first friend in America was a plucky boy.

Annie unwrapped the tissue paper that encased Miss Henrietta's wardrobe and carefully lifted each dress out of the trunk and placed it on a hanger. Even if her ladyship took little notice, Annie recognized each costume as a vivid illustration of fashion—fashion Annie was lucky enough to touch and appreciate, alter and mend.

But never wear.

This limitation didn't bother her. Everyone was born into a certain position. Even in the animal kingdom a cardinal was born to be with other cardinals and a sparrow with fellow sparrows. Both shared the same overarching category, and both were content with their situation—or if not content, accepting of it.

As the daughter of a laundress and a ne'er-do-well who was usually half-rats with drink, Annie held no aspirations to be a countess or a queen. Being a lady's maid to such a woman was ambition enough. *Order above all* was a notable and noted English tradition. Although she was intrigued by the idea of American freedom, it seemed a bit chaotic in its implementation. There was strength in knowing what was what and who was who. Or was it whom?

Annie worked very hard to speak and think as if she were educated, even though she was mostly self-taught. Her cause was aided by being a good mimic. She paid close attention when those of higher status spoke. Listening well was her school. To graduate would allow her to move up in the world.

She would be ready when the door of opportunity opened.

Her thoughts were interrupted by Miss Henrietta as she rose from her dressing table, her hair freshened to go down for tea. She was assisted by Miss Dougard, whose black dress was a jarring swath against the sage-green silk that adorned every surface of the bedroom from wall to ottoman.

"I do hope this dress isn't too tight," Miss Henrietta said, using the pinched voice that signaled she was readying to hold her breath.

Miss Dougard glanced at Annie, and they shared the knowledge that Annie had recently—and not for the first time—let out the seams of the robin-blue afternoon dress. It was well known that the Kidds' only daughter had a tendency to overly delight in her scones and clotted cream. Annie had even overheard the Misses talking about their last trip to the fashion houses in Paris, where they'd given instructions that the seam allowances be extra generous to allow for future alterations.

Speaking of, Annie noted that the color of the let-out area along the newest altered seam differed ever so slightly from the rest of the dress, but she doubted anyone else would notice if they weren't spotting for it.

With an intake of breath on Miss Henrietta's part, the dress was put on and the hooks and eyes secured. Only then did she let out the breath, hesitate a moment, and smile. "I must be losing weight."

Miss Dougard did not respond but secured the clasp of a moonstone choker around the young lady's neck. The ensemble complete, Miss Henrietta headed to the door. "I wish to wear my rose chiffon for dinner. I forgot to mention before we left home, but the beading under the arms is quite abrasive."

"I'll see to it, miss," Miss Dougard said with a nod.

Annie nodded, her eyes downcast. As soon as their mistress was gone, Miss Dougard scanned the room—which was littered with clothes. "That girl is as fickle as a bee buzzing from flower to flower." She retrieved a mauve dress of faille silk, put it on a hanger, and handed it to Annie. "When the hooks on the wall are filled, use the few in the armoire."

There weren't enough hangers. There weren't enough hooks. It was clear six weeks' worth of clothing that would provide Miss Henrietta at least three changes a day would fill the lush bedroom to overflowing. "I wish we had a dressing room like we have back home," Miss Dougard said.

"At least it isn't winter," Annie said.

"Why would you wish that—other than the obvious fact that no one likes the cold?"

"Winter clothes would be bulkier and heavier than these—and there would be more layers to let out."

Miss Dougard's laugh renewed Annie's feeling that someday, when Annie was also a lady's maid, they might be friends.

Their work was interrupted when Miss Miller entered. She inspected the room with a single glance then said, "Miss Dougard, come. It's time for tea in the servants' hall."

"But Miss Henrietta asked that some beads be adjusted in her evening dress and—"

Miss Miller waved away her concern and said to Annie, "See to it, girl."

Annie expected as much. "I'll get to it right after tea."

"You'll get to it now. And you still have unpacking to do in this room *and* Lady Newley's."

But she was famished. Annie hadn't had a thing to eat since this morning on the ship.

"Don't give me that plaintive look. Work comes before pleasure. I'll have one of the under maids bring you something. The unpacking and mending must take precedence."

"Yes, Miss Miller."

Miss Dougard gave Annie a sympathetic look but showed her true allegiance by leaving for tea without fighting on her behalf.

The benefit of their departure was a chance to sit down. Annie fell into a brocade chair near the fireplace and closed her eyes. With all the family occupied on the ground floor and all the servants in the basement, the lone sound was the *ticktock* of the mantel clock.

Annie hadn't enjoyed silence since they'd left England. On the ship they'd endured the constant undulating pulse of the engine. Now she could only hear the occasional horse or automobile going by outside. The wide avenue in front of the Friesen mansion was a world away from the chaotic streets they'd passed through earlier.

Her mind raced, wanting to take advantage of the quiet, wanting to land on a peaceful thought that would offer rest. But in its racing it created an inner racket of to-dos and should-dos until Annie had no choice but to sit upright and address it. *Yes, yes. To work.*

She decided the unpacking should be attended to first, as there would be large heapings of trouble if she was found altering the dress when the bedrooms were in disarray. Once Miss Henrietta's belongings were in place, Annie moved to the bedroom of the viscountess. It was larger than the daughter's and had a small alcove assigned as a closet. There were only two gowns hung up, so Annie set to work. She was just about to move her ladyship's underthings from trunk to bureau when there was a knock. "Come in."

Danny appeared in the doorway holding a tray. "Tea is served, milady."

She laughed and curtsied then pointed to a table next to a chair. "Over there, if you please."

He set it down, and she saw it was indeed a pot of tea and three biscuits. The sight of them ignited her hunger and she fell into a chair. "You are a godsend." She poured a cup then wolfed down two of the biscuits in short fashion. Annie noticed the boy was still standing and had the most enjoyable twinkle in his eye. "Thank you for bringing me the tea, Danny—and the biscuits." When he didn't make a motion to move, she said, "Dare you sit with me a minute?"

"I'm always up for a dare." He claimed a seat. "And over here, they're called cookies."

Annie acknowledged the bit of information with a nod. "Did you miss your tea to bring me mine?"

"I volunteered." He stretched out on the chair enough for his hand to reach deep into his pocket. He pulled out his own three cookies. "But don't worry a smudge about me. I never miss a chance to eat."

"You sound like my little brother," Annie said. Her thoughts clouded. "You remind me a lot of Alfred. He was just your age. . . ."

"Was?"

"He died."

"Sorry," the boy said through a mouthful of biscuit. Cookie. "What'd he die of?"

"His appendix burst."

"Sounds awful. Were you close?"

"We were. But let's talk about happier things."

"I'll do my best." Danny stuffed a cookie in his mouth, tried to talk, but ended up coughing. Crumbs spurted all over the carpet. Annie offered him some tea, and as soon as he was in control, he knelt on the floor to pick up the crumbs. "How long have you worked for the Kidds?"

"Five years. When I was fourteen I got a job at Crompton Hall. Ma and Pa didn't approve, but I did it anyway."

"Why wouldn't they approve? Being in service is a good thing—if there's no other thing, that is."

"There wasn't any other thing," Annie said. "My parents were always complaining about what they didn't have and how life wasn't fair. It was always someone else's fault. If the hen laid two extra eggs they complained it wasn't three." She took a breath. "I grew weary of it. I wanted to prove to them that there was more to be had if a person went after it."

"I'm betting they were proud of you."

She smoothed her skirt, as if making the fabric nice would make her memories the same. "They said I was nutters to try."

"But working for a highborn family like the Kidds. . .that's something."

"They didn't think of it that way." Annie remembered an incident to illustrate her mother's disdain for all those who *had* what she didn't. "One time the Kidds drove by in a fine carriage and everyone in the village stopped what they were doing and bowed and tipped their hats and such. Ma got peeved about it and said it didn't seem fair, them having everything and us having next to nothing." Annie adopted her mother's voice. "'I'd like to see them wash clothes or mend a fence.' But I saw it differently. I said it was good the Kidds didn't do those tasks, because it meant they had to pay us to do them. We had jobs because of them."

"What'd she say to that?"

"She said, 'Whose side are you on?'" Annie sighed. "I suppose my parents are one of the reasons I want to be a lady's maid. Maybe then they'll be proud of me."

"But you're not a lady's maid."

"Not yet."

"Have the Kidds said you can rise up someday?"

"They implied it."

"But you're just a housemaid."

He was squashing her dream, and she didn't like it. "I came in as an under housemaid just to get my foot in. And now I'm an upper. I worked hard to earn that title."

"But you're still just a housemaid."

"This from a hall boy?"

Danny fell back in his chair and popped a handful of crumbs into his mouth. "I'm not going to be a hall boy forever."

I would hope not. "What are you to be, then?"

"An adventurer."

She couldn't help but smile. "Do you have any specific adventure in mind?"

"I'm open to whatever comes my way. I refuse to jiggy up my life by making hard 'n' fast plans."

"You're a chancer." When he gave her an odd look, she explained, "You take risks."

"That's me. Wild and free. Free in spirit now, and free in body eventually."

"So you *do* have a plan."

He hopped to his feet, raising his right fist to the sky. "I plan to be deliriously happy!"

"You make *me* happy. You make me laugh."

He turned his declaration into a bow. "Then the main task of my day is successfully completed."

Task completed…Annie remembered all the tasks yet to complete. She drank the rest of her tea, put a cookie in her apron pocket, and handed Danny the tray. "I have to get back to work." As he headed to the door, she asked, "By the way, where did you take my satchel? Where is my room?"

"In the attic, milady. Where all captive princesses reside."

She returned to her work, feeling rejuvenated by the food and the friendship.

❦

The unpacking was complete, the alterations to Miss Henrietta's dress finished, and the dress worn to dinner. While the Kidds and Friesens enjoyed an after-dinner brandy in the drawing room, the servants had a short window of time for their own supper.

Upon seeing the bowls of beef, potatoes, beans, and bread that were spread upon the dinner table in the servants' hall, Annie's stomach growled loudly.

A footman standing close by grinned. "That's pleasant."

"I apologize for my stomach's anticipation."

He leaned close—too close—and whispered. "If you need anything, you call me. Grasston's the name. Got it, pretty filly?"

She got it. And rejected it. There was something about Grasston that made her want to be wherever he was not.

Annie waited to be told where to sit. At home there was a distinct seating chart, with the butler at the head, the housekeeper to his right, and the earl's valet, the lady's maids, and the first footmen next, followed through the ranks, ending with the kitchen maids and hall boy. Yet surely in democratic America, things would be different.

"You sit here, Miss Wood," instructed the housekeeper as she walked past Annie's seat to the head of the table, where she sat. . .to the right of the butler.

So much for democracy.

Annie settled in among the other housemaids and watched as the Misses took their places of honor at the other end. The situation made her feel oddly deflated. Hadn't America fought against the British to gain their freedom? Why copy what *was* when you had the chance to create something new and better?

When all were settled, the butler stood. "We'd like to welcome our visitors, Miss Miller, Miss Dougard, and. . ." His eyes scanned the table for Annie. "And their helper, Miss. . ."

"Miss Wood, sir," piped Danny.

"Yes, Mr. Dalking. I knew that." The butler nodded at Annie. "Miss Wood. You are also welcome."

She nodded, pleased at the extra attention—though with it came a crease between Miss Miller's eyes.

"Very well, then," the butler said. "Let us give thanks."

As he led them in prayer, Annie caught Danny's eye, mouthed *Thank you*, and received a wink in return.

❦

If Annie could have climbed the stairs to the attic with her eyes closed, she would have done so. Every inch of her body ached and begged for sleep. If the steps weren't so narrow and steep, she might have considered curling up right there.

But she didn't dare close her eyes, for the stairs were shadowed and the upper landing scowled in darkness. She had searched for a light switch at the bottom of the stairs but had found none. Which was surprising. She accepted sporadic electrical upgrades back at the Kidds' Crompton Hall that had been built in the 1700s, but she'd expected everything to be modern here.

When a figure appeared on the landing above, Annie nearly fell backward.

"So sorry," the girl said. "I didn't mean to scare you." She held an oil lamp high. The odd shadows made her face appear years older than the young tenor of her voice. "I heard you coming. Sorry there's no electricity up here. Guess they didn't think those of us in the attic were worthy of the expense."

"Us?"

"Just me anymore. They've taken to using the rest of the rooms for storage. Come on, I'll show you to our room."

Our room? Annie didn't even have her own room?

"I'm Iris. I saw you at dinner. I'm Danny's older sister. You're Miss Wood, yes?"

"Annie." She remembered seeing the towheaded girl, but they hadn't spoken. As expected, supper conversation had been dominated by the butler, the Misses, and their American counterparts.

Annie leaned against the wall. "If you don't mind. I'm knackered." She nodded toward the attic.

" 'Course. Silly me."

Annie followed Iris to the first room on the right. It was like entering a cave. When Iris set the lamp on a dresser, it did little to improve Annie's first impression.

"We do have us a window," Iris said, displaying the curtained panes as though the darkness outside would benefit the darkness within. " 'Course it ices in winter something awful, so I cover it with a quilt, but in summertime I'd suffocate without it."

Sounds lovely.

Iris pointed to Annie's satchel sitting against the wall. "I didn't look inside. I promise."

"Nothing to see," Annie said as she moved the satchel to the only chair. She pulled out her nightgown.

"I emptied two hooks for you."

Annie hung up her one day dress and her formal uniform. She looked around for a washstand.

"Sorry. There's no water up here, neither. We have to share the bath with the female servants one floor down. But there is a pot." From beneath the bed Iris pulled out a chamber pot with a nicked rim.

All the comforts of home.

Needing sleep more than modesty, Annie began to undress. She shook out the uniform she'd been wearing since. . .had they only arrived today? It seemed weeks had passed since they'd left the ship.

Iris also began to undress and hung her uniform on a hook behind the door. "At least it's quiet up here."

That it was. Too quiet and very different from the quiet she'd enjoyed earlier in the day. Here in the dark attic the silence surrounded her like an ominous fog. "It's like we could be forgotten."

"They shan't forget us long. Not when they wake up and there's pots to empty and grates to sweep."

Annie decided to forgo washing her face, and she removed her corset, taking a full breath for the first time all day. She let the folds of her nightgown fall over her like a familiar shroud. "I'm glad I don't have housecleaning duties while I'm here. I'm assisting Miss Miller and Miss Dougard."

"How do you assist them?"

"I sew and mend for both the viscountess and Miss Henrietta."

"Ain't that a task for the lady's maids?"

"They're not very good at it. And I don't mind because it's making me indispensable and shows my mistresses that I can be a lady's maid, too."

"They'll let you do that? Rise up from housemaid to lady's?"

Annie slipped between the sheets and was grateful she didn't have to share a pillow. "Miss Miller is over sixty. I've heard her talk about giving it up, and then Miss Dougard will rise from serving the daughter to the mother, leaving a space for me. At least I'm hoping that's how it will work."

"Hmm." Iris sounded skeptical.

"Miss Miller is always complaining about the stairs and talks about going to live with a sister in Brighton. I'm not going to be a housemaid forever."

Iris stood at her side of the narrow bed and braided her hair across her right shoulder. "I'm not, either."

"Do you want to be a lady's maid, too?"

"Not me. This world is too small, and I'm seventeen already. I want to work where I can meet people. I want to work in a shop." She exploded the *p* with special emphasis.

Annie thought of the tiny shops in the village of Summerfield back home. None held any appeal. "What kind of shop?"

"It don't matter to me, as long as I don't have to clean it." Iris pointed to the lamp. "Ready?"

Darkness swallowed the room.

Iris climbed into bed. When their hips touched they both moved an inch toward the edge. " 'Night," Iris said.

Yes, it was.

CHAPTER TWO

The preacher's sermon echoed through the grand cathedral like the voice of God coming down from the heavens. Annie let her gaze move upward to the grandiose altar area with its brilliant stained-glass windows and intricately carved pulpit. The vaulted beams overhead captured the sounds of the service and returned them tenfold. Surely God lived in such a place. Their small country church back in England could fit inside this cathedral four times over. But as in England, the Kidds sat up front with the Friesens and other wealthy New Yorkers, while their servants sat in the back rows. Was the preacher talking to them first and the servants second? Or did his words rise toward God and the rafters, wrapping around them all equally?

Suddenly the preacher's voice echoed loudly through the sanctuary. "Praise, O ye servants of the Lord, praise the name of the Lord! From the rising of the sun unto the going down of the same the Lord's name is to be praised!'"

Danny leaned close. "Maybe after we get our work done."

He received a shush from the housekeeper farther down in the pew. Yet his words rang true. The servants of the Friesens and the Kidds were up with the rising of the sun and worked until it set—if not long into the darkness. It was a daily burden. The preacher was saying that the Lord's name was to be praised during all that? Annie had to admit she didn't think much about God during the day. She said her prayers at night and had done her share of praising Him on the trip to New York, but as the to-dos of the day demanded her attention, thoughts of God seemed very far away.

The preacher finished, and the massive organ played the introduction to the final hymn. The congregation stood and they began to sing together: "'Take my life and let it be consecrated, Lord, to Thee. Take my moments and my days, Let them flow in endless praise. . . .'"

Praise. There it was again.

After finishing the midday meal, Annie stood on the basement stairs, staring out the small window on the landing. Rain pelted the glass.

"What's wrong?" Danny asked, as he and Iris came close.

"We have a free afternoon, but it's pouring. I hoped to see some of the city. I haven't been outside this house other than church this morning."

Brother and sister exchanged a glance and a grin. Then Iris took Annie's hand. "Follow us."

Annie expected them to detour on the main level, perhaps to some back covered stoop where they could bemoan the rain. Instead Iris led Annie up two more flights, to the attic. Annie hung back. "I'm sorry, but I don't want to spend the day up in our room. There's barely enough space to move around and—"

At the landing Danny edged past her and headed down the narrow attic hall. He swung open a door and stood aside, sweeping an arm to invite them in. "Enter, ladies!"

Iris went in first, running to a row of three dormer windows. "Welcome."

Annie walked through an aisle created from discarded furniture and trunks. Near the window she discovered a space hollowed out among the Friesens' discards, with two chairs framing a table, an oil lamp, a scattering of books, and an island of cushions, pillows, and coverlets on the floor. "What is all this?"

Danny flopped onto the cushions and immediately adjusted one under his head. "It's our hideaway."

Iris pointed to a chair and sat in the other one. "It was Danny's doing. One Sunday afternoon he got me exploring the storerooms up here, and we had the idea of making a place for us to spend our free time."

Annie scanned the room, which was larger by two than the bedroom she shared with Iris. "Why don't they let us have this room as ours and put their leftovers in our room?"

"Their things would never fit," Iris said. She retrieved three books. "And look at these: *Robinson Crusoe*, *Pride and Prejudice*, and *The Three Musketeers*."

"The last one's my favorite," Danny said. "Just like us. We're the Three Musketeers. All for one and one for all!"

Annie leafed through the pages and looked at the spines. They were fine editions. "Where did you get these?"

"I borrowed them from the master's library. He'll never miss 'em."

"And if he does?"

Danny shook his head. "Nobody ever comes up here. This is the castoff room, right, bug?"

Iris nodded.

His term of endearment made Annie ask, "Why 'bug'?"

Iris answered. "Cuz I hate 'em. Can't stand the crawly things and how they crunch when you step on 'em."

Annie laughed. "Brothers do like to pester, don't they?"

Danny winked at his sister. "I wouldn't pester you if I didn't love you." He looked to Annie. "Did your brother pester you?"

She thought a minute. "He used to hide my hairbrush."

"Any reason?"

"Because *he* always got in trouble for not combing his hair, he was such a yob, wanting me to get in trouble with him."

"I'll have to remember the brush thing," Danny said.

"No, you don't!"

Annie spotted a row of gilt-edged chairs, stacked two each. "You say this is the castoff room, but those chairs are posh."

"They were posh enough until Mrs. Friesen decided to redo the dining room last year."

It seemed like such a waste, yet who was she to complain? The Friesens' fickleness made for a fabulous nest among the rafters.

She eyed Danny's makeshift bed. "Maybe I could sleep in here so we wouldn't have to share a bed."

"We don't dare," Iris said. "If someone came for you in our room and you weren't there. . . We don't want anyone to ever find out about this room. It's our secret."

"A secret you shared with me."

Danny sat upright. "I do believe you've proved yourself trustworthy."

"And how have I done that?"

Danny moved to the window and pressed his hand against the glass as if challenging the raindrops to touch him. "You want something *more*. Just like us."

She remembered. "A shopgirl, an adventurer, and a lady's maid."

Danny wrinkled his nose. "Your dream is too small. At least Iris and I want to be something besides a servant."

Servants. . . "Did you hear the preacher talk about being servants of the Lord?"

"Sure. Getting up early and working late." Danny huffed against the pane then wrote his name in the fog.

"It's got to mean more than that. He was talking about it for everyone, not just us."

"The Friesens being servants? I don't think so." Danny rubbed the condensation off the window with his sleeve.

"God is their master just like they are ours."

He shook his head. "Too many masters."

Iris took her turn on the pile of cushions, not seeming to mind that her calves showed beneath her jumble of skirt and petticoat. "Being God's servants sounds high and good, but surely there's more for us than emptying chamber pots, or keeping the brass shining, or scrubbing a tub. None of those things sound like they're God's orders for us. At least I hope not."

Danny lifted his arm toward the sky and proclaimed, "I will strike you down for that, Iris Dalking! How dare you question Me!"

"Sorry, Lord," Iris said. "I know I shouldn't complain about what we do, and how hard it is. After all, God worked hard creating the world and all that."

Annie smiled. "And all that."

"But our work does get old, boring, and pointless. We do the chores then have to do them again the next day. A circle of chores that never ends."

"Don't you think there are repetitive tasks working in a shop?"

"Of course. But stocking shelves and getting to be around pretty things. . . and every day new customers will come in. That won't be boring at all."

Annie moved to the window next to Danny's, and Iris joined them at the third window. They could see the mansion across the street but were up too high to view the street below, or much of anything else beyond the roof and a few chimneys. "I would so like to see New York while I'm here."

"Next Sunday," Danny said. "I promise." He huffed on the pane again and wrote his name a second time. "See? I give you my signature, now you give me yours."

Annie did the same on her pane, and Iris followed suit.

"As I said, we're the Three Musketeers," Danny said.

They laughed together as their names faded away.

❧

Miss Henrietta stood before the full-length mirror in her room as Miss Dougard attempted to fasten the hooks at the back of the lavender day dress. There was a good half-inch gap between hook and eye. After grunting and groaning, Miss Dougard gave up. "Perhaps the blue lawn?"

"I want this dress. I want to wear my straw hat with the lilac sprigs, so it has to be this dress." Miss Henrietta nodded to Annie. "You're a strong girl, you try."

Miss Dougard stepped away with a "you have a go" look. Annie took a fortifying breath then realized how insulting that might have seemed to her mistress. Luckily, Miss Henrietta didn't seem to notice.

Minding the impossible gap, and knowing there wasn't time to remove the bodice and tighten the already tight corset, Annie got an idea. "Would you please try to make your shoulder blades touch, miss?"

"What?"

"Put your shoulders back as far as they will go."

Her mistress thrust her ample chest forward and did as she was told. "There now," Annie said. "Hold that." She hurriedly fastened the hooks. The one at the waistline was the most difficult, but even it was secured. "Done! You can relax. Carefully, please."

Miss Henrietta slowly drew her shoulders forward. The hooks and eyes strained but held. She turned to face Annie. "Well done! Thank you. Now for the hat."

Annie assisted Miss Dougard by holding the hat pins. It was a lovely hat, so she could understand why her mistress wished to wear it to the tea at Mrs. Belmont's. Annie chastised herself for not checking the fit of the lavender dress before they sailed for New York.

For there was still a problem. While seated, Miss Henrietta's bosom became the focus of her presence, as it was pressed to overflowing atop the squared neckline. The lace inset leading to the high collar strained against it. Annie vowed to alter the dress after this day's wearing was done so it would be ready the next time.

"I'll need my reticule and my shawl," Miss Henrietta said.

Annie had gathered the purse when the bedroom door burst open and Lady Newley strode in. "Come, Henrietta. You are making everyone late."

With a fit and fluster, Miss Henrietta grabbed the purse from Annie and followed her mother downstairs.

"She does not look seemly," Miss Dougard said as she tidied up. "She looks like a sausage overflowing its casing."

It wasn't that awful—though nearly. "I'll take out the dress when she returns."

"I don't think there's a smidgen left in the seams. I was against her bringing that dress at all."

"Perhaps I could add a gusset in the side seams?"

Miss Dougard eyed her over her glasses. "What do you know of gussets?"

Annie wasn't sure where she'd heard the term. "It would work, would it not?"

"You have no fabric to match."

"Perhaps we could go out and get some."

"Where?"

"I don't know where, but if there's a fashion problem, it needs to be addressed. She'll want to wear the dress again."

"The fashion problem has nothing to do with the dress and much to do with the lack of self-control of the woman wearing it."

It was a cruel statement, though Annie couldn't contest it.

Suddenly she spotted the shawl draped over a chair. "She forgot her shawl!"

"Run on then. Catch them if you can."

Annie sprinted down the stairs to the front entrance where Mrs. Friesen and Lady Newley were just entering a carriage, with Miss Henrietta last in line. Annie stepped forward. "Your shawl, miss."

Henrietta smiled. "Thank you, Annie."

Annie retreated toward the door, but as she passed Grasston, the footman said, "I hope that shawl's big enough to cover the big fat hen."

Annie was so shocked she stopped to face him. "How dare you. Show some respect."

He shrugged. Annie glanced to the carriage and saw by the look on Miss Henrietta's face that she'd overheard the rude words.

If Annie could have gotten away with slapping him, she would have left a mark on his cheek.

◈

Annie was just finishing a cup of tea in the servants' hall when she heard the call bell for Miss Henrietta's room. "That's me," she said. "They must be back."

Once upstairs she rapped lightly on her mistress's door before entering, and was surprised to see that Miss Dougard was not present. "Yes, miss?"

Her mistress was still wearing her hat and had not begun to change clothes for the afternoon. She extended the shawl toward Annie. "Thank you for bringing my shawl."

"You're welcome." Annie folded it smooth. "Would you like me to help you change?"

She gave a quick shake of the head then a nod. "Yes, but first. . . I want to thank you for defending me this morning."

Annie wasn't sure what she was talking about.

"That footman?"

Ah. "Please don't take to heart anything he says. He's a bounder. From what I've seen he has the manners of a dustman—though perhaps that's offending the latter."

Miss Henrietta smiled. "Be that as it may, I know what people think of me. I'm too young to be so. . .corpulent. Mother says I'll never find a husband if I don't trim myself up."

Annie could imagine Lady Newley saying such a thing—and not kindly. Especially since *she* was still a very handsome woman.

"Many men prefer a voluptuous woman," Annie said.

Henrietta looked down at her chest. "Voluptuous is fine, but fat is not."

Annie wasn't sure what her mistress wanted from her. Unfortunately, the vast menus that would fill the family's dining fare in New York would test Miss Henrietta's willpower past its limit.

"The dress can be altered to fit."

Miss Henrietta shook her head. "I don't want any more adjustments. I want to fit into this dress—which is one of my favorites. Perhaps overhearing the footman's comments was what I needed, for it has spurred me to take action and become a better, more desirable woman."

Annie admired her attitude but was distressed regarding its core. "You do whatever you wish to feel good about yourself, miss. But know that as you are, you have much to offer any man."

Miss Henrietta looked to the floor. "You are sweet, and I appreciate your words." She moved to the dressing table and allowed Annie to remove her hat.

After the evening meal, Annie headed toward the back stairs. Suddenly Grasston grabbed her arm and dragged her into the laundry. Two women ironing sheets looked up. He put his back to them and faced Annie. She yanked her arm away. "What are you doing? Leave me alone."

"Sorry," he said under his breath so the workers wouldn't hear. "But you've made that impossible."

"What did I do to you?"

"You made Mr. Brandon give me a reprimand."

"I did no such thing."

"Someone did. I've been demoted to second footman for a week."

So the news of Grasston's nasty comments had made their way to the butler's ears. "It serves you right for being so rude. Miss Henrietta is a wonderful woman and a guest in this house."

He took a step toward her, his grin smug. "A big, fat, ugly guest."

"You are the ugly one. Ugly inside and out."

Grasston grabbed her chin and squeezed it hard. "You'd better watch out, Annie Wood. You can't hide from me." He let go of her chin then swatted her behind before exiting the room.

Annie didn't know what to do. The two washerwomen stared at her, their eyes revealing their shock and compassion. But to acknowledge what they'd seen would make it worse, so Annie left the room and fled to the safety of the hideaway.

"Here you are," Danny said as he entered their attic gathering place. "Your mistress has been ringing for you, and Miss Miller sent me to find you."

Annie sat upright on the pile of cushions. "I needed some time alone."

"Not allowed. Not before the family goes to bed. You know that."

She nodded and held out her hand. He helped her to her feet, and she smoothed her skirt and apron. "Thank you for coming to get me."

He put a gentle hand on her arm. "What happened to upset you?"

Annie shook her head and left to find Miss Miller. Telling Danny about Grasston would not better the situation.

Nothing would.

CHAPTER THREE

After breakfast, Annie noticed the butler and housekeeper talking one-on-one with Danny. The butler handed him a note and with a hand upon his shoulder and the point of his finger gave him some instruction. Danny nodded, turned to walk away, and then turned back and asked a question. Both adults looked in Annie's direction, though past her. She turned around and saw Iris at the doorway. She heard a few more mumbled words then saw Danny leave the conversation with an enormous grin on his face.

"Come on," he whispered as he passed Annie. Danny corralled his sister, and the three of them found some privacy in the basement corridor.

"Why are you grinning so?" Annie asked.

"Mr. Brandon asked me to take a message to the Franklins, and Mrs. Grimble wants me to pick up a recipe for raspberry meringue pudding from their cook."

"You get to leave?" Annie said. "Lucky bloke."

"I asked if Iris could come along and they said yes—as long as she got her chores done."

Iris kissed him on the cheek. "I'll work at double speed."

Annie was happy for them but sad she was being left behind. But then Danny said, "Can you do *your* chores at double speed, Annie?"

Hope sped through her like a breath of fresh air. "Me? You want me to go, too?"

Danny glanced down the corridor where other servants bustled about the day's chores. "Just don't say anything to the rest of them."

Annie made a locking motion at her lips. "What time should we go?"

They each took a moment to weigh their tasks. Annie was the first to speak. "The Kidds are going to a charity luncheon at one. Perhaps after they leave?"

"One fifteen, then," Danny said. "Meet at the kitchen entrance."

"Outside the kitchen entrance," Annie said. "It will increase my chances of not being noticed."

Suddenly the butler's voice echoed down the corridor. "Mr. Dalking? Miss Dalking? Have you nothing to do, because if you don't, I'm sure Mrs. Grimble can find something—"

"No, sir. Yes, sir. We're going."

Yes, they were.

⚍

Annie was torn.

Should she ask Lady Newley for permission to leave with Danny and Iris? Or should she ask Miss Miller for permission? Or...?

Miss Miller's headache determined the answer to both questions. With Miss Miller indisposed—with instructions not to be disturbed—it was up to Annie and Miss Dougard to help their two mistresses get dressed for their outing. Lady Newley was the easier of the two, as the time helping Miss Henrietta was once again consumed with getting her dresses to fit. The chance for Annie to do any asking for anything at any time never presented itself.

As soon as the ladies were on their way, Miss Dougard informed Annie she was going to take a nap and she, too, wished not to be disturbed, thus closing the final door on permission.

Permission or not, she was going.

Annie rushed up the back stairs to her room to find Iris already getting changed into her street clothes.

"Isn't this exciting?" Iris asked.

Annie wasn't sure *exciting* was the correct term for a simple errand, but she was very happy to be able to get out of the house. In a dash both girls were dressed and ready. At the last moment, Annie removed her hat. "I don't want to draw attention to myself. I'll put it on when I get outside."

"Should I go first?" Iris asked.

Perhaps. Annie let Iris leave the room and waited a short time before venturing out behind her. Her stomach was in double knots. She wasn't doing anything wrong by leaving for a short time, yet she knew she wasn't doing anything right, either. In spite of it all, she found bending the rules exhilarating.

What was it about America that made her think beyond what was into what could be?

As she approached the basement, Annie walked on her toes, slowing to check for witnesses. She heard the sound of workers in the laundry and saw a scullery maid moving from the storage closet to the kitchen. But otherwise the coast was clear. Tucking her hat beneath her arm, she slipped outside. She spotted Danny and Iris, but as she moved toward them, Grasston stepped out of the shadows.

"Well now. Who have we here?" He dropped the stub of his cigarette and ground it with his toe.

Annie ignored him, strode past, and linked arms with Iris.

"I'll see you later, Annie Wood."

She walked faster. As soon as they reached the street, Iris asked, "What did he do to you? You're practically trembling."

Danny stepped in front of the girls, stopping them. "If he hurt you in any way. . ."

The fact Danny assumed such a thing spoke volumes. "Has he hurt other girls?"

Danny's glance at Iris revealed the truth of it.

"Did he hurt you, Iris?" Annie asked.

"Not hurt me, but bothered me in a way I didn't like. At all."

Annie's ire rose. "Men like him should be stopped."

"How?" Iris asked, motioning for Danny to move so they could start walking again. "He's got the high position in the house. We don't."

"When I confronted him about Iris, he laughed at me," Danny said.

Annie wasn't surprised.

"He dared me to tell Mr. Brandon."

"Did you?"

Danny shook his head. "But when I get bigger, I'll take care of him no matter what he says. Our pa was six-foot-three, so I'll be tall like him someday."

Again Danny reminded Annie of her brother, Alfred, full of honor and high hopes.

"Enough of him," Iris said. "We have some time away, so let's enjoy it."

"Where is this house we have to go to?" Annie asked.

"A few blocks up Fifth. If we hurry and get that done, then I know a special place I want to show you."

Iris perked up. "Really, Danny? Do you think we have time to go to Macy's?"

"What's Macy's?"

Danny grinned. "Mrs. Friesen calls it 'a palace of product, pleasure, and profit.' And she's right. You have to see it."

Annie still wasn't sure what it was.

"It's a department store. Eight floors heaped with things to buy."

"But I don't have any money."

"Neither do we, but it's fun to look. Come on! We need to hurry."

❧

The three young people finished the task at the Franklins' in quick fashion and soon found their way over to Herald Square. "There it is," Iris said, as if viewing a holy relic. "Macy's."

The store loomed over the street corner, taking up more than an entire block. Windows ran the length of the building, with glorious displays of goods from iceboxes to boots to baby prams.

They stood in front of the window display of women's dresses. "Will you look at that blue dress," Annie said. "Don't you love how the lace on the bodice hangs free, making the waist look tiny? I'd add a bit of beading at the edges of the lace, though. It looks a bit raw."

"You care about the fashion of it," Iris said. "I don't care what the fashion is. I just want the chance to sell it, to be around it all day, to be around people."

"You're around people at the Friesens'," Danny said.

"I'm around other servants. I'm not around the family. They don't want to even see me, they just want to see my work."

It was a true statement. The majority of the servants were supposed to be invisible to the family they served, hence the back stairway and the careful timing of the chores so rooms were cleaned and beds were made while the family was elsewhere.

Once inside the store, all thoughts of the Friesens evaporated as the threesome entered a land of plenty. Every kind of bits and bobs were on display. They walked through wide aisles that showcased glass cases of hats, shoes, gloves, lace, fabrics, and. . .

Annie stopped to gawk at a sewing machine. "May I help you, miss?" a clerk asked.

"I'm just looking. Admiring."

"Do you sew?"

"I do, but always by hand. To have a machine. . ."

"Would you like to see how it works?"

"Yes, I would, but. . ." Annie noticed Danny and Iris motioning her to move along. "Perhaps I can come back?"

"Of course. I am always here." She handed Annie a card with her name on it. "My name is Mrs. Holmquist. Feel free to ask for me."

Annie slipped the card in her pocket. If ever she could come back, she would.

❧

There was no denying it was hard returning to the Friesens'. After experiencing a bit of New York and Macy's, Annie felt like a bird who'd jumped from the nest and learned to use its wings. She wanted to soar and explore, not return and yearn to be free again. Yet what choice did she have?

The three of them came in the back way, and Danny and Iris immediately detoured to report to Mr. Brandon regarding the message he'd had them deliver, and give Mrs. Grimble her recipe. Annie headed upstairs to her room to change back into her uniform. But as she reached the landing on the floor of the family bedrooms, she was surprised by Grasston, who popped out from a dark corner and pulled her into it. He pushed her back against a wall, angling her arm behind her. He loomed close. He smelled of cigarettes.

"You think you can come and go as you please?"

Annie glanced down the hall leading to the bedrooms and kept her voice low. "I am not beholden to you."

"They noticed you were missing. I made sure of it."

What? How dare he!

Fueled by anger, Annie pushed against him, but Grasston pinned her tightly against the wall, forcing her to turn her head to the side to avoid his warm breath on her face. He whispered in her ear. "I always wanted to taste an English tart."

He bit her earlobe. Then he stepped back, gave her a wink, and retreated downstairs—into the bowels of Hades where he belonged.

Her strength drained out of her, and Annie found the wall a necessity. Her thoughts ricocheted with the bad news that her mistresses and the Misses knew she had left without permission, the lingering memory of

Grasston's hands, and the fear it would happen again. Or worse.

She heard female voices in the hallway. Lady Newley's words rushed down the hall to her ears. "Annie is where?"

Miss Miller answered. "I have no idea, my lady. But I assure you I will find out."

Her wings clipped, Annie hurried upstairs to change into the clothes of a servant again.

She had just tied her apron when Iris came in their room, also ready to change back into her maid uniform.

"Mr. Brandon didn't say a thing about us being gone too long, so everything worked—"

"They know I left."

Iris put her coat on the hook. "How do you know they know?"

She decided not to mention Grasston—yet. "I overheard Lady Newley and Miss Miller in the hall."

Iris removed her hat and sat on the bed. "What are you going to tell them?"

"The truth. I have no feasible lie."

"What will they do to you?"

"I have no idea."

"They can't send you home. It's too far away. Can they?"

Surely such a punishment would be an overreaction. What had she done wrong except fail to ask permission?

Annie chose to check in with Miss Henrietta first. She knocked on her door and waited for permission to enter. Henrietta sat at the dressing table, removing her earrings.

"Good afternoon, miss. Did you have a pleasant time at your outing?"

Annie received a pointed stare. "Did *you*?"

Annie's insides flipped.

"The footman let us know of your absence."

Once again Annie was stunned by Grasston's gall. Yet it was best to face the issue head-on. She moved to help Henrietta with the removal of her other jewelry. "Actually, I had a very pleasant time. I haven't been out of the house except for church since we arrived."

"Really? Didn't you have Sunday afternoon free?"

"It was raining."

Miss Henrietta's nod eased Annie's nerves. Then she locked her gaze with Annie's in the mirror. "You should have asked permission."

"Agreed, miss. But both the Misses were indisposed and didn't want to be disturbed."

"Perhaps you should have left a note."

Why hadn't she thought of that? "You are right. I should have. But I thought I would be back before you returned."

"Ours *was* a shorter outing than I'd hoped it would be. But Mother seemed peeved at the way the charity work was being handled, so she wanted to come home." She stood. "It was far too dramatic. I need a nap. I don't wish to wait for Miss Dougard. Help me undress."

That task accomplished, Annie fluffed the pillows and readied an afghan as Miss Henrietta lay down. "Did you come upon anything exciting on your outing?" she asked Annie.

Annie wasn't certain she should mention where they went, as it was out of the way from their initial errand, but decided to share because surely Miss Henrietta would be interested in Macy's. "The outside windows hinted at what they had to offer. Then once inside there were thousands of items to buy, floors and floors of pretty things."

Miss Henrietta snuggled into the pillows. "You haven't been to London with us, have you? You've never seen Harrods department store."

"It has display windows and many floors?"

"It does indeed." She yawned. "The window displays entice you inside to buy. It's quite impossible not to be lured in."

"They know what they're doing with that."

"Indeed they do. Now go. But tell Miss Dougard to wake me for tea."

Annie slipped out, feeling lucky to have no consequences.

"Annie Wood!"

She spun around and found the Misses exiting Lady Newley's room. Miss Dougard had a rose-colored dress on her arm.

Annie readied herself for another scolding but put a finger to her lips. "Miss Henrietta is resting."

The three women moved away from the bedroom doors. Then Miss Miller said, "Perhaps Miss Wood is exhausted from her own excursion? It seems you like to break the rules when others take a kip."

Annie stifled a sigh but repeated her explanation and her apology. "I should have left a note. I am sorry."

"You should be. Lady Newley is quite upset by your insubordination."

"It shan't happen again." As she said the words she felt a wave of sadness. She wanted to go out again. And again. And again. On any day of the week, not their free Sunday afternoon when nothing was open. Mrs. Holmquist and the sewing machine were waiting for her.

"Here," Miss Miller said, grabbing the dress from Miss Dougard's arms. "As punishment we have some extra work for you. Add some beading to the bodice of this dress. Lady Newley has realized the fashion of Mrs. Friesen overshadows her own."

If this was punishment, Annie would gladly accept it. Sewing for the Misses was nothing new. "Where do I get the beads?"

"Come to my room. I brought a store of them from home."

Annie held the dress at arm's length. "Any special instructions?"

Miss Miller pointed to the scooped neck bodice. "Something along there, but not like the beading you did on her sage dress. Something different."

"Use your imagination," Miss Dougard said.

That was hardly punishment.

⌘

Up in the hideaway, Annie enjoyed having time alone to do the beading. While she did the work, she pondered two disparate issues: her newly born pleasure of exploring the city and her newly born fear of Grasston. As they were due to stay at the Friesens' for six weeks, she hoped for more weekday outings. To the other issue, she was wary of Grasston's unwanted attention. In the short time she'd been in residence, he'd shown a disturbing aggression that would probably get worse rather than better.

To fight back the fear, she reminded herself that he wasn't the first male who'd assumed too much and been too grabby. She might be only a maid, but she was a *maid* in the truest form of the word and planned to keep it that way. She'd known other girls who'd succumbed to temptation. Nothing good came of it. The only result was a ruination of their lives—never love. Annie wanted to fall in love someday, but not with someone who was merely handsome and charming. She wanted a man who challenged her, made her want to be more than she was alone, a true partner.

She finished the beadwork, tied off the thread, and cut it. She held the dress to inspect her work. "Lovely. As usual."

If she didn't say so herself. Yet if she didn't say it, who would?

Chapter Four

Upon hearing Mr. Brandon's chastising voice, Annie paused on the last step of the stairs leading to the basement. She didn't want to embarrass another servant by witnessing a scolding.

"Really, Mr. Grasston, this is the second time you've arrived for service without the proper gloves. I fail to understand what is so difficult about maintaining your proper uniform."

"I'm sorry, sir. I don't know what happens. I remove them to do other work and—"

"And they disappear?"

There was a pause. "They do, sir."

"Are you saying we have spirits in the house, Mr. Grasston?"

"No, sir."

"Are you accusing others of stealing your gloves?"

"Well. . ."

"Passing the blame is not acceptable. Unless you have proof that others are pilfering your gloves—which I have difficulty imagining—you must take responsibility. But know this, Mr. Grasston: I am giving you a warning. If you come on duty again without the proper gloves, I will dock your pay for a dozen pair. I believe that should rectify the matter if you cannot."

"Yes, sir."

"Very well then. You have work to do in the dining room."

In a split second, Annie realized Grasston would be using the stairs. She considered retreating upward but knew her footsteps would be heard. Best to continue down. She quickly backtracked three steps then came downstairs, passing Grasston as he started upstairs. Neither greeted each other, but after a few steps she heard him pause and felt chill bumps up her spine as she headed down the corridor. Was he wondering if she overheard?

She smiled at the thought. Let him squirm.

Then, ignoring common sense, she turned to look at him. "Lose something, Mr. Grasston?"

Only the sound of footsteps on the stairs saved her from his retort.

Or worse.

~❧~

The Kidds and the Friesens were set to attend a formal dinner, which required extra care in the ladies' toilette. Annie moved between the rooms of Miss Henrietta and Lady Newley, assisting the Misses. She was thrilled to see that Lady Newley was going to wear the dress Annie had beaded. It was some of her finest work.

When Miss Miller left her ladyship's bedroom to retrieve her jewels from the Friesens' safe, Annie was left alone with her.

Ask her how she likes the beading. Now's your chance.

"Fetch my gloves, Annie," Lady Newley said.

Annie did as she was told, but as she was buttoning the twenty buttons that edged the inner seam, Annie took a chance. "I hope the new beading on your dress pleases you, my lady?"

Lady Newley put her free hand upon the beads. "It does. Miss Miller does such fine work. I couldn't ask for a more talented lady's maid."

Miss Miller's work?

Upon hearing the words of betrayal, Annie stopped buttoning the gloves.

"Annie? Come now. Finish up."

They didn't give me credit?

Two more questions came next, ricocheting against the first. *Have they ever given me credit? Do my mistresses truly attribute all the fine detail on their dresses, all the hours and hours of work, to the Misses?*

Somehow Annie finished buttoning the gloves. But then Miss Miller came in carrying two velvet boxes of jewels and shooed Annie away. "Go on, girl. There are towels to clean up in the bath."

"And I'd like a fresh pillowcase, if you please," her mistress said.

Annie walked into the hall in a daze. They truly thought of her as a housemaid. Nothing more.

That's because you are a housemaid. Nothing more.

All her hard work learning the details and intricacies of sewing and dressmaking so she could rise to the position of lady's maid... Had she ever had a chance? Or had she created her own dream and her own scenario that had never owned any basis in fact?

Annie went into the bathroom and cleaned up the towels, wiping down the floor. Maid's work. Anger stirred inside even as her body accomplished the work. She felt like a fool who'd been duped into striving for something that was impossible. She had more chance of building a skyscraper than she did of building a life as a lady's maid.

"They shan't get away with this" became her mantra as she scrubbed the tub. By the time her work was finished and the towels were taken downstairs to the laundry, she knew what she had to do.

Annie stood outside Miss Miller's room, her heart pounding in her ears. Inner warnings that she should let the betrayal pass collided with the need for justice and the unrelenting desire for her emotions to be released.

Please, God. Help me.

Help her what? Confront Miss Miller?

For better or worse.

With a fresh breath Annie knocked on the door, her first knock more forceful than the next two.

"Yes?" Miss Miller said.

Annie stepped inside and closed the door behind her. Miss Miller sat in an easy chair, reading a book.

"If you're wanting another outing, the answer is no."

"I need to talk to you."

With a dramatic sigh, Miss Miller shut her book and removed her spectacles. "But I don't need—or wish—to talk to you. I need you to leave. I've had a hard day."

"Doing what?"

"What did you say?"

"What have you done today—or any day—that constitutes hard work?"

Miss Miller rose from her chair, the book thudding to the floor. "Leave!" she said, pointing to the door. "I insist you leave this minute."

Suddenly the door opened behind Annie, and Miss Dougard slipped in, closing the door behind her. "What's going on in here?" she whispered. "I could hear you in the hall."

"Annie was just leaving."

"I will leave as soon as I've said my piece."

"Your piece?" Miss Miller said. "You're the one in trouble."

"Not anymore." She cringed at her own word choice. It was too late to stop now. Annie drew in a breath and began. "I object to both of you taking credit for my beading work—for all the sewing work I've done for Lady Newley and Miss Henrietta. I thought they knew *I* was doing the work."

"And why would they know that?" Miss Miller asked as she retrieved her book.

It took Annie a moment to recover from shock. "Because you'd tell them. Because you wouldn't take credit for work you didn't do."

"You liked doing the work," Miss Dougard said. "You have a talent for it."

"I do like it, and I do have a talent for it," Annie said. "But that doesn't mean you should pass it off as your work." She pointed to a painting of a mountain scene on the wall. "The person who hangs the painting doesn't take credit for painting it."

"I don't like your tone."

"My tone?" She looked from one to the other, incredulous. "I did the work and deserve the credit. I did the work as training for when I become a lady's maid someday."

Miss Dougard looked at Miss Miller, and then the latter began to laugh. "You? A lady's maid?"

Miss Dougard shook her head. "Lady's maids are women of breeding and education."

"Not a girl who grew up cleaning pigpens and chicken coops."

A pit grew in Annie's stomach. "When I applied for a job at the manor house, I told them I was good at sewing."

Miss Miller was not fazed. "But you were hired as a maid. An under housemaid."

"That's the only position they had open. But they saw my potential, I know they did. There are many who apply to work with the Kidds and not all are taken."

"They are if the vicar insists on it," Miss Miller said.

"What?"

"You'd just lost your brother and your father was a known drunkard. The vicar heard you were applying for a job and strongly suggested the Kidds take you on."

The foundation of Annie's position in the household cracked. "They were impressed by my sewing ability. I brought them examples of dresses I'd made for Ma and some neighbor ladies. I told them I wanted to be a lady's maid someday."

Miss Miller chuckled. "You had nerve, that I'll give you."

"Did they tell you being a lady's maid was a possibility?" Miss Dougard asked.

Annie's mind rushed back to her interview with the housekeeper at Crompton Hall. She remembered a vague *"We'll see, child"* but nothing else. Had those few words been an attempt to humor her, nothing more? Had Annie planted her hopes on the polite patience of a housekeeper who'd been instructed to hire her out of pity? As a charity case?

Miss Dougard touched Annie's arm. "Don't feel bad about it. They hired you. People were looking after you."

Miss Miller pointed the book at her. "You should be thankful, girl. You have a job. You have a future with the Kidds."

"As what?"

Miss Miller looked taken aback, as if she didn't understand the question. "As a housemaid. It's an honorable position in an honorable house. I know dozens of girls who would fight for that honor."

The pit in Annie's stomach dug deeper. Why had she ever thought she could rise above her station? The Misses had never encouraged her. No one had.

"Go on now," Miss Miller said, opening the door. "Get up to the attic until we need your help when the ladies return home."

Miss Miller nudged Annie out the door and closed it on her heels. From the hall she heard their laughter.

She also heard the soft click of more than one other door in the servants' hallway.

Her humiliation was complete.

Annie went through the rest of the day and evening as if walking underwater, her movements slow, her gaze blurry. More than one person asked if something was wrong. She had no answer for them. For there were a thousand things wrong, yet nothing at all. Nothing that could be shared. Nothing that would matter to anyone but herself.

When it was time to retire she returned to her attic room, longing for the oblivion of sleep. She dreaded seeing Iris, for Iris would sense something was amiss, and Annie didn't want to share the details of what a fool she'd been. She remembered the words of Iris and Danny when she'd first shared her dream. *"They'll let you do that? Rise up from housemaid to lady's maid?"*

Even young Danny had known what an impossibility it was. Why hadn't Annie realized as much? She'd been dumb as a plank for not seeing the truth.

Annie got ready for bed and slid under the covers, praying for sleep to come quickly. But her mind wouldn't let her body go, reliving every horrible moment again and again.

She heard steps outside the door and quickly closed her eyes, feigning the sleep that eluded her.

Iris came in with a lamp. "Oh," she said, immediately turning down the wick.

Annie was just about to congratulate herself on her ruse when she heard Iris crying—and not just a little.

She turned over to see her. "What's wrong?"

Iris shook her head back and forth. "Nothing. Really. Go back to sleep."

Annie pushed back the covers and went to her.

Iris fell into her arms. "He's such a brute. I hate him!"

"Grasston?"

Iris nodded. "He grabbed me and. . .and rubbed up against me, and. . . I don't know why he's bothering me."

Annie led her to sit on the bed. "I'm afraid I am to blame. I've rebuffed him more than once and got him in trouble about his rude comments to Miss Henrietta. If he can't get to me, he'll go after you because he knows we're close. I'm so sorry."

Iris nodded then put a hand on her upper arm as though it was sore.

"Did he hurt you?"

"He pinched me hard."

"Let's look at it." Annie helped remove her arm from the dress sleeve, revealing two distinct red finger marks on the outside and a thumbprint on the inner arm. "It's going to leave a bruise. We should show Mrs. Grimble or Mr. Brandon."

"No!" Iris said. "Nothing will come of it. And then he'll come after me more."

"We have to do something."

"I just want to go to bed."

Annie helped her then got in on her side.

Sleep would come, but the problem remained.

CHAPTER FIVE

You must leave.

Annie sat up in bed, jarred awake by the words. Her bedroom was still dark but for the moonlight that cut a swath across the bed. Iris lay sleeping beside her, though she stirred at the alteration of the covers.

Annie took a fresh breath and blinked herself awake. Had she heard the words? They echoed in her mind as if they had been shouted.

You. Must. Leave.

Leave the Kidds?

Leave the Friesen household?

To go where?

Annie pressed a hand to her chest and made herself calm down. *God? Is this You talking? Am I really supposed to leave?*

Iris turned over and opened her eyes. "What are you doing awake?"

"I'm not sure."

"Then go back to sleep. It will be morning too soon."

She felt another prodding. "I can't sleep. And neither can you."

With a sigh Iris sat up. "What are you talking about?"

If only I knew for sure.

Needing to see if light dispelled the dream, the voice, the directive, or whatever it was, Annie lit the lamp then returned to the warmth of the covers.

"Your eyes are so bright, as if you've been lit from inside," Iris said.

"An idea has been lit. A big idea that includes you—and Danny."

Iris adjusted her pillow. "What is it?"

"It's hard to explain without sounding daft. But I was awakened by three words: *'You must leave.'*"

Iris glanced around the room. "In your dream or outside it?"

"I don't know. But they were clear enough for me to wake up."

" *'You must leave.'* Leave here?"

Annie's heart beat faster, and she said another quick prayer. *Yes, Lord?*

Receiving no nudge to tell Iris to go back to sleep, Annie continued, "Leave everything. Leave here, leave my job, leave the Kidds. Everything."

"And go where?"

"I have no idea."

"It would have been nice if the voice shared the details."

Agreed.

Now that Annie was fully awake the one idea expanded into many, like branches of a tree growing from its trunk. "The first day we met you told me you planned to leave, that you and Danny were saving up for it. You want to be a shopgirl."

"Someday."

"Then why not now? What's stopping you?"

Iris made a face, clearly thinking hard. Finally she said, "I know *here*. I don't know *there*. It's scary."

Annie felt the same fear but didn't tell Iris that. Instead she tossed the covers aside and faced her friend. "I'm going. That's why you and Danny should go, too. We'd be three instead of one. Being three would make us strong."

Iris's nod was weak.

"There's nothing for any of us here."

"What happened to becoming a lady's maid?"

Annie told her about the Misses taking credit for her work. And their derisive laughter when she confronted them. "I've been a fool, thinking I could rise up."

"So you think you could rise up out *there*?"

"Isn't America the land of opportunity?"

"To some, maybe. But for the three of us?"

Annie felt doubt threaten. She forced it away. "Why not us?"

Iris hugged her pillow. "What makes you think Mr. Brandon and Mrs. Grimble will let Danny and me go?"

"You're not going to ask."

"We're going to sneak away?"

"You can leave a note." Annie made a decision. "That's what I'm going to do."

"They'll never give us references if we leave like that."

"You want references so you can be a maid again?"

Iris bit the corner of the pillow.

"And remember Grasston. I doubt things will get better with him—for either of us."

Iris's shudder was the seal on it. They had to leave, or suffer under Grasston. Annie could probably handle him, but Iris. . .

"When do you want to go?" Iris said.

Annie let out the breath she'd been saving. "So you'll go with me?"

"If I don't go now I'll never go."

"What about Danny?"

"He'll be first out the door."

They laughed softly, knowing it was true. Then they looked at each other and sighed at the same time, which elicited another laugh. "When do we leave?" Iris asked again.

Annie made a quick decision. "Tomorrow afternoon. My ladies have a function to go to, so the Misses will take their naps."

"Will you help me write a note?"

Annie glanced at the bureau. The Friesens provided their servants paper and pencil to write to their families. She gathered a piece of paper and the Bible to support it, and together they began their farewell notes.

⬦

With their departure day upon them, the notion of revenge grew. Each hour the details were refined, culminating in this moment when Annie stood in the hall of the servants' floor, looking at the door that divided the women's bedrooms from the men's.

"Boo!"

Her heart dropped to her toes as she turned to confront Danny. "Don't do that!"

"A bit jumpy, are ya? Just three more hours and we'll be free."

"I know. But first. . ." Maybe Danny could help. "I need you to do me a favor."

"Is it dangerous?"

"It could be. If you're caught."

He grinned. "What do you want me to do?"

45

The Kidd and Friesen ladies left for the afternoon. On cue, Annie saw the Misses go off to take their naps. The coast was clear.

She slipped into Miss Henrietta's room and paused a moment to reread the note she was leaving:

Dear Miss Henrietta,

   Please share this with your mother.

   I am leaving your family's employ and am venturing out into New York City to find my new path. I am sorry to do this in such an abrupt fashion, but I have realized that as a housemaid there is no place to go, no ladder to climb. I have a stirring within me that forces me to take this drastic step. I know it is a risk, but it is a risk I must take.

   Please forgive the trouble this causes, and know that I truly appreciate your family's past kindness. Also know that I have greatly enjoyed serving you. Especially you. I wish you all the happiness in the world, Miss Henrietta, for you deserve it.

Sincerely,
Annie Wood

Annie had considered tattling on the Misses but hadn't wanted this final note to be tainted by a complaining tone. Besides, Miss Henrietta and her mother would find out soon enough that their lady's maids had no sewing talent. Being appreciative was the honorable way to leave.

She leaned the note against the dressing table mirror and closed the door behind her.

Annie was nearly through packing her few belongings when Iris came in their room, out of breath.

"Are you ready?" Iris asked.

Annie closed the clasp on the carpetbag. "I am now."

Annie helped Iris remove her uniform and put on her one shirtwaist, jacket, and a straw hat. Iris held up the apron. "I won't miss this. I vow to never wear an apron again."

Annie smiled but suffered a glimmer of dread. It might be a hard vow to keep.

"Do I leave my uniforms?" Iris asked.

"Did you pay for them?"

"No."

"Then you leave them. I had to provide mine, so I'm taking them with me. Perhaps I can alter them."

Iris carefully laid the clothes on the bed, stroking a sleeve to make it lie flat. She retrieved her note for the butler and housekeeper and placed it on top.

"Well then," she said.

Their bags packed, they looked around the room they had shared. "Our last chance to change our minds," Annie said.

Iris let out a breath. "Onward. Quickly. Before I chicken out."

⨳

The plan was to meet Danny outside the kitchen door, behind the coal bin, hopefully out of sight.

Please don't let anyone see us. Please, God.

Iris and Annie waited in an alcove in the basement until the only noise came from the kitchen—which was unfortunately near the exit.

"I'll go first," Annie said. "Wait until I give you the signal."

Iris nodded, but her eyes were frantic with worry. Annie put a hand on her arm. "It will be all right."

Hopefully.

With one last look and listen, Annie walked quickly down the corridor. Cook was busy giving directions about how to slice carrots and had her back to the doorway. A kitchen maid looked up, but Annie didn't wait to be accosted.

At the door she motioned for Iris to follow. Iris ran on tiptoes, clutching her bag to her chest. Together they exited the home and ran behind the coal bin.

"You made it," Danny said.

"So far," Iris said. "Let's go before someone sees us. I feel like ants are crawling up my spine."

Annie led the way toward the street. She turned around and whispered, "Walk quickly. Don't run."

Somehow they managed to do so and turned left to walk away from the Friesens'. A delivery wagon passed them, and the driver gave them a second look.

As soon as they reached the end of the block Danny yelled, "Run!"

So run they did.

❧

"Thanks for the ride, mister!" Danny said as the three young people hopped off the back of his wagon.

The man tipped his hat and went into a haberdashery to make his delivery.

They took a moment to look around the narrow, busy street, which even in the late afternoon was in shadow. "Where are we?" Iris asked.

"I don't care," Annie said, "as long as it's away from *there*."

"I'll tell you where we are," Danny said. "We're at the starting point of our adventure."

Iris tucked her hand around his arm, looking very vulnerable even if she was four years older than him. "There are so many people."

"Ah, don't be a baby. We've been to department stores before. We've been around loads of people."

"But we've never been around people when we don't have anywhere to go home to."

Annie had not expected to hear her doubt so soon. "Do you want to go back?"

"I just want to *be* somewhere, not here, out in the middle of nowhere alone, with all these strangers around."

What had the girl expected?

Danny patted her hand. "You have us, Iris. None of us are alone."

His strength fed Annie's.

"I'm hungry," Iris said.

"Never fear!" Danny said. He opened his satchel and took out a large roast beef sandwich and an orange.

"How did you manage this?" Annie asked.

"It pays to have friends in low places who appreciate that I'm a growing boy." He shrugged. "Cook likes me."

They sat on the stoop of a building full of apartment flats. Street vendors closed up their carts for the night. Annie heard a baby cry from inside the building and watched as a horse fouled the street. The city was shutting down.

Lovely.

Danny took out a pocketknife and divided the sandwich into thirds while Annie peeled the orange and did the same. There were ten sections, so she gave Iris the extra one.

"Our first meal on our own," Annie said, adjusting the bread around her meat. She shooed a stray dog away.

"But where will our next meal come from?" Iris asked.

"We all have a little money, yes?" Annie asked. "You said you've been saving for this."

"We have a little," Iris said. "Very little."

"We'll use our money to get a room for the night and tomorrow we'll find jobs."

"Where?" Iris asked.

Annie was weary of her helpless attitude. "You and I will get a job in a shop."

Danny took an enormous bite of his sandwich. "As for me? Give me a job and I can do it."

Annie appreciated his attitude. "I believe you."

Danny licked his fingers noisily. "Let's count how much money we have between us."

They each retrieved their coins, and Annie suddenly realized that she didn't have dollars and cents but pounds and pence. "What good will this do me?" she asked aloud.

"There's got to be a place to change it," Danny said. "Most everybody here came from somewhere else."

Another task for tomorrow. But for today. . . "Just counting yours we have $11.52."

"Is that enough for a room?" Iris asked.

"I don't know what boarding rooms cost."

"We probably shoulda checked into that," Iris said.

"Too late now, bug," Danny said. "We'll just have to—"

Suddenly a boy ran toward them and grabbed all the coins out of Annie's hands. "Hey!" she cried.

Danny ran after him as Iris picked up the few coins the boy had dropped. Annie rushed toward the people on the street. "Please! He stole our money!"

She received a few sympathetic looks from passersby and scanned the street for a bobby.

No police anywhere. All she and Iris could do was look in the direction the boy and Danny had run and hope for the best.

A minute later, Iris said, "There's Danny!" She rushed to meet him. "Did you catch him? Did you get our money back?"

Danny opened his palm to reveal two coins. "He dropped these, but I couldn't catch him. It's gone. Our money is gone."

Iris began to cry, and Danny put his arm around her. "Don't cry, bug. We'll get jobs tomorrow and everything will be fine."

Annie knew he was overstating it but didn't want to make Iris more upset. Especially when evening was upon them. They had to find a place to sleep. Soon. They'd regroup in the morning.

She looked around for a church. It would be a safe place to stay.

But she couldn't spot a steeple in any direction. Shops and housing closed in around them, blocking out the last of the sun.

Men walked by and entered a pub with BEER on the signage. She didn't want to be anywhere nearby when they came out drunk.

"Let's find a quiet alley out of the way where no one will bother us," she said.

They walked up and down the street, checking for a suitable choice, but many stunk from rubbish or rows of privies serving the flats. A woman heaved a bowl of table scraps out an upper window, and stray dogs rushed forward to clean the mess. Annie longed for the tidy streets of Summerfield village, where everyone knew everyone and lights illumined the cozy cottages as day moved into night.

"We should have stayed home," Iris said. "This is disgusting."

And though Annie agreed with her, she said, "Every day will get better. You'll see."

"How will it get better?" Iris asked.

"Because it can't get worse," Danny said with a laugh. He linked his arm through hers. "Did you really think our adventure would include soft beds and hot running water?"

"Yes."

He looked to Annie, apparently waiting for *her* to answer. "I didn't think about it much—at least not what would happen the first night or two."

"And we never could have predicted that our money would be stolen," Danny added.

"But it was. And so we'll make do. After we get jobs, everything will be fine."

Iris looked unconvinced. So be it. Annie had little patience for whiners.

"Come on, now," Danny said. "Let's keep looking for an alley. Maybe one paved with gold, eh?"

They finally found one that seemed the best of the worst. Danny rearranged some crates, moving them away from the brick wall, creating a hiding place for them to spend the night. They huddled together, Danny at the open end.

"Don't be afraid, girls," Danny said. "I hereby vow to protect you forever!"

Annie wasn't sure what a thirteen-year-old boy could do against the dangers of the world, but she appreciated his confidence.

She looked upward and saw the darkening sky between the four-story buildings on either side. Windows looked down on them. Laundry dried on clotheslines strung between the buildings, hanging limp and still in the autumn air. *At least it's not winter.*

Iris drew her knees to her chest, tucking her shoes under her skirt. She put her hands beneath her arms for warmth.

That gave Annie an idea. "I have a present for each of us." She dug into her carpetbag and retrieved three pairs of white gloves. "Here. At least our hands can be warm."

Iris turned a pair over in her hands. "These look like footman gloves."

"Because they are footman gloves. A particular footman's gloves." Annie smiled conspiratorially at Danny. "Danny did the deed."

"But it was Annie's brilliant idea."

Iris's eyes glowed with understanding. "These belong to Grasston?"

"Belonged," Danny said.

"He'll get in dire trouble with Mr. Brandon."

Annie nodded. "His trouble will be a small bit of justice against the trouble he caused us."

Iris put on the gloves—which were far too large. She spread her hands, grinning at the sight of them. "I'll take great pleasure imagining how it played out at dinner service—him with no gloves."

The pleasure was all Annie's.

CHAPTER SIX

*O*oh, the cook made bread.

A groaning sound made Annie open her eyes. She wasn't at home at Crompton Hall. She was lying against a building, in an alley in New York City, with Iris's elbow in her stomach.

Danny lay on the outside of the three, the protector. He must have sensed her movement because he opened his eyes, blinked a few times, and then said, "I smell bread."

"Me, too," Annie whispered.

The two of them inched their way to sitting, causing Iris to lose her support. The girl opened her eyes. "It's morning? I smell bread."

Danny stood then helped the girls up. "We need to follow our noses and find the source."

"But we don't have money to buy any," Annie said, brushing off her jacket and skirt.

"Maybe the smell alone can ease the ache in our stomachs," he said.

Iris stretched. "I want to eat it. Lots of it."

They gathered their things and left the alley in search of bread. All they had to do was follow the scent and the trail of people walking toward their morning sustenance.

The Tuttle Bakery was a block south, a narrow storefront with a window displaying rolls, biscuits, and bread. There was a line out the door. People with money.

The trio stood outside, gazing at the wares they couldn't buy.

Iris finally turned her back to the window, leaned against it, and pressed her hands against her stomach. "I'm starving!"

"You are not starving," Annie said, pulling her away from the bakery. She wanted to remind Iris that as a girl of seventeen she should act more mature than her younger brother, but Annie didn't think it would do any good. Maturity often had little to do with age.

The line lessened as people left the bakery with their goods and went on their way to work or home.

"I'm going in," Danny whispered.

"To do what?" Iris asked.

"To get us some breakfast."

The girls didn't have time to ask him more as he entered the bakery. They peeked through the window and saw him talking with a woman behind the counter, gesticulating with his arms, and finally pointing right at them.

The woman saw them, and Danny motioned them inside.

Annie and Iris went in, and Danny came to greet them. "This is my sister, Iris, and our friend Annie. Girls, this is Mrs. Tuttle."

That Danny had learned the name of the woman in such a short time was amazing. "Hello, Mrs. Tuttle," Annie said.

The woman wiped her pudgy hands on her flour-sprinkled apron and nodded at them. "Hello, girls. Danny says you've had your money stolen and are in need of some food to fill your stomachs."

Annie laughed. "It appears he's shared much in quick order." She wondered how much else he'd said. Surely he hadn't shared the full truth of where they came from.

Danny shrugged. "No need to dally around when we're hungry. Or starving." He gave Iris a pointed look.

"No need to be either when there's fresh bread. What will be your pleasure?"

She was giving them a choice?

"A bap would be wonderful," Annie said. "Thank you."

"I'd like the one there, with apricot jam," Iris said. When Annie nudged her she added, "Please. And thank you."

The woman handed over the rolls then looked at Danny. "And you, lad?"

"If you please, I think a loaf of bread would be wise. We could save part of it for lunch and dinner."

Mrs. Tuttle nodded and wrapped up a loaf, but her forehead was furrowed. "Where are you staying? I've not seen you in the neighborhood."

Annie tried to think of what to say, but Danny did the choosing for them. "We got laid off from our work—working for a family, we were. We slept in the alley last night."

Mrs. Tuttle blinked. "I don't like hearing that. Not at all. Where is your home?"

They glanced at each other, and this time Annie answered. "We are on our own, and our task today is to find jobs so we'll never have to ask for charity again."

"A work ethic, have you?" she asked.

"We *are* hard workers," Danny said. "All three of us."

There was a decided thump overhead then the sound of a scuffle and children crying. "My boisterous brood. They know better'n to misbehave during the morning rush." Then, with a blink, she looked at the girls. "I could use some help with 'em."

"I love children," Iris said.

Annie was less enthused. "How many?"

"Seven."

"Seven?"

"The two oldest are my husband's children from his first wife before she passed. After he and I got hitched, we had five in quick succession. They're the ones who need tending. You interested?" She looked directly at Iris.

"How much does it pay?"

"Room and board. And maybe a little more if you handle it well."

Iris checked in with Danny, who nodded. "Yes. Please."

"Glad for the help," Mrs. Tuttle said. "Would you like to help around here, too?" The woman looked at Annie.

Although Annie had hoped for a job in a shop that sold clothing or hats, she certainly wasn't going to turn the offer down. "I would."

"Count me in," Danny said. He flexed a muscle. "I can do the heavy work."

Mrs. Tuttle laughed. But then Annie wondered if they'd asked for too much. "Are you sure you could use all three of us? We don't want to be a burden."

Mrs. Tuttle wiped some crumbs off the counter onto her palm. "After child number three came along, I came to the conclusion that it wasn't that hard to add another one to the pile. Family is precious, and helping three young people in need is the Christian thing to do."

Annie had never met someone so generous. "We'll work hard. We'll not let you down."

"I know you won't." A customer came in the store. While he was looking at the baked goods, Mrs. Tuttle pointed toward the back. "There's a storeroom off the kitchen. See how you can arrange it for a space to sleep."

Danny led the way back through a kitchen where two men—one elderly and one less so—worked with a boy and girl aged about twenty and a little less. They looked up from their work, but briefly. Apparently three strangers walking through didn't faze them.

They spotted the storeroom. There were shelves of pans, bowls, and utensils. Sacks of flour and sugar were stacked on the floor. "There's not much space here at all," Iris said.

"We can sleep on the floor between the shelves," Danny said. "Maybe Mrs. Tuttle has a few extra blankets. We can use our carpetbags as our pillows."

He was being optimistic, yet Annie was pleased to have a roof over their heads.

Mrs. Tuttle popped her head in. "It ain't much, but I'll get you some blankets and maybe you can arrange some of those pallets as beds."

"We appreciate it, Mrs. Tuttle," Annie said. "You're very kind."

"Don't thank me yet. Not until after you meet the hellions upstairs."

❦

The five Tuttle children stopped jumping on the bed and throwing toy blocks at each other and eyed the three strangers warily.

Their mother stepped forward and removed a brush from a girl's hand—a brush that was en route to whack a sibling. "Children, I'd like you to meet three new friends who have come to help us. There's Danny and Annie who will help us in the shop, and Iris who will help take care of you."

Annie was relieved her name wasn't mentioned in the latter task.

The children were named and their ages given: Nelly, Nora, Nick, Newt, and Joe were aged eight, seven, six, five, and two.

Iris scooped Joe into her arms then sat on the floor near the largest pile of blocks. "Let's see how tall a tower we can build."

Shockingly, the children gathered round.

"Well then," Mrs. Tuttle said. "Would you look at that." She put a finger to her lips and motioned Danny and Annie out of the flat and down the stairs to the store.

Once again the two young people looked up from their work, though there was one less, as the older man could be seen up front manning the counter. "Family, I'd like you to meet Danny and Annie who are going to be staying with us and helping in the store. Iris is upstairs saving the children from themselves." She nodded at the duo then at the man. "This is my husband, and the two others are our eldest."

Mr. Tuttle looked over his glasses. "They're staying in the storeroom?"

"I thought you could arrange some pallets for them. Maybe fill some old flour sacks with straw."

The expression on his face showed his exasperation at the arrangement and extra work but quickly changed to resignation. "Yes, m'love." To the guests he said, "Welcome."

The young man stepped away from his kneading, his eyes locked on Annie in a way she'd seen before. "Hello. I'm Thomas."

She gave him a nod, felt herself blush, and then looked past him and said to the girl, "And what's your name?"

The girl seemed to prefer the view of the floor over making eye contact. She let her floured hands fall upon her apron and mumbled something.

"That's Jane," Mrs. Tuttle said. And to the girl she said, "I've repeatedly told you to speak up."

"Yes'm," she said softly.

Annie felt sorry for her. In a family of seven children, the quiet ones would have a harder time of it. Annie gave her a smile—which was returned.

"Gramps works with us, too," Mrs. Tuttle said, nodding toward the front. "But his knees get to hurting something awful so he needs to be spelled more often than most."

"I can do that," Danny said.

Mrs. Tuttle laughed. "I'm sure you can, but I think the best use of your young muscles is delivering."

"In a wagon?" Danny asked, his eyes wide.

Mr. Tuttle answered, "Unless ye want to haul the fifty-pound bags of flour and sugar on yer shoulders."

"I get to be out of doors?"

"In good weather and bad."

Danny looked as though he was about to burst. "When can I start?"

He earned their laughter, and even Jane smiled.

"Ye know how to tether a horse and drive a wagon?" Mr. Tuttle asked.

"No, but you'll teach me, yes?"

Mr. Tuttle offered him a wink. "I'll teach ye, yes."

Thomas nodded toward Annie but looked to his stepmother. "What's Annie going to do?"

Mrs. Tuttle put a finger to her chin. "I'm not sure yet, but we have plenty of work to be done, that's for certain."

Annie was a bit disappointed that the other two had been specifically chosen for a task, but she used it as an opportunity to interject, "I was thinking of working in a store that sells dresses or shoes or hats."

Mrs. Tuttle gave Annie's outfit a once-over, clearly judging it for its lack of fashion. "More power to ya. But until then, how about cleaning that stack of pots and pans over there?"

Over there was a sink with a hand pump and an enormous stack of dirty kitchen utensils.

The bell on the front door dinged twice in quick succession, causing Mrs. Tuttle to say, "I needs to get up front and help Gramps. Back to work, everyone."

Mrs. Tuttle left them, and the other three went back to their baking.

Leaving Annie to tackle the pots.

Joy.

❧

Dinner was served in the kitchen of the bakery, on the table where the bread was made.

Before the meal, Annie hadn't noticed the two benches pushed under the worktable, but as the bakery closed up shop and Mrs. Tuttle put on a huge pot of stew, the benches were pulled out and the table set.

The children descended from upstairs like a herd of cows coming in from a pasture. They were accompanied by Iris, and with little to-do everyone took a place. Mr. Tuttle sat at the head using an upturned crate as his throne.

"Grace," he said. That one word caused all talking to stop and all heads to bow. In unison the family prayed, "We thank the Lord for happy hearts, for rain and sunny weather. We thank the Lord for this our food and that we are together. Amen."

Annie was moved by the simple table grace. It seemed to suit the Tuttles. She imagined their lives to be more full of sunny weather than not and felt an aura of gratitude even amid their hard work. Annie was thankful for the chance to work at all, and mostly that they were all together. She much preferred this prayer over the longish ones the butler at the Hall used to say, the prayers that offered gratitude as a duty rather than a joy.

Mrs. Tuttle served up bowls of stew, and bread was passed. Annie was ravenous.

"Did ye work up an appetite?" Mr. Tuttle asked.

She forced herself to slow down. "I did."

"Nothing wrong with that." Thomas gave her a sympathetic smile. "We worked you hard today."

Annie rubbed her red and chapped hands. "At least it's done."

"Until tomorrow," Jane said softly.

"Aye," said her mother. "Unfortunately, that's the way of it. Every day it starts over again." She pointed to Annie's hands. "I have some salve. Jane can attest to its value on chapped skin."

So Jane's task had been the washing? Somehow knowing she was easing the girl's load made the work a little easier to endure.

"I worked hard, too," Iris said, with a look to Thomas.

He glanced at her and nodded. "Didn't say you didn't."

Iris's brow dipped.

"I'm going to drive the wagon tomorrow," Danny said.

"With my help," Gramps said. "Though ye do seem a natural at it. The horses liked ye well enough this afternoon and that's important."

"Everyone likes me well enough," Danny said.

"That's because you're so humble," Annie said, taking a bite of bread.

Thomas passed the jam across the table. "Try this apple butter. It's as sweet as you."

Annie felt her face grow hot and looked around the table. The flattery had been noted by all the adults.

Everyone but Iris was smiling.

<hr />

From beading gowns to stitching straw mattresses.

Annie tied off the thread, finishing the last of the six fifty-pound flour sacks they'd filled with straw, and took it into the storage room.

Danny and Thomas set empty pallets on two sides of the room, while Iris placed the makeshift mattresses on the pallets, two to each.

Jane arrived from upstairs with three quilts and one pillow. "Sorry there's only the one."

Thomas took it from his sister and handed it to Annie. "You can have it. I want you to be comfortable."

Iris put her hands on her hips. "And what about me?"

Danny lightened the moment by mimicking her. "And what about me?"

Annie didn't appreciate Thomas's obvious favoritism—though she did like having the use of the pillow. "We'll take turns." She put the pillow on one of the beds. "Actually I'm so tired I think I could sleep directly on the floor."

"Sorry the work was so hard," Thomas said.

Although she'd enjoyed his extra attention, it began to grate. "I'll be well enough."

"Me, too," Iris said.

"Me three," Danny added, unlacing his shoes.

The oldest of the younger children appeared in the doorway. "Iris, Mama wants help getting Joe to bed. She says he's taken a liking to you and he never goes quietly for her."

Iris sighed dramatically. "'Man may work from sun to sun, but woman's work is never done.'" She brushed her shoulder against that of Thomas when she left the room.

"My, my, that girl has a chip on her shoulder," Thomas said.

Danny was already stretched out on his mattress, punching and pushing the straw to find some comfort. "Chip or not, she's working as hard as any of us."

Thomas looked as though he wanted to say more but, with a nod to Annie, left them.

Annie released a breath she'd unwittingly saved.

"He's sweet on you," Danny said.

She sat on her mattress and removed her shoes. "You saw it, too?"

"Everyone saw it." He turned on his side to face her. "Trouble is, Iris likes him."

"She can have him."

"You're not interested?"

"Face the wall so I can get undressed."

Danny did as he was told. "You didn't answer me."

Annie unbuttoned her blouse. "I could be interested. He's a nice enough boy, and maybe a few days ago I would have been. But now I'm just not."

"He's not good enough for you?"

She stepped out of her skirt and hung it from a nail. "It's not that." She unhooked her corset, relished the freedom of full movement, and put it out of sight in her bag. She put her nightgown over her head. Then she lay down and arranged the blanket to cover herself. "You can turn around now."

Danny faced her. "Finish what you were saying about Thomas."

Putting it into words was like trying to catch the mist. "I have a feeling there's something out there for me to do, to be. Something that's beyond anything I can imagine."

"I believe it. You certainly have a fire in your belly that goes beyond washing pots and pans."

His belief in her gave her courage. "I have no idea what *it* is."

"Maybe you don't need to. Maybe it will find you instead of you finding it."

She lay on her back and noticed water stains on the ceiling. "I do like the sound of that. It takes the pressure away, as if it's fate, not just folly." She looked at Danny. "Tomorrow I'll do my work here, but I'm also going to find a job in a store."

"Macy's?"

She hadn't thought of it, but yes, why not Macy's?

CHAPTER SEVEN

There was a detail Annie hadn't thought about before going to sleep in the storeroom the night before: bakers have to get up early to make their breads. To make their breads, they need supplies in the storeroom.

The door swung open, flooding the room with lamplight.

Thomas did the honors. "Sorry to wake you, but we need flour."

"No sorry to it," Mr. Tuttle said from behind his son. "People won't wait for their bread. We could use yer help."

Iris squinted at them. "What time is it?"

"Half past four." Thomas set the lamp on a shelf.

"That's earlier than we got up at the Friesens'."

Thomas looked at his father. "The Friesens? The banking Friesens?"

"I sees their name in the paper off and on," Mr. Tuttle said. "Surely ye didn't leave a position in a family as wealthy as them."

They couldn't renege on the name, so Annie went back to their original lie. "They didn't need us anymore, so they let us go."

"That's not very kind of them," Jane said from the kitchen. "Times are hard. What with all their money you'd think they could keep you on."

Annie wished they would leave so she could dress. They were having this discussion while she and Iris had their blankets pulled up to their chins. "Come in and get what you need and then we'll dress and get to work."

Sacks of flour, sugar, and dried milk were obtained, and the door was closed. "You get up first, Danny," Iris said.

Iris and Annie averted their eyes, and Danny dressed and was gone. The girls dressed and went outside to the communal privy in the dark alley. The stench was horrific, and Annie longed for a flush toilet, a bath, and warm water.

On their way back inside, she asked, "When you were upstairs with the

61

children, did you see a bath or running water?"

"Only water is downstairs in the kitchen. Mrs. Tuttle said Saturdays are bath day."

Annie hated to ask. "Where is this done?"

"In the kitchen. A tub's brought in. Water is heated."

The thought of it harkened back to her childhood, when her family shared a weekly tub at the fireside in the kitchen. Once she started work at the Kidds', she was happy to find they'd had indoor plumbing added to the centuries-old mansion, which included designated bathrooms for both family and servants. The Friesen household in New York was even more modern with tile walls instead of wallpaper, fancy painted water closets, and sinks with brass faucets. To go from those comforts to the primitive facilities at the Tuttles' was definitely a step back.

Wait until you get a job. Then you can let a proper room, with a proper bath.

The thought made her remember that today she needed to find another job. She'd work extra hard this morning to earn the chance to leave this afternoon. Surely they wouldn't object.

Upon reentering the bakery, Iris went upstairs to help with the children, and Danny left to see to the horses.

Annie approached Mr. Tuttle, who was measuring ingredients into an enormous crockery bowl. "Sir? Mr. Tuttle?"

He gave her a glance. "We'll have dishes to wash soon enough."

"It's not that, I—"

"Ye want breakfast ye'll have to wait till the bread's done. Unless ye want some day-old in the cupboard."

"I can wait." He was making this difficult.

Finally he stopped his work. "What is it then, girl?"

"I need to be gone this afternoon to apply for a job in a shop."

His eyebrows rose. "This shop ain't good enough for ye?"

"I'm not implying that. But since my talents lie in sewing and fashion, I thought it would behoove me to get a job more suited to my abilities."

"Well now. Aren't ye the fancy one?"

"Fashion?" Jane asked. "You know about fashion?"

Her father pointed a finger at her. "None of that wasted dreaming of fancy dresses, lass. Ye have no need for fashion other than some simple clothes on yer back."

Jane nodded once and slunk away. Annie wanted to defend Jane's natural female desire for pretty things but knew now was not the time. Her new job had to come first or there'd be no fashion for anyone.

"Where are you going to apply?" Thomas asked.

"Macy's."

"That's a grand store."

"Yes, it is. A grand store that has many employees. I hope they have an opening."

"If they don't you'll still work for us, won't you?" he asked.

The need to get another job increased. "I'm not one to give up easily," she said.

"Neither am I."

Oh dear.

❧

With her chores at the Tuttles' accomplished, Annie walked to Macy's on Thirty-Fourth and Broadway. It was hard to believe that she and her friends had been in this very store a few days earlier. They'd been three servants out on a lark, seeing how the other half lived.

She wasn't a servant any longer.

She was a scullery maid.

She *had* to get a job here.

Annie entered the store at one of the three entrances on Sixth Avenue and saw it with new eyes. It wasn't just a palace of products she couldn't afford, it was a place where she could prosper as a person. She was guessing a clerk didn't make a lot of money, but the money was secondary. The goal she was pursuing had a larger name: purpose. The pit of her belly stirred, begging to discover what she'd truly been born to do. To be.

Annie considered seeking out Mrs. Holmquist in the sewing machine department but balked because she knew nothing about the product. Yet there were other products she *could* sell. . . .

She walked among aisles of merchandise that screamed, "Buy me!" There was the untrimmed hat department, which led to the vast display of flowers and ribbons to adorn them. Hosiery, jewelry, lace and embroideries, handkerchiefs, ladies' collars and cuffs—with similar products in a men's section seen across the store. Gloves, linens, curtains, and a vast shoe department that could have easily—and stylishly—shod the entire village back home.

Annie passed a display case of buttons and dress trimmings. *I can sell these.* She was drawn to the dress goods in every color and quality from silks, satins, and velvets, to cottons and worsteds. Signs announced the prices and the special sales: NOVELTY DRESS SILKS! 49 CENTS A YARD/VALUE $1.00 A YARD. Even she was drawn to the bargain though she had absolutely no use for silk—and no money to buy it.

And then she saw it. A sign on a counter: SALES HELP WANTED.

Her stomach pulled, then danced, causing her heart to pound. This was it. This was her opportunity. Her destiny.

She stepped toward the counter and waited for a clerk to notice her.

A middle-aged woman approached. "May I help you, miss?"

Annie nodded toward the sign. "I would like to apply for a position. The sales position."

The woman's gaze fell upon Annie's clothes then met her eyes. "It's a position that requires a knowledge of sewing, dressmaking, and... fashion."

The last word was said with a hint of disdain.

Annie stood taller. "I have extensive experience with alterations of fine gowns and the use of proper accessories."

"Where did you gain this experience?"

It was a challenge more than a question. "I worked for a viscountess and her daughter." *As a maid.*

The woman eyed her warily, and Annie could tell she took her words as a lie. "If you held such a position why would you leave it?"

Please give me the words. With her next breath she was fueled by a sudden surge of confidence. "I left England and came to America to follow a dream."

"And that dream is...?"

"I want to become all I can be. I have a talent for sewing and designing and altering fashion to make it suit its wearer." She spread her hands and took a step back to showcase her own meager ensemble. "As a working girl I have no funds to apply what I know to my own clothing, but that will change once I find a job. I want to help women dress in ways that will make them feel on top of the world." She stepped closer, lowering her voice. "Please give me a chance. I shan't let you down."

The woman glanced at Annie's hands, which were clasped against her breast. "You don't have the hands of a seamstress."

Annie looked at her hands—which were chapped and red. She put them at her sides, out of sight. "I've been helping a neighbor with some cleaning."

A customer approached, and the clerk gave Annie one last look. "You need to speak to Mr. Jones, the superintendent. He'll get you set up."

"So I have the job?"

"It's not for me to say." She suddenly craned her head then said, "He's over there. By the thread."

Annie saw an older gentleman with a large gray mustache. Annie looked to the woman, who nodded.

"Good luck," the woman said with a smile. "And tell him that Mrs. MacDonald approves."

Annie bounced twice on her toes. "Thank you so much, Mrs. MacDonald." But as Annie approached the man, she found herself focusing on something other than the need for good luck. *God? Please help me get this job. Please open this door for me.*

Mr. Jones was jotting something in a small notebook. Annie stood nearby and waited until he was finished and looked up. "May I help you find something, miss?"

"No. I mean. . ." A fresh breath brought courage. "My name is Annie Wood, and Mrs. MacDonald over there. . ." She paused to nod toward the notions counter, where Mrs. MacDonald offered a discreet wave. Annie turned her attention back to Mr. Jones. "I spoke with Mrs. MacDonald about the clerk position. I gave her my qualifications, and she said I need to finalize my employment with you."

That wasn't exactly what was said, but Annie hoped the implied confidence would work to her favor.

Mr. Jones eyed her clothes a bit more discreetly than had Mrs. MacDonald. "There is a certain standard required of a Macy's clerk. A certain code of dress."

"I realize that, Mr. Jones. And if I could be advanced a small sum, I would be happy to buy an appropriate ensemble."

When he smiled his mouth disappeared beneath the swag of his mustache. "You're already spending your wages?"

"For the benefit of the position, sir."

His left eyebrow rose. "I admire your spunk, Miss Wood."

"Does that mean I have the job?"

"As I am busy today, and the need is great. . .it does. Follow me to my office and I will take down your information. Then report to the floorwalker, Mrs. Gold, and she will explain how things work."

Annie nearly curtsied but remembered she was in America. Instead she held out her hand and Mr. Jones shook it firmly. "Work hard, Miss Wood. That is all we ask." With a sweep of his arm he led them to the elevator and to his office.

She was officially a shopgirl!

Mrs. Gold read the note from Mr. Jones and then wadded it up in her palm. "Well then. I will have to assume you have been thoroughly vetted, but honestly, I have my doubts."

"I assure you, Mrs. Gold, I will not be a disappointment."

"Hmm." She strode toward the women's wear section and waved toward some black shirtwaists and skirts. "Choose two of each. And two white lace collars from that department."

"That is generous."

"It is not generous. A bit will come out of your wages until it is paid off. But take note that the proper costume is imperative. As a sales clerk you are the primary point of contact between the store and the public. Macy's reputation depends upon the manner and method in which you perform your work."

Mr. Jones had repeated the same lines—almost word for word. "I understand."

"Did Mr. Jones explain to you about wages?"

"Six dollars a week to start, with the chance of bonuses if I sell my quota."

"Which is two hundred dollars a week. Sell above that and you will get an additional one percent."

"I will achieve that quota—and then some."

Mrs. Gold shook her head. "Don't get cocky on me, girl. Collect your uniform then report to Mrs. MacDonald tomorrow by—"

"Twenty past eight."

"By eight o'clock since it's your first day."

"Yes, ma'am."

Mrs. Gold peered downward. "Let me see your shoes."

Annie lifted her skirt enough to reveal her well-worn but still functional boots.

"They will do. Go on, then. Gather the essentials and get a good night's rest. You will need it."

Annie was bursting with joy and longed to let out a whoop of rejoicing. Instead, she turned her gratitude inward. *Thank You, God! I shan't let You down!*

She hurried to the women's department to shop for ready-made clothes. It was a first. Her maid uniforms at the Kidds' were stitched on-site, though the shoes and undergarments were ordered from London. Annie had never shopped for herself other than to spend a few pennies on a stick of candy or a handkerchief at the Summerfield mercantile.

"May I help you, miss?" a clerk asked.

With full pride Annie was able to say, "I have just been hired as a clerk in the sewing department and I need to dress the part."

❦

"And who is going to wash the pots and pans now?" Mr. Tuttle asked.

Annie set the parcel containing her clerk uniforms aside and glanced at Jane. Jane's hands were covered with flour, but the task of washing would once again fall on her.

She looked at Thomas to see his reaction, but he was focused on forming the dough into rolls.

"I'm sorry for the inconvenience, Mr. Tuttle, but aren't you happy for me? I'm proud to work at such a prestigious store as Macy's."

"So we ain't good enough for ye?"

"You know that's not true. I appreciate you taking us in like you did, but I made it clear I was seeking another job." She noticed the sink overflowing with pots and pans. "I'll still do the washing today."

"We wouldn't want to put ye out." His voice dripped with sarcasm.

She ignored his tone, tied on an apron, and set to work. If she clanged and clattered a bit more than necessary, let them complain.

Jane came up behind her and whispered, "I'm happy for you."

"I'm sorry about the dish washing."

Jane shook her head vehemently. "Don't be. You getting a job at Macy's is ever so exciting."

"Girls?" Mr. Tuttle barked. "Work."

Jane had one last thing to say. "Be a grand success, Annie. For both of us."

❧

The awkwardness continued when the rest of the Tuttles came to the kitchen for dinner. Mrs. Tuttle was at the stove, and Iris was busy getting the children set at the table. Annie wanted to tell Iris when they were alone, but with the Tuttle clan teeming around them, it wasn't possible.

Just as the adults were sitting down, Danny and Gramps returned from deliveries.

"Smells great, Mrs. Tuttle. I'm starved to near wasted away."

"You are always starved, boy. Eating us out of house and home, you are."

He gave her a peck on the cheek before washing his hands at the sink.

Gramps sat at his place with a noisy *oomph*. "Don't get af'er the boy. He earns his keep."

Mr. Tuttle glared at Annie—implying she was *not* earning her keep. She might as well share her news now rather than later. "I was hired at Macy's. I start tomorrow."

Her news was received in silence. Danny was the first to respond. "Congratulations, Annie. It happened just like you hoped it would."

She looked at Iris, who was just sitting down with the baby on her lap. "Are you happy for me?"

"Of course. Good for you."

That was all?

Mrs. Tuttle finished spooning out the soup. Only then did she look at Annie. "You're putting us in a bind."

How? Until two days ago Jane washed the pots.

"We let you have a room here if you worked for us, but now. . ."

"Once I get a paycheck, I will pay you rent."

Mrs. Tuttle exchanged a look with her husband. He was the one to answer. "One dollar a week for the room, and one dollar for the meals."

That would be a third of her paycheck. "I'll be eating the noon meal at Macy's," she said. "Apparently, they have an employees' cafeteria with reasonable prices."

"Seventy-five cents, then," he said.

How could she haggle? "Consider it done."

Done for now. One day she'd have a proper working-girl flat.

Annie draped her new uniforms over some bags of sugar in the storeroom. She carefully set her lace collars on top—one white and one ecru.

Iris came in. "Fancy shopgirl clothes."

"They're not fancy," Annie said. "But they are the uniforms worn by all the girls. I bought two skirts, two blouses, and two collars."

Iris ran her fingers along the batiste fabric as if it were the finest silk. "You got the job I always dreamed of."

Annie hadn't thought of that. "You can get a job there, too. Mr. Jones says they have over five thousand people on staff."

Iris pulled her hand away from the temptation of the outfits. "I haven't seen five thousand people in my life."

"You know what a big store it is. Eight floors of pretty things to buy."

"Things you can't buy if you don't have any money."

Annie didn't want her to be miffed. Or discouraged. "The Tuttles said they would pay you something in addition to the room and board."

Iris shrugged. "Actually, *I* wanted to work in a small sort of shop with just a few clerks."

Her stipulation removed some of Annie's guilt. "Then Macy's isn't your cup of tea."

Their conversation was interrupted by two distinct pounds coming from the floor above. "Mrs. Tuttle needs me."

"That's how she calls you? She stomps on the floor?"

"I have to go."

As she left the room, Danny came in. "Well I'll be. Look at your fine duds."

"It's a uniform. All the clerks wear black with a collar."

"Fancy." He slumped onto his blanket. "I am happy for you, Annie."

"I am happy for me, too. But I don't want Iris to be green about it."

"Ah, don't mind bug. Though she won't admit it, I think she likes taking care of the children."

Annie sat on the straw bags that were her bed. "I couldn't do what she does. There are so many of them."

"Don't you want to be a mother someday?"

The dreams of her future had never strayed in that direction. "I know I *should* want that."

"No *should* about it. And you don't have to decide now. What are you? Eighteen?"

"Nineteen, and no, I don't have to decide that yet. Besides, a husband needs to come first."

He grinned. "I know someone who's interested."

"I am *not* interested in Thomas."

He lay on his back, linking his hands behind his head. "New York is enormous. I didn't know how big it was till I got the chance to drive the streets."

"Do you like your work?"

"I do. I like being outside and driving the wagon. I like Gramps, too. He reminds me of my own granddad: feisty and full of good stories."

"Do you see him? See your own granddad?"

"Nah. He died. Grandma and our parents, too."

Annie felt a wave of compassion. "I'm so sorry."

"It happens."

"But all of them? What did they die of?"

"Some fever. Iris and me were spared because we were working at the Friesens'."

The implication was sobering. "Those jobs saved you."

He shrugged. "Those jobs, and now the jobs we have here."

"And at Macy's."

"It seems the lot of us are right where we ought to be."

"So it appears."

"God did a pretty good job arranging it, didn't He?"

Annie had no complaints.

Chapter Eight

Annie tried the entrance door at Macy's, but it was locked. She moved to another one and found it, too, was locked. She felt panic rise within her. How could she be on time if she couldn't even get in?

But then a man inside noticed her, came to the door, and talked through the glass. "Store opens at eight thirty, miss."

"I'm a new clerk. Today is my first day."

The bald and bearded man studied her a moment then unlocked the door, letting her in.

"A little eager, are we?" He pulled a pocket watch from his vest. "It's only quarter of eight."

"A little eager, yes. And nervous."

"No need to be. Macy's wants you to succeed."

She liked the sound of that. "I never thought of it that way."

He leaned close, as if sharing a confidence. "If you succeed, Macy's succeeds."

She laughed. "I will do my very best."

"Which department?"

"Dress goods and sewing supplies."

"Are you a talented seamstress?"

She considered this a moment. "I am a seamstress with aspirations of talent."

"Work hard and you will attain your aspirations."

For the first time Annie noticed that not all the lights were on. Was it this man's job to light the store? "I'm sorry," she said. "Did I take you away from your work?"

"Nothing takes me away from my work."

The door opened behind them, and Mrs. MacDonald entered. "Mr. Straus. Miss Wood."

71

"Good morning, Mrs. MacDonald. It appears you have an eager new clerk."

"I do, sir."

"Carry on, then. Good day, ladies." He left them.

"You are one lucky girl." Mrs. McDonald said.

"Lucky?" Annie asked.

"To meet Mr. Straus on your first day."

"Who is Mr. Straus?"

Mrs. MacDonald gawked. "You're joshing."

"I'm not. I don't know who he is."

"He's our boss. He's the owner of Macy's."

Annie looked back. "But he was so nice."

Mrs. MacDonald took her arm and got them walking. "He is nice. And he cares about his employees and their families. Among other things, he's the one who stopped the practice of keeping the store open until ten or eleven o'clock on the ten evenings before Christmas so we could spend more time with our families and stay in better health. Before then, I remember not getting home until midnight and then having to be back to work at eight. The new policy is much better for everyone."

"That was nice of him."

Mrs. MacDonald stepped onto some moving steps leading upward. Annie balked.

"Haven't you ever seen an escalator before?"

"I hadn't been in an elevator until yesterday."

Mrs. MacDonald was halfway to the next floor. "Come on. Don't be scared. Take the handhold and step on."

Annie watched the steps ever moving from flat to full. If she timed it just right. . .

She stepped on and grabbed the hold, only bobbling a little. Mrs. MacDonald stood at the top, laughing. "My, my, you have been in the sticks."

Annie wasn't sure what she meant by the comment but ignored her ribbing, as the stair was ending and she had to concentrate on stepping off without incident. As she did so, Mrs. MacDonald applauded. Annie responded with a bow. And a sigh of relief.

"By the time we get to the floor that houses the employee lockers, you'll be an expert."

They finally reached the area where they put their hats and jackets in lockers. Mrs. MacDonald nodded toward some other rooms. "Employee restrooms are in there. The public ladies' is on the second floor, right next to the boys' clothing department. But we are to use these facilities and leave the other to the customers."

"Understood." *Anything is better than the privies at the Tuttles'.*

Mrs. MacDonald checked her hair in a mirror. "There are also shower facilities for employees."

"Really?" Annie had never had a shower, and the last bath she'd had was at the Friesens'. "Have you used them?"

"I prefer baths. But it's there for you to use. Men's and women's, of course."

"Of course." Annie tucked a few stray hairs behind her ears. "It seems Mr. Straus has thought of everything."

"Most everything. I'll tell you more as we go along. Come, now. Let's get to work."

⌘

"Miss Wood, I would like you to meet Miss Krieger, the other clerk in our department. Mildred, meet Annie."

Annie extended her hand to a petite girl in her early twenties, whose sharp and pinched facial features made her look cross. Surely when she smiled, the look would fade.

Unfortunately, the smile did nothing to soften her expression. On the contrary, the smile seemed false, as though it was only for show and there was malice behind it.

Mildred ignored Annie's hand. "We don't need another clerk."

Mrs. MacDonald's eyebrows rose. "That's not for you to say."

"She'll just make it harder to sell over our quota, taking away any chance of a bonus."

With such a tetchy attitude, Annie wondered why any customer would buy from Mildred.

Mrs. MacDonald moved on. "Please watch the counter as I teach Annie the sales procedure."

Mildred had the audacity to shrug. How did she ever get hired with such an attitude?

Mrs. MacDonald brought out two sales books. "This one is for Monday,

73

Wednesday, and Friday, and this one is for Tuesday, Thursday, and Saturday. When you have a sale, you list the items and their cost and then collect the payment and put it, along with your sales slip, in one of the pneumatic tubes over there." She pointed to a creeper vine of brass tubing on the wall. "It is sent to cashiers in the tube room, who send back change and your sales slip, stamped to show that payment was made. You call a parcel boy to wrap the package for the customer."

"What do I do with the paid sales slip?"

"You put it in your book for the proper day and turn them in at night to be checked against the money received. That's why you need a different book for alternate days."

It was all very logical. "It gives them time to do the checking and get the book back to us."

"Exactly. Well understood. Follow the rules and make shopping a pleasant experience for the customer and—"

"And a profitable experience for Macy's."

Mrs. MacDonald beamed. "I'm glad you were hired, Miss Wood."

⁓

Annie ran her hand along a bolt of gold shantung. The weave of the silk caught the light, making the cloth sumptuous.

A customer—her very first customer—strolled by, eying the bolts. "May I help you with your choice today, my. . .madam?" She'd caught herself before saying the familiar "my lady."

"I'm looking for cloth suitable for a walking suit. Something for autumn."

Annie chose the gold bolt and unrolled a yard or two of the fabric to best showcase its depth and texture. "This color mimics the rich hues of the season." She noted the woman's auburn hair. "It would also complement your coloring beautifully."

The woman blushed and put a hand to her cheek. "Do you think so?"

"I do, Mrs. . . ?"

"Reinhold."

"Would you like to look at suit patterns and find a style that pleases you, Mrs. Reinhold?"

The woman ran a hand over the fabric as if they were getting to know each other. With a final pat she claimed it as her own. "I would. Thank you."

Annie led Mrs. Reinhold to the Butterick pattern catalogs and turned to the suit and coat section. Mrs. MacDonald was watching and gave her a nod of encouragement.

"Are you making this yourself or having it made?" Annie asked.

"Myself," Mrs. Reinhold said. "I haven't sewn my own clothes much, but in the past year we've had a few setbacks and my husband wants to cut. . . wants me to be thrifty and wise."

"That is always a worthwhile goal." Annie sensed that a simpler pattern would be the best choice. "What about this one?" she said, pointing to a drawing of a streamlined three-quarter-length coat. "You could use a gold velvet for the stand-up collar and cuffs, and perhaps some wash braid sewn into a curved design down the front and along the bottom. See how clean the back silhouette is?" *Clean, meaning simple to sew.*

"I do see," the woman said, leaning close to the page to see it better. Annie hoped she had spectacles at home, or sewing anything would be difficult.

The woman stood upright and finalized the decision with a nod. "This one," she said. "I think I can conquer this one."

Annie smiled at her terminology. "I'm sure you can. Would you like a skirt to go with it? Let me show you another pattern that would complement the coat."

They quickly found a pattern for a simple A-line skirt to be sewn in brown lightweight wool, and the customer approved of Annie's choice of a chocolate-brown soutache braid as an accent to be applied in a loop design.

While Annie measured and cut the fabric, Mrs. Reinhold studied the illustration on the pattern envelope. "I do like her hat. And with brown gloves. . ."

"I would be happy to accompany you to the hat department and see if they have anything to your liking. If not, Macy's has an extensive trim, ribbon, and silk flower department so you can make your own hat that will be every bit as grand as the one in the picture."

"Ooh. I'd like that."

It took an hour to complete Mrs. Reinhold's transaction. With the fabric, trim, pattern, thread, basic hat—and the silk flowers and ribbon bought to recreate the one in the picture, Mrs. Reinhold's total was $9.45. Plus fifty cents for brown gloves—$9.95.

Annie sent the receipt and the money up to the tube room where change would be made. A boy collected the goods to wrap as Annie and Mrs. Reinhold chatted.

"If you have any questions about the construction, come back and ask."

Mrs. MacDonald joined them. "I couldn't help but see the lovely ensemble you're going to make. The color is very becoming."

"Thank you," Mrs. Reinhold said. "I couldn't have done it without Miss Wood's help."

Mrs. MacDonald put a hand on Annie's shoulder. "She is a prize."

The change was made, the hat and its trims were safely in a hatbox, with the fabric wrapped in brown paper, tied on top to form a handle. "I think I'm ready," Mrs. Reinhold said. "I can hardly wait to get home and get started. Thank you, Miss Wood."

"You are utterly welcome."

As the customer walked through the store toward the exit, Annie felt as if she would burst with pride. "I did it. I knew I could do it, but I actually did it."

"That you did," said Mrs. MacDonald. "You seem to have an eye for fashion and design. And because of your suggestions, she also purchased hat supplies and a pair of gloves. Well done."

"Thank you."

The floorwalker, Mrs. Gold, walked toward them. "Things going well, Mrs. MacDonald?"

"Very well, thanks to Miss Wood." She gave Mrs. Gold the details.

"A notable first transaction, Miss Wood," the older woman said. They all spotted a woman approaching the display of batiste blouse fabric. "Don't stop now," she said to Annie.

"I wouldn't think of it."

※

Annie pinned on her hat and gathered her jacket and purse to leave. Her first day was finally finished. As was she. It would take the rest of her stamina to get home.

Just as she left the locker room, Mildred stepped in her path. Although they'd been introduced, Annie had been so busy throughout the day that they'd never had a chance to get to know each other.

"Hello, Mildred. Are you as knackered as I am, because—"

"Because you hogged all the customers?"

"I did no such thing." Annie had second thoughts, trying to remember if she'd stepped up when she should have let Mildred handle a sale. "Or if I did, I apologize. It being my first day I was probably overly zealous."

"You ruined everything." Mildred took a step closer, making Annie want to step back. But something about the girl's stance and the way she scowled made Annie understand that it was important to stand her ground. She'd dealt with bullies before and knew strength was the best deterrent. Besides, Mildred was six inches shorter than Annie.

"I don't recall ruining anything," Annie said. "In fact, Mrs. MacDonald and Mrs. Gold commended my work."

"Bootlicker."

"Excuse me?"

"Don't think you can come into my department and take over, acting like a know-it-all."

Annie took a step back and then another, turning toward the mirror to adjust her hat. "I don't believe it is anyone's department—unless you are Mr. Straus." The hat properly adjusted, she faced Mildred. "When I saw him this morning he said if I worked hard I would attain all my aspirations. He's such a nice man."

Mildred's expressions revealed her battle between anger, frustration, and a tinge of envy and fear. "I've met him, too, you know."

"Jolly for you."

Mildred moved close and held a finger in Annie's face. "Watch it, Annie Wood. You don't want to cross me."

No, she didn't. With difficulty Annie masked her nerves with a smile and turned on her heel. "If you'll excuse me, I need to go home and rest up for another successful selling day tomorrow."

Annie left the room with a stride of bravado. Yet as she made her way toward the exit, she suffered a shiver. It was never good to make an enemy.

❧

Annie didn't get home until nearly seven. Jane was washing the dinner dishes.

"You missed the meal."

"I apologize." She locked the bakery door behind her.

"I kept a plate warm for you." Jane removed a plate of roast beef and potatoes from the oven and set it on the table.

Annie removed her hat and jacket and sat at the table with a thud. "That's very kind of you."

Jane brought her a glass of water. "How was your first day?"

"Long."

"As a maid you're used to long days. Longer days than this, yes?"

Annie cut a piece of meat and chewed on it, along with her response. "Working at the store seems longer because my day is out in public. As a maid I worked hard, but I was alone much of the time." She rubbed her cheeks. "My face is sore from being cheery."

Jane laughed. "My hands are sore from washing."

"Again I'm sorry for giving you a respite then taking it away so quickly."

"From the moment I met you I knew you were destined for big things."

"How did you know that?"

Jane shrugged. "You have an air of success about you."

Annie liked the sound of that.

◆❧◆

Annie was already in bed when Iris and Danny came down from the Tuttles' living quarters.

"I didn't know you were back," Iris said.

Danny sat on his bed. "You should have come upstairs. We had a rousing game of Whist."

"I don't have the energy to hold the cards." She wished they would turn out the light.

"Was being a clerk everything you thought it would be?" Iris asked.

Annie was unsure what Iris hoped to hear. She was too tired to come up with anything but the truth. "Actually, it's quite glorious. I enjoy helping customers put together a new ensemble from pattern to cloth to accessories. But it's also grinding work. My feet are throbbing."

Danny doused the lamp so he and Iris could get undressed. "I got to drive the wagon all the way to Chinatown today. It's like going all the way to China itself."

She heard the rustle of the straw mattress as he got under the covers.

"How about you, Iris? What did you do today?" Annie asked.

There was a long patch of silence. "I learned how to play jacks."

"What's that?"

"It's picking up little pieces of things before a ball bounces twice. I got to fivesies. And Nelly is an expert at doing the horse before carriage. But little Joe kept stealing the ball and. . ."

Annie had no idea what she was talking about, nor did she want to know. Sleep. Sleep.

Chapter Nine

Walking through Macy's on the way to her department, Annie paused at the display of sewing machines. She spotted Mrs. Holmquist, the clerk who had talked to her on her first visit to the store.

Mrs. Holmquist was setting up for the day and smiled at Annie. She began to give her the customer pitch: "May I interest you in the time-saving, high-quality aspects of our latest sewing machine? It is a must in any household that has an eye for custom fashion."

"That's a good line," Annie said.

"Thank you. I think the 'custom fashion' phrase is the clincher."

"Because every woman wants to think her fashion style is one of a kind?"

She touched the tip of her nose. Then she stared at Annie. "I've met you, haven't I?"

"I came in the store a few weeks ago, and you gave me your card."

Mrs. Holmquist looked at her more closely. "You're dressed differently, but it's more than that. You seem more. . .grown up."

Annie had to chuckle. "Life does that. And yes, I *am* more grown up now. And now I work here. Two weeks now. I'm Annie. Annie Wood."

"Edna Holmquist. And I've been here since bustles made our bottoms look enormous."

Annie liked her immensely. She glanced toward her department, not wanting to be late. "I am interested in learning how to use a machine. I know the basics of dress construction, but I've always sewn by hand."

"Are you hungry today?"

"Pardon?"

"Come by during your lunch break and I'll show you the basics."

"But you'll miss your lunch, too."

Mrs. Holmquist put a hand on her ample midsection. "I have stores enough to miss one meal."

They both saw Mrs. Gold coming down the aisle. "I'd better dash," Annie said. "But I'll be back."

⟨⟨⟨⟩⟩⟩

Annie thought about the sewing lesson all morning. It seemed a bit sneaky to ask another clerk for lessons behind Mrs. MacDonald's back—not to mention Mrs. Gold's eagle eye. So Annie decided on the up-front approach.

"Mrs. MacDonald, may I speak with you a moment?"

As they walked away to gain some privacy, Mildred eyed Annie suspiciously. Mildred was always eyeing Annie suspiciously. She seemed to have two expressions: suspicion and a false smile she pasted on when helping customers.

"Yes, Annie?" Mrs. MacDonald asked.

"I thought it might be advantageous if I knew how to run a sewing machine."

"You don't know how to use one?"

"I've only hand sewn."

"Dear, dear. I don't know how that point was missed during your interviews."

Did this mean her job was at stake? If only she hadn't brought it up. "I assure you I am a fast learner, and Mrs. Holmquist has agreed to teach me during my lunch break."

"Oh, she has, has she?"

"I think it would be advantageous to know as much as I can about sewing a garment from start to finish to best help the customers with specific questions, don't you?"

"I do. Of course I do." She looked toward Mrs. Holmquist's department then back. "You *are* familiar with using patterns."

It was a statement. A challenge. Annie couldn't lie. "I've studied the envelopes. I've noted the different pieces that are involved in making a garment."

"But you've never actually pinned them to fabric, cut them out, and sewn them together."

Suddenly being sneaky about her lessons seemed the better option. "No. I haven't." When Mrs. MacDonald's eyes grew large, Annie added, "I'm going to learn that, too. Since I've received my first paycheck, I plan to buy some fabric and a pattern so I can start a garment from scratch, just like my customers have to do."

Two customers approached, thankfully ending their conversation. For now.

❧

"You slip the edge of the fabric just so," Mrs. Holmquist said, "then lower the presser foot to keep it in place. Left hand behind, right hand in front. But first use your right hand to move the wheel on the side forward, and then let your feet get the treadle going, making the needle create the stitch."

Before Annie started the seam, she took a deep breath. "So many things to remember."

"With just a little practice it will become second nature."

Annie began, at first making the needle go too fast with a surge then getting control so it made the stitches with a steady rhythm. "I did it!"

"You certainly did. You're a natural."

They stopped what they were doing when a customer approached and looked at another machine. Annie experimented with reverse and pivoting at corners, and she loved the sense of taming a machine. She'd never used a machine—any machine. It made her feel bold and strong and confident, as if the world was hers to conquer.

Mrs. Holmquist returned. "How are you faring?"

Annie lifted the presser foot and snipped the threads. "I'm enjoying this."

"You should. Creating something from scratch is very satisfy—"

"Ahem."

They turned around and saw the floorwalker close by, her hands clasped behind her back.

"Good afternoon, Mrs. Gold," Mrs. Holmquist said.

The elder woman ignored the greeting. "What's going on here?"

"I'm giving Miss Wood a lesson in using a sewing machine."

"On company time?"

"During our lunch break," Annie said. "Mrs. Holmquist is a wonderful teacher."

"That may be, but I want no more lessons on the selling floor. Is that understood?"

"Yes, ma'am," Annie said.

"Yes, Mrs. Gold."

Annie stood. "I'm disappointed. I need to learn all of it. And Mrs.

MacDonald informed me I need to learn how to use a pattern and sew a garment together from scratch."

Mrs. Holmquist spread her arms. "Then I'm your woman."

"But we can't—"

"We can't have the lessons here, but I have a machine at home. And a dining table that's perfect for cutting out patterns. Come to my place after work a few evenings a week and I'll make you an expert in no time."

Annie thrilled at the thought. "I'd be happy to pay you for your time."

"Nonsense," Mrs. Holmquist said with a flip of her hand. "I'm a widow and my son lives in Pittsburgh. You would be doing me a favor by providing me with companionship and conversation beyond the sound of my own voice—for it seems I've taken to talking to myself."

Annie smiled. "Are you a good conversationalist?"

"Not really. I argue too much."

Annie noted the time. "I need to get back. Would tonight be too soon?"

"Just soon enough," the woman said.

Elated, Annie took a detour before returning to her duties in order to use the Macy's pay phone. She called the Tuttles and told them she would be late getting home.

All that accomplished, she returned to work, not needing food, not needing any fuel beyond anticipation.

❧

During the rest of the afternoon, while helping customers choose patterns, fabrics, and notions, Annie had a chance to peruse the Butterick fashion catalogs with her own needs in mind. She decided on a shirtwaist blouse and a five-gored skirt—very practical, yet stylish—and during a free moment she retrieved the two patterns from stock.

Her fabric choice was made while helping a woman find the proper dress goods for an afternoon dress. A brown broadcloth would do well for Annie's skirt, and an ivory cotton with a faint print of leaves would make a lovely blouse. On a whim she decided to create a cummerbund from some burnished-orange velveteen. Elated by the purchase for herself, she bought a length of three different colors of ribbon for Iris, Mrs. Tuttle, and Jane.

When Annie saw Mildred was occupied, she approached Mrs. MacDonald. "Would you cut my fabric, please? And make me a ticket?"

"You were serious about sewing yourself a garment, then."

"Of course I was. Mrs. Holmquist has offered to take me through the process at her home, starting this evening."

"That woman is a gem. You should feel very lucky to have such a teacher."

The fabric was cut and buttons and thread added to the purchase. Annie got the package boy to wrap up the goods. "When you're done just slip the parcel under the counter, Robbie."

It felt wonderful to pay for the goods out of her own earnings. During all the time she'd worked for the Kidds and earned wages, there had never been much to spend it on in the village of Summerfield. She'd saved up twenty pounds over the years, but it could have been two hundred for all the access she had to it now that she'd run away and left it behind in England.

She truly was starting from nothing. Wasn't that the American way? Pulling oneself up by one's bootstraps and making a success of it? Annie liked the sound of that challenge. And now, for the first time in her life, it all seemed very possible.

"There," she said, placing the coins in Mrs. MacDonald's palm. "All paid."

❧

At the end of the workday Annie was hungry—after all, she'd skipped lunch for the sewing machine lesson—but she was not at all tired. Rather, she was eager to go to Mrs. Holmquist's for the sewing lesson.

She gathered her jacket and hat from her locker, and on her way out, she stopped to retrieve her parcel from under the counter.

Suddenly a man grabbed her arm. "We'll take that, miss."

Annie had seen the man in the store previously and had been told he was a plainclothes security man. His main job was to catch shoplifters—

"You think I'm stealing?" she asked.

He took the parcel from her and opened it on the counter. "We've been so informed." He seemed disappointed at the contents. "Sewing supplies?"

Annie was incensed. She saved the spool of thread from rolling off the counter. "Yes, sewing supplies. Supplies I paid for. You can check my receipt book from today."

Mrs. Holmquist approached, putting on her gloves. "What's the issue, Mr. Horace?"

"We were informed Miss Wood was stealing."

"I assure you she is not." She spotted Mrs. MacDonald and motioned her to join them. "Velma, tell Mr. Horace that Annie paid for the goods."

Mrs. MacDonald's face passed from confusion to anger. "She most certainly did." She pointed to the parcel. "Wrap it back up, Annie."

"But we were informed—"

"You were informed wrong," Mrs. MacDonald said. "And who, may we ask, was your informant?"

"I prefer not to say."

"I insist you do say," she said.

"As do I," Mrs. Holmquist said.

"As do I," Annie said.

He looked reluctant but leaned close and said, "Miss Krieger."

"Mildred?" Annie wasn't surprised.

"I'll deal with her tomorrow," Mrs. MacDonald said. "Now then, let us go home in peace."

Mr. Horace nodded and let them go.

The three women made for the exit. "That girl," Mrs. MacDonald said. "I don't know what to do with her. If it's not lollygagging in the department, it's scowling when she should be smiling, or. . ."

"Has she done anything like this before?" Mrs. Holmquist asked.

"No."

"She took a dislike to me the moment I started work," Annie said. "I have no notion why. I've tried to be friendly."

"She has a chip on her shoulder, that one does," Mrs. MacDonald said.

Mrs. Holmquist opened the exit door and held it for the others. "Maybe it's time to knock it off."

"I know it's necessary," Mrs. MacDonald said. "But I'm not looking forward to the repercussions."

"Repercussions?" Annie asked.

They turned south on Broadway. "She is a relative to one of the buyers."

"Relative or not, Macy's holds its clerks to a certain standard." Mrs. Holmquist said. "Falsely accusing another clerk of theft is unacceptable."

Mrs. MacDonald nodded. "I'll speak with Mrs. Gold about it tomorrow."

"That's settled then," Mrs. Holmquist said.

Annie had a bad feeling about it. Nothing about Mildred seemed "settled."

❧

"Forgive the walk-up," Mrs. Holmquist said as they reached the landing for her third-floor apartment.

"I'm used to stairs," Annie said. "As a housemaid I used to—"

Mrs. Holmquist stopped in front of her door, key in hand. "You were a housemaid?"

"All my life."

"Until when?"

They heard another tenant on the stairs above. "I'll tell you the entire story inside."

Mrs. Holmquist used the key. She flipped a switch and turned on the lights. "It's not much to look at," she said. "But it was enough for my Ernie and our son."

Mrs. Holmquist hooked their coats and hats on a coatrack by the door.

"This is far more than I've ever had," Annie said. She strode through the parlor, past a table with four chairs and a small kitchen beyond. There was a hallway leading to the right.

"Two bedrooms, indoor plumbing, and electricity. And plenty of windows for natural light—though with working the hours I do, I don't get to see much of the sun."

"It has all the comforts of a loving home."

"All the comforts that Ernie and I needed to bring up our boy."

"You said your son was in Pittsburgh?"

"Steven is an English teacher there. I'm very proud of him."

"As you should be."

Mrs. Holmquist stepped into the kitchen. "I have some leftover stew and bread. Care for a quick supper?"

"That would be grand. I'm famished." Remembering the reason she was so hungry, she added, "You must be, too, for you gave up your lunch break to help me."

"It adds to a person's character to be hungry once in a while." She pointed to one of two chairs next to a tiny table. "Have a seat."

"I'd be glad to help."

"Keep me company while I work."

Annie took a seat and watched as Mrs. Holmquist took a bowl of stew out of a small icebox. "You have an icebox?"

"Wouldn't do without one. Ernie liked to buy me the latest equipment." She moved to an odd-looking stove. "But this is my pride and joy. It's an oil cookstove." She pointed to the three receptacles beneath the burners. "See here? I put the oil in, light it at the top, and voila! I can cook." She lit the wick, and a blue flame appeared.

"That's marvelous. Back at the manor the cook still uses an enormous cast-iron stove."

"I had one of those while Steven was growing up. But it took up too much room, and since I don't have reason to bake anymore. . ."

She sounded wistful about it, and Annie could sense her loneliness.

The smell of stew began to fill the room.

"Would you like some coffee, too, Annie?"

"That would be lovely. At least let me help with that." Mrs. Holmquist gave her the coffee grinder then put a pot of water on to heat.

She let Annie help with more than the coffee, showing her where the dishes were. Soon the meal was ready and they sat to eat in the dining room. "It smells delicious," Annie said, taking up her spoon. "Thank you for all you're doing for me, Mrs. Holmquist."

"You're welcome. And the name is Edna." She held out a hand and clearly expected Annie to take it. "And since you've thanked me, let us thank God." She bowed her head and Annie did the same. "Come, Lord Jesus, be our guest, and let Thy gifts to us be blest."

"Amen," Annie said.

But Edna wasn't through. "And thank You for the blessing of friendship. Amen."

"Amen again," Annie said. "The dinner grace makes me think of the Tuttles. They are probably sitting to eat this very moment."

"That's the family you live with?"

"Stay with."

"There's a difference?"

Annie wished she hadn't pressed the issue. "If I explain the difference I'll sound ungrateful, and I'm very grateful to them, for they took the three of us off the street when we had nothing and nowhere to go, and—"

"Three of you?"

"Danny and Iris are brother and sister. The three of us sleep in the storeroom of the Tuttles' bakery, amid the stores of flour and sugar. Before I was hired on at Macy's, I scrubbed their pots and pans. Their daughter was relieved of the duty, but then she had to go back to it when I got my job, and their son acts like he's interested in me, but I'm not interested in him—Iris is—and. . ." She sighed. "It's complicated."

"Thank God you've moved up in the world."

"I have, and I do thank Him for it."

Edna passed a jar of apple butter, and Annie spread it on her bread.

"How long have you known the two friends staying there with you? Iris and. . . ?"

"Danny. He's her little brother. We'd only known each other a short time when we all ran away from service together."

"You mentioned being a housemaid? This sounds like a story I need to hear."

And so, Annie told it. All of it. From her life in England as a housemaid, to her dreams of becoming a lady's maid for the Kidds, to the exciting trip to America, to the betrayal of the Misses, the tension with Grasston, escape, and being saved by the Tuttles.

By the time she was finished, they were done eating—and then some. They were on their second cup of coffee. "Iris, Danny, and I are the Three Musketeers. We're in this together."

"To begin with, perhaps. But you've moved on."

"But I am still their friend."

"Of course." Edna stood. "As *we* are friends. And as your friend, I think it's time I give you your first lesson on using a sewing pattern."

Their conversation had been so refreshing that Annie had nearly forgotten why she was there. She helped clear the table and was told not to mind washing the dishes. Edna moved the dining chairs away from the table, giving them full access. "Now show me the pattern and fabric you bought."

⁂

It was after ten when Annie stepped off the streetcar. The door to the bakery was understandably locked, but she rapped softly on the glass. Danny came and let her in.

" 'Bout time," he said.

"I know. Sorry."

He locked the door behind them. "They were worried."

"I called. I told them I'd be late."

They walked back to the storeroom where Iris was just getting into bed. "You're late."

Annie held back her impatience and shooed Danny into the kitchen so she could get undressed. She kept the door open so they could still talk. "How was your day?" she asked.

"As if you care," Iris said.

"Bug...," Danny said from the other room. "Be nice."

Iris got under the covers. "We never see you anymore. You've moved on and are making new friends and having adventures without us."

So that was the problem. Annie hurriedly unhooked her corset and drew her nightgown over her head. Then she sat on the bed beside Iris. "I'm not sure *adventures* is the right word. I'm working—working very hard."

"But you have other friends."

"I have one friend, Mrs. Holmquist, and she's old enough to be my mother."

The crease in Iris's forehead eased. "Oh."

Annie took the ribbons out of her purse. "I bought something for the three women in the house, but you can have first choice."

Iris's face softened, and she chose the ribbon of emerald green. "Thank you."

Annie took the girl's hand. "You will always be my special friends. My first friends in America."

Danny knocked on the doorjamb. "You decent?"

"I am."

He came in and stood nearby. "Remember, we each have to make the most of today. Even if it's not doing the same thing in the same place as each other."

He was such a dear. "I agree," she said. "Make the most of today."

Chapter Ten

Upon entering the sewing department, Annie spotted Mildred speaking with the security man, Mr. Horace. Mildred was shaking her head as he pointed his finger at her.

"If Mildred disliked me before, she'll hate me now," Annie said under her breath.

Mrs. MacDonald overheard. "You have made an enemy."

"Unless they sack her."

"I doubt that will happen. After all, she can give the defense that she was watching out for the best interests of Macy's by trying to catch a thief."

"But I'm not a thief."

She shrugged. "I'll keep an eye on her."

Annie wasn't sure Mrs. MacDonald's care would be enough to save her from Mildred's wrath.

Luckily for Annie, the day was a busy one. With a constant stream of customers there wasn't any free time for her to interact with Mildred.

And then, Annie's day brightened. A handsome man with sandy hair and a winning smile entered the department. "May I help you, sir?"

His eyebrows rose, and he gave her a mischievous smile. "I am the one to help you, Miss...?"

"Wood," she said.

He set a large sample box on the counter. On the outside was stenciled Butterick Pattern Company.

"You're the Butterick salesman?"

"I am." He held out his hand, "Sean Culver, at your service." He leaned his forearms atop the case and grinned at her. "What next, Miss Wood?"

She felt herself blush. "I don't know what to say. I don't know the procedure."

"The procedure is that I win you over in such a grand fashion that you'll go the extra mile to sell Butterick patterns above all others." He leaned close and spoke behind his hand. "We show utter disdain for the McCall's product."

"But isn't competition the essence of American business?"

"By your accent I can tell you're not from around here. I bet you're from. . . Brooklyn perhaps?"

She had no idea where Brooklyn was but knew he was teasing. "I am from England. Kent, to be exact."

"You worked in a store there?"

She chose her words carefully. "I worked for the Kidds at Crompton Hall. Lord and Lady Newley and their daughter and son."

He eyed her a long moment, and she feared he would guess her past lowly position. To distract him, she said, "Do you need to check our pattern stock, Mr. Culver?"

"It seems you've caught on to the procedure quite well, though far too quickly, for I would have enjoyed chatting a bit longer."

In spite of his blatant flattery, she liked the twinkle in his eye. "We can chat while we check the stock, can't we?"

"I can think of nothing better."

He came behind the counter and pulled out drawer after drawer of numbered patterns that were kept in a large oak cabinet. "Care to hold the clipboard for me and mark the numbers?"

"Isn't that making me do *your* job?"

"Part of it."

She looked across the department and spotted Mildred staring at them. Scowling. Since there were no customers to occupy Annie's time, if she left Mr. Culver to himself, a confrontation with Mildred would surely be imminent. "I would be happy to help you."

◈

Annie entered the employee cafeteria and chose a glass of milk, a turkey sandwich, and a bowl of vegetable soup. She paid her dime and took her tray toward a table. She spotted Mildred, nearly finished with her meal, and thought of joining her. The stress of waiting for Mildred's wrath made her want to push for a confrontation so she could be done with it. Or—miracle of miracles—make peace.

But as she approached Mildred's table, the girl left.

So be it.

Mildred glared. Mildred stared.

And though Annie tried not to, Annie cared.

Her nerves got the best of her midafternoon, and she fumbled a box of buttons, scattering them over the floor. Mrs. MacDonald moved to help, but Annie waved her off. "I'm the fumble fingers. I'll get them."

She was nearly through when a man knelt beside her and said, "You missed one."

"Thank—"

"Hello, Annie."

Annie's heart flipped. She stood and stepped away from him. "Grasston."

"I'm glad you remember me."

"What are you doing here?"

He moved to the counter and fingered some lace. "I was just walking through, passing the time since I now *have* so much time. You see, I am no longer employed by the Friesens."

"What?"

"It seems that losing three pairs of gloves tipped the scales against me. I was sacked."

Because of the gloves I took?

"I'm sorry to hear that," she said, even though she wasn't. "Are you looking for other employment?"

"Actually, I'm looking for something more satisfying than employment."

She remembered his inappropriate behavior against herself and Iris. "Move along, Mr. Grasston. There will be none of that."

"You flatter yourself. I wasn't talking about *that*, I was talking about something even better."

She didn't want to ask.

"I'm talking about revenge."

Her breath caught in her throat, and she decided to feign ignorance. "Revenge for what?"

"For someone setting me up, for ruining my reputation."

He knew. For who else would have taken his gloves?

"I'm sorry my joke caused you—"

"Joke?" he said, taking a step closer.

His voice had risen, and people looked toward them.

"I meant no harm." *Not this much harm.* "Now please. . .go away."

She saw Mrs. MacDonald speaking with Mr. Horace. Help was on the way.

But Grasston saw it, too. With the parting words "We're not done, you and me," he quickly walked toward the exit.

"Are you all right, Miss Wood?" Mr. Horace asked. "Was that man harassing you?"

No. And yes.

"I can go after him, if you'd like."

The last thing she wanted was for Grasston to hold more against her. "I'm all right. No harm done."

"Who was he?"

"Just an acquaintance from my last employment."

"He seemed to take issue with you."

She smoothed the lace Grasston had touched then pulled her hand away, remembering that he'd touched it. "I believe Mr. Grasston takes issue with many more persons than me. It's his nature."

"There are those sorts," Mr. Horace said. "I'll leave you to your work, but let me know if you see him again."

"I most certainly will, and thank you for your concern."

As soon as he left, Mrs. MacDonald came over, and Annie repeated her rendition of the event.

It was a mixed blessing that Mildred stayed away. But instead of bothering Annie, Mildred kept looking in the direction Grasston had gone.

The customer perused the Butterick catalog. "I don't like the sleeve in this dress but I do like the neckline and the skirt."

Annie made note of it then said, "Excuse me a moment, but if we go back two pages. . ." She found the pattern illustration she was looking for. "Is this the sleeve you like?"

"Yes, it is. But I don't like that pattern's bodice or skirt."

"Then combine the two patterns into one garment," Annie said.

The woman studied the pictures of both patterns, back and forth between the pages. "I can do that?"

"Of course you can. See how the set-in of the sleeve is the same? This sleeve will fit into this other pattern and you will have exactly the fashion you want."

"Brilliant!" the woman said. "I'll take both."

"Now let's find you some fabric."

❧

Annie perused her sales receipt book at the end of the day. She mentally added the numbers. It had been a good day. Her best ever. At this rate she'd get a bonus.

"Don't gloat."

Annie looked up to find Mildred standing in front of her. "Gloat?"

"You're stealing the best customers."

"I am doing no such thing. And how would either of us know who is a good customer versus a bad one until they start looking?"

Mildred huffed this off. "You got me in trouble and I don't appreciate it."

Annie had to back up her thinking. Was she talking about Mr. Horace? "You shouldn't accuse me of stealing when you know very well I paid for the items."

"I didn't know that. You hid the package like you were guilty."

"I put it under the counter, out of sight from the customers. If I wanted to steal, would I get Mrs. MacDonald to cut the fabric for me?" Annie was done, fully done with her. She crossed her arms in front of her chest. "Is there anything else you have against me? For if there is, let it out now. I want to know."

Mildred's expression was a mask of confusion. Had no one ever called her out on her behavior?

When she didn't say anything, Annie said, "Then I would appreciate it if—"

"Your flirting with Mr. Culver is disgusting."

This was unexpected. "If you must know, he flirted with me. And any banter between us is none of your business, and above all, is not disgusting or inappropriate or any other word you care to fling at me."

"Why does that button man hate you?"

Button man? Then Annie realized Mildred was talking about Grasston, who had helped her pick up the buttons. She'd had enough. "If you would spend more time focused on your own clerking skills and less on me, we'd both be happier and more successful."

Mildred shuffled her shoulders. "I'm a fine clerk."

"Good for you. Now if you'll excuse me, I want to get home."

The gall of some people.

Annie first felt the *presence* as she waited for the streetcar, a distinct feeling that someone was watching her. She turned around, but the sidewalk was crowded and she saw no one out of the ordinary. The stop was populated by many Macy's employees, many who smiled or nodded at her gaze.

Then, she spotted a black-suited man slip around the corner of a building. Grasston had been wearing black.

The streetcar arrived and she was forced to let her suspicions go. She was being silly. A lot of men wore black suits. Most did. All of the male clerks at Macy's wore black.

She got on the streetcar and found a seat—which was a blessing, for the car was overloaded and many had to stand. She made small talk with her seatmate and let her nerves subside.

Until she was almost at the bakery door. Suddenly fear crawled up her spine. She spun around and scanned the street.

And saw no one.

But with all the alcoves and doorways, it would be easy for someone to slip out of sight.

Gathering her senses, she hurried to the door, entered, and locked it.

Iris ran to greet her. "You're home for dinner! I'm so glad. I have much to tell you."

Annie let the tension outside be overshadowed by her friend's enthusiasm—which was a marked improvement over Iris being so irritable.

"I'd love to hear all about it," Annie said.

But then Mrs. Tuttle and Jane asked for help with dinner, so the conversation had to be postponed. Yet Annie noticed they were each wearing a new hair ribbon—Mrs. Tuttle's was royal blue, and Jane's was red. And Iris wore her green one. Annie was glad she'd thought to buy them the small gift. It would hopefully ease the friction of her working such long hours.

But then during dinner, Annie thought she saw someone looking in the window from the street. It was dark out, and hard to see, but she couldn't help but wonder if Grasston was out there. Waiting for her. Waiting for his revenge.

"Goodness, Annie," Mrs. Tuttle said. "Your face is pale as a baby's, the blush gone from your cheeks entirely. Has something frightened you?"

It showed? "I missed your fine cooking last night and am in dire need of it."

With that, the discussion moved to Edna and her lessons. "How often are you going to have those lessons?" Danny asked.

"Every other evening," she said. "We have the skirt and blouse cut out, but next I have to learn how to sew it all together—on a machine, not by hand."

Mrs. Tuttle nodded. "Mrs. DiSalvo down the street has a machine. She's offered to sew some dresses for the little ones."

"In exchange for bread, I hope," Mr. Tuttle said.

"Yes, dear. I know the rule. Barter is better."

"I'd like to barter for a new horse," the elder Tuttle said. "Old Moss is limping."

As talk turned to other things, Annie tried not to glance at the window. Tried not to be afraid.

~∽~

After the lights were out in the bakery, Annie ventured near the window, needing the darkness to cover her interest. She peered out and saw no one besides a couple walking together, and another man hurrying home late from work.

She started when Danny came up beside her. "You scared me!"

"I see that. The question is, why are you scared?"

He deserved to know, for he'd been a part of it, too. "I saw Grasston."

"How is the clod?"

"Angry." She faced him. "He got sacked because of the gloves I pinched."

"Sacked for gloves? That can't be the only reason. Others besides us musta seen the kind of man he was."

"Whether they saw or not, he's blaming me. He wants revenge for costing him the job and ruining his reputation."

"He did that on his own."

"Tell him that."

"I will tell him, if I see him."

Annie felt a terrible foreboding. She put a hand on Danny's arm. "You will not tell him anything. If you see him you will give him a wide berth. Do not involve yourself."

"Too late. I am involved. Remember I promised to protect you forever."

She slipped her hand around his arm. "Are you sure you're only thirteen?"

⧉

Annie was dozing by the time Iris came down from upstairs. "Baby Joe would *not* go to bed. And his ma makes it worse by coddling him. Annie? You awake? Remember I have things to tell you?"

"I'm awake."

But only for a moment.

CHAPTER ELEVEN

Danny nudged her. "Get up! It's morning."

Annie heard him awaken his sister next then heard the door to the storeroom open and close.

The night had been too short, for she had been plagued with nightmares about Grasston popping out of hidden corners, being everywhere. A constant threat.

She tried to force the latest bad dream away. The details faded but the essence remained.

"Good morning, Iris," Annie said as they both got out of bed.

"She speaks."

"What?"

Iris smoothed the blanket on her makeshift bed. "Remember last evening how I wanted to tell you something important?"

Oh dear. "I'm sorry. I was preoccupied with—"

"With your very important life. I know. Sorry to intrude."

Annie kicked herself. With all her Grasston worries, she'd completely forgotten her friend. "I'm the one who's sorry. Tell me your news."

Iris grabbed her clothes off a shelf. "If you'll excuse me. I'll dress elsewhere."

Again, the door opened. And closed.

Annie stood in the room alone. She sank onto her bed. She'd been so caught up in her new life she'd ignored the old one. Her old friends. Her best friend.

She looked upward when she heard the patter of children's feet overhead. The Tuttles were up. Iris was busy.

The thought of enduring breakfast with the lot of them made her lose her appetite. Iris wasn't good at hiding her feelings, and there would be more tension.

"I can't take more tension right now."

And so, Annie hurriedly got dressed and left early for work. It wasn't the courageous thing to do, but it was the best she could do.

❦

It was too early to go to work, so Annie strolled around Herald Square. The elevated train that loomed above the street seemed ominous, especially considering her mood, so she walked to the Herald Newspaper building at the crown of the square. It was already humming with commotion. She could even look in the windows and watch the presses.

A young boy approached, a stack of newspapers under his arm. "Paper, lady?"

"No, thank you."

"Don't you care nothing for the World Series?"

"I'm afraid I don't know what that is."

He gawked at her. "Baseball, lady. The New York Giants are playing the Philadelphia Athletics. Third game is today up at the Polo Grounds at two twenty-five. We're tied one game to one."

Annie knew nothing about baseball, but the boy's passion made her believe it was a lack of knowledge that needed to be rectified. "You convinced me. I'll take a paper."

"Remember, two twenty-five. No need to even go because thousands stand right here outside the offices and get a play-by-play."

"I'll be working." She nodded toward Macy's.

"Just listen for the roar of the crowds. They'll let you know how we're doing." He tipped his cap and left to do his job.

Speaking of. . .

She checked the clocks on the Herald building and saw it was time to go to work.

❦

"Good afternoon to you, Miss Wood."

Annie was glad to see Mr. Culver. "I'm surprised you're here," she said.

"Why?"

"Doesn't the baseball game start any minute?"

His eyebrows lifted. "You're a Giants fan?"

She retrieved the newspaper from under the counter. "Not yet. But I'm learning."

"Highly commendable. And you've caught me. I purposely timed my day to be around the Herald offices during the game. They have a Play-O-Graph posted outside that shows a miniature baseball diamond. They get the results telegraphed inside and then post the plays on the board."

"How ingenious." She didn't want to admit she had no idea what a baseball diamond was, or any details about how the game was played. But she was happy he was impressed with her interest.

"What can I help you with, Mr. Culver? I don't believe we've depleted our Butterick stock since your last visit."

He set his sales case on the floor at his feet. "Actually, I've come because of a complaint."

She put a hand to her chest. "About me?"

She saw him glance in Mildred's direction.

"Mildred is the complainant?"

"I assure you there isn't cause for worry, but my superiors insist that I—"

"Everything about that girl is cause for worry," Annie said, more to herself than to him. "How did she make this complaint?"

"She sent a note to the Butterick office, and they sent me to deal with it."

"Meaning?"

"I'm supposed to talk to you. See if there is any basis in the complaint."

Annie's heart pumped double time—not out of fear but anger. She hadn't done anything wrong, and the gall of Mildred to imply otherwise was unacceptable. "Since Mildred leveled the complaint, I insist she be present during your accusation. Mrs. MacDonald, too." Annie didn't wait for him to say yea or nay but called the two women over.

"What is it, Miss Wood?" the older woman asked as she joined them. "Afternoon, Mr. Culver."

Annie pointed at Mildred, who approached warily. "It appears Mildred has lodged a complaint against me to the Butterick Company."

Mrs. MacDonald's brow dipped. "Is this true, Miss Krieger?"

Her shrug turned into a nod. "When I witness wrongdoing I feel it is my duty to report it."

"Wrongdoing like the fabric I *didn't* steal?"

"I agree with your point, Miss Wood," Mrs. MacDonald said. "Miss Krieger, you do seem overly concerned with Miss Wood's behavior."

Annie's thoughts returned to Mildred's complaint. "There has been no wrongdoing. How can there possibly be wrongdoing selling sewing patterns?"

They all looked to Mildred. At least she had the decency to blush. "I. . ." She passed it off to Mr. Culver. "He has the complaint. Let him read it."

Coward.

Mr. Culver unfolded a piece of paper. "'Miss Annie Wood has denigrated the Butterick product to customers by declaring their designs insufficient and inferior.'"

"What?"

Mr. Culver lifted a hand and continued, "'Noting a customer's dissatisfaction with the fashion design of a pattern, Miss Wood did not try to sway her by mentioning the pattern's attributes, but openly discussed its flaws. This disloyalty should not go unpunished.'"

Annie laughed. Then she laughed harder. "That's the all of it? That's your complaint?"

Mildred pointed to the note. "It's true. I witnessed you with that customer wearing the blue coat, talking with her about the flaws in the pattern designs."

This was absurd. "She didn't like a certain sleeve, but *did* like the bodice and skirt of a dress pattern. I suggested she combine two patterns to get the look she desired. In the end she bought two patterns instead of one. I doubled the sale."

Mildred blinked twice then took sudden interest in the cuffs of her blouse. "I. . . I stand by my complaint."

Mrs. MacDonald shook her head. "Miss Krieger. Really."

"But she—"

"I'll deal with you in a moment." She turned to the others. "Please forgive Miss Krieger her falsely placed. . .whatever it is. Miss Wood? I congratulate you on doubling the sale. Keep up the good work. Mr. Culver, I assume this is a nonissue with your employer?"

"It is now."

"Very good. Now if you'll excuse us." She took Mildred's arm and led her away. After they slipped behind a display of woolens, Annie could see Mildred get a good ear bashing.

"She's hated me since my first day," Annie said.

"With good reason—no one likes her, and everyone likes you."

"How do you know that?"

"Oh, I know. You want to know how I know?"

"I suppose."

He moved to block the view of Mildred's scolding. "Because *I* like you, Miss Wood. Because you're irresistible."

She blinked. "Where did that come from?"

"I could say 'my heart,' but that would sound too sappy, don't you think?"

"It would."

He tapped a finger against his lower lip. "So. . .from where did my fondness stem?"

"Mr. Culver, I don't think you should talk like this."

"You're against the truth?"

"I'm against flattery. You shouldn't flirt with me."

His face turned serious, his mischief gone. "I don't want to flirt with you, Miss Wood. I flirt all day to gain sales. It's part of the job. But with you. . ." He waited until she looked at his eyes. "I knew very quickly you were special."

She smiled. "Flattery again, Mr. Culver?"

He shook his head. "I admit that the first Sean Culver you met was the salesman, but the Sean talking to you now is just the man. And that man wants to know the woman, Annie Wood, beyond sales and work and customers."

She didn't know what to say.

He took her hesitance as a rejection. "I'm sorry. I've gone too far and said too much too fast. I don't mean for my words to be off putting or alarming, only to be honest and—"

She touched his arm for the briefest of seconds. "Shh."

He sighed. "Again I've said too much—I'm sorry."

She sighed, too. "You haven't said too much, you've said just enough."

Relief washed over his face. "Just enough for. . . ?"

"For me to be interested. In Sean Culver, the man." She was surprised at her own words, yet they were sincere.

He beamed. "You've made my day, Annie Wood. My week." He leaned close, becoming the flirt again. "Perhaps my life."

She laughed. "Shut it down, sir. Don't get carried away."

He put on his hat and retrieved his sales case. "I won't promise a thing. See you tomorrow, Miss Wood."

"What's tomorrow?"

"You and I are taking a late lunch so we can go outside and watch the game play out across the square."

Annie looked for Mrs. MacDonald, who was helping a customer. "I'm not sure I'll be able to get away."

"It's worth asking, isn't it?"

Yes, it was.

⤨

Thankfully, Mildred avoided even the proximity of Annie the rest of the day. Perhaps the humiliation and the scolding by Mrs. MacDonald had properly quashed her schemes. Annie began to relax, to breathe easier, to—

Annie did a double take when she noticed the customer Mildred was assisting. Odd enough that it was a man, but when he looked in her direction. . .

Grasston!

She gasped. How dare he come back here!

She looked around the store for Mr. Horace.

Grasston said something to Mildred then turned toward Annie, smiled, and waved.

Somehow his false friendship was more frightening than a direct threat.

Annie spotted Mrs. MacDonald, but she was busy with a customer. If Grasston approached, she would be on her own.

Only he didn't approach. He continued his conversation with Mildred and even got her laughing. He touched Mildred's hair, as if retrieving a thread from the tendrils near her face.

Don't you touch her!

Annie's heart beat in her throat. She didn't like Mildred, but the girl had no idea the sort of man she was flirting with. Annie stepped into the aisle when Grasston faced her and offered a proper bow and a tip of his hat. Then he walked toward an exit.

After watching him leave, Mildred looked at Annie and gave her a challenging smile full of contempt and satisfaction. *She doesn't know what she's doing.* Annie set aside her dislike and went over to talk to her. "What did that man want?"

"None of your business."

"Don't play coy with me. Now is not the time."

103

"Not the time because I happen to have a handsome man interested in me? You have Mr. Culver wrapped around your little finger. You want the button man, too?"

It was apparent that Grasston hadn't told Mildred his affiliation with Annie. "I know him better than you, and he's smarmy, a conniving dolt, and—"

"I will know him plenty well myself after we go walking this Sunday."

"No!"

Mildred blinked at Annie's outburst then busied herself with a rack of trim. "I don't need your permission to have a gentleman caller."

"He's not a gentleman. He's a cad."

"He is no such thing. He's very nice and said he's been in Macy's before and has admired me from afar. It took all his courage to approach me today and talk with me."

She was utterly blind. "He's not here for you, he's here for me."

Mildred straightened to her full five-foot-nothing height and glared at Annie. "How dare you think you are the only woman who can attract male attention."

"I don't think any such thing. It's just that I know him. He's out for no good. He wants to hurt me. He's paying attention to you to get to me." Annie saw a flutter of pain cross Mildred's face. "I don't say it to be mean but to save you from grief, from heartache, and. . .and maybe worse."

"I don't need your warnings. I am quite capable of taking care of myself."

"But—"

Mildred glared at her and lowered her voice. "You wonder why I hate you? You come into Macy's and act as though you are the queen of the store. You can do no wrong and everyone loves you."

"Maybe if you didn't have such a sour look on your face all day and weren't such a dosser they'd—"

Mildred pointed toward the other end of the department. "Go on. Go back to your counter and stop trying to take away my chance at happiness."

Annie was stunned.

"Go!"

"Just be careful of him, all right?"

Mildred turned on her heel and walked away.

Annie returned to her post, saying a prayer of protection for Mildred. She might not like the girl, but she wouldn't wish Grasston on anyone.

❦

It was closing time, and Edna stopped at Annie's department on her way out. "Are you coming over this evening for another lesson?"

Annie looked around at the mess in her department. "I will as soon as I clean up from my last customer. She bought dress goods for three ensembles, but it made quite a shambles of everything."

"Do you want me to wait for you?"

"Go on home. I'll be there as soon as I can."

"I'll stop at the butcher's to buy some pork chops and get supper going."

After the drama of the day, Annie was famished. "You are too good to me."

❦

On the way to Edna's home, Annie found a seat on the streetcar and closed her eyes. Even a few minutes of rest would be helpful, for her day wasn't over. Tonight she was going to learn how to set in sleeves.

Instinctively, Annie sensed when her stop was close, opened her eyes to confirm it, and got out. But as she walked toward Edna's flat, she felt uneasy. The familiar sound of people walking behind her intensified and became significant.

She glanced over her shoulder and saw others making their way home after work, everyone intent on their own thoughts and their own destinations.

But then she saw him. A face intent on *her*. Staring after *her*.

Grasston.

She quickened her pace, needing to get to the safety of Edna's. She still had two blocks to go and the crowd behind her was thinning out. They were her buffer against him. Surely, he wouldn't do anything surrounded by witnesses.

But then she felt a swell of anger rise up. Unlike Mildred, she was not going to be a victim. She knew the truth about him, and with truth came power.

And so she stopped walking and turned to face him.

A few other walkers looked surprised at her action but handily sidestepped around her. But other than the lifting of his right eyebrow, Grasston wasn't fazed. He stopped in front of her and smirked as if nothing she did would rile him, and even worse, as if everything she did stirred him in a way Annie didn't want to think about.

"Mr. Grasston," she said. "Two times in one day? Really? Don't you have anything better to do with your time than—"

He grabbed her upper arm with a shocking strength and pulled her close to his side. Then he led her into an alley. She could feel his warm breath in her ear. With each step away from the community of the street, her fear intensified. *He's going to hurt me! Lord, please don't let him hurt me!*

She frantically looked around for an escape, but the alley was closed at the end and only grew darker at its terminus. She looked upward but only saw clothes hanging like flags on lines strung over the alleyway. The few windows were closed against the evening chill.

The possibilities of what could happen threatened to crush her. But then she thought of Iris and Danny and all they'd been through losing their family, and their courage combined with her own that had thrust them out of servanthood and into lives full of hope and opportunity. The thought of them gave her the power to shove aside her fear and ignited her choice to fight. She would not let this bully have his way.

With a surge of energy, she twisted her arm out of his grip and ran toward the street.

But he ran faster.

He caught the hem of her jacket and yanked, making her fall. He fell on top of her, turning her over, securing her flailing arms.

"Come on, Annie. Gimme what I want."

Please, God, help!

The weight of him. . .she found it hard to breathe. She knew his brute strength was no match for her own. And so she used all her energy and what oxygen was left in her lungs to do one thing. She screamed. "Help! He's attacking me!"

He released an arm to cover her mouth, but she bit him and continued calling for help.

She heard a commotion at the entrance to the alley; then two men pulled Grasston off her. He ran toward the street and one man went after him. "Police! Police! Stop him!"

The other man, and then a woman, knelt beside her. "Are you all right?"

They helped her sit then stand. "I'm fine. Thank you, thank you so much."

No one asked what Grasston was doing to her. There was no need. His aberrant intention had been clear.

And she had been saved from it. God had heard her cries and saved her.

The couple helped her to the street, where a police officer rushed toward them. The man who'd run after Grasston returned and said he'd lost him. Annie thanked the couple and the man profusely, and they stepped away as the officer asked her for details of the assault. She did not hesitate to give him Grasston's name, though she hated that she didn't know where he'd been living since being sacked. "He's been harassing me at work and following me home. He blames me for losing his job."

"Where is your home?" the officer asked.

"Far from here, but I was going to my friend's flat a block away. Take me there, please."

She gave him the name of the Tuttles' bakery and her department at Macy's should he want to ask further questions. He accompanied her to Edna's, chaperoning her all the way to the door.

Edna opened the door saying, "I was wondering when you would get—" She looked taken aback by the officer's presence. "Sir? Annie? What happened?"

Annie turned to the bobby. "Thank you, Officer. I'll be all right now."

He tipped his cap and said, "The name is Officer Brady, miss. I suggest you stay here the night if you could. At least until we catch him."

Annie looked to Edna, whose eyes were wide with questions. "I can stay, can't I?"

"Of course, of course. Come in."

As soon as the door was closed behind her, Annie's legs faltered. She fell into the arms of her friend.

<hr/>

Dinner was eaten, the story was told, and the sewing lesson set aside. The horrors of what could have been consumed Annie and sapped her remaining energy, leaving her barely enough to button the nightgown Edna lent her. The palms of her hands stung from the scraping they'd taken when she fell, and her muscles ached from the impact and the fight against Grasston. Even her face was sore from his hand trying to cover her mouth.

Edna finished smoothing the bedding in a small bedroom that used to belong to her son. "There now. Your bed is ready, and the Tuttles have been called and assured of your safety. There is nothing left for you to do but rest. Tomorrow is another day."

If only it were so easy. Annie lay down and let her friend tuck a sheet and blanket around her. "You've been so kind."

Edna ran a comforting hand over Annie's forehead. "Everything will be all right. They'll catch him."

"How? They don't know where he lives. He's but one man in an enormous city."

Edna nodded then gathered Annie's hands into her own. She bowed her head. "Father, thank You for saving Annie from that evil man. Help the police find Grasston and arrest him so he no longer causes harm to my dear friend, to Mildred, or to any other person. Give Annie the rejuvenating gift of sleep, and the courage and strength to deal with tomorrow, tomorrow. Amen."

"He *did* save me," Annie said. "God."

"Yes, He did. Now sleep."

She would try, but when she closed her eyes, Grasston's face loomed large and fierce.

Chapter Twelve

"Are you sure you want to go to work today?" Edna asked Annie. "You have good reason not to."

She let Edna board the streetcar first and waited to answer until they were seated. "I have good reason to go in. I will not let Grasston stop me from earning a living."

"What if he comes back to Macy's? What if he follows you home tonight?"

She had no answer.

"Perhaps you should come and stay with me again," Edna said. "He doesn't know where I live."

"Can we be sure of that?" Annie asked. "I wouldn't put it past him to run away last night but circle back to see where I was heading. You may be in as much danger as I."

Suddenly Edna turned her head and looked at everyone in the streetcar. "I'm not sure I know what he looks like."

"He looks like evil," Annie said. She was tired of talking about him, thinking about him, dreaming about him.

"As soon as we get to work, you must inform Mr. Horace. He's seen him and talked to him. Have him be on the lookout."

It was a wise idea. As the streetcar jostled her to the left and right, forward and back, Annie closed her eyes and let the movement take her where it wished. Why fight it? She was clearly not in control.

❧

Should I tell her?

Annie considered telling Mildred about how she'd been attacked. But every time she thought of it, Mildred would glare at her or blatantly turn her back.

"So be it," Annie finally said aloud. Luckily a customer came by and she was distracted. The busier the better.

She spotted Mr. Horace strolling by. He'd been true to his word that morning and made diligent rounds through Annie's department hourly. Every time he passed, he gave her a nod. His presence gave Annie a tentative peace.

A peace that could be shattered in a blink.

"Excuse me, miss," a customer said. "I asked for the blue ribbon, not green."

"Oh. Yes. I'm sorry." It was not her first error.

"What happened to your hands?" the woman asked, pointing to Annie's scraped palms.

"I fell." *I was tackled to the ground by a man who meant to force himself on me.*

"Put a potato poultice on them."

Annie had never heard of such a thing but thanked the woman and sent her on her way.

Mrs. MacDonald approached. "Go home, Annie. You've been through a very traumatic experience. No one expects you to act as though nothing happened."

Suddenly the stress of keeping a stiff upper lip combined with the stress of her attack, and she began to cry.

Mrs. MacDonald led her behind a pattern display and handed her a handkerchief. "That's it, then. You're going home right now." She looked around the store then called to Robbie, the package boy. "Robbie, I want you to accompany Miss Wood home. She's not feeling well. Can you do that for me?"

"Sure, Mrs. MacDonald." He looked at Annie. "You sick or somethun?"

Mrs. MacDonald reached into her pocket and gave him a few coins. "Here's money for the streetcar to her house and back. Now go up to the lockers and get her jacket, hat, and purse. Number...?" She glanced at Annie.

"Number 387."

"Go on now. I'll make sure you stay on the clock."

He nodded and ran toward the stairs.

Annie dried her eyes. "I'm sorry to be such a bother, but I do think home is exactly where I need to be."

⊗

"My ma will love getting some fresh bread," Robbie said as he walked Annie from the streetcar to the Tuttles' bakery. "That's mighty nice of you to offer."

"It's nice of you to interrupt your day to bring me home," Annie said.

"Interrupting is good." Robbie walked with one foot in the street and one on the curb. "I likes getting out. Whenever they needs anyone to go on an errand, I'm their boy."

He was delightful. Actually, she thought of introducing him to Danny. Both boys had the same charming manner.

They approached the bakery, and Annie got her wish, as Danny was outside, painting the trim around the window.

"Annie! What are you doing home so early? Are you all right? We got the call last night from Mrs. Holmquist and were worried."

The thought of rehashing all that had happened made her stomach turn.

"She's not feeling good," Robbie said. "I brought her home. Got paid for it, too."

Annie hurried past his comments. "Danny, I'd like you to meet Robbie. He works at Macy's with me. Robbie, this is Danny, a very good friend who makes deliveries for the bakery."

Robbie's eyes grew wide. "You get to drive a wagon?"

"I do. And I get to paint, too, until the next delivery is ready."

She'd been right about their affinity for each other. She left them to talk and had her hand on the doorknob when she looked inside. Grasston was buying some bread from Mr. Tuttle.

She pulled her hand away and stepped back.

At that moment, he spotted her. He looked right at her and grinned. Then he tipped his hat as if nothing had happened.

Danny moved to her side. "What's wrong?"

Everything. She pointed at Grasston. It took Danny a moment to recognize him. "How did he get in there? I didn't see him go by me."

It didn't matter how, it just mattered why. "He's the one who attacked me last night." She held up her palms as evidence. "I called the police on him, but he ran away."

Robbie took a step toward the window to see him better. "Is he the man Mr. Horace told us about?"

She needed to make Robbie leave. She took him by the shoulders and turned him toward the streetcar stop in the next block. "Go on now. Get back to work before you get in trouble."

"But—"

"Go!"

Robbie reluctantly ran down the street.

Grasston chatted with Mr. Tuttle. Was there no end to his nerve?

Danny pulled the door open and, before Annie could stop him, stepped inside. "You!" he shouted, pointing a finger at Grasston. Annie followed him inside.

Grasston looked surprised—for a brief moment—then his smirk returned. "If it isn't Danny the hall boy. What'd you do? Run off with Annie? Isn't she a little old for you?"

Danny shoved him into the counter, making him drop his bread.

"Danny!" Mr. Tuttle said.

Thomas moved close, his hands covered with flour, his eyes alert.

Danny talked to the Tuttle men. "His name is Grasston and he used to work at the Friesens' with me and Iris, and—"

Grasston smoothed his coat and looked toward the back of the shop. "Is Iris here with you? I'd really like to see her. *Really* like to see her."

Although he was a good six inches shorter than Grasston, Danny swung to hit him in the jaw.

Grasston grabbed his wrist. "What do you think you're doing, you dumb kid?"

Danny yanked his hand away. "You attacked Annie last night. You hurt her."

Thomas moved closer, and Mr. Tuttle asked, "Is this true, Annie? This is the man?"

"Show 'em your hands," Danny said.

She did just that.

Mr. Tuttle called Jane from the back of the bakery. "Run down the street and get the police, Jane. Tell them to hurry."

She rushed past, giving Grasston a wide arc. Upon her exit Danny stood in front of the door, barring Grasston's escape. Thomas stepped around to Grasston's side of the counter.

He was cornered. The police would get him, lock him up, and Annie would be safe again.

But then Grasston whipped out a knife, pointing it at each man. "Back away!"

Thomas raised his hands. "Annie, come here."

Gladly. She took cover behind him.

With a surge of motion, Grasston grabbed Danny's arm and yanked him away from the door so violently that he bounded off the wall and tumbled to the floor. He rushed outside and turned right, while Jane had turned left.

Annie ran to Danny's side. "Are you all right?"

Danny moaned as he got to his feet but immediately made for the door. Annie caught his arm, holding him back.

"Let me go! I'm not going to let him get away with this."

Annie held firm. "He has a weapon and he'll use it. Let the police handle it." *Hopefully they'll catch him this time.*

A customer came in, studied their faces a moment, and then asked, "You open?"

Mr. Tuttle ran a hand through his hair then said, "What can I get for you?"

⌘

Life goes on.

It was an odd fact to realize that Annie's crises did not change the world. Or stop it.

After Grasston ran from the bakery, there was still bread to get out of the oven, pans to wash, deliveries to make, and customers to serve.

After speaking with a constable, who assured Annie that Grasston would be caught, Mr. Tuttle suggested Annie go upstairs with the family. She could rest up there.

It was a nice thought, but impossible. With five children under the age of nine, there was seldom a quiet moment. They weren't naughty; they were just children.

Mrs. Tuttle was down in the bakery most of the time, leaving Annie alone with Iris and the brood. Iris got the older two girls interested in drawing pictures and the younger three boys playing with blocks: Nick and Newt built a tower, and two-year-old Joe knocked it down.

Iris brought Annie a cup of tea as they sat in the only two chairs that had cushions. "I'm sorry to hear Grasston is back."

Annie held the cup beneath her chin, enjoying the warmth and fragrance of its rising vapor. "He's not just back, he's vowed revenge. He's evil, Iris. Fully and completely evil." She noticed Iris wasn't drinking. "Aren't you having some?"

She shook her head. "Actually... can we move to the other room? I have laundry to take in."

They entered one of four small bedrooms and sat upon an oak chair in the corner. Iris opened the window and pulled in the laundry that had been drying on a line.

"I can help," Annie said, setting her tea aside.

"No, you sit. Relax. Talk to me while I fold it."

Annie felt guilty for sitting yet didn't feel up to doing much more.

"Do you really think he would have. . .forced you?" Iris asked.

"I do. He wants to hurt me. Shame me."

"As you shamed him?"

Annie was taken aback and was going to protest but realized Iris was right. "I did shame him, didn't I?"

"You took his gloves on a lark, but if it made him lose his job. . ."

She felt her defenses rise. "But he hurt you, too. He pushed himself on you, too."

"After you told on him about Miss Henrietta and he was scolded."

After I told. After I took his gloves. The wave of regret fell upon Annie's shoulders. "I never thought I'd say this, but he has a right to be angry with me."

"Angry is one thing, violent is another."

It was a relief to have it confirmed that despite his reasons, Grasston had gone too far.

Iris spread a shirt on top of the dresser and turned to Annie. "Sprinkle these shirts and aprons for me. Then roll them up to keep until I can iron them."

Annie took up the Coca-Cola bottle with a sprinkle attachment corked in the top and did as she was asked. Suddenly she remembered that she still hadn't heard Iris's news. "Tell me your news. I've been so consumed with my own troubles that I—"

"Yes, you have."

Annie accepted the rebuke. "I'm sorry I haven't been here for you."

Iris drew a clean nappy to her chest and faced her. "I was the one who wanted to be a shopgirl."

Annie suffered an inward sigh. "We've gone over this. The other day you said that Macy's was too large a store for you."

Iris nodded and looked to the floor then at Annie. "It was, and it is, and. . ." She smiled broadly. "The truth is, I've given up the notion of ever working in a shop. My future is set."

It sounded both ominous and hopeful. "How so?"

Iris looked past her to the main room. The children's voices could be heard, but none were close by. "Thomas proposed to me."

The sprinkle bottle slipped from Annie's hand, but she caught it before it hit the floor. "When did this happen?"

"A few days ago." She beamed. "He says he loves me."

If he did, Thomas had made quick work of it. Annie couldn't help but remember his initial interest in herself. "Do you love him?"

There was a moment's hesitation. "I think I do."

"*Think* you do?"

"I do. I do."

Annie hoped Iris wasn't getting married to be married. She was only seventeen and had only known Thomas a short time.

"Don't doubt me," Iris said. "Don't make me doubt myself. That's not fair. You've found yourself a new life, so don't begrudge me doing the same."

Annie pushed her doubts aside and embraced her. "Congratulations. I'm very happy for you. When is the—"

Annie's words were cut off by a horrific scream coming from the bakery below. It sounded like Mrs. Tuttle. Annie and Iris rushed down the stairs, with the children close behind. They nearly ran into Jane, coming up to get them.

"What happened?" Annie asked. "Is your mother all right?"

Jane's face was a mask of panic. "It's not her, it's. . ." She looked to Annie and then Iris. "It's Danny."

The girls ran into the bakery, looking this way and that for Danny. But he wasn't there. No one was. Everyone was outside.

Annie got there first. She fell upon Danny sprawled in the back of the delivery wagon. He was covered in blood.

Thomas held Iris back as she screamed, "No!"

So much blood, too much blood.

"Is he. . . ?" Annie asked.

"Yes," Gramps said. "He's dead. Beaten and stabbed."

Annie stared at Danny's bruised and bloodied face and torso. How could this broken being be her vibrant Danny? She took Danny's hand in hers. "Sweet boy, dear Danny. I'm so sorry."

"Why are *you* sorry?" Mrs. Tuttle asked.

Why couldn't they see the obvious? "It's Grasston. He did this. He was angry with me but took it out on Danny."

Iris broke away from the comfort of Thomas's arms and hurled herself toward Annie, pounding her with her fists. "You did this! This is all your fault!"

Thomas pulled Iris away so Annie was saved from her pummels.

But not from the truth.

❧

Annie hugged herself and looked to the floor as she answered the constable's questions. If only she could disappear or wake up and find it was all an awful dream.

"What is this Mr. Grasston's first name?"

Shocked at the question, she looked up. "I don't know."

"Hmm. You say he had a grudge against you? What for?"

"He worked for the Friesen family as a footman. He bothered me and Danny's sister, Iris, and—"

"Bothered?"

It *was* too soft a word. "He made inappropriate advances on us."

"Oh."

"He did worse to me last night. He's been following me for days, showing up at my work, coming in the bakery just to intimidate me."

"So he was after you, not the young man."

There was the truth of it. "He blames me for him losing his job at the Friesens'."

"But hadn't he also 'annoyed' Mr. Dalking's sister?"

"I was the one who stood up to him." The rest of it would sound petty, but she had to say it. "I took his footman's gloves when the three of us left service, and he got in trouble for it. Told me that was the reason he was sacked."

The officer blinked. "Over gloves."

Annie realized how daft it sounded. How far fetched and false. She could honestly add, "I'm sure it wasn't just the gloves." She stood straighter and looked at the officer, emboldened by this truth. "He was a horrible man. He attacked me last night as I walked to a friend's house. He knocked me to the ground and would have..." She needed to just say it. "Would have had his way with me if my screams hadn't brought others to save me." She showed him her scraped palms. "See?"

His eyes grew wide. "I'm so sorry for your pain, Miss Wood."

"Thank you. I spoke with an Officer Brady. You might talk to him about it."

He nodded. "But the question remains, why would this Grasston kill Mr. Dalking if his beef was with you?"

She thought of Danny and his declaration to keep the two girls safe. "Danny was protective by nature. I'm sure he died defending me."

The officer nodded to the elder Mr. Tuttle. "That's what the old man said. Said a man approached them and started harassing the boy. Went away, but then must have caught him when he was alone."

To get to me. "You see what a despicable man he is? Instead of talking to me, why don't you go out and find him. Please. Before he hurts someone else."

"We're doing that, miss." He closed his notebook. "If I have any more questions, I'll come back. Until then, you have my condolences."

As the officer left, Annie did a double take when she saw Mr. Culver on the street nearby. He walked toward her.

Impulsively, she flew into his arms. "He killed him! He killed Danny!"

Mr. Culver held her close. "I'm so sorry."

Annie let his warmth and strong arms comfort her. She leaned her head against his shoulder and closed her eyes. *Don't let go. Don't ever let me go.* "Why are you here? How did you know where I live?"

"I went to Macy's for our baseball outing and—"

She pulled away. "I'm sorry. I should have sent word."

He shook his head, brushing away her apology. "Obviously that pales in relation to this horror. When I heard you'd gone home and pressed Mrs. MacDonald for why, she gave me your address so I could check on you. I hope you don't mind."

She longed to return to the safety of his arms. "I'm glad you're here."

He touched her arm. "I'm so sorry for this, and for what you endured last night. They'll catch him. I know they will."

Annie knew no such thing.

She spotted Iris coming toward them, her face sagging with grief and tears. Annie feared another pummeling and was surprised when Iris held out her arms.

Annie was glad for the embrace. "I'm so sorry, Iris," she whispered. "I never meant for any of this to happen."

Iris began her nod even before she left the embrace. "None of us did. He's an evil man. Our Danny died as he lived, protecting those he loved."

Annie drew in an enormous breath and let it out, relieving herself of the guilt that had restricted her breathing. "You forgive me, then?"

Iris nodded. "Of course I do." She returned to Annie's arms for a second embrace.

CHAPTER THIRTEEN

And God cried.

That's what it seemed like during the week of Danny's death. The morning after he died, the skies opened with the tears of every mother and sister and father and brother. God may have welcomed Danny into His everlasting arms, but those left without him couldn't grasp the whys of it.

There was no answer to that.

Annie had few memories of the wake and the funeral. The rain created a somber veil keeping the pain inside. She had vague memories of visits from Edna, Mrs. MacDonald, and Mr. Culver. Sean. For his care had shoved aside all formalities. He was Sean and she was Annie.

Annie awakened to commotion in the main bakery, and only by that sound realized it was time to get up. The first morning that Danny hadn't awakened her, she'd slept so long that Jane had been forced to come in the storeroom to get her up—for they were in need of more flour.

Not wanting to be embarrassed again, she'd started to sleep with the door ajar so she could hear them earlier. Hearing them now, she quickly rose, lit the lamp, and dressed. As she buttoned her work uniform, she worried about her day. She was going back to work for the first time since Danny's death. Macy's had been very understanding about her time off, but she could not take advantage of their largesse any longer. The Tuttle family and Iris had buried the dear boy, had found a proper pocket to keep their grief, and had gone back to work. Could she do any less?

Her eyes fell to the makeshift beds that used to belong to Danny and Iris. The covers and pillows were gone now. For even Iris had left her, moving upstairs to be with the family she now claimed as her own.

She paused in her buttoning. "I'm all alone here. I'm not family." And finally, as a natural conclusion to her statements, she said, "I can't stay here anymore."

The realization forced her to sit. Where could she go?

Edna's.

With the force of the answer Annie stood. She would ask her friend if she could be a lodger and felt totally assured Edna would take her in.

She finished dressing, and as a period to her decision, folded the linens of her bed and took them out to the bakery.

"Good morning, Annie," Jane said. Her eyes grazed over the linens. "Would you like me to wash them?"

Annie cleared her throat, needing all of them to hear. "I am moving out."

Mr. Tuttle, Gramps, and Thomas all stopped their work. "You're leaving us?"

She'd stated it too plain, without the proper preamble. "I am ever so grateful for the welcome you gave me and Iris. . .and Danny. The place to sleep, the meals, the care and sense of family."

"You are family," Jane said.

After a moment's hesitation, Annie shook her head. "Iris and Thomas are going to be married, and I am happy for them. It's a joyful event that will help ease our current pain. But. . ." She had no hard and fast reason. "I need to move on."

"But where will ye stay?" Mr. Tuttle asked.

"I've made a good friend at work. Mrs. Holmquist. I stayed with her the other night."

Mr. Tuttle nodded. Then Jane said, "We're going to miss you."

"And I will miss you. I am forever in your debt."

The sounds of the rest of the family coming downstairs for breakfast interrupted the conversation. Annie dreaded telling Iris, but the decision was made. The deed was done.

As the children swarmed around the table and took their places, Annie took Iris aside.

But instead of an argument, Iris said, "Are you sure?"

Annie felt the hint of disappointment rise then fall away. "I am."

Iris glanced at Thomas. "You will come to the wedding, though?"

"Of course. And I'll visit. Edna's isn't that far away."

With a nod, Iris hugged her. "Good-bye, then."

The finality of her words made Annie wonder if Iris still held Annie accountable for Danny's death.

So be it.

Since the good-byes had already been accomplished, Annie decided to forgo breakfast. She quickly packed her bag, took the hot roll offered by Mr. Tuttle—and a loaf to give to Robbie for seeing her home from Macy's a week ago—and left the bakery.

As the door shut behind her, she felt as if more than a door had been closed. A chapter of her life had ended.

And a new chapter had begun.

"Of course you can move in with me," Edna said.

Annie hadn't realized she'd been holding her breath. She breathed free. "Thank you so much. I shan't be any trouble, and I'll be a proper lodger and help with expenses."

"Not a worry. When can you move in?"

"Straightaway? Tonight?"

Edna chuckled. "You are a girl who makes quick decisions."

She hoped it wasn't a rash one.

It was odd being back at work, waiting on customers, smiling. Helping a woman choose a pattern and fabric seemed frivolous compared to the life-and-death situations she'd endured the past week.

Her only relief was that Mildred had kept to herself. Though others had offered condolences and wanted to know the lurid details and whether Grasston had been arrested—which he had not—Mildred offered accusatory glances. Accusing Annie of what, she wasn't sure.

It didn't matter. Mildred Krieger had no part in Annie's life. She was an annoying fly on the back side of a window.

As Annie was finishing up with a customer, she spotted Mildred talking to Mrs. Reinhold, the customer she'd helped during one of her first days on the job. She saw the woman pointing at Annie, and Annie waved. With a nod, Mrs. Reinhold said a few more words to Mildred and then came over to Annie's counter.

"Good morning, Mrs. Reinhold," she said. "I'll be with you in just a few minutes."

"I will wait," she said.

As Annie wrote up the other customer's purchase, Mrs. Reinhold addressed the woman. "You are smart to let Miss Wood help you with your sewing purchases," she said. "Look at what she helped me put together." She spread her arms and turned in a circle.

Only then did Annie realize she was wearing the gold coat and brown skirt they had designed together. "What a fine job you did," Annie said. "You are a very talented seamstress."

"And you are a very talented fashion designer. From skirt to coat, to hat and gloves."

The other customer pointed to the hat. "Did you make that, too?"

"I did—with Miss Wood's design expertise."

The new customer turned to Annie. "I'd like to make a similar hat to go with the fabric I am purchasing. Can you help me?"

Annie feared the extra time required would offend Mrs. Reinhold. She need not have worried. "Don't concern yourself with the delay, Miss Wood. I have the time. And if you don't mind, I'd like to add my two cents to the process."

The other woman beamed. "I'd welcome your opinion."

Annie proceeded to help the ladies.

While Mildred stewed nearby.

❧

Annie was cleaning off the cutting table when she looked up and saw the owner of Macy's standing before her.

"Mr. Straus."

"Good day, Miss Wood."

She put a hand to her hair, hoping the stray strands were neatly tucked away. "What can I do for you, sir?"

"Continue on as you have been doing," he said. "I've heard good things about your work."

"Thank you, sir."

His face grew serious. "I wanted to check to see how you were after the death of your friend. I offer my sincere condolences."

"Thank you, sir. I am coping. And I want to thank you for the time off. I enjoy working here, so to have my job still available after being gone a week is—"

"Paid time off," he said.

She gawked. "Paid?"

"It is the least we can do for our employees in their time of need."

"Oh, sir. Thank you so much."

"You're quite welcome." He looked embarrassed and quickly said, "Carry on."

She watched him walk away, his hands clasped behind his back. He greeted many of the clerks and customers, the store's attentive father.

⟡

Soon after Mr. Straus's visit, Sean stopped by. Annie was busy with customers, but he quickly wrote something on a slip of paper and handed it to her. When she was free she read it: *Skip lunch and let's have our baseball date today at 2:30. At least we can hear part of the game.*

They were still playing the World Series?

Annie asked Mrs. MacDonald about it. "Oh yes," she said. "They played the first three games, but then because of constant rain, game four in Philly and today's game here were postponed. Tomorrow is the last game—in Philadelphia. Unless we win both, and then they'll have to play a seventh game."

Annie was getting confused. "Are we winning the series?"

"We need a win today to stay alive. Philadelphia is ahead three games to one."

The only detail that mattered was that the Giants needed to win today, and Sean wanted her to be there. With him. She showed Mrs. MacDonald the note. "May I go? For a short while?"

The woman smiled. "Of course you can. You need some frivolity in your life."

The morning flew by, and soon she held Sean's arm tightly as they made their way through the crowd in front of the Herald Newspaper offices. A police officer shooed them up onto the curb and sidewalk, trying to keep Broadway clear. But both sides of the street were shoulder to shoulder.

"There," Sean said, pointing to the building. "That's the Play-O-Graph. See the diamond on it?"

"But what does it mean?"

He explained the game: bases, outs, strikes. He received help from men wedged on either side of them.

"I think I have it," she said, truthfully. "It's a bit like cricket where they hit a ball and run while it's being fielded."

One of the men laughed. "You could be right, miss. I don't know cricket, but your quick understanding of baseball means you've done better'n my wife. I've been trying to get her interested for ten years but she won't have nothing to do with it."

"You have a fan," Sean whispered in her ear.

"I hope I have more than one."

He winked at her.

She enjoyed the crowded conditions, for it enabled her to stand close to Sean without fear of seeming too fresh. She stood in front of him, enabling her ear to be near his lips. He put a protective arm around her, keeping her safe. And happy. It felt good to be happy.

But Grasston is still out there.

She shoved the thought away. He wouldn't dare bother her with thousands of witnesses.

A man stood beside the Play-O-Graph, getting news that was relayed from inside. "Miller on first!"

The crowd roared. And Annie's heart soared.

∝

"Seeing you three times in one day is quite the treat," Sean said.

Annie retrieved her carpetbag from her locker and put on her coat. "You don't have to help me move to Edna's," she said. "All I have is this one bag— which I can easily carry."

Nearby, Edna secured her hat with a hat pin. "Quiet, Annie. If a man offers to help, you let him help." She winked at Sean. "Especially a handsome man."

"Are you flirting with me, Mrs. Holmquist?"

"Was I? Who knew I still had it in me. Come now, you two. I want to stop at the butcher's and get some beef. I'm going to make you Swedish meatballs."

"You don't have to feed me," Sean said. "I work for free."

"If a woman offers to feed you, you let her feed you."

Annie's few belongings were moved into Edna's extra room, and then dinner was enjoyed by all. Annie was impressed by how easily Sean kept the conversation lively. Between his stories about growing up in Brooklyn, Edna's stories about her early days at Macy's, and Annie's stories about working as a maid at Crompton Hall, time flew by.

Edna shoved her third cup of coffee away and stood, groaning as she arched her back. "Sitting so long makes these old muscles tighten like a clothesline in the winter."

Sean stood, too. "I should be getting home myself. Tomorrow is a workday."

Annie hated to see him go. "I thoroughly enjoyed today," she said.

"Especially since the Giants won the game."

"It was fun to lark about and see a portion of it, and then hear the crowd cheering even after I was back at work."

"I'll make a fan of you yet," Sean said. He moved toward the door but detoured to the sewing machine where Annie's blouse was being sewn. "Is this the product of your lessons?"

"It is," she said. "And you'll be pleased to know I used a Butterick pattern. Sort of."

"What do you mean 'sort of'?"

She took up the blouse—which only had one sleeve set in. "Since I'm a bit taller than most women, Edna showed me how to alter the patterns to fit. Plus, I wanted to try a tight sleeve to the elbow and let it go into a wider flare and—"

"I'm not sure I understand."

Annie took up a pencil and paper and sketched it for him. "See? The upper sleeve is straight, but the bottom half billows out at the elbow and is secured again at the cuff." She studied it a moment. Something was missing. She took the edge of the pencil and smudged a bit of lead on the underside of the sleeve to better show it off. "There. That's better."

"I'm impressed."

"It was just an idea I had and—"

"I'm impressed by your sketching ability." He took the page and showed it to Edna. "Did you know she could draw like this?"

"I did not. Annie, why didn't you tell me you were an artist?"

"I'm no artist."

"You most certainly are," Sean said. "Look at how you captured the design with just a few lines. You even added shadow. You must have had some training."

She laughed at the thought. "I've been a housemaid since I was young. I've never had time or the inclination to draw anything, much less become an artist."

"I'm even more impressed," Sean said. "To have a talent you don't even know you have?" He shook his head. "Fascinating."

Edna handed the drawing back, and Annie looked at it with new eyes. It *was* good—though next time she would add the entire bodice to the drawing to give it context.

Sean put on his coat and hat. "You are full of surprises, aren't you, Annie-girl?"

Apparently.

※

Before Annie turned out the light in her room at Edna's, she stepped across the hall and rapped on the other bedroom door. "You still awake?"

"I am. Come in."

Edna was sitting up in bed, reading the Bible. "Do you have everything you need?"

That one innocent question punched a hole in the wall Annie had built around herself, letting her emotions rush out in a torrent. She fell into Edna's arms.

"Oh my. Oh sweet girl."

"My best friend is dead!"

Edna stroked her back. "I know."

Annie thought of more. "I don't have a spot at the Tuttles' anymore."

"I know."

"Grasston's still out there. Who knows if he'll find me again and hurt me."

"I know."

Annie sat up to face her. "Iris is getting married."

"The gall."

The change in Edna's answer made Annie blink. "I'm not saying it's a bad thing. I'm happy for her."

"Are you?"

"Of course."

"You don't sound happy. You sound peeved."

Annie stood beside the bed. "I never expected her to find love—at least not so quickly."

"Before you."

The words could have stung, but oddly they did not. "I'm not seeking marriage."

"Was Iris?"

Annie didn't know. "She wanted to work in a shop, but then the Tuttles needed her help with the children, and. . ."

"And she was happy doing that?"

"I suppose."

Edna peered at her over her glasses.

"Yes. She was happy."

"Isn't that what you want for her?"

"I do." Annie didn't like how Edna flipped her grievances over upon themselves. "But Danny is dead!"

"A true tragedy. But are you upset because he died so young and lost the chance at a fuller life, or because he left you?"

"You're turning everything around."

Edna removed her glasses and set the Bible on the bedside table. "I'm merely pointing out that everything you mentioned had *you* as the focus. The truth is, it's not just about you."

"That's rude."

"Truth can be rude, but that doesn't stop it from being the truth." Edna patted the side of the bed, and Annie sat. "Yes, your best friend died, but he's the one who had his young life taken from him."

"I didn't mean to belittle his loss, but—"

Edna raised a hand, stopping her words. "It's true you don't have a room at the Tuttles' anymore—or perhaps, even a place in their family. But you are not on the street, not destitute. You do have a room—a real room with a bed to sleep upon, not a makeshift bed on some flour sacks."

Shame took a turn. "I'm sorry. I don't mean to downplay all you've offered me. I truly appreciate the room. Actually, I've never had a room of my own."

Edna cocked her head. "Never?"

Annie let her thoughts trail through her life. "When I was small I shared with my brother, and when I got a job with the Kidds I shared a room with another maid. Even here in New York I shared a room—and a bed—with Iris." She was shocked by her realization. "And at the Tuttles' I shared a room with Iris *and* Danny."

Edna spread her arms. "You have risen up in the world."

Why hadn't she thought of it like that? "Thank you, Edna. For everything you've done for me. Befriending me, giving me sewing lessons, feeding me, giving me the room, encouraging me. . ."

"I did all those things—do all those things—because I care for you."

Annie took her hand. "I care for you, too. Immensely. You're like the mother I never had."

"You mother wasn't around?"

A snicker escaped. "She was around in body but had none of your loving and generous character."

"I *am* exceptional," Edna said with a laugh.

Annie clasped her hand harder. "Actually, you are. My parents begrudge the world its every smile or bit of happiness. They feel due, as if everyone and everything owes them. They can't see that they have nothing because they give nothing. They don't understand it isn't just about them."

Edna's left eyebrow rose, and Annie realized Edna had just said it wasn't all about *her*.

She tried to recover from the similarity. "But they are leeches, sucking the world dry. Nothing is ever good enough or enough enough. It's left them gorged with pessimism."

"I'm so sorry. What a horrible way to live."

Annie squeezed her eyes shut, ridding her mind of the memories. "Their attitude is why I went into service when I was fourteen. I had to get away *from* them or be pulled under *with* them."

"All the more reason to count your blessings. You are here, across the world, fully free to be all you can be."

"I am free, aren't I?"

"Completely. You have a job you enjoy, a warm bed, the most fabulous landlady—"

"Absolutely."

Edna held up a finger. "And you have a newly discovered talent to draw."

The idea was still hard to fathom. "I never knew I could do that."

"A talent uncovered is a talent recovered."

"Recovered?"

"It's always been with you, Annie. You just didn't know it was there. It's a known fact that God's gifts can't be returned."

God gave her that gift? It made her wonder what other talents lay hidden.

"You've forgotten one other blessing in your life."

"What's that?"

"*Who's* that?"

"Ah. Sean."

"Yes, ah Sean. He's a good man who likes you very much."

"But—"

"Before you discount his interest, think about all he's done for you in the short time you've known him. He's defended you to his company against Mildred's complaint."

"A stupid complaint."

"Let me finish. After Grasston assaulted you, Sean sought you out to check on your well-being."

"He did."

"That took effort. He also was a comfort after Danny was killed, yes?"

She nodded. "He came to the Tuttles' every day. He accompanied me to the funeral."

"Which shows how much he cares."

It does.

"And," Edna said, "he took you out to listen to a baseball game during the World Series."

Annie laughed. "I never would have experienced that without him."

"I'm betting there are many things you can experience together." Edna's smile spoke beyond the words.

"I am not ready to be courted."

"You may not be ready to be courted, but you *are* being courted. By Sean and by someone else."

"Who?"

Edna lay a hand on her Bible. "The Almighty is working all around you if you just open your eyes. He's waiting for you to notice Him."

Annie wanted to respond but couldn't find the right words. "If you say so."

"I do." Edna squeezed Annie's hand. "Now go to sleep, girlie. And may all your dreams reveal wonderful surprises."

❧

Annie snuggled amid the covers of her very own bed, in her very own room. Edna was right. Even through the hard times of the past few weeks, there had been good times, times of great blessing.

"The Almighty is working all around you if you just open your eyes. He's waiting for you to notice Him."

She was still a bit baffled by Edna's words. She believed in God. She even prayed occasionally.

When I need something.

Wasn't that all right? Didn't God want to hear her needs so He could provide for her?

More of Edna's words returned: *"It's not just about you."*

She sat up in bed. "Then who's it about?"

"Me."

The thought surprised her. What also surprised her was the unexpected knowledge that "Me" was God. God was claiming that *He* wanted the attention? That it was all about *Him?* Wasn't that selfish?

"Come to Me first. You are Mine and I am yours."

The words that were unspoken yet felt frightened her. The concept of a God who gave Himself to her and drew her close was beyond any father-child relationship she'd ever experienced. Fathers weren't loving. They were judgmental, disparaging, and cruel.

"I love you, Annie."

God. God was telling her He loved her? This was too strange. Things like this didn't happen to her.

Annie lay down and pulled the covers close.

Chapter Fourteen

Annie looked up from a display case of scissors to see two police officers standing in front of her. One of them was Officer Brady, who'd spoken with her after her assault. Memories of that attack and Danny's death forced themselves to the front of her thoughts.

"Officer Brady, is everything all right?"

The two bobbies touched the brims of their hats, and Officer Brady said, "I believe it is, Miss Wood. For we have caught your assailant."

The fear that had rushed forward retreated like a tide going out to sea. "Grasston."

"Oscar Grasston, yes, miss," the other officer said.

"So he's going to jail forever?"

The officers exchanged a glance. "For assault, no."

"But he killed Danny."

"Allegedly," Officer Brady said. "We've not found a witness."

"Yet," the other officer said.

"But he's guilty! He did it! Gramps saw them arguing then found Danny stabbed. All after Grasston threatened him with a knife at the bakery."

Officer Brady made a "calm down" motion with his hands, and Annie realized she'd raised her voice. She saw Mrs. Gold approach Mrs. MacDonald to talk, her eyes on Annie and the officers.

This was neither the time nor the place.

"We need you to come to the precinct and pick him out of a lineup."

"But I know he assaulted me. I don't need to identify him." She leaned over the counter and lowered her voice. "He knocked me down. He was on top of me."

Did bobbies blush? Both of them looked down, cleared their throats, and then looked back at Annie. "It's just a formality, Miss Wood, as we do have statements from others at the scene. You confirm he's the one and we'll take care of the rest."

Annie noticed too many eyes watching. She needed them gone. "May I come after work? Around six?"

"We can hold him that long."

That long? He needed to be jailed forever.

Brady handed her a card that showed the precinct address, and they left.

Before they were even out of the store, they were accosted by Mr. Horace and another plainclothes security man. As that was happening, Mrs. Gold approached Annie. "Miss Wood, this sort of attention is not welcome in Macy's."

"It's not attention, ma'am, it's police work."

"I realize that, but uniformed officers disturb the customers."

"I don't understand why. They should feel more secure seeing officers here."

"I will not play tit for tat with you, Miss Wood. I merely mean to impress on you the need to maintain an enjoyable shopping experience."

Annie understood, but it rankled her. "If you're interested, they caught the man who assaulted me, the man who killed my friend. I will be visiting the precinct to identify him."

"On your own time, I assume."

"On my own time." This was wearying. "You're treating me as if I caused all this."

Mrs. Gold's hesitation was telling. "Carry on, then, Miss Wood. But please inform the officers that next time they need to speak with you, they can send you a note."

The silly thought of the two burly officers writing a note made her smile.

"Do you find this amusing, Miss Wood? Because I assure you I take it very seriously."

"I take this seriously, too, Mrs. Gold. After all, my friend and I were the victims."

With the lift of an eyebrow the supervisor walked away, only to be quickly replaced by Mrs. MacDonald—and Mildred, who'd somehow made her way from fabrics over to the sewing notions section, where she busied herself sorting tape measures. Annie was beyond caring. Let her listen in.

"So?" Mrs. MacDonald asked.

"They caught him." She looked directly at Mildred. "They caught your friend, Grasston. He's been arrested for assault and murder." She forgave herself the embellishment.

Suddenly Mildred stopped her sorting and came close, her forehead furrowed. "He. . . he's arrested?"

"He is. I tried to warn you. I hope you didn't spend any time alone with him."

Mildred shook her head vehemently. But then she began to cry.

Tears? "What did he do to you?" Annie asked.

"Nothing."

"Then why are you crying?" Mrs. MacDonald asked. "Did he hurt you?"

Mildred retrieved a handkerchief and dabbed at her eyes and nose. "Thankfully, no. He wanted to take me out, but we never went anywhere. He gave me attention here at the store and led me on then disappeared and never came back."

So it was an issue of pride. "He disappeared because he'd killed Danny."

Mildred turned away from them and blew her nose. When she turned back she said, "I'm crying because I finally get a man interested in me, and he turns out to be a criminal."

That *would* hurt.

Annie let Mildred cry on her shoulder.

Would wonders never cease?

⊸⊱⊰⊷

"You're treating me as if I caused all this."

Although Annie's previous words to Mrs. Gold were said in her own defense, and though Mrs. Gold had not confirmed them, they hung over Annie the rest of the day as her own private condemnation.

For it was true. She was to blame for all the problems Grasston had caused, and who knew how many more people he had—or would—hurt because he was angry at *her.*

Oddly, during her lunch break in the cafeteria, she saw men talking among themselves—their glances revealing that she was the subject of their discussions. And the women. . . When she went to sit with some girls from the shoe department, they quickly left.

Now I know how Mildred feels eating alone. She had the notion to take her tray and eat in the locker room.

While she ate her soup and buttered her bread, her nerves tingled as if she were being electrified. When a group of young male clerks started giggling as they looked at her, she'd had enough. Annie pushed her chair back with a titter of its legs against the floor. She stood—though the moment she stood, she told herself to sit back down before she did something stupid.

She didn't listen to her own warning. Instead, she scanned the room and said, "Attention! I'd like your attention, please."

She got what she asked for. Talking stopped and all eyes were on her.

"I am ever so glad to provide you with your daily dose of gossip. But know this: the man the police have arrested, the man they want me to identify after work this very evening, is evil. Oscar Grasston attacked me, followed me for days, harassed me, threatened me, and stabbed a dear friend to death when he came to my defense. He killed Danny, a thirteen-year-old boy who will never have the chance to grow up and become the fabulous man he was destined to be. So if you wish to chunter on and giggle and talk behind your hands, at least get the story straight. Otherwise, keep your nonsense to yourselves."

She was glad the chair was there, because her last words did her in. She was about to pull the chair back toward the table to finish her meal when a man came close and helped her scoot it in. "Well said, Miss Wood."

As he stepped away, the rest of the cafeteria began to applaud. There were even a few shouts of "Go get 'em, Annie!"

The notion of eating in the locker room returned. But then someone joined her at the table.

"Mildred."

"I thought you could use a friend."

Well, then. Would wonders never cease?

⚓

"I think that lace would look lovely on your blouse, Mrs. Dresden. How many yards would you like?"

As Annie's customer did the calculations, Annie spotted Mr. Straus walking by. After her outburst in the cafeteria she hesitated to make eye contact. Surely he'd heard about the woman gone off her trolley, making a scene.

But as he strolled past, he caught her glance and in return offered her a wink and a thumbs-up.

She laughed aloud. Would wonders never cease?

❦

Sean took her hand as they left Macy's at the end of the day. "This is not how I planned to spend our evening together. Although I will say visiting a police station is a unique outing."

"And not just visiting," Annie said, "but making sure an evil meater stays in jail."

"Meater?"

"Coward. For he is that, you know. Only a coward would hurt women and children."

Sean pulled her hand around his arm. "Don't be nervous. I won't let him hurt you."

"I *am* nervous because I'm afraid not you or anyone can stop him if he's set loose."

"Then we'll have to make sure he's not set loose."

"But they're only wanting me to identify him as the man who assaulted me, having nothing to do with Danny's death."

Sean stopped walking and looked at her. "I thought this was for—"

She shook her head. "They have no witnesses for it."

"But we all know he did it."

She shrugged. "Without witnesses. . ."

Justice would not be done.

❦

Annie clung to Sean's arm as the men were lined up in a viewing room at the police station. They each held a number in front of them. Although they were in the light and she was standing in the dark, she knew she could be seen.

Grasston could see her.

And just as she zeroed in on him, he did the same for her. His jaw clenched, and his eyes bore into hers for just a moment before he looked away.

"Number three," she said immediately.

"Wait a minute, miss," the officer said. "I haven't even asked the question yet."

Sean intervened. "Then ask it, sir."

"Which man best resembles the man who attacked you on October 17?"

Annie wasn't sure she had air enough in her lungs to answer again, but she dug deep and said, "Number three is the man. He's the one who hurt me—and killed my Danny."

She saw Grasston flinch. Let him.

"He's not here for that, miss. But thank you. That will be all."

She couldn't get out of the room fast enough. The officer led her down the hall to the precinct offices. "So what now, Officer? When will he be tried?"

"Can't say at the moment, Miss Wood. We'll let you know. You'll have to come back and testify."

Annie let out a sigh. "Isn't identifying him enough?"

" 'Fraid not. But we thank you for coming down."

She needed more from them. "What about the murder of my friend, Danny Dalking? Have you found a witness yet?"

"Not that I'm aware of, miss. But be assured we're doing our best."

She left with Sean, feeling spent. "I fear their best will not be enough." The image of Grasston showing up at times and places of his own choosing haunted her. "Even if he's convicted of assault, that won't keep him in jail very long." She voiced a thought that had niggled at her for days. "Sometimes I wish he'd really hurt me. That way he'd be put away longer. Or maybe it would have delayed him enough so they would have caught him right then and there. Maybe he wouldn't have been free to kill Danny."

Sean put his arm around her shoulders. "Don't say such a thing. We have to be thankful he didn't hurt you more than he did."

She was unconvinced. "I would gladly suffer if it would bring Danny back." Tears took over, and she let herself be comforted.

CHAPTER FIFTEEN

It was done. Her testimony against Grasston for the assault was over. Being in the same room with him, feeling the heat of his stare...

Now it was up to the judge.

Sean accompanied her out of the courtroom. "You're shaking."

An inner quaking started deep inside and overflowed to her extremities. She held her hand out, and seeing the result, pulled her fingers into a fist to stay them. "I don't know why I thought telling the truth would be easy."

They walked down the courthouse steps arm in arm. "I saw how he glared at you the entire time. But he had no defense. Explaining your fall by saying you tripped? Making him trip on top of you? Very lame."

As if minding Sean's words, Annie tripped on the steps. Without his help, she would have ended up at the bottom.

"I'm a jumble," she said. "The lid is off the teapot. My life is boiling over, making the fire go out."

Sean laughed. "I've never heard it described that way. How British of you."

"How would an American say it?"

He was quiet a moment then said, "Your life is a mess."

"That it is."

"I have a way to change all that," he said as they headed back to Macy's.

She felt a surge of panic. The only drastic *change* she could think of involved him proposing marriage. She was nowhere near ready for such a question. "I think I'm afraid to ask."

"You don't trust me?"

"I'm not certain how to answer that."

He pulled his hat off and thrust it against his chest. "I am utterly crushed. And just for that, I'm not going to tell you my idea."

"Now you have me curious."

"Too late," he said, returning his bowler to his head.

She was too drained to play games. "Please tell me. I do want to know."

"I think I'll tell you at dinner tonight, when I have the proper time to explain my idea."

"Explaining an idea" didn't sound like a phrase associated with a proposal. Her mind eased.

∽≈∾

After taking time off to testify against Grasston, Annie rushed directly to her department at Macy's. She folded her jacket around her purse and set her hat on top, all under the counter. She checked her reflection in a hand mirror, tucking the stray strands of hair where they belonged.

"So?" Annie turned around to find Mildred standing before her.

"I testified. Now it's up to the judge."

"He'll go to jail, won't he?"

The strained look on her face reinforced Annie's feeling that something *had* gone on between Grasston and Mildred beyond what she'd admitted. "I'm sure he will." *For how long is the issue.*

For Mildred's sake, Annie gathered a smile she did not feel. "Enough of Grasston. Let's not let the likes of him cloud our day." She looked around the department. "Have you been busy?"

Before Mildred could answer, Annie spotted Iris walking down the store aisles. She rushed to greet her friend, kissing her on the cheeks. "Iris! I'm so glad to see you."

"And I you," Iris said. She looked around the store. "Remember when you and I and. . .and Danny came to Macy's, exploring?"

"I do," Annie said. "That outing sparked the idea to work here." She wasn't sure whether she should mention Danny further, but it seemed wrong not to. "How are the Tuttles? How is everyone faring without him?"

Iris pulled an envelope from her pocket. "This is for you. Open it."

Annie broke the seal and removed a hand-lettered card. "It's an invitation to your wedding?"

Iris pointed to the card. "December 23. The church is a few blocks from the bakery."

It was only six weeks away. Annie embraced her. "I'm happy for both of you."

Iris's smile faded. "You don't think it's improper to get married so soon after Danny's death?"

"I think he'd want you to be together as soon as possible."

Iris nodded, making the daisy on her hat bob. "That's what we thought. Plus, we decided to marry soon because there's an apartment coming open in the building across the street, so we needed to make a quick decision and grab it up."

"Your own apartment. . ."

"I know. And me being married. Ain't it strange?"

"It's wonderful. You deserve some happiness." Annie spotted Mrs. Gold giving her a disparaging look for chatting instead of selling. "May I interest you in a dress pattern, Miss Dalking?"

Iris looked confused then saw the supervisor. "I'd like that very much."

Annie led her to the catalog, and they leafed through it. Suddenly Annie got an idea. "What if I made you a wedding dress?" She turned the pages to the illustrations of fancier dresses.

"Ooh," Iris said. Then she shook her head. "I don't have the need for a fancy dress—nor a white one. But a new one I could wear to church Sundays? Yes, please."

"Perfect." Annie was a bit relieved. She's just finished her first skirt and blouse from scratch. To tackle a dress of satin and lace would have tested her abilities. Since the pricey fabrics were out of the mix, Annie had another idea. "In fact, I will pay for everything *and* do the work. As my wedding gift to you."

Iris flung her arms around Annie's neck. "You're so good to me. Thank you!"

Annie pulled out a chair so Iris could sit and properly peruse the pattern illustrations. Luckily, she wasn't choosy and quickly picked out a pattern for a dress. Annie studied it a minute to make sure she could sew it, and decided she could. The dress had a slim sleeve and silhouette that was popular. The neck was scooped with trim along the edge. The dress itself hung straight from a slightly higher waist, and an overskirt was cut short on the diagonal from knee to ankle, revealing the drapery of the main skirt beneath.

"I don't want a train," Iris said, pointing to the slight train of six to eight inches in the back. "I wouldn't want the risk of getting it mucked up on the street."

"That change is easy enough." Luckily, they had the right size in stock. "Now, for the fabric. What's your favorite color?"

"Blue," Iris said, without hesitation.

Annie made a beeline for the perfect piece, a dusty-blue moss cloth, a mixture of wool and silk that felt like a soft moss. Iris ran her hand over it, caressing it. "It's beautiful."

"You'll be beautiful in it—and it has enough body to hang nicely." *And sew easily.* "Perhaps the underskirt could be a crepe that would drape, and the wide decorative strip on the bottom of the overskirt could be a matching satin?"

"I put myself in your fashionable hands," Iris said.

They finished gathering the notions Annie would need—with her keeping track of the cost for her own sake—when Officer Brady approached.

A verdict already? Annie greeted him and introduced Iris—but he already knew her from the murder investigation. "Good news I hope?" Annie asked. "How long is his sentence?"

He swirled his mustache and did not meet her eyes. "I hate to tell you this, ladies, but Oscar Grasston escaped custody."

Annie and Iris exchanged an incredulous glance. "He's loose?" Annie managed.

"I'm afraid so."

"How could that happen?"

"As he was being led from the jail to the courtroom for sentencing, he pushed an officer down the stairs and ran out a side entrance—handcuffs and all. We ran after him, but he. . . Well, he slipped away."

He's free.

Mr. Horace approached and was filled in. "Do you think Miss Wood is in danger?"

"I do," Officer Brady answered. "He knows where she works and has come here before."

"He also knows where *I* live," Iris said. "He came in the bakery the day he killed Danny." She clutched her drawstring purse, her eyes darting. "He doesn't like us, either. You interviewed all of us after Danny died." She looked at Annie with panicked eyes. "He's going to come after us!"

Brady sighed and spoke to Mr. Horace. "I think it would be best if we accompany both of these girls home to the bakery, for their own safety."

"I. . . I don't live there anymore," Annie said. "I have a room with another clerk."

"Does Grasston know where you live?"

She thought a moment. "I don't think so. He assaulted me nearby, but ran in the opposite direction after help came."

He twirled his mustache again, obviously thinking. "I think you can go back to your place, then. But I will provide an officer to accompany you."

Annie shook her head. "A male friend is coming to get me after work. He will see me home safely."

"But what about here at the store?" Mr. Horace asked Brady. "We certainly don't want that man coming in here and causing trouble."

"I'll put officers at the doors, and you make your security men aware." He turned to Annie and Iris. "We are heartily sorry, ladies. We are doing our best to catch him." He spoke to Iris alone. "Are you ready to go home, miss? I will fetch an officer to accompany you."

"I can finish up here," Annie said. The girls embraced and wished each other well.

Mr. Horace left to alert his men. As soon as they were gone, Mrs. MacDonald and Mildred came close. "He's free?" Mildred asked under her breath.

"He is."

Her head shook back and forth, back and forth. "What if he comes after me?"

"Does he know where you live?"

She bit the nail of her thumb. "No. We met elsewhere."

"Then you should be all right."

Mrs. MacDonald had a solution. "I'll accompany you home tonight, Mildred."

Everyone was covered—as well as they could be.

⬥

Sean was a good sport about postponing their dinner so Annie could get safely home. Although Annie wanted to enjoy the time alone with him, she could not get Grasston out of her mind. Even as they got on the streetcar she searched the crowd for her tormentor. She held the parcel containing the supplies for Iris's wedding dress tightly against her chest, like a shield.

Sean must have noticed, because as soon as they were seated he said, "Surely he wouldn't be stupid enough to show his face."

"He's not stupid, he's obsessed. With me. With revenge."

"All because you took his gloves."

"And cost him his job."

Sean shook his head. "A footman could dye his gloves purple and it

141

wouldn't be enough to get him sacked."

"You don't know the butler."

"Neither do you. How long were you visiting at the Friesens'?"

She had to think. "Five or six days."

"Less than a week."

"Yes."

"So in less than a week, as the maid of a guest, you single-handedly were responsible for making the head footman—which is a prestigious position— lose his job? You have that sort of power?"

It did seem far fetched. "But he blamed me. In person, the first time he came to Macy's."

Sean looked out of the streetcar window a few moments before turning back to her. "Perhaps he's simply one of those people who have to blame someone—anyone—for their own shortcomings and mistakes."

That made her feel better, until the truth pressed forward. "Be that as it may, Grasston's character flaws do not change the fact that he attacked me, did something to Mildred she won't talk about, and killed Danny. We could determine with one hundred percent certainty that the reason he's perpetrating these crimes is because he hates his mother or can't stand cloudy days. The whys behind his actions do little good other than help us wrap our minds around his actions. They do not *change* his actions."

Sean let out a sigh. "Where did you get your keen, logical mind, Miss Wood? It's quite impressive."

Accepting the compliment spurred her to answer with confidence. "I have done more than my share of dissecting character while trying to figure out my parents. I quickly learned that such an analysis—though interesting— made it clear that I had little choice but to accept them for who they are and make choices based on logic rather than emotion."

He leaned slightly against the outer wall of the streetcar to better study her. "Tell me about them."

"This is peculiar," she said. "I rarely think of them, yet just the other night Edna had me talking about them, and now you."

"Why don't you think of them often?"

She placed the parcel in her lap and laid her hands upon it. "I shouldn't be here in America."

"They disapprove."

"They don't know."

"*That* is peculiar."

She nodded. "By saying I shouldn't be here, I mean that the opportunity to travel or to work in a fine store like Macy's are achievements I never dreamt of as a child, because I couldn't even conceive of such possibilities. I grew up poor."

"There's no shame in having meager beginnings. Many of us did."

Us? She'd ask him more about his roots later. She wanted him to understand hers. "Being poor in status is one thing. My family was poor in spirit. In their attitude." She looked at him, needing to see his eyes. "It *is* possible to be happy and poor." She put a fist against her chest. "Happiness comes from in here, doesn't it?"

Sean was quiet for a moment. "It should. But often the outer details of life complicate and cloud happiness. They stir people up and feed their discontent."

Annie nodded. "I know it's not as simple as I make it out to be, but I think there has to be a certain amount of will involved. People need to *will* themselves to be happy so the harsh particulars won't faze them."

Sean nodded. "God gave us free will to choose our own way."

"To choose happiness?"

"To choose Him and His way—which will give us that deep-down happiness and contentment, no matter what happens."

"Now, *you* make it sound too easy."

"It's not that difficult to say yes to Him. And the subsequent yeses get easier."

Annie remembered her last encounter with God at Edna's, when she felt His presence and love. *"Come to Me first. You are Mine and I am yours."* God wanted her to say yes to Him. Now Sean was telling her to say yes to Him. Surely it couldn't be as simple as that.

"Annie?"

She changed the subject. "Back to my parents—"

He smiled. "You're willing to talk about a flawed father rather than a perfect one?"

"I know the one better than the other."

"That's too bad."

She huffed at him. "Do you want to hear my story, or not?"

He gave her a by-your-leave with his hand.

"Where was I?"

"Being happy in here." He put a fist by his own heart.

Her thoughts sped across the ocean to her family home. "I was determined to be happy, but my parents were just as determined to be unhappy, to be dissatisfied, to be victims of life, with no hope of changing it or making things better." Before he could respond, she finished her point. "Yet they did worse by begrudging everyone else of *their* happiness, wanting to pull the rest of us down into their hole to moan and complain."

"So you moved away from that hole."

"I ran from it. I ran to a life that offered hope and a chance to be something more, first with the Kidds, and now on my own."

He took her hand in his. "You've done well, Annie Wood."

His words filled her up. "I hate that your compliments mean so much to me."

"Why?"

"It's hard to explain."

"Do you want me to tell you why?"

She was amazed at his audacity. "Be my guest."

"To accept compliments means someone else has seen into your world and has judged it."

"I'm used to being judged."

"In the negative."

She felt the sting of tears and nodded.

"Having others point out the good in you means *you* need to acknowledge the good in you."

She swiped a stray tear away. "Where did you get your keen, logical mind, Mr. Culver? It's quite impressive."

⌘

Edna arrived home before Sean and Annie and was at the stove when they entered. The delicious smell of sausages and onions filled the flat.

"Dinner will be ready soon," she said. "Not as fine as in a restaurant, but I made bubble and squeak to honor Annie's British roots."

Sean hung his coat and hat on a hall tree. "I have no idea what that is."

Edna pointed at the stove. "Sausage served with mashed potatoes, cabbage, and onions."

"Thank you, Edna. It's one of my favorites." Annie began setting the table.

"Why the 'bubble" and why the 'squeak'?" Sean asked.

Edna smiled. "Listen." She leaned her ear toward the pan. The onions bubbled and the sausage squeaked.

Sean laughed. "Food that makes music. I know it will taste as good as it sounds." He took on the job of slicing bread. Annie loved how he pitched in without asking.

"So, Sean," Edna said as she stirred the onions. "Annie said you were going to take her to dinner and share some great idea?"

Annie felt herself blush. She'd told Edna about it, never intending for Sean to know. What *if* his idea was of a more personal nature? He wouldn't want to share it here. "If you don't want to tell me tonight—"

"With me in the room," Edna said.

"You don't have to," Annie said. "I can wait."

"But I can't."

His enthusiasm fed her own and eased her mind about the subject matter. Within minutes they sat at the table, said grace, and set to work eating dinner.

"Hmm. The bubble and squawk is now a favorite."

"Squeak," Edna corrected.

Sean winked.

"Oh you," she said. "But enough about the food. Annie's dying to know your idea."

"Dying might be too strong a word. I'm interested."

"That's all?" Sean said, pretending to be annoyed.

She played along. "Very interested." *Just tell me.*

Sean ate another large bite to fuel himself, then stood. He stepped into the parlor and returned with Annie's drawing. "This sketch is going to change your life."

Really? "You have my attention."

"After seeing your talent, I approached my superiors at Butterick and told them about you, about your fashion sense, and your artistic ability."

"I hardly think helping a few customers choose the materials for a dress or skirt reveals any acute fashion sense."

"But you did more than just choose the materials; you looked beyond the patterns that were shown in the catalog and innovated a new piece of fashion altogether. You designed something that previously didn't exist."

"You did do that," Edna said.

Did I? "So what did your superiors say?"

"They want to hire you to work at Butterick in the pattern design department."

Annie felt her jaw drop. She pointed to the parlor. "I've only used two patterns. Ever. How am I going to help create new ones?"

"They are willing to hire you and help you learn."

It was all too much. "But why? They don't know me. They haven't even seen my sketch—my one sketch. Why would they risk so much on a girl who two months ago was a housemaid in England?"

He returned to his chair. "I can be very persuasive. And, there's an opening in that department."

Her thoughts collided, one into the other. "Let us say I am able to do a good job at Butterick. . . . What about Macy's? They've been nothing but kind to me, and have been so understanding about letting me take time off to deal with Danny's death and Grasston. I can't just leave them."

Her point was met with silence.

"Actually, you could," Edna said. "Clerks come and go all the time. It's the way of it."

"But you've been there many, many years."

"Because I found my niche selling sewing machines. Do you really think your destiny lies in selling fashion? Or designing it?"

The thought of abandoning Macy's overwhelmed: Mrs. MacDonald, Mildred, and even Mr. Straus. . .

"There is another reason you should take the new job," Sean offered.

Annie pressed a hand to her forehead. "More? I'm already at sixes and sevens."

"The other reason is that Grasston is loose. He knows where you work. But if you worked at Butterick, he couldn't find you and hurt you."

"Oh my," Edna said. "He's right."

It would be such a relief to not have to look for Grasston lurking around Macy's anymore.

Edna interjected. "If Annie is interested—which she most certainly *should* be—what is the next step?"

"I can't take any more time away from Macy's. I'm sure someone at Butterick would want me to come to their offices and interview and—"

"I thought of that. I got them to agree to an interview on the telephone." He retrieved a slip of paper from his pocket. "Here is the name and number of Mr. Burroughs. Call him tomorrow during your lunch break."

Annie stared at the number. "You've thought of everything."

"I've certainly tried." He took her hand. "I want you to become all you can be, Annie-girl. I also want you to be safe. Accepting this job will bring about both goals."

She thought of their discussion on the streetcar, the talk about free will, choosing God's way, and saying yes to Him. With a surge of certainty, Annie found herself saying, "Yes. I say yes."

Sean jumped out of his chair, pulled her to her feet, and encased her in a hug. Then it was Edna's turn.

"Once again, Annie makes a quick decision," Edna said.

"I hope it's the right one."

"I assume it is." Edna turned to Sean. "That's some idea you had."

He nodded but only had eyes for Annie. "You've made me very happy—in here." He put a fist to his chest.

She mimicked his motion, pressing a hand against her own happy heart.

CHAPTER SIXTEEN

Annie skipped lunch to call Butterick. As she stepped into the telephone booth in Herald Square she was glad she hadn't eaten. Her stomach clutched and rolled.

This one phone call will change my life.

Did her life need changing? She had already endured so many changes: coming to America, leaving her job as a maid, taking refuge with the Tuttles, getting a job at Macy's, moving to Edna's, losing Danny to Grasston.

Grasston was one of the biggest reasons she wanted to change her place of employment. Leaving Macy's would gain her much-needed distance from the threat of him.

She retrieved a coin from her purse and thought of yet another huge change in her life: Sean. If someone asked her to pinpoint when their relationship started, she would have a hard time giving them an answer. In so many ways Sean always *was*. He was indelibly linked to her time at Macy's. And now he would be a part of her time at Butterick.

If I get the job.

If she didn't make the call, there was 100 percent certainty she'd get a no. She had to risk asking the question.

But as she risked, she found herself turning to the One who knew all the answers. *God? Is this You at work? If so, let it happen. If not, I'll get back to work and be satisfied at Macy's.*

Annie hesitated a bit after realizing that her prayer was a bit confrontational, as if she was demanding God do the work to get *her* life where it needed to be.

Yet that's what she wanted Him to do. Sean had talked about saying yes to the Almighty. Doing so required surrender on her part but also demanded work on His part. Was He busy right now? Did God have more important things to do besides listen in on her phone call?

She shook the theological musings away. Whether God had time or not was out of her control. What *was* in her control was putting the coin in the slot, dialing the number, and saying "Hello" when someone answered.

With one last intake of breath, Annie did just that. "Butterick Pattern Company, may I help you?"

"I would like to speak to Mr. Burroughs. Please."

"I'll connect you."

Annie took advantage of the delay to breathe deeply. She saw a man standing outside the booth, waiting to use the phone. She covered the receiver and said, "Sorry, but I am going to be a while."

He shrugged and went on his way—which was for the best. She didn't need an audience.

"Burroughs here."

Annie's heart skipped a beat. "Yes, sir, Mr. Burroughs, my name is Annie Wood, and I was told by Sean Culver to—"

"Yes, indeed, Miss Wood. Mr. Culver has told me all about you."

What was she supposed to say to that? "Good things, I hope?"

"Very impressive things. Apparently you have a talent for fashion?"

She regretted that Sean may have overstated it. "I have an interest in fashion." She thought of something to add. "And a desire to learn about the business."

"Very good. What is your background?"

She wanted to fudge about the maid part, but not knowing what Sean had told him, she had to tell the whole truth. "I was a housemaid for the Viscount Newley and his family in England."

"Not much fashion involved there."

"At first, no, sir, there wasn't. But I quickly became involved in making alterations to the ensembles of her ladyship and her daughter."

"That doesn't sound like the usual duties of a housemaid."

"It wasn't. But I had an interest and helped the lady's maids do *their* jobs."

"So they taught you how to sew?"

Had they? "Not really. I learned by doing. By studying the dress construction of Lady Newley's couture gowns and dresses."

"Couture?"

She wasn't sure why he was asking the question. "She has all her clothes made in Paris after attending the fashion shows at the couture fashion houses."

"Your knowledge of such construction might come in handy."

Annie tried to contain her surprise. "I'm glad you think so. I am also currently working at Macy's and—"

"Mr. Culver has told us about your ability to sell multiple patterns to one customer."

She couldn't help but laugh. "I must admit I didn't do it to gain sales as much as to fulfill the needs of the customer."

"That's a good answer."

Since he seemed impressed, she offered her own question. "What does the position at Butterick entail?"

"That depends on you."

"I. . . I'm not sure how to respond."

"Let's just say that with Mr. Culver's hearty recommendation and our conversation today, I am intrigued by the possibilities of having you work for our company. Are you interested, Miss Wood?"

And there it was. A *yes* or *no* stood between Annie and the path of her future. She found herself praying a very simple prayer: *Yes, Lord?*

With but a moment between the prayer and her answer, she heard herself saying, "Yes, Mr. Burroughs. I think I would be very interested."

"Very good. When can you start?"

Today would be ideal. But then she thought of Mrs. MacDonald and Mr. Straus. . . . "I will give my notice today and let you know. I don't want to cause Macy's more trouble than I have to." *Than I have already caused with the Grasston business.*

"Although I'd like you to start immediately, I find your loyalty and work ethic commendable. We shall be in touch."

"Thank you, Mr. Burroughs. I shan't let you down."

"I don't believe you will, Miss Wood."

Annie hung up and bowed her head in gratitude.

❧

Annie needed to talk to Edna or she would burst with excitement. Luckily, Annie was helping a customer who was interested in sewing machines, so she had the chance to go to Edna's department.

As the woman tried a new Singer, Annie whispered to Edna, "I did it. I took the job."

Edna's eyebrows rose. "Congratulations. Have you informed Macy's yet?"

"I will as soon as there's a lull."

The customer looked up from the machine. "How do you make it go in reverse?"

Annie left her in Edna's care and returned to her own counter, eager for the chance to wrap things up. If only the customers would go home so she could talk to Mrs. MacDonald.

Finally, there was a lag in business, and she had her chance. "May I speak with you a minute, please?"

Mrs. MacDonald nodded, but the furrow in her brow revealed her concern. "Is everything all right?"

"It is. Yet. . ." She'd best just say it. "I need to give notice."

Mrs. MacDonald's head drew back. "I thought you liked it here."

"I do, and I appreciate everything that you and Macy's have done for me."

"Do you have another job?"

She nodded. "I'm going to work at the Butterick Pattern Company."

Mrs. MacDonald smiled, her face glowing with a revelation. "I'm betting this is Mr. Culver's doing."

Annie felt a bit of a pull in her stomach. "Yes, it's true he initiated it, but I had an interview and—"

Mrs. MacDonald waved her defensiveness away. "I'm sure you got the job based on merit. You *are* a very talented girl, there's no denying it."

Annie was embarrassed for overreacting. She touched her friend's arm. "I learned so much from you. I'm sorry to leave, but I can't ignore this opportunity."

Mrs. MacDonald patted her hand. "Nor should you. Have you spoken with the powers that be?"

"I have not."

"Best go do it. Mildred and I will cover for you until you get back."

Annie was going to miss this place.

❧

Annie spoke to the person in charge of employees and resigned. It was as painless as such an act could be. They asked her to finish out the week. Only three more days. . .

But on her way downstairs, Annie spotted Mr. Straus standing outside an office. Of all people, he deserved to be told in person.

She walked toward him and waited until he was finished giving his secretary some instruction. He looked up, saw her, and smiled. "Miss Wood. How are you today?"

"I'm fine, sir, but may I speak with you a moment?"

He blinked once then nodded and led her into his office. "Have a seat."

She would have rather stood but didn't want to offend.

"What's on your mind?"

"I. . . I am leaving Macy's for another position."

His left eyebrow rose. "Is there a reason? Were you unhappy working here?"

She scooted forward in her chair. "Oh no, sir. Not at all. I am very thankful for the experience you've given me. I will be forever grateful for that, and for your kind sympathy and patience after Danny was murdered."

"Murdered," he repeated. "Have they found his killer?"

"They know who did it, but they don't have enough evidence to convict him." She considered telling him that Grasston was on the run but didn't want to go into it further.

"I'm sure he will be judged and jailed."

"I hope so, sir."

"So who is the lucky company who's stolen you away from us?"

"Butterick Pattern Company."

"A thriving company for certain. They just built a sixteen-story building. Very impressive."

Annie was unaware of these details but was glad to know them.

"What position will you have?"

She bit her lip. "I'm not sure. *They're* not sure where they're going to use me."

Mr. Straus laughed. "Which most likely means they see a myriad of talents in you and need to take time placing you to their best advantage."

It was a wonderful thought. "I hope so."

He stood and extended his hand. "I wish you the best of everything, Miss Wood. Don't be a stranger to us."

She was moved by his gracious farewell. She only hoped the people at Butterick would be so kind.

❦

As soon as she saw Mr. Horace walking toward her, Annie felt her entire body tense. The grim look on his face made her wary.

"Good afternoon, Miss Wood," he said.

"Good afternoon. Is something wrong?"

"Something isn't right." He handed her a note. "This is from Officer Brady. He didn't want to come inside because he knew his presence tends to disrupt business."

"How thoughtful of him."

"Read it," he said.

The note said: *Miss Wood, An update: Grasston is still at large. Continue your vigilance as we continue our efforts to capture him. Officer Brady.*

She sighed deeply, folded the note, and put it in her skirt pocket. "I was so hoping. . ."

"I know. We all were. You are being careful when you go home?"

"I am. I hope he still believes I live at the bakery." She thought of something. "Are the police watching the Tuttles? Watching for him there?"

"They are. But what about your new residence with Mrs. Holmquist?"

"I still don't think he knows about it."

"He could follow you after work."

Thanks for reminding me. "Did you hear I gave my notice today?"

His eyebrows rose. "Did he scare you off?"

"Partly. But I also received an exciting job opportunity I could not refuse."

"Good for you. Good for you in ways beyond the opportunity. Hopefully Grasston never finds out where you work."

"That was one consideration in taking the job."

He extended his hand for her to shake. "It has been nice knowing you, Miss Wood. I wish you a well and safe future."

Annie suffered a shudder. She wouldn't feel truly safe until Grasston was caught and convicted.

❦

"I have a confession to make," Annie told Sean as they entered the restaurant.

"Is it something incredibly juicy and naughty?"

She batted him on the arm. "Sorry to disappoint. I was simply going to confess that this is the first time I have ever eaten in a restaurant."

"Ever?"

"Ever. When I was young we were too poor—and there were no restaurants in Summerfield anyway. In service for the Kidds I ate with the servants. On the ship over to America I also ate with the servants, as I did at the

Friesens'." She looked around the restaurant, which glowed with soft electric light and the sparkle of crystal and silver. "I have never ordered from a menu. Actually, I have never had much choice regarding what to eat at all, unless you count the cafeteria at Macy's."

"I don't count the cafeteria as proper restaurant dining." Sean pulled her hand around his arm and held it there. "I am honored to be the one who gives you a proper initiation."

A man dressed like a butler led them to a table and held out her chair, then Sean's. He placed a linen napkin in her lap with a flourish.

"Finally, our dinner out," Sean said with a wink.

"Are you saying Edna's dinners are lacking?"

They received menus. "I'm saying no such thing, and don't you ever imply that to her. I'm simply happy for the time alone with you."

She smiled at him then hid behind the menu lest he see her blush.

He guessed her ploy and pushed it down. "Is the feeling reciprocated?"

Annie pointed to the day's specials. "The codfish looks enticing."

Sean pressed the point. "Don't be coy with me, Annie. Or elusive. Or flirtatious."

"Then what should I be?"

"Open. Honest. And. . ."

"And?"

He looked at the menu. "I think I might try the mutton chops."

"You are so cheeky."

"I can be," he said. "And will no doubt continue to be." He set the menu aside and extended his hand on the table, waiting for her to take it.

Which she did.

"What I want from you, *for* us, is not a courting game that involves meaningless chitchat about nothing, but something very real that involves meaningful discussion about everything."

She was moved by his sincerity yet also a bit frightened by it. "I want that, too," she said.

"I hear a 'but' hanging nearby."

"But. . .everything in my life is happening so fast. Too fast. A very short time ago I was a housemaid. Then a clerk. And now a pattern artist."

"Your quick journey reveals your true inner talent."

"It's not just my career that has moved quickly, it's my private life, too. I went from knowing the Kidd family and the servants in the house to knowing Iris and Danny, to the Tuttles, to Edna and Mildred, and. . .and you."

"Saving the best for last."

She loved how he could make her smile. "I have no one left from my *before* life. Every friend is a new friend."

"That doesn't make us bad friends."

"Not at all. It's just. . ."

The waiter came and took their order. They stuck with their initial cod and mutton chops.

"It's just?" Sean prodded.

She adjusted the napkin in her lap, trying to return to the previous thought. "It's just that everything in my entire life is new. Even my so-called talent is new. I'm not sure who Annie Wood is anymore. I don't recognize her. I don't know her."

He found her hand again and squeezed. "But I do. Would you like me to introduce her to you?"

She laughed. "Are you going to make me blush again?"

"I certainly hope so." He let go of her hand and cleared his throat. "Annie. . .What's your middle name?"

"Louise."

He cleared his throat again. "Annie Louise Wood, aged. . .?"

"Nineteen, but nearly twenty."

"So old." He continued, "Annie Louise Wood, aged nearly twenty, is an extraordinary modern woman. She knows her own mind, is not afraid to share it—even when she's wrong, and—"

"Blimey."

He held up a finger, stopping her objection. "*And* she has the ability to make everyone she's with feel special. She sees the world with wide-eyed eagerness, open to whatever life throws at her."

The thought of Grasston came. And went.

He had more. "She makes friends easily, has an incredible work ethic, and has excellent taste in male companions." He grinned. "I couldn't resist, but only because it's true."

"Are you finished?"

"You want *more* praise?"

"You have more?"

He sighed with feigned drama. "Annie Louise Wood has an amazing, fascinating, and surprising life in front of her. She will succeed in everything she does—with God by her side. There," he said. "Satisfied?"

"It sounded a bit like a eulogy. I'm not dead, you know."

"In a way you are. The old Annie is dead and a new Annie has risen in her place."

His words took her aback, for they were full of truth.

⸎

Annie set her fork down and leaned back in her chair. "I cannot eat another morsel."

Sean did the same. "The apple tart crowned the meal—and then some."

She sipped her coffee. "The dinner was brilliant. I thank you for the meal, your delightful company, and for my new job."

"Your phone call with Mr. Burroughs cinched it. I merely put the idea in his head."

Remembering the interview. . . "Did you tell him I used to be a maid?"

"No. I didn't know if you wanted that mentioned. I focused on your work at Macy's, and your drawing ability. But—"

"Drat," she said. "Not knowing whether you mentioned it or not, *I* mentioned it. I hope he doesn't think less of me for my humble beginnings."

"You didn't let me finish. I spoke to Mr. Burroughs after your interview and he said that your experience as a maid under Lady Newley was the tipping point in giving you the job."

She was confused. "Why would that help my cause?"

"You told him you've altered couture gowns?"

"Well, yes. Lady Newley and Miss Henrietta went to Paris every spring to see the newest fashion. They had their clothes custom made. Of course I never went with them. But their lady's maids did."

"Ah. Paris. I'm betting that was the clincher for Mr. Burroughs."

"Why would the Kidds going to Paris matter?"

"Because Butterick sends handpicked employees to those same fashion shows."

"Why?"

"To make sketches that we turn into knockoffs for our home sewers. You play your cards right and you might get to go to Paris, too."

She had to laugh. "Me? Going to the fashion shows in Paris?"

"You, working as a pattern artist in the largest pattern company in the world?"

Annie put a hand to her heart and felt it pounding. "Why are good things happening to me?"

Sean studied her a minute. "What did you tell me yesterday? That you thought it possible to *will* yourself to be happy? That's what you're doing now."

"Am I?"

"You are. You're not letting the pain of Danny's death and Grasston rule your life. You've chosen joy and hope."

"Have I?"

He laughed. "You are either searching for more compliments—which I shall be happy to provide—or you're simply not allowing yourself to enjoy and accept the very marvelous woman you are."

Annie's heart swelled at his words—because they encouraged—but also because they revealed him to be an extraordinary man.

"There is one more thing I choose," she said.

"And what's that?"

"I choose you."

He leaned over the table and kissed her, sealing the moment.

CHAPTER SEVENTEEN

T ake a deep breath, Annie."

Annie did as Edna instructed, putting a hand upon her midsection. One breath then two for good measure. "I've got the collywobbles."

Edna smiled. "I've never heard that term before, but I understand completely. It's natural to be nervous about your first day on a new job."

Annie smoothed her new skirt. "Do I look all right?"

"You look lovely. They'll certainly be impressed you created your outfit with Butterick patterns."

She had second thoughts. "Is it too obvious? As though I'm a toady?"

"A what?"

Americans didn't use that term? "A flatterer. Buttering them up?"

"Ah," Edna said. "Don't point it out to them, but if they notice, you can certainly say something." She pointed to the toast on Annie's plate. "Eat. You need a good breakfast."

Annie wasn't sure her stomach was up to food, but she nibbled at the bread and drank her tea.

&

Sean had said it was approximately two miles from Edna's to the Butterick offices at Spring and MacDougal Streets. It should have taken her forty-five minutes at a brisk pace, but she'd taken a wrong turn and had to backtrack.

She was late. She hated being late.

The Butterick building loomed at the west end of Spring Street like a massive monster intimidating the three-story buildings around it. Its presence spoke volumes toward the company's importance and success.

Before she entered the building, she dabbed at her face and neck with a handkerchief. To "glow" prettily was one thing. To be sweaty was another. She looked at her reflection in a window and smoothed the stray strands of hair that announced her frenzied walk. Then she forced herself to take some deep breaths, hoping to calm her pulse. *Please, God. You brought me here. Help me do my best.*

She entered the lobby and approached a front desk. "Excuse me, but I'm a new employee. Today is my first day and I don't know where to go."

"Of course, miss," the receptionist said. "What is your name?"

Annie was instructed to go up the elevator to the fifth floor and report to Mrs. Downs.

As Annie walked away, the girl said, "Welcome to the Butterick Company, Miss Wood."

Her politeness reminded Annie to move out of her self-focus and reciprocate. "Thank you for the welcome and your help."

The girl's smile was genuine. "Don't be nervous. We don't bite."

Annie's laughter eased her nerves. "That's good to know."

The elevator operator greeted her warmly. "First day?"

"Is it so obvious?"

"Just a bit. Don't worry. You'll be fine."

The doors opened up to an enormous room filled with oak desks piled high with papers.

A man whose desk was in the front row asked, "Looking for someone?"

"Mrs. Downs? I'm Annie Wood. I'm new."

His gaze took in the whole of her, but she couldn't tell whether he was impressed or appalled. "We heard you were coming. Follow me."

By the way he said it, it seemed they'd been *warned* she was coming. She hoped her instincts were wrong.

"Mrs. Downs," the man said to an older woman with a pinched face. "This here's Miss Wood, come to work."

The woman eyed her, yet her gaze avoided Annie's face and took in her clothes. "I recognize the skirt—pattern number 8358, and the blouse is 3758, yet not completely."

Annie was impressed but immediately regretted altering the sleeve to her own design. "I changed the sleeve."

Mrs. Downs moved close and inspected it. "I do like the sleekness here, and the cuff. . . It is an interesting alteration."

"Thank you." Annie hastened to add, "It wasn't that I thought the initial blouse pattern faulty, I just had an idea and—"

"You are here to design, Miss Wood. To create. To take what does not exist and make it real."

Annie realized she'd been holding her breath. "I am eager to get to work."

"Hmm," Mrs. Downs said. "Come with me."

Annie was led into another room that contained an extremely long layout table in the center. Along the window wall were smaller tables, each four feet in length. A half-dozen women sat at those tables, while others fitted pattern pieces or fabric on headless dress forms that wore muslin ensembles in various stages of construction. A girl stood at the long table, using a curved ruler to mark on some paper.

Mrs. Downs clapped her hands to get everyone's attention—an act that was unnecessary as Annie had everyone's eyes from the moment she'd come in the room. As the man said, they knew she was coming.

"Ladies, I would like to introduce you to Miss Annie Wood, who has come to fill the position vacated by Agnes. As you've been informed, she has artistic ability illustrating designs, as well as an innovative eye. I trust you'll make her feel welcome." She pointed at the girl who was fitting some muslin on a dress form. "Maude? I place you in charge of Miss Wood."

"How grand. I've always wanted to be in charge of someone."

Mrs. Downs pointed a finger at her. "Be kind. Show her around the building and then lead her through the design process." She looked at Maude over her glasses. "Don't make me regret choosing you for the task, Miss Nascato."

Maude put a hand to her chest and feigned indignation. "I wouldn't dare."

Annie was shocked by her boldness. Yet Mrs. Downs must trust Maude or she wouldn't have chosen her.

As soon as the older woman left, the room erupted in giggles and comments such as "She lets you get away with murder, Maude" and "Be nice to Miss Wood, Maude" and "You'd better behave yourself, or. . ."

Maude turned to the last speaker. "Or what?"

The girl went back to her table. "One of these days. . ."

"I agree," Maude said. "One of these days I'm going to get what is coming to me: fame, wealth, and unimaginable happiness."

Her words quieted the girls and they returned to their work. But as Maude turned her attention to Annie, Annie wasn't sure what to think of her guide.

Maude stuck some stray pins into a cushion then headed for the door. "Come along, Annie Wood. Let me show you what you've got yourself into."

⬩⬩⬩

Annie was shown the press room where they printed up the envelopes for the patterns, as well as the pattern catalogs and copies of the *Delineator* magazine—which—Maude informed her, was the most successful women's magazine in America, with a circulation of 1.3 million readers. Annie had no concept of such numbers.

The sound in the press room was deafening, and the constant frenetic motion of the massive machines was almost frightening. Also frightening— in its own way—was the attention of the men manning the presses. They winked at her, whistled, and laughed among themselves.

Maude was not fazed. "Behave yourselves, boys," she called out above the noise. "She's not your type."

"How 'bout you, Maudey? Is you me type?"

"Nobody is your type, Calvin."

Another man yelled out, "You two are the jammiest bits of jam I's seen."

Annie was flattered and had to admit that she and Maude were a pretty pair. Maude was petite, dark, and curvy, and she, tall, slim, with creamy skin.

As soon as they were clear of the presses, Maude said, "Don't let their fresh ways intimidate you. They're good enough fellows. Actually, you won't have much contact with them."

"But you do?"

Maude grinned. "I have contact with everyone."

"Why?"

"Why not?"

"Then maybe I should know them."

Maude stopped walking and faced her. "Keep to the design department, Annie. There's only room enough for one know-it-all in this company, and that's me."

Annie studied her face a moment, trying to determine whether Maude was threatening her or teasing.

Maude flicked the tip of her nose. "Lighten up, chickie. Life's too short."

Annie wasn't sure what to make of the woman. She liked her, but she was also intimidated by her.

Maude led the way to another floor that was populated by dozens of desks, and dozens of workers. Each desk was piled high with letters. "This is the correspondence center. We get thirty thousand letters a week from women asking questions about our patterns, sharing ideas, or needing help with their sewing."

Again the numbers overwhelmed. "You answer them all?"

"Every one. A company doesn't have the money to build a huge building by ignoring the customers. And to let you know the massiveness of our jobs, Butterick puts out between seven hundred and nine hundred patterns per year. Patterns *we* have to design and create."

"That many new ideas? How do we do it?"

"You'll get the hang of it. And remember it's not just women's day fashion, but evening wear, sleepwear, undergarments, children's wear from layette to teen, and men's, too."

"I know nothing about the construction of men's clothing." *And little enough about women's.*

"We stick to the nontailored clothes for men. Shirts, vests, nightshirts."

"That's a relief. I can't imagine tailoring a suit."

Maude raised a finger and a point. "Neither can the average home seamstress."

It was a good point to remember.

"Don't worry about any of it. Nobody starts out knowing what they're doing—no matter what the job." She gave Annie a mischievous glance. "Unless you're...special."

It sounded like a challenge—one Annie was not willing to take. "I'm not special. Not at all."

"Noted, and filed for future reference."

They visited a floor where women were folding tissue patterns and stuffing them into printed envelopes. Maude shouted over the chatter of the workers. "Ladies! Meet Annie Wood, a new designer."

A chorus of "Hello, Annie" ricocheted off the tall ceilings.

"You *do* know everyone."

"Of course." She walked to a table and showed Annie a stack of pattern pieces. "I'm sure you're familiar with the patterns."

"I am. My skirt is number 8358, but the blouse is a variation of 3758."

Maude touched the sleeve. "You changed it."

My, these people were observant. "Do you like it?"

"It has possibilities." Maude turned back to the workers. "A cardboard template is made of each pattern piece, and then layers and layers of tissue paper are cut at once. And perforations are added to indicate the darts, the matching points, and to create identifying letters for each piece."

"Those perforations are very handy," Annie said.

"There's another department that takes what we've designed and what pattern pieces have been created and writes instruction sheets that go in the envelope."

"Another handy tool."

They took the elevator to the next floor where Maude announced, "This is the sales floor where—"

Sean rushed toward them, his face beaming. "Annie! My protégé!" He kissed both her cheeks.

Maude put her hands on her hips. "Ahem."

"Good morning, Maude." He winked at her. "You're looking especially lovely this morning, Miss Nascato."

She flipped his compliment away. "Too little too late, boyo."

"Don't say I didn't try."

"I'll let Sean show you around his department." To Sean she said, "Ticktock, Sean. Don't take too long."

"Yes, ma'am." Sean saluted her.

Sean showed Annie around, explaining how mail orders came in for fifteen cents and how there were agents like himself who called on stores to replenish their stock.

He was all business, so though she longed to take his arm, she dared not. Obviously he hadn't shared the more personal side of their relationship with people at work. She accepted that arrangement. In a way it was freeing. Annie wasn't certain she could handle dealing with a new job *and* a suitor on the job.

Sean led her back to her starting point, where they found Maude chatting with another salesman. Sean finished up by saying, "We have actual Butterick storefronts in Paris, London, Berlin, and Vienna. I am the lucky chap who gets to call on them in person."

"You get to go to Europe? For business?"

"I do. I'm going there in April. I'll attend the Paris fashion shows, too, getting ideas for the company." He grinned. "You want to come along?"

He'd already teased her with this possibility. "You know I would."

Maude approached, her hands beckoning Annie to follow. "Yes, yes, enough of the sales department. We need to be moving along. Ta-ta, Sean."

"Ta-ta, Maude." He gave Annie a special smile. "Miss Wood."

Maude led her to the stairs instead of the elevator. "The next bit takes some exertion. Are you up for it?"

"Of course," Annie said.

As they climbed floor after floor, Annie became winded. "Aren't we running out of building?"

"Almost."

They reached a landing with an exit door. Maude opened it, and Annie found herself on the roof of the building. "You really are giving me the complete tour, aren't you?" She noticed enormous glass skylights cut through the middle of the roof.

"Natural light?"

"Two stories high. Saves on electricity." Maude pointed across the expanse. "No tour would be complete without seeing the famous Butterick sign in person." She swept a hand toward the east end of the building. They viewed the back of the sign amid extensive bracing. It was enormous.

"It's the largest illuminated sign in the world. The *B* is sixty-eight feet high—about the height of a five-story building. The smaller letters are fifty feet high. And it lights up at night." Maude led Annie to the side of the *B* where she could see hundreds of bulbs outlining the letter.

"How many bulbs are there?"

"Fourteen hundred—give or take. There's a man here who spends most of his time changing 'em out. Dwight takes his job very seriously, not wanting some letters to go black, lest the sign say 'butter' or 'ick" or worse yet, 'butt.'"

Maude was clearly gauging Annie's reaction to the slightly crude comment. Annie was not going to bite. "Protecting the company's reputation is a noble job."

"And here I thought I'd get an indignant rise out of you."

"I'm not so easily scandalized."

"Good for you."

Maude led the way to a clear view of the city. "To the west there is the Hudson River, and Dwight says when he's up on the sign he can even see the Statue of Liberty, way down that way." She pointed to the south.

Suddenly Annie felt a little dizzy and took a step away from the edge. "You all right?"

"I just realized I've never been so high."

Maude laughed and led the way back to the door. "Being in my presence will do that to a person."

Annie couldn't argue with her.

They made their way down the stairwell all the way to the floor that held the design department. But Maude paused at the door. "Are you sweet on Sean?"

Annie didn't know what to say, so she turned it around on her. "Are you?"

Maude flipped the notion aside with a hand. "Don't worry about me. I have no interest in Sean Culver."

Annie was taken aback by her tone. "You make it sound like the notion is revolting."

"Nothing against Sean, mind you. I simply have no interest in the men who work here."

Annie caught the distinction. "So is there a man in your life? Who doesn't work here?"

Maude leveled her with a look. "You're getting mighty personal for the first day, don't you think?"

"You started it. You asked *me* about my personal life."

Maude tilted her head. "So I did." She opened the door and they were back at work.

Annie couldn't help but notice Maude hadn't answered her question.

❦

"Enough of tour time," Maude said. "Now it's time to create some fashion." She stood with Annie in front of the huge layout table in the workroom.

It looked intimidating. There were rolls of paper, rulers, curves, pencils, scissors, and bolts and bolts of muslin. Annie had been assigned one of the tables that were set perpendicular to the wall of windows and had her own dress form.

"You do know how to use patterns, yes?" Maude asked.

Annie hesitated. "I have a basic knowledge." She remembered her lessons with Edna. "I have altered a pattern to fit my taller frame, and as you noticed, I changed a sleeve."

Maude stared at her, offering a slow blink. "That's the extent of it?"

Annie looked around the room, seeing that many of the girls were listening. She lowered her voice, hoping to reach Maude alone. "I want to learn. Teach me. Please."

Maude studied her a moment. "All right, then. Let's get to work." She moved to a muslin dress on a form. "Every dress has the same design elements to work with: the neckline, neck edge, armhole, sleeve shape, cuff, waistline, hem length, and skirt silhouette."

"All that."

"All that." She pulled a chart close. "These are the basic body measurements for our patterns. And over there are the basic patterns for our dresses, skirts, and blouses. We can start there and adapt the existing pieces to our ideas." She cut off a length of tissue paper and placed it over a bodice pattern piece on the table. "Let's say we want to have a scoop neck. We can draw it with the curve and trace over the basic piece." With a sweep of a pencil along the curved edge, Maude showed how it was done.

"You make it look easy."

"It can be—with practice."

Annie pointed to the finished dress. "How do we get from this to that?"

"Trial and error. After we make the new pattern we carefully cut it out in muslin, sew it together, and fit it on the dress form—seam-side out. That's where we make adjustments and alter the pattern until it's right. Only then is it made up in real fabric so the art department can make sketches for the catalogs and the *Delineator*. Then it goes into production."

Annie took a deep breath and let it out slowly.

Maude laughed. "It will be fine. You will be fine."

"I'll take your word for it."

The rest of the day went by in a blur. Annie worked with Maude on a blouse pattern with an interesting wide collar. They had trouble getting the collar to lie just right. It was a tedious process but one that provided much satisfaction. Creating something from nothing was a new experience, one Annie embraced.

The girls were nice enough: Suzanne, Wilma, Dora, Sofia—or was it Sophie? Annie tried to remember their names, but by the end of the day, with all the information thrown at her, she took the safe way out and said her good-byes without using their names.

"You survived," Mrs. Downs said when Annie clocked out.

"I did. But there's so much to learn."

"'All I know is I know nothing.'"

"What?"

"Socrates."

Annie had no idea who that was but had the feeling she *should* know. "Thank you for the opportunity, Mrs. Downs."

"Don't thank me yet. You'll need to prove yourself, prove the buildup is true to your talent."

"Buildup?"

"Mr. Culver was beyond complimentary as to your potential."

"I hope he didn't overstate."

"So do we, Miss Wood. See you tomorrow."

✦

Sean waited for her in the lobby. "Would you like some company on your walk home?"

"Of course."

They left the building amid the crowd, and only when they were a block away did he pull her hand around his arm. "So. Tell me everything."

She laughed. "I'm not sure I could detail the color of the sky at the moment. My mind is a-jumble with new things I need to learn."

"You'll do it. I believe in you."

"Which brings up the point. . . I hope you didn't oversell my talent. I have very little experience. I fear they expect a Rembrandt while I am but a crude sketcher."

"I'm betting Rembrandt was a crude sketcher at one time. As Butterick is giving you a chance to excel, you need to give yourself a chance to excel and grow."

She leaned her head against his shoulder. "I don't know what to do with you, Sean Culver."

"I'll think of something."

✦

Annie started up the steps of Edna's building then noticed Sean wasn't following her. "Won't you come to dinner?"

"Not tonight. I have some paperwork to do back at my place."

A new thought made her freeze in place. "I don't even know where you live compared to here."

167

"It's a ways away."

She descended the steps to face him on the sidewalk. "How selfish of me to never realize that you coming here, and walking me home, might be an inconvenience."

He touched her hand. "You're worth it."

Annie didn't feel worth it. She pressed the palm of her hand to her forehead. "I'm so angry at myself for not thinking of you, for only thinking of myself. I'm so sorry."

"You're forgiven." He kissed her cheek then turned to leave. "I'll come by tomorrow morning to walk you to work."

"But you said it's out of your way."

"And I said you're worth it."

She stood on the sidewalk and watched him walk away, his hands in his coat pockets, a spring in his step. "What did I do to deserve you?"

"Pardon?" said a man walking by.

"'Evening." She went into the building and up the flights to Edna's—to *her* home.

At the sight of Edna in the kitchen, making dinner, Annie was faced with another failing. "I can make dinner sometimes," she said. *Though I have little idea of how to cook.*

"I know you can," Edna said, stirring a pot. "And once you're settled in your new job I'll take you up on it. Now, tell me about your day."

"What did I do to deserve *you*?" Annie said under her breath as she put her hat and jacket on the hall tree.

"What?"

"I'm noticing what good friends I have in you and Sean."

"We are a golden pair, aren't we?"

Annie wouldn't let her flip the compliment away. She went to the stove and stopped Edna's stirring with a hand. "I mean it. If it weren't for you two, I might be heading back—" She stopped herself. *Oh no. Could it be?* "What is today's date?"

Edna hesitated a moment. "The thirteenth, I believe."

Annie took a step back, stunned by the fact.

"What's wrong?"

"Tomorrow is November 14."

"So?"

Annie's legs puddled beneath her, and with Edna's help she found a chair. "The Kidds sail back to England on the fourteenth."

Edna took the pot off the stove and sat at the table. "Your ride home."

"My ride home."

Edna wiped a few crumbs from the tablecloth onto her hand, where she held them captive. "You could still go."

"Could I?"

"I don't believe 'could' is the right word. *Would* you go? Do you want to go?"

Annie pressed a hand to her chest, trying to calm her frantic heartbeat. "I don't know."

Edna's eyebrows rose. "Really?"

Her question—and her surprise—was justified.

"I wouldn't think you could leave, Annie. Not with your new job, new friends—a special male friend."

Annie's nod had no strength in it.

"You're not agreeing with me," Edna said.

Annie rose from the chair, needing her body to move along with her thoughts. "I love my new life here, and appreciate everything about it."

"But. . . ?"

Annie stopped pacing and wrapped her arms tightly around herself. "Letting the Kidds go, and not being on that ship, is so final."

"A closed door."

"A locked door."

Edna shook her head. "Not locked. You can always return to England on your own."

"Perhaps."

"The larger question is what would you be returning *to*. Surely you don't want to be a maid again."

"Of course not. Never."

"Do you wish to go home and live with your family?"

"Of course not." *Never.*

"Do you have other job prospects there?"

"In Summerfield? None. It's a tiny village."

"How about in a city? London?"

She was embarrassed by her lack of experience. "I've never been." She returned to her chair. "I've never been anywhere but Summerfield and here."

"A village to New York City is an enormous jump."

"An enormous leap."

"Of faith?"

Annie was taken aback. "Is that what it is?"

"Seems so to me. You left the Kidds with the expectation you'd find something better."

"I had no idea what I'd find."

"Exactly. You took the leap—on faith—that there was something better out there. And there was."

"I did that."

"Is that a question or a statement?"

"Both."

Edna retrieved a Bible from her bedroom. She leafed through it then handed it to Annie, her finger pointing at a verse. "There. Hebrews 11:1. Read it aloud."

"'Now faith is the substance of things hoped for, the evidence of things not seen.'" Annie put a hand on Edna's forearm. "I just got the shivers."

"I always take such shivers to mean that God approves of what I'm thinking. As if saying, *'Yes, Edna. You've got it.'*"

"Surely not."

"You want to argue with me? Or Him?"

Annie's soft laugh broke through the seriousness of the moment. "I do like the notion that God is right here, letting me know I'm on the right go of things."

"So you're all right with staying? With turning your back on what was and fully investing in what could be?"

Annie let a deep breath come and go. "Sean said the old Annie is dead and a new Annie has risen in her place."

"Has she?"

This time Annie's nod was filled with certainty. "She has."

"Very good, then. Give God a 'thank You,' and welcome to *now*."

Now seemed a very good place to be.

Thank You, God.

CHAPTER EIGHTEEN

Annie was deep at work, trying to perfect the pattern for a draped overskirt on a dress, when suddenly all the girls in the department turned toward a sound in Mrs. Downs's office.

Through the glass window of the office Annie could see a visitor, a woman wearing a lavender wide-brimmed hat with a plume. She was talking very loudly to Mrs. Downs, gesticulating wildly with her hands.

"Who is that?" Annie asked Dora.

"That's just Mrs. Sampson, a rich lady with too much time on her hands."

"At it again, I see. Or rather, hear," Suzanne said.

The other girls giggled.

As the woman's voice grew more animated, Annie turned to Maude for a more detailed answer. "What's the story with her? She's a giddy kipper for sure."

There was a pause, and then the girls laughed. "Giddy kipper?"

"She's overly excited."

"That she is," Maude said. "Always is."

"She comes here often?"

"Too," Suzanne said.

"What are they arguing about?"

"She's a fashion rebel," Maude explained. "If she had her way we'd all go around naked."

More giggles.

"If she's for nakedness, why is she visiting a company that designs clothes?"

"Don't take me too literally," Maude said. "She's one of the rational-dress reformers, those who are against corsets and clothing that binds."

"I'm against corsets, too," Annie said, adjusting the pinch of boning under her arm.

"But you wear one," Dora said. "We all do."

Suzanne shook her head. "It's improper to do otherwise."

"Scandalous," another girl said.

The subject got her thinking. "I know that's the way it's always been, but wouldn't it be nice not to be bound up? When I was a—" She caught herself before she admitted to being a maid.

"A what?"

She found a different tack. "When I was younger I was all excited to wear a corset, not knowing what a discomfort they could be."

"A torture."

"A cruelty to women."

As if on cue, all the girls made adjustments to their corsets.

Maude put a halt to the subject and pointed at the designs at hand. "Back to work, girls. After dealing with Mrs. Sampson, Mrs. Downs will be in a foul mood. We'd better be getting something done."

The four girls returned to their work. Maude looked over Annie's shoulder at the pattern pieces for the skirt and offered no suggestion. Then she placed a sketch in front of her.

"What's this?" Annie asked.

"Mrs. Downs wants us to add more hobble skirts to our catalog."

Annie looked at the drawing. The skirt of the dress was wide at the hips but at the knee narrowed drastically toward a tight tube above the ankles. "I've seen a few women around town in these, but they look ridiculous."

"It's fashion," Maude said. "From Paris."

"I don't care where it's from," Annie said. "Women can't walk in them. I saw a woman trying to get in a cab and she had to receive assistance, and then virtually had to lift the skirt quite high to get in." She pointed at the ankles of the woman in the illustration. "She's showing her ankles even before she tries to get in a cab."

"It's the fashion of women's rights," Maude said. "No more heavy petticoats. No more tripping on our skirts."

There was no "right" to it. It was illogical. "So we are free from the length, but create a new restriction in the width?"

"It's modern," Suzanne said from her table.

"It's silly."

"Yes it is. My point exactly."

None of them had noticed Mrs. Sampson leave Mrs. Downs's office until she stood beside Annie. "It's nice to hear the voice of reason in the design department." She gave Annie a look-see. "Are you new?"

"I am. Very." Annie caught Mrs. Downs's scowl. "Since I don't know much about fashion yet, I probably shouldn't voice my opinions."

"Of course you should voice them," Mrs. Sampson said. "We need a clear voice of reason in this company." She nodded at Mrs. Downs. "This is exactly why I continue to delight you with my visits. Think of me as the woman repeatedly coming before the judge in the Bible, wearing him down." She gazed directly at Mrs. Downs. "I *will* wear you down."

Mrs. Downs swept an arm toward the elevator. "Thank you for your visit, Mrs. Sampson, but the girls have work to do."

"Fool's work, if they're creating more patterns for that insipid fashion."

Mrs. Downs was insistent. "If you please."

With a dramatic sigh, Mrs. Sampson turned to leave. Then she paused and turned back to Annie. "What is your name, miss?"

"Annie. Annie Wood."

"I look forward to winning you over to my side. Carry on."

When she left she took a good portion of air with her.

"She exhausts me," Mrs. Downs said, pressing a hand to her brow.

"She seems interesting," Annie said.

"You will *not* be swayed by her rantings."

"Some of what she says makes sense." Annie pointed at the drawing. "This isn't a fashion for the everyday woman who needs to move about easily in order to get through her day. Home sewers don't want this."

Annie heard Dora gasp. And Suzanne took a step back. Maude crossed her arms and shook her head.

Now I've done it.

Mrs. Downs glared at her. "You are an instant expert as to the needs and desires of our customers? We've been in business since 1863, we have over a hundred branch offices and over a thousand agencies, and are second only to the United States government in the size of our publishing department, yet you know best?"

Annie wanted to hide under the table. "I'm sorry. I misspoke."

"Indeed you did. Focus on our company's goals, Miss Wood, not the absurd rantings of a rebellious malcontent." Mrs. Downs stormed into her office and shut the door hard enough to rattle the glass.

"Oh dear. I dropped a clanger on that one."

Maude laughed. "That you did."

Dora and Suzanne moved back to the main table. "I do see your point," Dora said. "The hobble skirts *are* a silly fashion."

Suzanne shook her head. "They may be silly, but if it's good enough for Paris and the Wright brothers, then—"

"The brothers who invented the aeroplane?" Annie asked.

"Rumor is they's the one who started it," Suzanne said. "They were taking some ladies up in their planes and tied a sash around their skirts below the knees so the fabric wouldn't flap around."

It made an odd sort of sense. "But very few women go on aeroplanes."

Dora shrugged. "Doesn't seem to matter. It became fashion."

"And as such, we need to work with it," Maude said.

As they turned their attention back to the drawing, Annie had one last question. "If Mrs. Downs doesn't like Mrs. Sampson, why does she let her in?"

"She and her husband have more money than spit," Dora said.

"That's hardly a nice way to put it," Suzanne said.

"It's all I could think of on short notice."

"She and her husband are friends with the Astors and Vanderbilts," Maude said. "Powerful families. Powerful businessmen."

"With power comes a voice that demands to be heard?" Annie asked.

"Exactly."

"You are right about one thing, Annie," Dora said.

"What's that?"

"Mrs. Sampson *is* a giddy kipper."

※

With work going well, there was still another issue that needed to be addressed, and a phone call to make.

Since the people at Butterick knew nothing of Annie's personal life—beyond her friendship with Sean—she didn't want to risk anyone overhearing the call, so she left the building and found a phone booth. She held a business card for reference and dialed the number. When the call was answered, she asked, "May I speak to Officer Brady, please? Annie Wood calling."

While she waited for him to pick up, she recognized a few coworkers walking on the sidewalk, gave them a nod, and then discreetly turned away.

"Miss Wood," the officer said. "I *am* glad to hear from you."

Her hopes swelled. "You've caught him?"

"Uh, no. I was wanting to check to see if you'd seen him."

There was something pitiful about his question. "No."

"That's good."

"It is, but as I explained, I changed jobs. He doesn't know where I work."

"That's a plus."

"It is, but. . .the reason I called is this. I need to go to the Tuttles' to fit a wedding dress for Iris. But now that I hear he's not been caught, I'm hesitant to show myself there."

"You have reason to be hesitant. My men *have* seen him near the bakery."

"Then why haven't they caught him?"

"Seeing and catching are two different things."

His words were the antithesis of encouraging. "I'm not sure what to do. I really need to see Iris. Plus, I want to visit the rest of the family."

"This won't solve the latter issue, but perhaps Iris can come to you for the fitting?"

"Wouldn't Grasston follow her?"

"Not if he doesn't know where she's going. Since she left the Friesens' he's never been after Iris, has he?"

"Just me. And Danny." *And Danny's dead.*

"Then if she's aware and wise—and if someone accompanies her—I think it's a valid solution. I'd prefer that you stay away from the places he used to find you. No Macy's. No bakery. I'm sorry, but until we catch him. . ."

What choice did she have?

Annie thanked him—for what, she wasn't sure—then called the bakery. Saturday would be a good day for the fitting.

Thomas answered. Thomas, Iris's perfect chaperone.

⚬⚬⚬

A boy ran into the workroom, an envelope to his chest.

"Yes, boy?" Maude asked.

"I got here a message for a"—he read the envelope—"a Miss Wood? And I's supposed to wait for a reply."

"That's me," Annie said, raising her hand.

There was a chorus of oohs and teasing comments. "A secret admirer, perhaps?"

"There's no secret. It's Sean Culver who admires her."

"Maybe this is a rival."

"Girls!" Maude said, shushing them. "Enough speculating." She turned to Annie. "Read the note."

"Thank you," Annie said.

But Maude wasn't through. "Then let us know what it says."

"Thatta way, Maude," Suzanne said.

Annie enjoyed their banter because it made her feel like one of them. She stepped toward the window and dramatically turned her back to read it. She assumed it was from Sean and planned to chastise him for being so bold.

But when she saw the elegant cursive of her name on the front of the envelope, she knew it wasn't from him. It was a female's hand. Maybe a note from someone at Macy's?

Inside was a letter written on fine stationery, folded in two. There was a printed letterhead.

Eleanor Sampson.

What would Mrs. Sampson want with her? They'd only met this morning, with Mrs. Sampson being a blustery wind that had blown in and out of the room.

"Come on, Annie," Dora said. "What's it say?"

She hadn't gotten that far—yet the message was short: *You've impressed me, Miss Wood. I invite you to dine this Friday with myself and my husband. Eight in the evening. You may bring a companion. Relay your answer to the boy. I look forward to getting to know you better.* There was an address at the bottom.

"Come on, chickie," Maude said. "Spill."

Annie was hesitant. It had been made very clear that Mrs. Sampson and her rebellious ways were not looked upon kindly at Butterick. Plus, there was the question of why the woman would want to meet with *her*.

Before she could make the decision to share or not share, Maude plucked the letter from her hands.

"Wot! That's personal."

Maude read it quickly. "Why would she want to meet with you?"

There were many questions of "Who?"

The cat was out of the bag—and running about the room. "Mrs. Sampson."

Maude handed the note back and addressed the others. "Annie's been invited to dine." The last word was expressed with a haughty tone.

"Mrs. Sampson is giddy rich," Dora said.

"Very," Maude added. She gestured toward the letter. "They live at 451 Madison Avenue."

"Ooh," Suzanne said. "La-di-da."

Annie was intrigued by their response. "That's a posh address?"

"The poshest."

Annie was rather embarrassed with her first thought. "I don't have a thing to wear. I have work clothes, not dinner dresses."

"Miss?" It was the boy. "I needs an answer?"

Maude did the honors. "She says yes."

"And thank you," Annie added. The boy left Annie staring at the letter. "Why does she want to talk with me?"

"You and a companion," Dora said. "Who you taking with you?"

"I know," Suzanne said in a singsong.

Annie didn't like that they thought Sean was a foregone conclusion. "Perhaps I'll bring my landlady. She's a dear friend."

"A landlady?" Dora said. "Don't be ridiculous. You must go with a man on your arm."

"And Sean's your man," Suzanne said.

They were right. If she asked Edna, Edna would be just as nervous as Annie. Sean's presence would hopefully keep her calm. "Fine," she said. "I'll ask Sean to go."

"Now *there's* a modern woman for you. She's doing the asking." Maude motioned toward the other girls. "We best get back to work or Mrs. Downs will have our heads."

"She still needs something to wear," Dora said, going back to the dress form she was draping.

"There's no time to make anything," Annie said.

Maude stared at the door, a hand to her chin, her thoughts clearly whirling. Annie left her alone. If anyone could find an answer, it would be Maude.

An hour later, Maude came to Annie's workstation and said—more loudly than necessary, "I'm afraid I was negligent about the tour of Butterick. Follow me, Miss Wood. There's one more area I'd like to show you."

"But where—"

"Shh."

When they were in the stairwell they could talk. "Where are you taking me?"

"To your very own personal closet."

"What are you talking about?"

Maude's face glowed with excitement and adventure. "We often fully make up the patterns with nice fabrics. Some are for fashion shows, and some for photographs, but all are stored together in a large closet."

Annie took the knowledge to its logical conclusion. "Do you think they'll let me borrow a dress?"

Maude started up the stairs and answered over her shoulder. "We aren't going to ask."

Annie tugged on the back of Maude's skirt. "But shouldn't we?"

Maude looked down at her from two steps up. "Do you want to risk a no?"

"Do I want to risk my job? And yours?"

Annie saw a moment's hesitation in Maude's eyes. "Opportunities such as yours don't come often into a working girl's life. You can't *not* go."

"I could still go, and just wear a blouse and skirt."

Maude shook her head. "Mrs. Sampson said you impressed her. So do that. Impress her by wearing something fashionable, something that shows you appreciate the invitation and are aware of what's proper and what's not."

"It's very tempting."

Maude put a hand on her shoulder. "They don't go through the closet often. The dresses that have already been utilized are just sitting there, gathering dust. We can choose one, borrow it, and you can bring it back on Monday."

The thought of dressing up—really dressing up—was enticing. Yet once again reality reared its head. "How do we get it out of the building?"

Maude glanced past Annie, revealing that this was an issue. Then her eyes brightened. "Occasionally I take home a garment to work on the design with my own machine."

"They let you do that?"

"I choose to do that, to get the thing done so I can move on to something else. I put the dress in a garment bag to take it home."

Annie nodded, understanding. "We could slip the dinner dress behind the other one?"

"It would work."

"But then you'd have to work. At home. On your days off."

Maude grinned. "So it is. My only payment will be hearing about everything—in detail—on the Monday morning after."

Consider it done.

CHAPTER NINETEEN

I *am not meant to be a thief.*

Annie hated that word. She preferred "borrower." Yet in all honesty, that term indicated an open arrangement, an ask-and-be-told-yes arrangement.

To just take the dress without asking...

She had to trust Maude. Maude had worked at Butterick for years. She knew the ropes. She knew the people. She knew the ins and outs of every department.

Maude knew how to steal a dress, but more importantly, Annie hoped she knew how to wangle not getting caught.

Maude's plan to slip the dinner dress behind a work-in-progress dress in a garment bag seemed possible. As long as something didn't muck it up.

When it was nearly quitting time. Annie's stomach flipped and grabbed. She put a hand to it and took a deep breath.

"Gracious goose, Annie," Maude said as she came close. "It's not good form to look guilty before the crime."

Crime?

Maude held up a garment bag where she'd placed the dress she was going to finish at home. "I'm ready for the other one, and have even slipped a second bag in this one, so you won't be carrying a bare dress around when you go to your home, and I to mine."

Annie made sure no one else was looking. "Did your man, your contact...?"

"Bertie, and he's just a boy. And yes, the item should be in a box in the storeroom on fifth, just where we arranged."

Annie needed this over and needed to be safely away. "I haven't been this nervous since I ran away from—" Once again, she'd nearly said too much.

"Ran away from what?"

She quickly put it to rest. "You don't need to know everything about me, Maude Nascato."

"Of course I do." Maude retrieved their jackets and hats. "But that will wait for another time."

Annie and Maude left with the other girls of the department, many chatting about their plans for their days off. No one mentioned the garment bag.

"Good night, Mrs. Downs," Maude said as they passed their boss.

"Good night, ladies." Mrs. Downs glanced at the garment bag but said nothing more.

As they entered the stairwell and made their way down two floors, Annie was impressed by Maude's confidence. She had a way about her that implied she knew exactly what she was doing and had full authority with what she was doing, which meant there was no reason to question her.

The girls detoured from the stairs into the fifth-floor offices, going against the tide of workers exiting toward the stairs.

" 'Night, Maude," a few of them said.

" 'Night, ladies." Maude strode toward the far side of the large room, and with a glance around, stepped inside a storage area, tugging Annie in with her.

And there it was. A box.

Maude lifted the lid to reveal the lovely peach gown Annie had chosen from the company's closet. But before she could admire it longer, Maude put the dress in a garment bag.

"I'm certainly glad it's not one of those old-fashioned dresses with huge leg-o'-mutton sleeves. I'd never get it to fit. Hand me the other dress."

Annie did as she was told, and within seconds the garment bag within a garment bag was completed.

"By the way, you owe Bertie a bag o' sweets."

"Who?"

"The boy who brought this down here for you."

"Certainly." But then she had a question. "Why didn't we just get it directly from the closet upstairs?"

"Because it was upstairs." Maude nodded in the direction of the stairwell. "It would be a mite hard to explain the two of us going *up*, against the tide going *down*. I had to get it to a floor below ours."

Annie was impressed. "You think of everything."

"I try." She draped the bag over her arm. "The hard part is done. Are you ready to go?"

"More than ready."

When they exited the storeroom they found the entire floor empty. They rushed to the stairwell and joined the sea of workers going home.

☙

Maude was smooth. Maude was unflappable.

When Annie met Sean outside the building—as per their routine—Maude walked with them for a while, giving no indication that anything was awry. As the corner approached where Maude would go north when they continued south, Annie felt a wave of panic.

For she had not told Sean anything about the dress. Although she felt she knew him well, to ask him to ignore their scheme was asking a lot.

"Down here," Maude said, stepping into an alley.

"What are you doing?" Sean asked.

"Close your eyes, Seanie," Maude said. "That way you won't be held as an accomplice."

"Accomplice to what?"

Maude already had the garment bag open and removed the second bag. She handed it to Annie. "There you go. Wear it in good health."

Sean's forehead was furrowed. "What just happened here?"

Maude offered a dramatic sigh. "You're accompanying Annie to the Sampsons' for dinner tonight, yes?"

"I am."

"What are you wearing?"

"I suppose I'll wear my Sunday suit. I haven't thought about it much."

"Of course you haven't," Maude said. "But Annie has given great thought to her attire. She wants to wear something pretty and appropriate for such a grand dinner."

"I expect she would."

Annie couldn't take their vague banter any longer. "I had nothing to wear so I borrowed a dress from the Butterick closet and will bring it back on Monday."

Sean's gaze moved from Annie to the bag she was holding. "That belongs to the company?"

"It does."

"It does now, and always will," Maude said. "She's not keeping it, she's just borrowing it."

His eyebrows rose skeptically. "That's a fine line."

182

"Not fine at all," Maude said. "She wants to make a good impression. You can't fault her for that."

"Did you get permission?"

"Well. . .no."

He shook his head. "Breaking the rules, Annie. Really?"

Annie shoved the garment bag back into Maude's arms. "He's right. I can't do it. If the Sampsons don't like what I'm wearing, that's too bad. They know I'm a working girl and only have ordinary, functional clothes. They can't expect me to wear a dress that's so. . .totally lovely." She gazed at the bag, remembering the fine detail of the dress inside.

"There," Maude said, presenting Annie's words as a cause to be championed. "Do you wish for our dear Annie to feel ordinary and functional, or totally lovely?"

Sean gave Maude the look she deserved. "There is no harmony between what's right and the answer you wish to hear."

"Of course there is. Choose the woman over the rule."

It was time for Annie to make her final petition. "I *would* love to wear it. Just this once. I promise I'll be exceedingly careful with it."

Sean looked from Annie to Maude then back again. "I am surrounded."

"And won over?" Maude asked.

"Stampeded is a better word."

Maude slapped him on the back. "Good for you, Seanie. Now take our Annie home, and have a marvelous time at dinner." She walked out of the alley to the street and then turned back to Annie. "Please don't spill anything on it."

Her departure showcased the silence. "Thank you," Annie said to Sean.

He took possession of the garment bag and offered her his arm— along with his reluctant consent to look the other way.

❦

Annie stood before the mirror on the bureau. The dress made her feel lovely and sophisticated. She almost didn't recognize herself.

It was created from a peach-colored dupioni silk with a high waist and a daring scooped bodice that gained modesty with a dark brown chiffon covering the upper chest. The neckline was adorned with a wide flat collar of brown satin, with matching cuffs on the three-quarter sleeves. The shorter overskirt was edged in the brown satin that curved from the center front to the back, ending in a short train. Annie had never worn anything so beautiful. To go from wearing the uniform of a housemaid to this?

But then she remembered the source of the dress, and her elation waned. "Oh, Edna. I hope it's worth the risk."

"You're testing the bounds, that's for sure."

Annie wished Maude were here. Maude could convince Edna just like she'd convinced Sean. Even Annie could use an extra dose of convincing, because every time she thought about borrowing the dress, she felt a stitch in her stomach. Yet the anticipation of the evening always put a salve on the stitch, calming it.

For the moment.

Edna gave a little gasp. "Wait! I think I have the perfect accessory." She opened a bureau drawer and pulled out a worn velvet box. Inside was a necklace of golden-brown stones. "Wear this."

Annie let Edna hook the clasp at her neck. "It's beautiful. What are these stones?"

"Amber. It was my mother's."

"It's precious to you. I don't think I should."

"You should, because *you* are precious to me. I insist."

Annie pulled Edna into an embrace. "You are so good to me. You are the mother I always wished for."

Edna whispered in her ear, "And you are good to me. Good *for* me, the daughter I never had. I thank God for you."

Annie held back happy tears and whispered back, "As I thank Him for you."

There was a knock on the door.

Edna pulled back, flicking a tear away. "There's your escort."

Annie took a deep breath, wanting to hold on to the moment a little longer. For the first time in her life she felt fully complete and whole. She didn't need a fancy dinner or gorgeous dress to feel special, she only needed the presence and love of this dear, beloved friend. She had a fleeting but profound impression: of all the people who would move in and out of her life to come, the one she would treasure the most was Edna.

"Are you ready?" Edna asked.

Annie smoothed her skirt. "I am."

Edna answered the door, and Sean stepped in. As soon as he saw Annie his jaw dropped.

"Say something, man," Edna said.

"You're lovely. Breathtaking."

Annie felt her face flush. "Thank you. You look quite smart yourself."

Edna handed Annie a brown wool shawl. "There you go now. I don't want you to catch your death."

As they were leaving, Sean said, "Go to the window, Edna. I want you to see something."

Together Sean and Annie walked downstairs. "What do you want to show her?"

"You'll see."

Outside there was a motorcar with a driver. "What's this?" Annie asked.

"I hired him for the evening. I decided we needed to go to dinner in style."

Annie looked upward and saw Edna fling open the window sash. "Well done, Sean!"

He tipped his hat then helped Annie into the car, and the driver closed the door behind them.

"I've never been in a motorcar."

"Me neither," he said. "I hope this is the first of many new experiences we share."

Annie could think of nothing better—or no one better to do it with.

⸎

"Oh my."

It was all Annie could say when their car motored in front of 451 Madison Avenue. It was not just one building, but three built in a horseshoe configuration with a courtyard between.

"This is one family's home?" Sean asked.

"I don't know. I assume so, but I know very little about Mrs. Sampson."

"You know her enough for her to invite you to dinner."

Suddenly the absurdity of the entire evening fell about her. "We shouldn't go. I met the woman once—in passing. We've only exchanged a dozen words. Why would she invite me here?"

Sean looked out the window at the immensity of the home. "Perhaps she's lonely. I think a person could get lonely in such a place."

The driver opened the door for them. "So?" Sean asked. "Are we going in?"

"We are." Annie would forever regret it if she didn't.

When they exited the car, Annie saw that they were directly across the street from an enormous cathedral. "What church is that?"

"St. Patrick's," Sean said. "How would you like such a monument for a neighbor?"

The next issue was finding the entrance. Sean asked the driver, "Where do we go in?"

"I believe you enter through that gate, sir. Then to the right."

Annie saw the ornate metal gate with a lantern hanging at the top of it.

"What time should I come to retrieve you, sir?"

He looked to Annie. "Ten. . .thirty?"

She nodded. If the dinner was done sooner, they'd go sit on the cathedral steps to wait.

The driver tipped his hat. "Enjoy your evening, sir. Miss."

As the driver drove away, Sean offered Annie his arm. "Shall we, *mademoiselle*?"

She gathered her courage. "We shall, *monsieur*."

They walked through the gate into a courtyard with manicured hedges. Electric lanterns lit the entrance on the right-hand building.

Annie was not encouraged when she heard Sean say under his breath, "Lord, help us." But his entreaty spurred her to add her own.

They didn't need to knock on the stained-glass door as it was opened as they approached. A butler nodded to them. "Good evening, Miss Wood, sir."

They entered a room where every surface was decorated, from the mosaic tile floors, to the marble walls, to intricately carved wood moldings, to columns that looked to be inlaid with mother-of-pearl. The furniture was secondary and consisted of a few chairs that were upholstered in a silky fabric with designs of orange and yellow.

"Blimey," Annie said, finding no other word adequate.

"This is just the foyer." Sean's eyes were wide, taking it all in.

"May I take your coats?"

As soon as Annie removed her shawl she was glad she'd borrowed the dinner dress, for her surroundings demanded posh attire.

"Right this way," the butler said and led them through a reception area into a drawing room. Annie couldn't help but compare it to the drawing room at Crompton Hall. The present room won the comparison with an intricate coffered ceiling, more columns clad with mother-of-pearl, and an inlaid wood floor.

"Miss Wood." Mrs. Sampson rose from a chair of golden velvet and came to greet them, her arms outstretched. She took Annie's arms and kissed her cheek.

This was completely different from how Lady Newley would greet an acquaintance. There was little touching among the titled in England. But in America—where no titles existed—such boundaries were obviously crossed.

"You look lovely, my dear."

"Thank you." Annie left it at that.

A mustachioed man joined them and shook Sean's hand. "And you are?"

"Sean Culver, sir."

"Glad you could join us."

Mrs. Sampson led Annie to a settee and shared the seat with her. "I am so glad you accepted our invitation. And that you brought a. . .friend?"

Annie hastened to explain. "Sean *is* a friend, but he also works at Butterick. He was instrumental in getting me the job."

"He obviously recognized your talent."

"I did," Sean said, standing by the fireplace with Mr. Sampson. "Annie has an innate design and artistic ability. She didn't even know she had the talent."

Mr. Sampson looked confused. "How could you not know?"

Annie glanced at Sean, not sure how much she should say. She knew so little about their hostess.

Mrs. Sampson touched her arm. "This is America, Annie. Humble beginnings are a badge of honor. It's not where you begin, but where you end up."

"Hear, hear," her husband said.

The butler returned with a footman, and hors d'oeuvres were offered. And wine. Annie took a glass to be polite, took a sip, and tried not to make a face when she disliked the taste.

"Now then," Mrs. Sampson said. "Back to humble beginnings?"

There was something about the woman that spurred Annie to share. "I was a housemaid in an English country estate. I started when I was fourteen."

"My, my," Mrs. Sampson said. "You have come a long way."

"Very commendable," Mr. Sampson said, "but I do believe I have you beat, Miss Wood. I started out shining shoes on the street. The horse dung I had to wipe away. . ."

"Yes, dear. That's enough of that."

Annie was impressed with his candor. "I've had my share of such unpleasantries in the form of chamber pots."

"Oh, the things we have dung," he said with a chuckle.

"Stop it, Harold. Really."

Annie could tell that their banter was something they enjoyed about each other.

She had her own question. "If I may ask, what do you do now? How did you get from there to. . ." Her eyes scanned the room. "To here?"

"Shoes, Miss Wood. Shoes. As a boy I saw thousands of men's shoes and learned which ones were well made and which ones were going to fall apart. I decided to make quality shoes, and—"

"Sampson Fine Shoes!" Sean said. "I know of them."

With a glance to Sean's shoes, Mr. Sampson said, "I'll see you get a pair. Size ten?"

"How did you guess?"

He spread his arms. "It's my business."

"Now then," Mrs. Sampson said. "Back to Miss Wood's accomplishments."

Annie was more at ease talking about the shoe business. "It's a short list," she said. "I've only worked at Butterick a week, and before that, I worked at Macy's." She looked down at her dress. "This dress isn't even mine. It's borrowed. I don't own anything near this nice."

"Wearing your work clothes would have been fine," Mrs. Sampson said. "Just be who you are, Annie. Who you are is enough."

"But I want to know more, be more."

"You can add wisdom to your list of accomplishments."

Suddenly the flattery was too much. "I appreciate your kind words, but really, I know very little about a very little."

"More wisdom."

She sighed. "Why did you invite me here?"

Mrs. Sampson shared a laugh with her husband. "To the point. I like that."

"You warned me she was a feisty one."

"That she is," Sean said.

The three of them continued the discussion a few moments longer—as if

Annie wasn't even there. It made her nerves rise to attention. The stress of the invitation coupled with the tension of borrowing the dress. . . "Stop. Please."

Silence.

"We don't mean to upset you, dear," Mrs. Sampson said.

"I'm not upset," Annie said. "Just confused. You talk about talent and being feisty and accomplishments when I haven't done anything to deserve your praise. Truly, I'm just starting out, trying to wend my way from being a maid to a working girl. I know bits about life, and am scared to pieces about all I *don't* know." She took a breath. "Why am I here? Tell me. Please."

Mrs. Sampson took her hand in hers and let both rest upon her knee. "You may be feisty, but I have been accused of being a whirlwind."

"Or a hurricane," her husband said.

She continued, "We speak of talent. My talent is identifying a spark in people. When I see it—as I saw it in you during our brief encounter the other day—I waste no time fanning that spark into a flame."

Annie was still confused. "What spark did you see?"

"The spark of practicality, creativity, and conscience."

Annie tried to remember the circumstances of their first meeting. "We were talking about hobble skirts."

"Exactly," she said. "You pointed out how ridiculous they are. Impractical. And I believe you called them—"

"Silly," Annie said, remembering. "They are silly. How is a woman supposed to live a normal life, hobbled in such ridiculous fashion?"

Mrs. Sampson looked at her husband. "You see, Harold? I told you she was the one."

Annie blinked. "The one what?"

"The one to champion our cause."

"What cause is that?"

Mrs. Sampson opened her mouth to speak then closed it and raised a finger. "Have you ever heard of the Reform Dress Movement?"

"No."

"It started in the 1840s, rejecting the unhealthy confinement of the female form, and promoting practical clothing. Harold and I agree with its principles." She stood and set her plate and glass aside as if needing her hands free to make her point. "If women want the freedom to vote, then shouldn't they be allowed to wear fashion that offers them freedom of movement? Now is the time to let women break the bonds of corsetry and the confinement of petticoats!"

"Step off your soapbox, dearest," her husband said.

Mrs. Sampson nodded and took a fresh breath. "It's a steep step down. I apologize."

"Don't apologize," Annie said. "I like what I hear."

"Actually, I do, too," Sean said. "At least in theory."

"But there you have it," Mrs. Sampson said. "It has to be more than theory. Freedom of dress needs to become the new wave of fashion. And you, Annie Wood, are just the one to bring it into being."

At that moment, the butler entered the room. "Dinner is served, ma'am."

Sean accompanied Mrs. Sampson, and Mr. Sampson offered Annie his arm and a whispered "To be continued."

She wasn't certain whether to be eager or petrified.

❧

Every surface of the Sampsons' dining room was embellished with carving, tile, mother-of-pearl, gold, brass, or silk. The item that was most unadorned was the top of the enormous dining table, which had its own decoration within the swirling grain of the polished oak.

Where the oak left off, the painted china took over, as each gold-edged plate—there were four different plates so far—presented a different exotic bird in its middle, with sweeping leaves and floral sprays surrounding it. The goblets were intricate cut glass, and the sterling silver flatware was far from flat as the handles were created through an interweaving of curlicues dotted with flowers.

Although awed by the decor and finery, Annie was heartily glad she knew which knife and fork to use. Although she'd never sat at such a fancy meal, she'd been exposed to a proper place setting at Crompton Hall. Sean seemed less informed and looked to her for guidance. She picked up the proper utensil, and he followed her lead. It was rather satisfying to know something that he did not.

The conversation about freedom of fashion did not resume until well after the fish course, as they were enjoying a fine cut of lamb.

"So, Annie," Mrs. Sampson said. "May I call you Annie?"

"Please."

"And you may call me Eleanor."

Annie was taken aback. "I'm not sure I can do that."

"Why not?"

She raised a hand a few feet off the table. "You are here, and I am..." She lowered her hand to just above her plate. "Here."

"Nonsense," Mrs. Sampson said. "Harold told you about our humble roots."

"It was very nice of you to share that. I like to hear such stories. They give me hope."

"A question, Annie. Do you wish to have a house such as this?" Mr. Sampson asked.

She knew the answer straightaway but didn't want to offend, so she chose her words carefully. "I wish to be successful at something, but I don't much care if it brings me wealth."

"What would you like it to bring you?" Mrs. Sampson asked.

"Satisfaction." She let the word stand on its own.

Sean had his own requirement. "And a sense of purpose. I'd like to think I was doing what I was supposed to be doing."

"According to whom?" Mrs. Sampson asked.

Sean glanced at each of their faces before answering. "God."

Mr. Sampson slapped a hand on the table, making them jump. "Well said, sir. Well said."

Annie was surprised. She'd been taught never to talk about God or politics or the latest cricket match at the dinner table. The butler and housekeeper at Crompton Hall had been very strict about this during the servants' meals.

Mrs. Sampson leaned back in her chair so the footman could serve her more brussel sprouts. She nodded after receiving four. "So you believe there is a divine plan, Sean?"

"I do." He looked at Annie and nodded once. "I believe we each have a unique purpose—a God-given purpose. The trick is to find out what it is."

"Now *that's* a good trick," Mrs. Sampson said.

"But not impossible," he said.

It was Annie's turn to ask a question. "So how does one know they are on the right path?"

Sean answered with confidence. "Practice and peace."

Mr. Sampson cocked his head. "You have my attention."

Sean's face reddened, and he refolded the napkin in his lap. "I am no expert, but from what I've ascertained from personal experience is that I need to pray for direction, be aware of the nudges the Almighty sends me, and act on those nudges to the best of my ability. If I'm on the right path, I feel a sense of peace."

"A very businesslike way of approaching the spiritual," Mrs. Sampson said.

"It's practical. And it works. I am proof of it."

Mr. Sampson made a motion to the footman to replenish the drinks all around. "I love a good story. Proceed."

Sean's blush deepened. "I didn't mean to take the attention away from Annie. She was the one you invited here. I am simply her dinner companion."

Mrs. Sampson smile was a wee bit wicked. "Oh, I think we have all determined you're more than just that."

Annie deflected her own heated cheeks by taking a drink of water.

Sean looked across the table at her. "If it's all right with Annie for me to tell my story?"

"Of course it is," she said with full sincerity. "I'd love to hear it."

Sean set his fork down and took a cleansing breath. "My life has been a series of stepping-stones, one step leading to another until I reached a door."

"A door you opened? Mr. Sampson asked.

"And walked though."

"In order to tell the story, I need to go back eight years. I was thirteen and working at my father's general store in Brooklyn. I was good at sales. He'd order in too many match safes and would ask me to push them until our stock was depleted. Or bowler hats. Or wire whisks—he overbought terribly the wire whisks."

"You were a salesman then as you are a salesman now," Annie pointed out.

"It seems that is my talent."

"Your purpose," Mrs. Sampson said.

"Not completely. Just a part of it."

Mr. Sampson motioned for the dinner plates to be removed. "Don't interrupt him, ladies. Let the man continue."

Mrs. Sampson made a locking motion to her lips, which made Annie smile.

Sean took up where he'd let off. "I befriended Ebenezer Butterick, who lived in Brooklyn, too." He must have seen Annie about to speak because he added, "Yes, the founder of our company. He was retired then, in his mid-seventies. A frail man, but very wise and sharp of mind. He lived quietly and simply, and gave much of his wealth to good causes. He had a soft heart for children—he created the first sized patterns to fill a need for home-sewn children's clothes."

"I didn't know that," Mr. Sampson said.

"Shh!" Mrs. Sampson said with a wink.

"Ah. Yes. Hush."

Sean smiled, too. "Mr. Butterick created his highly successful company from a single idea. In the early years they'd cut and package the patterns on their kitchen table in Sterling, Massachusetts."

"More humble beginnings," Mrs. Sampson said.

There were nods all around.

"The year we met, the company was constructing the building where Annie and I work. Mr. Butterick was very proud of how the business had grown, and attributed its success to God."

"A wise man."

"Very wise. That spring he grew ill. I made deliveries from the store to him, and he said I reminded him of his nephew, and we would talk. A lot. He seemed to need someone to talk to. His wife had died decades earlier, and his son in infancy. His only daughter, Mary Ellen, came to visit, but he seemed to like my company."

"I understand that." Annie's compliment was heartfelt.

"We talked about business, and sales, and using our success to help others."

"He sounds like a wonderful man."

Scan confirmed this with a nod. "We also talked a lot about God and how there's no such thing as a coincidence. He said that my making a delivery to his house was God's plan to bring us together. And when his health grew worse, he made me promise to go to his company and apply for a job. He even wrote a letter of recommendation."

"You went, and you got the job," Mrs. Sampson said.

"I did—against my father's wishes. He saw no reason for me to take a job in Manhattan when we lived in Brooklyn and I had a perfectly good job in the family store. But I really felt this was the path I was supposed to take, so I walked across the Brooklyn Bridge—and back—every day for five years until I got my current sales position, which allowed me to afford my own apartment closer to work. I was in the stockroom at first, but I worked my way up to sales. It all came about from me working in my father's store, from *me* making a delivery to Mr. Butterick instead of the other boy who worked for us. One thing led to the other. One stepping-stone led to the next and to the open door."

"And you felt it was right," Annie said.

"I knew it was right because of the peace I felt inside. I still feel that peace."

"What a marvelous story," Mrs. Sampson said.

Sean looked to his plate, which now contained a piece of multilayered chocolate cake. "I don't know if it's marvelous, but it's my story." He looked at Annie. "I think Annie is on her right path, too. The door to Butterick opened for her just as it did for me."

"Because you recommended me," Annie said.

"How could I not?" he said softly.

"I will not contradict you, Sean," Mrs. Sampson said. "But we asked you here tonight to open another door that leads to another room."

Mr. Sampson nodded. "I do believe it is time to get to the point. Go ahead, my sweet."

Mrs. Sampson took a large bite of her cake, pushed the plate aside, and then dabbed at her mouth. "Harold and I have been looking for a new beacon in the fashion industry, someone who can design for real women who live real lives. Someone who dares to be unconstricted by the designs of others who show more care for fad over function."

"Ooh, I like that, Eleanor," Mr. Sampson said. "Fad over function."

"Thank you, dear one," she said before continuing. She looked directly at Annie. "We believe you are that beacon."

Annie was confused. "You met me once—on my first day on the job. You know nothing of my talent or lack of it."

Mrs. Sampson shook Annie's logic away. "As I stated, my talent is having a sense about people. I am an extremely good judge of character. When good character and a zest for new ideas show themselves in a person, I will not remain silent. I must make every attempt to tap into it for the common good."

Annie looked to Sean for his reaction. His eyes were slightly wide, his eyebrows raised. He looked as confused as she felt.

"I know how odd this is," Mrs. Sampson said, "but before we move on, I need to finish it and put a cherry on its oddness. We want you to design a fashion line that combines style and utility." She looked to her husband, who nodded. "We will provide all the funding, and Harold has the business contacts for distribution."

"You will be paid well for your efforts," Mr. Sampson said.

"So what do you think of our grand scheme?" Mrs. Sampson said.

Annie had no idea how to respond. The idea was absurd.

Mr. Sampson looked across the table at his wife. "She needs time to think on it, my sweet—which again, shows her wisdom."

"Which further increases my desire to have her work with us." Mrs. Sampson stood, suddenly ending the evening. "We are so glad you took time out of your busy week to meet with us. And now you have the whole of the weekend to think about our proposal."

In minutes, Sean and Annie were out the door amid a flurry of thank-yous and good-byes.

"What just happened?" Annie asked.

"You were ambushed and they wanted us gone before you could object." Sean looked at his watch. "The car won't be here for a half hour. Shall we go across the street and sit on the steps of the church?"

Annie was glad for the suggestion because her legs felt weak. At the cathedral, Sean helped her sit upon a step before joining her. She tucked her skirt around her legs and wrapped the shawl close. The churning inner turmoil made the solidity of the stone steps a necessary foundation. Without it she would surely walk in an aimless circle, or faint away like some weakened woman of the past.

"They want me to quit my job—a job I just started. They want me to design clothes when I have no experience other than designing a different sleeve or collar."

"They want you to go against the entire fashion industry."

Annie remembered what Maude and Mrs. Downs had said about Mrs. Sampson. "They called her a fashion rebel, a nonconformist, and a zealous malcontent."

"Do you want to be associated with someone like that? Now, when you're just starting out?"

"No. I don't. I have too much to learn at Butterick to leave before I've started. Maybe at a later date, I'd—"

"So you'd consider it?"

She was surprised by the incredulity in his tone. "It sounds intriguing, and I like the idea of function over fad. You have to admit the hobble skirt is laughable and defies and denies all logical function."

"But that's what fashion is—a fad. Women like change. If fashion didn't change we'd still be designing hoopskirts or bustles."

"Two other fads."

Sean put his arm around her against the night chill. "Fads keep us employed."

"Even if what we're designing is wrong?"

The only answer he had for her was a shrug.

At this point it was as good an answer as any other.

CHAPTER TWENTY

There was no time to talk about the Sampsons' offer with Edna.

Annie had arrived home late from the dinner party the night before, and in the morning—being Saturday—she immediately dove into working on Iris's wedding dress. Today Iris and Thomas were coming over so it could be fitted. *That* was the task for the day. Pondering some far-off, far-fetched future as the Sampsons' "it" girl would have to wait.

Edna fluttered around the apartment moving a candlestick to the right an inch, dusting some porcelain chickadees, fluffing a pillow that had NIAGARA FALLS embroidered on the front.

Annie looked up from some seam-work on Iris's dress. "Be still, Edna. The place looks grand."

"It does not look grand, it can never look grand." She put a hand to her mouth, her eyes scanning the space for offending bric-a-brac. "I don't get many guests."

"Iris and Thomas are hardly guests."

"They're your friends."

"They are. And this apartment is far more than what they're used to above the bakery. Remember Iris was a housemaid like me." Annie stopped her seaming and went to her friend, taking hold of her upper arms. "Be calm. Relax. They are coming so Iris can try on the dress, not to inspect your home."

"All right. *You're* right." Edna stepped to the couch and turned the pillow upside down. "How's that?"

Annie laughed. "I dare you to keep it like that."

Edna stared at the pillow as if it were a threat. There was a knock on the door, and Edna rushed to the pillow and turned Niagara right-side up again.

Annie opened up the door and made the introductions.

Thomas looked around the apartment then pointed to the pillow. "My father and stepmother went to the Falls after they were married. Jane and I went with them."

Edna took up the pillow, gave it an extra fluff, and then returned it to its place. "My husband and I visited there after our marriage, too." She looked at the couple. "And now you will be married. Congratulations."

"Thank you." Iris wove her hand around Thomas's arm and looked up at him adoringly. "We are very happy."

Their love gave Annie's insides a little twinge. She wanted such a love, even as the thought of it frightened her. Sean was a good man, and all evidence suggested their friendship could be much more. But was she ready for that?

As if summoned by her thought, there was another knock on the door. Sean joined the group easily, as he'd met Iris and Thomas after Danny's death.

"I'm so sorry you had to come all the way here," Annie said. "But Officer Brady thought it best."

"I'm glad to come," Iris said. "Glad to get away from the bakery for a while." She looked at Thomas with a panicked look. "I mean no offense. I love your family."

He patted her hand. "No offense taken. And I agree with you. Any time I get to spend with you away from their prying eyes is a bonus."

Again, the loving looks. Annie took the subject in a new direction. "Have you seen Grasston?"

"Once," Iris said. "Gramps saw him standing in the alley across the street, staring at the bakery. He went outside, called a policeman over, and the coward ran away."

"Pa and I warned him never to go out there alone again," Thomas said. "I don't trust the wretch."

"Nor should you," Annie said.

"Ma didn't even want us coming today because she was afraid we would be followed," he said. "But I did a good scan of the neighborhood before I brought Iris outside, and we kept an eye out for him as we came here. We weren't followed."

That you know of. "I hope he doesn't know where I'm working now."

Edna smoothed the fringed scarf on the mantle. "We haven't seen him around Macy's. No reason to think he knows you aren't there anymore."

"Except if he's been waiting for me before and after work and hasn't seen me," Annie said. "Maybe he's asking around. Maybe he's figuring things out."

Sean put a calming hand on her shoulder. "Don't borrow trouble. We're being careful. So are the Tuttles. And Officer Brady is on top of things. There's not much more we can do."

"Except keep praying for safety," Edna said.

"And justice," Annie said.

"We're doing that," Iris said. "I've got all the children adding it to their bedtime prayers."

Annie was moved at the thought of all those little heads bowed in prayer.

Iris shook the subject a way with the flip of her head. "I came here to talk about my wedding dress, not Oscar Grasston. Where is it?"

"It's in the bedroom," Annie said.

Edna shooed the men outside. "It's time for the males of this company to take a stroll through the neighborhood."

"But I'd like to see Iris in the dress," Thomas said.

"Not until the wedding," Edna said. "You know it's bad luck."

Annie had heard such superstitions but thought them preposterous, yet practical for today since there was work to be done.

She was nervous about Iris seeing the dress for the first time.

Her fears were unfounded when Iris put her hands to her mouth and gasped. "It's the most beautiful dress I've ever seen."

It was an overstatement yet also a relief. "Let's see how it looks on you."

The high-waisted dress of gray-blue moss cloth had straight three-quarter sleeves, a scooped neckline, and a straight overskirt with a diagonal hem, edged with a twelve-inch band of satin. The overskirt was short enough to reveal the soft drapery of the crepe underskirt. There was little trim, just some braid at the cuff of the sleeve and neckline.

Annie was glad she'd cut it a bit big. "Have you gained a bit, Iris?"

The girl sucked in—which removed an inch from her midsection. "I suppose it's possible. Working at a bakery makes it hard not to nibble the wares. Can you fit it?"

Annie tugged at the back seam and found there to be just enough. She took pins from a pincushion and pinned it shut. "It doesn't have the hem in yet, but you can get the feel of it. Go in Edna's room and take a look-see."

The three women moved into Edna's bedroom, and Iris had her first look. She touched the neckline, the cuffs, the curve of her hips underneath. "I look all growed up."

"That you do," Edna said.

That you should be if you're getting married.

Suddenly Edna bounced on her toes. "I have the perfect accessory!"

She stood on a chair and retrieved a hatbox from the top of her chifforobe. With a flurry of tissue, she removed a wide-brimmed straw hat with an ivory ostrich plume on it. There were pink silk roses in a spray on top of a wide blue ribbon. "Voila!" Edna said, presenting it to the ladies.

Annie took possession, giving it a good study. "It's very lovely. I think the pink flowers complement the blue of the dress perfectly."

She handed it off to Iris, who held it reverently. "I've never worn anything so. . .so *chick*."

"It's pronounced 'sheek,'" Edna said. "And yes, that hat is indeed chic. I don't wear it often, but when I do, I feel quite glamorous."

"You wouldn't wear it during the wedding," Annie pointed out.

Edna agreed. "But for the occasional Sunday. . .you can borrow it sometimes, if you'd like."

Annie helped place it on Iris's head, tilting it back just a bit so her pretty face could be seen. "There."

Iris looked at her reflection and began to cry.

"What's wrong?"

"It's the most lovely I've ever looked. I am so blessed to be marrying Thomas and becoming a part of the Tuttle family." She turned toward Annie. "It was a good thing we ran away, wasn't it?"

Annie pulled Iris into her arms but couldn't help but think of Danny— Danny who would still be alive had they not run away.

⟨≫⟩

Annie peered out the front window of Edna's apartment, looking for the men. Oddly, she saw them coming out of the brownstone across the street. Sean was carrying a piece of paper, and they were talking with a middle-aged man. Sean shook his hand.

What was going on?

Annie opened the window and called to them. "We're done, boys. Come back up."

Within seconds they heard feet on the stairs in the hall, and with a burst of energy, Thomas and Sean came inside.

"You'll never believe what just happened," Sean said, holding the piece of paper behind his back.

"You'll never believe what Sean just did," Thomas added.

"Do tell," Edna said. "But don't start until I get some coffee water on the stove."

The four of them sat in the parlor, with Iris and Thomas sharing the sofa. Edna quickly returned and stood at the mantel. "So, Sean. What is this amazing feat?"

"It's not a feat," he said. "But it is amazing. It's God's doing, plain and simple." Sean's smile couldn't get any wider. "While Thomas and I were sitting on the front stoop getting to know each other, I saw a man come out of the brownstone across the way. A Mr. Collins."

"Mr. Collins?" Edna asked. "The landlord?"

Sean nodded. "He was posting this on the door." He pulled the piece of paper front and center. It said APARTMENT FOR RENT. "All of a sudden I'm walking across the street and talking with him. And then I looked at the place and rented it. It's mine!"

"Were you looking for an apartment?" Edna asked.

"I wasn't. But I was swayed because it's so close to here, to Annie."

"That was quick work," Iris said.

Sean nodded at their reaction but looked to Annie. "Aren't you pleased? Now when I walk you to and from work I only have to cross the street to be home myself."

Annie knew what she should say, but for some reason the words wouldn't come. As each second passed without her reaction, Sean's smile diminished until it was extinguished completely.

"I thought you'd be happy for me. Happy for us."

A glance to Edna nudged Annie to respond—if not with total honesty, at least with the words Sean needed to hear. "I'm very happy for you."

"For us."

"That, too."

His brow dipped, but he was clearly too excited to let his mood be dampened too long. "Mr. Collins and I shook hands on it, and I'm moving after work on Monday. Luckily, I have very little to move so it won't be much of a bother."

"I'm going to help," Thomas said.

The sound of water steaming in the pot was heard from the kitchen. "Coffee's coming. And some scones." Edna nodded to Iris. "Would you like to help me, Iris?"

With a glance at Annie, Iris left the room.

"I'll help, too," Thomas said.

Leaving Annie alone with Sean.

Annie immediately regretted the delay of her response. If only she'd given Sean what he needed and not hesitated to dissect her own contradictory feelings.

Sean moved to the chair nearest her. "I thought you'd be truly happy."

"I am."

"But?"

She couldn't go down that road just yet because it had no clear direction. "It *will* be much more efficient for you. I've felt guilty about you having the extra walking every day. You don't have to see me home. I am quite capable of—"

He popped out of his chair. "You're quite capable of making something I did because I want to be close to you into something completely pragmatic and convenient. Are you really so cold as to not be happy for the same reason I'm happy?"

She rose and touched his arm. "I'm sorry. I didn't mean to hurt you. You just caught me by surprise." She thought of something in her favor. "You caught yourself by surprise, too, correct?"

"I did. If Thomas and I hadn't been sitting on the stoop I may never have noticed the sign." His enthusiasm took over. "It's truly as if God put it together for me."

She said the words that would make him happy. "For us."

He beamed and kissed her lightly on the lips. "For us." He drew her into his arms where her doubts could be held at bay.

⸙

Iris and Thomas were gone. Sean, too. Annie had sent him away, claiming she had a bad headache.

She did. In a way. She suffered from a mental ache due to decisions left to make, and decisions already made by others.

"Would you like me to get you some aspirin?"

Annie took up Iris's dress and sat at the sewing machine. "I'll be all right."

Edna plucked the dress out of her lap and took Annie's hand, leading her away from the machine and to the sofa. "Sit."

"Did I do something wrong?"

"Lying is wrong. You lied about your headache to get Sean to leave—and don't deny it."

Annie drew the Niagara Falls pillow to her chest and leaned back with an expulsion of air.

"The question is why? You and he should be out celebrating his move to the neighborhood."

"I suppose you're right."

"Suppose?" Edna stood and stared down at her. "What is wrong with you, girlie? You have the interest of a wonderful man and you shoo him away like a mongrel puppy."

A wave of regret fell over her. "I did that, didn't I?"

Edna returned to the sofa. "You did. He was so pleased finding the apartment and you're acting as if having him close offends you."

"It doesn't offend me."

"Then what is it?"

Annie fingered the fringe on the pillow, giving herself time to find the right word. It came to her quicker than she expected. "It frightens me."

"Sean Culver is the least frightening man I've ever met. He's a true gentleman."

"I know."

"What other man would walk blocks and blocks out of his way—twice a day—to accompany you to and from work?"

"No one I know."

"Moving across the street will make life easier for him. Or don't you want things to be easier for him? Maybe you're a selfish flirt who wants to manipulate men to her bidding, keeping them on a leash she can yank at her every whim?"

Annie tossed the pillow aside. "I am not like that. I appreciate his extra care. I like having him around."

"But not too close."

Annie suffered a deep sigh. "I don't know what I feel about him. And then there's the Sampsons, offering me the world and—"

"What world? You haven't told me about the dinner party. What happened?"

Annie described the evening in detail, ending with the Sampsons' offer. "They want me to design a line of clothes for everyday women that combines function with style. They want me to leave Butterick."

"But you just started there."

"Exactly. And to add to the temptation they'll pay me well—better than what I earn now. By the looks of their mansion, I know they have the money to do everything they say."

"But it's an enormous risk. Going off on your own like that. . ."

". . .when I know so little about fashion and design. It's like leaping from scullery maid to housekeeper with no experience in between."

"So what are you going to do? You've been offered a new job and the love of a man. Two very large, very important decisions have been laid at your feet."

"Therein lies the problem. A few months ago I lived a life where every decision was made *for* me, where having a beau was frowned upon. Now I'm smack-dab in the middle of a life where *I* am in charge, where enormous life-changing decisions are mine to make. The responsibility overwhelms me."

Edna nodded and her face softened. "It was similar for me when Ernie died. Before his death he was in charge of most of the decisions of our life, and honestly, I was glad to leave him to it. But with him gone I was flung into a world where my happiness—and even my survival—depended solely on me."

"Spot on!" Annie said. "That's how I feel. How did you manage to get past it?"

"I didn't get past it, I trudged through it, one decision at a time."

"But how did you know which decision was the right one?"

Edna looked at Annie over her glasses. "You know the answer to that."

Ah. "I pray?"

Edna touched the tip of Annie's nose. "'A threefold cord is not quickly broken.'"

"What's that mean?"

"Think of a rope. One strand is good, two strands wrapped around each other is better, and three strands woven together is not quickly broken." She pointed to herself. "One." Then to Annie. "Two." Then to heaven. "Three."

Annie nodded with understanding and acceptance. "You have an answer for everything."

"I don't, but God does." Edna offered Annie her hand. "Let's begin."

Annie took her hand and their fingers intertwined, becoming strong. They bowed their heads.

The prayers of the two women wove their way to the Almighty, merging with His immeasurable, unbreakable strength.

CHAPTER TWENTY-ONE

The dress. Oh dear, the dress.

As it was borrowed, so it had to be returned. Yet there was a flaw in their plan. For going into work on Monday morning, Annie didn't have the help of Maude or Bertie. She was on her own.

Sean carried it for her as they walked to work. "How are you going to get it back where it belongs?" he asked as soon as they left their neighborhood.

It was the main problem of the day, yet she had to address something else first. "I want to apologize for my lukewarm reaction to the news that you are moving across the street."

"Tepid. Utterly tepid."

"I am sorry for it."

"Can you explain it to me?" He took her arm and helped her around some rubbish in the street.

"I can't explain it completely or well," she said. "I must leave it at the fact that I am unused to being around gentlemen who are kind and thoughtful and think of my needs over their own."

"I think there is a compliment in all that."

"There is." She stopped walking and faced him, stepping out of the flow of pedestrians. "You are a wonderful man, Sean Culver, and I appreciate all that you are, and our friendship."

"'Friendship' sounds too lukewarm for my taste."

Here was the difficult part. "I am a novice at being courted and wooed."

"I love that word, *wooed*. And *swooned*, too, if you ever choose to use it. Very descriptive words."

Annie smiled but would not be deterred from her point. "Recently I have been faced with many decisions, with more forthcoming. This freedom of choice is also new to me, and I don't take the blessing of it lightly. And so"—she took a fresh breath—"I wish to take the time to be wise. I am not saying no to everything you so generously offer me but am asking you to give me some time to choose wisely and right." She took his hand. "Is that acceptable?"

"Acceptable yes, but pleasing? No." He lifted her chin and looked into her eyes. "I am in love with you, Annie. If I had my way I would take you in my arms right here and give you a kiss that would create a public scandal."

She felt herself blush. "I didn't take you for a rogue."

"I am many things. Just give me time as I will give you time."

They resumed their walk, and Annie felt better for the discussion. At least that was taken care of. "Which leaves the dress...," she said.

"You should never have taken it. It didn't impress Mrs. Sampson. She said as much. You risked much for little gain."

"Although I enjoyed the wearing of it, it was a bad decision. Unfortunately, I am sure it will not be the last."

"Perhaps you should just walk right up to the closet where you got it, put it away, and hope no one sees you."

"Last time I checked, I was not invisible."

"I see no other way."

She did. "Could you go ahead of me, and make sure the way is clear?"

He didn't answer, and she realized she was also putting his job on the line.

"Never mind. I'll get it done myself."

Somehow. Some way.

◈

Annie slipped into the stairwell with the garment bag over her arm. Dozens of employees walked past her up the stairs, going to their respective departments. No one asked about the bag. Maybe she *could* just put it back without incident.

But what if I get caught? Surely I will lose my job. I will be shamed.

I should be ashamed. I am ashamed. I took what wasn't mine.

Then another word fell upon the rest, sinking heavily to the bottom like a pebble in a pond. *Confess.*

With the thought of confession came a hint of hope that all would not be lost. Confession was good for the soul, but was it good for the job?

"It's the only way," she said under her breath.

A man walking by said, "Excuse me?"

207

She shook her head and joined the others heading up the stairs. With each step she prayed. *Help me. Help me. Help me.*

At her floor, Annie strode toward Mrs. Downs's office.

"Good morning, Annie," the woman said, looking up from a desk full of paperwork.

Annie shut the door, making Mrs. Downs set her pencil down. "Miss Wood?" Her eyes fell upon the garment bag then met Annie's gaze. "Is there a problem?"

Annie draped the bag over the back of a chair. "Last Friday I borrowed a dress from the company's storeroom."

Mrs. Downs blinked. "Why?"

"I was invited to Mrs. Sampson's for dinner and had nothing suitable to wear."

"Mrs. Sampson. Mrs. Eleanor Sampson."

Annie nodded. "And her husband."

"What would they want with you?"

The full truth would not do. "As you are curious, so was I—which is why I accepted." She thought of a point that might make the entire excursion more legitimate. "Mr. Culver in sales accompanied me."

By the furrow in Mrs. Downs's brow it was clear this point made things worse.

"So Mr. Culver was in on the borrowing of the dress?"

Why did I mention him! She hurried to explain. "No. Not at all. Mrs. Sampson simply said I could bring a friend, so I invited him."

"Perhaps you should have invited me. After all, Mrs. Sampson comes to Butterick to speak with me."

But you hate her.

"I apologize for my oversight. I was flattered by the invitation—and curious. I'd heard the Sampsons were wealthy, and I knew my work clothes would not be smart enough, so. . ." She sighed. "So I borrowed the dress. My vanity overrode my common sense."

"How did you even know we had a cache of dresses?"

Annie thought of Maude and didn't want to get her involved, too. "I saw them when I had a tour of the building."

"Maude showed you."

Annie thought fast. "She showed me the printing presses, too. And the order room and shipping bays." She was running out of words. "I'm sorry. I know it was wrong, and I shan't do it again."

Mrs. Downs just sat there, clearly not knowing what to do. The silence was almost worse than if she'd yelled.

Finally she said, "This is unacceptable."

"I know."

"I'm not sure how to deal with you."

Mercy? Empathy? Forgiveness?

With a shake of her head, she flipped a hand at Annie. "Take it back where you got it and get to work."

That was the lot of it? Annie didn't wait to hear more. She retrieved the dress and scurried up the stairs to the company's closet.

As she was taking it out of the bag, a woman confronted her. "What are you doing?"

"Returning a dress," Annie said. "Mrs. Downs's orders."

The woman looked confused, but Annie folded the empty garment bag under her arm and left.

She hurried back to her floor, her steps light, her burden lifted. Confession had been the right choice. She'd never imagined getting off so easily.

When she entered her department Maude rushed toward her. "Mrs. Downs caught you?"

Annie kept her face neutral and her voice low for the sake of those who might listen. "I confessed."

Maude grabbed her arm none too gently and yanked her into the hall. "Did you tell them about my part in it?"

"I did not—other than to say I knew about the dresses because of the tour you gave."

"You didn't."

"I had to say that much. She asked how I knew the dress existed. But I did not tell her you came up with the idea, or your part in sneaking it out of the building for me."

Maude's chest heaved, and she stared at the air between them. Finally she looked at Annie again. "Why did you confess? Why not just put it back?"

"I feared I would be caught, so I chose to head it off by owning up to it."

"That was stupid."

Was it? "I feel better for having it in the open. I don't deal with fear well.

All day I would have worried someone would find out and I'd get in trouble."

"So you chose to get yourself in trouble?" She shook her head. "Don't ask me to help you again." Maude walked away.

But you suggested it. I never would have even known about it if it weren't for you.

Annie noticed people looking at her as she stood oddly in the middle of the corridor.

What was done was done. She went back to work.

❧

"Make sure the sleeve seam hits the cap of the shoulder just so," Maude said.

They stood before a dress form, where Maude taught Annie how to create the sleeve piece of a pattern. "How much seam allowance do you add?" Annie asked.

"Three-eighths of an inch."

It seemed an odd number. "Why not just make it an even half inch?"

Maude glared at her. "And they call Mrs. Sampson the fashion rebel?"

"It was just a thought."

Maude shrugged. "You haven't told me about your dinner Friday—which *was* part of our bargain."

"It was very nice. Delicious. And their house is truly a mansion."

"All vague details, and assumed. I want to know the reason she invited you in the first place."

Annie wanted to tell Maude the gist of things, and she would have valued her opinion about the Sampsons' offer, but there was still a tension between them regarding Annie's confession. Now was not the time.

"I'm not quite sure of her reasons," Annie fibbed. "Apparently when she was here that Monday I caught her fancy."

"Again, assumed. But why? Why you? Why not me? I'm far more interesting than you."

Annie was relieved to see Maude smile. Perhaps the tension was easing.

"You certainly have far more confidence than I."

"If I don't believe in myself, who will?"

They stopped their conversation when Mrs. Downs came in the room and made a beeline toward them. The woman stood with her back to the others and said, "You are wanted in Mr. Burroughs's office."

A wave of panic swept over Annie. "But I thought—"

"You thought wrong."

She set aside the muslin sleeve.

"You, too, Miss Nascato."

"Me?"

Mrs. Downs lowered her voice. "Don't make a scene. Just go."

The two girls had everyone's attention when they left the workroom. As they waited for the elevator, Maude said, "Your confession may be good for the soul, but it may also put us on the dole."

"Surely not."

Maude leveled her with a look. "One does not get summoned to talk to the boss if there are not consequences to be meted out."

They were being sacked? Annie found it hard to breathe. She'd known that was a possibility, but after Mrs. Downs's mild rebuke, she'd thought she was safe. Why hadn't she simply returned the dress in secret?

The elevator came. The operator gave them a nod. Without privacy there was no chance to say all that Annie wanted to say, except a whispered "I'm so sorry."

⌘

There were two chairs in front of Mr. Burroughs's desk. Maude sat in one, her hands in her lap. Her expression revealed nothing.

Annie adopted the opposite posture. She sat very straight and on the edge of the seat. Her nerves were on the alert. *Please help me, God. Please. I'm so sorry.*

Mr. Burroughs sat behind the desk, his silver mustache and neatly trimmed hair giving him the look of an older man of wisdom.

And mercy. Please mercy.

His secretary stood beside him, showing him some numbers in a large binder. The two perused the opened page, pointed at various items, and spoke softly to each other. When they were finished, the secretary glanced at the girls with a disapproving look then made to leave.

Suddenly she dropped the ledger. The sound made Annie jump.

"A bit skittish, Miss Wood?" Mr. Burroughs said.

"Yes, sir. I am nervous, sir."

"As you should be." He glanced at Maude, but Annie was his main focus. "I hear you took it upon yourself to borrow a dress from our stores?"

"I did, sir. And I'm very sorry for it. It was an imprudent thing to do."

"That it was." He straightened some papers into a tidy pile. "You could have asked."

Annie was shocked. "You would have let me borrow it?"

"No," he said. "With over two thousand employees we cannot allow such borrowing. Even *if* it was for a special occasion initiated by a wealthy New York family."

"Of course, sir." Annie chided herself for not thinking of all this before the act. "I was so caught up in the excitement of my new job here, and somewhat overly flattered by Mrs. Sampson's invitation, that I overlooked common sense."

"And right and wrong."

Her stomach flipped. "That, too."

Mr. Burroughs looked at Maude. "You've been with us a long time, haven't you, Miss Nascato?"

"Five years, sir."

"I hear you showed Miss Wood the closet."

"I did, sir. Mrs. Downs asked me to give her a tour of the entire building."

Annie chimed in. "It's quite an impressive arrangement you have here, sir. Sixteen floors. Very large yet very efficient."

Mr. Burroughs closed his eyes then opened them. "At times excessive flattery can be very unflattering, Miss Wood."

"I only meant to say that. . ." What did she mean to say? "I don't want Maude to get in trouble for something I did. I take the blame. I accept full responsibility for my actions." She risked a glance at Maude, but the girl was looking straight ahead.

Mr. Burroughs leaned back in his chair, his elbows on the armrests, his fingers tented. "What do you think I should do about you, Miss Wood? If you were me."

Annie didn't know whether to suggest leniency or a sterner punishment. "I would consider firing the offender, but I would decide against it because I would realize that the guilty party *did* confess and did apologize, and has great potential to be of benefit to the company if she were allowed to stay."

He smiled. "Great potential, you say?"

She felt herself redden. "Good potential?"

He leaned forward. "I prefer the 'great' designation. Prove me right, Miss Wood. Five dollars will be docked from your paycheck as a rental fee—a one-time rental fee."

"Yes, sir. I understand completely, sir."

"Be assured you do. Now carry on."

That was the full of it? They were free to go? With their jobs intact?

"Thank you, sir."

The two women stood, but Annie didn't dare risk a look to Maude. They opened the door to leave but saw Sean sitting by the secretary.

"You may go in now, Mr. Culver."

With only a glance, Sean walked by Annie into Mr. Burroughs's office. Had her mention of him to Mrs. Downs caused him to be in trouble, too?

She turned to the secretary. "Excuse me. Did Mr. Burroughs summon Mr. Culver, or did he arrange the meeting?"

There was a disapproving glint in the woman's eyes as she said, "He was summoned."

Annie's relief evaporated.

The girls took the stairs down to their floor, but not before Maude asked, "You got him called up, too?"

"I only mentioned him coming to dinner with me."

"Learn to keep your mouth shut, Annie Wood."

⟨❦⟩

At lunch, Annie saw Sean sitting at a table with two friends. There was an empty place across from him so she sat down. As soon as she did, the two friends excused themselves. *What have they heard? What do they know?*

"Hello," she said to Sean as she took a sip of milk. She wanted to ask him about his visit with Mr. Burroughs but wasn't sure how to go about it.

She didn't have to. "You've already had a busy day," he said.

Annie set her glass down. "Meaning?"

"Ruining your career, Maude's, and mine. Quite the accomplishment."

With a glance around the cafeteria she saw she had the attention of many others. So they all knew? She pushed her tray away. "What did Mr. Burroughs say to you?"

"He asked if I knew what you'd done. I had to tell him I did."

"But you didn't condone it. You were against it."

"Yet I let you keep the dress for the weekend, and accompanied you to a dinner where you wore the dress." He looked at his plate then up at her again. "I should have made you take it back immediately. I knew it was wrong."

"*I* knew it was wrong," she said. "It's my fault, not yours. I'm being docked five dollars as a rental fee for the dress."

Sean harrumphed. "A pittance compared to the fact our reputations *were* priceless. Now, they are tainted and tarnished. God's given us free will to make choices. We chose wrong."

"I'm sor—"

He shook his head. "All because you wanted to play dress-up and pretend to be someone you weren't."

Annie felt the breath go out of her. Was that what she'd done?

The truth of it made her next breath difficult. "You're right. But if that's true maybe working here is a farce, a part I'm playing. Maybe I should go back to being a maid."

He dabbed a napkin at his mouth and stood. "Maybe you should."

Annie was left alone at the table. Surely he didn't mean it. Surely *she* didn't mean it. Her days as a maid were over. She'd worked hard to get out of that life.

No, you didn't. You simply ran away.

But she'd worked hard to become a clerk at Macy's, and now a pattern artist.

Luck got you the first job, and Sean got you the second.

Now she'd ruined her biggest chance by putting on airs, *and* she'd hurt Maude and Sean.

It was Maude's idea.

She shook the thought away. As Sean said, she'd been given the choice. She could have said no when Maude first mentioned it. She could have said no when Maude showed her the dresses. She could have said no when Maude detailed the scheme or when she'd seen the dress where Bertie had placed it, or out on the street on the way home, or that evening when it was time to get dressed. She'd been given a dozen chances to say no.

Her shame increased with the gaze of her coworkers, their whispers and soft laughter.

Annie forced herself to stay and finish her lunch. The discomfort was just what she deserved.

⁂

Halfway through the afternoon, Maude came up behind Annie and said, "Move it along, chickie."

"Move what along?"

"Your mood." She pointed to Annie's wrinkled brow. "You want to look fifty before you're twenty?"

Annie pressed a hand on her forehead and could feel the worry lines there. She looked around the workroom, but luckily the other girls were busy. "You're angry at me, Sean's angry at me, Mrs. Downs is angry at me, Mr. Burroughs is angry at me, and I'm angry at me."

"As I said, move it along. It's over. Water under the bridge, the cookie's been crumbled, the train has left the station."

Annie chuckled.

"That's better," Maude said.

"So you forgive me?"

"Of course I do. It won't be the last time I get my hands slapped. And as I get to know you... I'm betting it won't be your last time, either."

"Oh yes, it will," Annie said. "No more borrowing dresses."

"I believe you. But something else will come up where you will cross some line—with two feet I'd guess."

Annie thought of the Sampsons' offer. Quitting would certainly be crossing a line.

But that was a decision for another day.

<hr>

"He'll be here," Maude said.

"I'm not so sure." Annie was doubtful Sean would meet her after work to walk her home. They hadn't parted on good terms at lunch. She'd caused him strife. She'd damaged his reputation and their relationship.

Beyond mending? Even though she didn't know exactly where she wanted their friendship to go, she valued the bond they shared.

Gazing through the mass of workers leaving the Butterick building, Annie didn't see him. He usually stood to the right of the main door, just outside.

He wasn't there. *Serves me right.*

But then Maude said, "There he is. As always."

There he was. Behind a group of men, talking.

He stepped out to greet them. " 'Evening."

"Yes it is," Maude said.

They began their walk home, but it wasn't "as always" at all. Sean did not draw her hand around his arm. Nor did he ask about her day, and she didn't dare ask him about his.

"This is a delightful conversation we're having," Maude said after a block walked in silence.

"I'm just tired," Sean said.

Annie nodded. She was tired, too. Drained. She glanced at Maude and made a short shake of her head, hoping Maude would let it go. Perhaps it was best to just let him be.

They approached the corner where Maude turned. "Have a nice evening, you two," she said. "If you can."

Why did you add that last bit?

"Maude, wait," Sean said. "I'm turning, too."

"You are?" Annie asked.

"If you remember, I'm moving today. Thomas is meeting me at my apartment to help." He looked her straight in the eye. "I'm moving to be closer to you."

It was not said with tenderness, but as a reminder of his sacrifice. What should she say? What could she say but "Thank you."

He blinked, as if surprised by her answer. His face softened. "Will you be all right getting home?"

"Of course."

He hesitated a moment. "Good-bye, then."

Although he'd said good-bye dozens of times before, this time seemed different. Final. "You don't have to move if you don't want to," she said.

His countenance fell. "You don't want me to?"

"Of course I want you to, but considering... I don't want you to feel you have to."

He broke their gaze and looked to the ground. "I'd better go."

She watched him walk away as Maude's voice resounded in her head: *"Learn to keep your mouth shut, Annie Wood."*

Then she walked toward home, her gaze down, her arms wrapped tightly around her body. *I certainly mucked that up.*

She started as a church bell began to strike the hour. . . . *Four, five, six.*

With the resonance of the bells still hanging in the air, Annie stopped walking and turned toward the church. She climbed the steps and took a seat at the top, pulling her skirt and coat over her legs against the cold.

She was immediately reminded of last Friday when she and Sean had sat on the steps of St. Patrick's. They'd discussed the job offer.

So much had happened since then.

She leaned her head upon her knees. *What should I do? I need direction.*

"Hey, missy."

She looked up and saw a disheveled man standing on the steps nearby. "Yes?"

"That's me place."

Even though it made no sense to do so, she stood and apologized. The man sat where she had sat then unwrapped a cloth and pulled out a heel of bread—half-eaten.

Annie dug a coin from her pocket and handed it to him. Then she headed in the direction of home.

❧

Edna had to work late, so Annie had the flat to herself. She put a pot of soup on the stove so they could eat later and then went to the window of the front room where she could see the brownstone across the street.

And then she saw Sean and Thomas walking up the street carrying two suitcases and a carpetbag. She was relieved to feel glad to see him. Perhaps she did want him to move close.

Then why haven't you told him that?

When he looked up at her window, she slipped to the side, out of sight. *Coward.*

Then she saw Edna going over to the men, greeting them. She pointed to her apartment, and Annie feared she was inviting them to dinner.

It would be the right thing to do.

But Sean shook his head and they parted. A minute later Annie saw the light in Sean's new apartment turn on.

"I'm home," Edna said, taking off her coat and hat. "I smell soup."

"It should be ready soon," Annie said as she went to stir it.

"How was your day?"

Annie paused in the stirring, deciding whether she should share. "It was fine," she said.

Edna had endured enough of her dirty laundry.

❧

Annie couldn't sleep. The knowledge that Sean was right across the street, and that he was angry at her. . .

She glanced at the clock. Two in the morning. There was nothing she could do about it now.

Or was there?

On a whim she tiptoed out to the parlor and retrieved a piece of stationery and a pencil from Edna's desk. She returned to her room and wrote a note:

Dear Sean,

Please forgive me for all the trouble I have caused you, and not just trouble but confusion and doubt.

I am very glad you have moved close, and I appreciate your constant care and concern for my well-being.

I suffer many regrets, but you are not one of them.

Sleep well.

She paused, unsure how to sign it: "Sincerely"? "Affectionately"? "With love"?

She decided on simply *Annie.*

She folded it in half then slipped on her shoes, a skirt over her nightgown, and then her jacket. Her hair fell upon her shoulders—totally unacceptable for a girl her age, but odds were, no one would see her.

Annie was glad Edna was a deep sleeper, but she left the apartment with as much stealth as possible and took the stairs in the same manner so as not to disturb the other tenants.

Being outside at this time of night reminded her of the first night she, Iris, and Danny had slept on the streets. This was a better locale than the alley they'd chosen, but there were still dangers about. Generally people who were out in the wee hours were up to no good.

Except her. Hopefully her note would do a lot of good toward mending the rift between herself and Sean.

She spotted two men talking at the far intersection, so she scurried across the street before they noticed her. The entryway was dark, with only one electric bulb on an upper landing. There were four stories to the building, and she'd seen that Sean was on the third. At the street side. She gathered her skirt and nightgown and made her way upward. There appeared to be four apartments per floor. She tiptoed to his flat and, with a kiss to the page, slipped it under his door.

It was done. There was nothing more she could do.

Her heart raced as she retraced her steps back home. But as she reached the street, she heard the sash of a window open. Sean's window. He leaned out. "Annie, wait," he whispered. He closed the window, and she stepped near the building, trying to be inconspicuous. Luckily, the men on the corner had moved on.

A few minutes later, Sean emerged, clutching his coat closed over his shirtless torso. He wore trousers and slippers. He looked wonderful. "I got your note," he said.

She could only nod. "You're moved in?"

"I am, but. . ." He shook the topic away. "Not everything can be fixed with an 'I'm sorry.'"

"But this *can* be? Please?"

He touched the hair around her face, letting his fingers glide its length. "This can be."

She fell into his arms, wrapping herself in his forgiveness, needing his strength. "Thank you."

He kissed the top of her head then gently stepped away. "Till tomorrow, then."

"Till tomorrow."

She noticed that he waited to go inside until she was at the door of her building. She waved. He kissed his fingers.

Thank You, Lord, for Your many mercies.

Finally, sleep could come.

CHAPTER TWENTY-TWO

What if we did something like this?" Annie drew a sleeve with a slight bell shape at the forearms. "Nothing drastic, but something a little more graceful than the usual tight sleeve."

Mrs. Downs perused the drawing. "It's not done. Slim sleeves are the norm."

"But isn't that the point?" Annie said. "Taking what exists and innovating it into something a bit new?"

Dora gave the sketch a glance then went back to her dress form. "Those sleeves will catch on things."

Annie listened yet ignored her. In the weeks she'd been working at Butterick she'd learned that Dora was the naysayer in almost every design. Annie offered her defense. "It will provide more ease of movement. And air. We're designing for summer. We're trying to show something new."

"Suit yourself," Dora said.

"Curb your attitude, Dora," Mrs. Downs said. "Butterick is rooted in innovation." To Annie she said, "Carry on. Piece it out for me."

"Yes, ma'am." Once again Annie was given the go-ahead to create a pattern from one of her designs. Not every idea had been met with enthusiasm, and some had been discarded for this reason or that, but the rejections only heightened the sweetness of each victory.

Annie had just cut a new length of muslin when Mrs. Sampson walked into the department.

"Mrs. Downs. Ladies," she said with a nod.

This was the second time Annie had seen her since the dinner and the job offer, yet far from the tenth time that the woman had contacted her via notes and even letters. She was nothing if not persistent, each time asking if Annie had made a decision. And each time—if Annie responded at all—she asked for more time.

Annie had been praying for an answer, yes or no, but so far hadn't received any heavenly nudge that sent her toward a certain decision with confidence. And so she'd hedged, waiting for God to make things clear.

As Mrs. Downs and Mrs. Sampson chatted in the office, Annie tried to focus on her work. She even called another girl over to the table, hoping her presence would deter a personal conversation with Mrs. Sampson. No one but Sean and Edna knew of the job offer, and Annie hoped to keep it that way.

Then why not just tell her no and be done with it?

She knew that was the only way to rid herself of Mrs. Sampson, but she just couldn't shut the door on the opportunity quite yet.

Her attempt at evasion was to no avail. The two women came out of the office, and Mrs. Downs beckoned Annie to join them.

"Mrs. Sampson wishes to speak to you alone. I've given her use of my office for the sake of privacy."

Annie was immediately alarmed by this assertiveness and regretted the attention it brought. Yet she had no choice but to comply.

Once in the office, they both remained standing, which Annie hoped was an indication the meeting would be short. She put on a smile for those watching from the workroom—which she had to fake—and a curious look, which she did not. "Yes, Mrs. Sampson?"

"You've evaded me long enough, my dear."

"I know. And I'm truly sorry. It's such a big decision. I simply need more time."

"I'm afraid you've run out of time. Tomorrow Harold and I are leaving on a ship bound for the warmth of Italy. We will be gone until the spring." She adjusted her gloves. "By the way, you know one of the other passengers."

"I can't imagine who."

"Mr. Straus and his wife. From Macy's. We know them quite well—and by the by, he speaks very highly of you."

Annie was glad for the compliment, yet Mrs. Sampson's ultimatum remained.

"I'd like to say it's now or never," the woman said, "but I'm afraid I'm too much of an optimist for that. Yet I do wish for your decision. It's the polite thing to do, don't you think?"

"I agree." Yet faced with the need for a decision, Annie still balked. But then, without her bidding, words began to spill out—words determining her future. "I can't leave Butterick. They've been so kind to me."

"Harold and I will be kind to you." Mrs. Sampson nodded toward the workroom. "Do they believe in you like we do?"

"I am giving them reason to. I am working very hard to learn from them."

"Learning to do their bidding."

"You wish for me to do *your* bidding."

"Touché, my dear." She straightened a piece of paper on the edge of the desk with a single finger. "Yet our bidding leads to the freedom to design what you wish to design. Do you have that freedom here?"

The word *freedom* held such power. "Partially."

Mrs. Sampson raised an eyebrow.

"Perhaps not true freedom to fully design. No. Not as yet."

"And you won't. Ever."

"Neither of us know that. But I do know my limits. I'm not proficient enough in design and construction to have full freedom. If I ever go out on my own, I need to know much more than I do now. To build anything you have to have a firm foundation."

"You are a practical sort."

"It's not a negative trait."

"I suppose not." She adjusted her gloves a second time. "I do wish you the best, Annie."

"I wish you the same. I will always remember the faith you had in me. Perhaps someday I'll be ready to deserve it." As the woman turned to leave, Annie asked, "What should we tell the ladies in the workroom about our conversation?"

"Leave it to me."

They walked out of the office, and Annie returned to her workstation. Mrs. Sampson thanked Mrs. Downs for the use of her office. "Alas, Miss Wood doesn't feel proficient enough to make me some dresses."

Dora raised a hand. "I'll sew them for you, Mrs. Sampson."

With a blink, Mrs. Sampson said, "Perhaps in the spring, after we return from Europe."

As soon as she left, Mrs. Downs clapped her hands. "Back to work, ladies. And Annie? You made a wise choice not to dive into dressmaking. You have much to learn."

"That I do, Mrs. Downs."

There was a general murmuring among the other girls about what they would have done with such an opportunity, and Annie was glad to let them chatter on. On her own part, she felt exhilarated. Although she had not expected to make a choice today, God had nudged her to the point of decision. The result? She felt a burden lifted. She felt. . .peace.

She remembered the dinner conversation at the Sampsons' when they'd discussed knowing when you were making the right decision. Sean had suggested "practice and peace." Through today's decision Annie had gained both.

Smart man, that Sean.

❧

On the last Thursday in November, Annie was awakened by the fragrance of nutmeg and cinnamon. But before she could wallow in the heady, cozy smell there was a knock on her bedroom door.

"Get up, girlie. I need your help in the kitchen."

Ah yes. Today was a holiday. Thanksgiving Day.

She'd been looking forward to this day ever since Edna had told her about it, for she had much to be thankful for. Plus, it would be a time when she could reveal her big decision to Edna and Sean. It had been hard to keep it quiet all week, but considering the weeks it had held her captive, she'd decided a more formal announcement on a day of celebration would be the proper time.

Annie got dressed quickly and joined Edna in the kitchen where she was putting a turkey in the oven. Fresh pumpkin pies sat on a sideboard.

"I do hope the turkey is large enough."

"There's enough there for many more than six. What time did you get up?"

"Four. I needed to get the pies in to free up the oven for the turkey."

"You should have awakened me."

"There's no need for two of us to be tired. Besides, I wasn't sleeping well. I am so excited to have a real party for Thanksgiving. It's been far too long."

Annie tied on an apron. "I'm excited, too—for it's my first holiday. Set me to work."

"You can shuck the corn then peel potatoes. I'm going to get the cranberries on the stove for the cranberry-fig chutney. And I need to punch down the dough for the rolls."

The friends made a good team, each intent on their work. "This is also my first holiday off," Annie said.

"What do you mean?"

"At Crompton Hall we had a free day every week, but as far as days free due to a holiday? The servants only got a few hours off for Christmas and Easter. We still had to work. The food did not cook nor the house clean itself."

"English Pilgrims started the Thanksgiving tradition over here. In the 1600s they celebrated good harvest with native Indians." She nodded to the cranberries. "I believe it was the Indians who introduced them to berries."

"So it's been a holiday since then?"

"Oh no, for *we* have not been a country since then. It was celebrated here and there but it was only during our awful Civil War that our president, Abraham Lincoln, declared it a national celebration."

"It's a good tradition. We have so much to be thankful for."

"That we do."

⌘

Annie was glad Sean was the first to arrive. She needed a moment alone with him and Edna before the other guests came for dinner.

The aroma of freshly baked rolls accompanied her announcement. "Can you stop a moment, Edna? I want to share something important with the two of you."

Edna gave the corn an extra stir then gave Annie her full attention. "Important?"

"I made a decision regarding Mrs. Sampson's offer."

"It's about time," Edna said. "I'd bragged that you were a girl who made quick decisions, but this one has dragged on for weeks."

Sean's eyebrows rose. "When did you decide?"

"Monday last. Mrs. Sampson came into work and gave me an ultimatum of sorts since they are traveling to Italy for the winter."

"And you said. . . ?" he asked.

"I declined their offer. I'm staying at Butterick."

Sean spun her around, nearly knocking over a chair. "I'm so glad!"

She hadn't expected his exuberance. "I didn't know it meant so much that I stay."

"I didn't either until I heard your decision. I like that we work together.

I like walking with you to and from. If you worked elsewhere, when would I see you?"

His point was well taken.

"What was your reasoning?" Edna asked.

"A pragmatic one. I need more time to learn about fashion before I can be held responsible to fully design it."

"Good for you," Sean said.

"You could always take the job in the future," Edna said.

"That's what Mrs. Sampson implied."

Sean's smile faded, and Annie felt a wee bit peeved. Did he truly expect her to stay at Butterick forever?

The moment was saved by the sound of footsteps on the stairs, voices in the hallway, and a knock on the door.

"Oh, the heavenly smells, Edna," Mrs. MacDonald said as she entered. "I'm eating before I'm eating."

Mildred nodded. "I haven't had a meal like this since I left home years ago. I thank you for inviting me, Mrs. Holmquist."

"You are quite welcome," Edna said.

"I thank you, too," Maude said, eyeing the pies.

"You're all welcome," Edna said. "Sean, take their coats, please."

The apartment was alive with happy chatter, with everyone pitching in. Finally it was time to eat.

Edna directed them to the dining table, which was decorated with gourds and small branches of brightly colored autumn leaves. "Let us give thanks, and then Sean, I was wondering if you would carve the turkey."

Sean eyed the bird on the platter as if it were a foe to be conquered. "It will be a new experience and may be more of a massacre than a carving. But if you're not choosy about the end result, I am your man."

"You're the only man," Maude pointed out.

They each took a seat around the table with Edna and Sean taking the ends. Then Edna held out her hands. Down the row the guests clasped hands then bowed their heads. "Dear God Almighty," Edna began, "thank You for the food upon the table, the roof above our heads, and the jobs to provide a living. But most of all, thank You for these friends, old and new. I want to say a special thanks for dear Annie, for she is the one who brought us together. Bless us and guide us to do Your bidding. In Jesus' name, amen."

Both Sean and Maude squeezed Annie's hands, and she felt herself blush at the extra mention. "Thank you," she said softly, looking at all of them. "Thank you for letting me be a part of your lives."

"Amen, again," Edna said. "Now to the turkey. Mr. Culver? If you please?"

Sean stood at his place and got to work, giving them their choice of white or dark meat. Annie had some of each. Then bowls of mashed potatoes, gravy, chutney, corn, and rolls were passed, and each guest filled their plates edge to edge.

More praise and thanks were offered as everyone enjoyed the bounty before them. When people began asking for seconds, Annie thought of something else to be thankful for.

"I am thankful that Grasston—though not caught—has not bothered us."

"Perhaps he's moved on to some other target," Sean said.

Annie noticed Edna, Mrs. MacDonald, and Mildred exchange glances. "What's wrong?"

"He was at the store the other day," Mrs. MacDonald said.

"Edna? Why didn't you tell me?" Annie asked.

"Mr. Horace and his men shooed him away and the police were called."

"Was he caught?"

Mildred shook her head. "If only."

Annie felt an all-too-familiar tug in her stomach. "I truly thought he had moved on."

Edna picked up the bowl of potatoes. "Who wants thirds?"

Annie had lost her appetite.

CHAPTER TWENTY-THREE

T his is the life," Sean said as he walked to church with Annie on one arm and Edna on the other.

"Oh, you," Edna said. In her free hand she carried a hatbox with a ribbon tied around it. The box contained her straw hat that matched Iris's dress so well—her gift to the bride.

Annie was happy to share Sean with her best friend. Today was December twenty-third. Today Iris and Thomas would be married.

It was hard to believe that little Iris, the immature housemaid whom Annie had met on her first day in America, was going to be a married. . .woman. Married or not, she was still a girl of seventeen.

Annie remembered their first conversation up in the tiny attic room at the Friesens', when Iris had expressed her desire to leave service and be a shopgirl. She wasn't picky about what kind of shop, just so she was around a lot of people.

The Tuttle family certainly fit that bill. From the very first day, Iris had been assigned the duty of taking care of their five small children. She'd fit with them and them with her as though they'd all been waiting for each other.

Danny had fit in, too. Getting to help Gramps with deliveries fulfilled Danny's desire for adventure, to be outdoors, drive a wagon, and make friends along the way.

"Danny would have loved this day," Annie said.

"I wish I would have known him," Sean said.

"He sounds like a delightful boy," Edna said.

"That he was." She raised her free arm in the air. "Make the most of today!" She lowered it and explained, "That was his rallying cry to Iris and me."

"*Carpe diem*," Sean said.

"What did you say?"

"It's Latin. Carpe diem. Seize the day."

"What an inspiring saying," Edna said.

"How do you know Latin?" Annie asked Sean.

"Mr. Butterick. He would say the line often. I'm afraid it's the only Latin I know."

"It's enough," Edna said.

"Danny had no reason to know the Latin of it," Annie said. "But he was wise beyond his years." The sight of the church up ahead forced her to set the sadness aside. Today was a day for joy.

As soon as they entered the narthex, Annie left Edna in Sean's care. Since she was responsible for the wedding dress, she wanted to find Iris and help in any way she could. She asked an usher and was directed to a room off the sanctuary near the front of the church.

She heard Iris's voice inside and knocked. Mrs. Tuttle opened the door. "Annie! Come help with the ribbons woven through her hair. Jane and I can't get them quite right."

Annie stepped into the room to help, but at the sight of Iris, she stopped. "Oh. Iris, you're beautiful. Truly and fully beautiful."

Iris turned toward her, smoothing the blue dress. "It's because of the dress. I can't thank you enough."

"It's not the dress," Annie said. "It's you. You're radiant."

Iris beamed, which added to her happy glow.

❧

With the words *I now pronounce you man and wife*, Sean squeezed Annie's hand.

The simple gesture surprised her. With that one squeeze was he truly saying he wanted to marry her? Pleasure and panic collided, and Annie found herself retracting her hand from his grip.

He gave her a questioning glance. She felt immediate regret, so she appeased him with a smile. He smiled in return, and she was struck by how much his mood was dependent on her own. There was power in that. But also responsibility.

The happy couple kissed and strode down the aisle with a confidence that two become one was a force to be reckoned with.

"I'm so happy for them," Sean whispered.

"As am I."

He held her gaze a moment, as though pondering his next words. Annie looked away, not wanting to encourage their release.

The ushers came to their row, indicating it was time to go to the church reception. Annie was glad for the distraction of getting from here to there. They were led into a large room scattered with tables. Several women set out various pastries around a two-tiered wedding cake—no doubt due to the expertise of the Tuttles. For an instant, Annie's thoughts flashed back to various party receptions at Crompton Hall when she'd helped out, dressed in her dress uniform of black with a crisp white apron. She'd come a long way—a world away. A lifetime away.

She thought of Lady Newley and Miss Henrietta. How were they getting on? And more to the point, how were the Misses handling the sewing work without her help?

"Let's greet the bride and groom," Edna said.

The three of them went through the reception line that consisted of the happy couple and Thomas's parents. It was rather sad that Iris had no family there to share her day. No parents. No Danny. The lack reinforced the special blessing of the Tuttles in her life.

The rest of the reception was a blur of Tuttle children running amok with other children of the neighborhood, the murmurings and laughter of friends celebrating one of life's milestones, the cutting of the cake, and numerous toasts with delicious spiced punch.

Annie sat at a table and closed her eyes, letting the noise of the party turn into a mesmerizing hum. If she let herself, she could easily doze.

Go outside. Now!

The inner nudge shocked her to full attention.

"What's wrong?" Sean asked from his seat nearby.

"Nothing."

"It was something. You jerked as if someone had shouted at you."

She put a hand to her forehead, trying to recapture the moment. "It was the opposite of a shout, but it *was* a voice—an insistent voice. From in here." She pointed to her heart.

"What did it say?"

"'Go outside. Now.'"

After only a moment's hesitation Sean stood. "Come, then. I'll go with you."

"I'm sure it's nothing. I don't even know what it means."

"Did you hear the words, or not?"

"I heard them."

"Then we go. You'll never know what they mean unless we go outside."

They collected their coats. When they passed Edna on the way out, Annie whispered, "We'll be right back." There was no need to get her involved in this bizarre goose chase.

They stepped outside, where a light snow was falling. Annie raised her shoulders against the chill. "It's too cold. Let's go back in."

"Just give it a minute," Sean said. "Look around."

Feeling ridiculous, Annie looked left, where she saw only pedestrians and carriages hurrying to their destination before the snow accumulated. And then right, where she saw more of the—

She gasped. "It's Grasston!"

"Where?" Sean said.

"He just ducked behind those barrels. He's over there!"

Sean ran after him.

"No, Sean! Don't!"

But it was too late. Grasston spotted Sean and escaped into a building. Sean ran after him.

Annie's thoughts dashed to horrible scenarios of Grasston lying in wait for Sean, hitting him over the head. Or did he have a knife? Or a gun?

She spotted a policeman talking to a street vendor who was closing up shop against the snow. "Officer!" she yelled. "Help!"

The officer came running, and Annie pointed at the building. "An escaped murderer, Oscar Grasston, just went into that building, and my beau ran after him. You have to catch him, stop him from hurting—"

"Is he armed?"

"I don't know."

The officer blew a whistle, summoning assistance. He instructed the other officer, "Go 'round back. Watch for a man. . ." He looked to Annie. "What's he look like?"

"Black hair, tall. Mustache. My beau is blond."

The officers nodded. One went down an alley toward the back, and the other went inside.

The whistle must have alerted the wedding guests, for a few of the men came outside and Annie filled them in. She was glad to see Mr. Tuttle and Thomas. "It's Grasston! He was here. He ran inside that building. Sean ran after him."

"Let's go," Mr. Tuttle said.

Annie took his arm, holding him back. "There are two constables involved. I think it's best we stay back."

But the two men would have none of it. "He's a slippery one. We can't risk him getting away yet again."

"That's my building," another man said. "There's a way out in the back. Come with me, men."

The women gathered close around Annie. It was surreal to see Iris with a coat around her shoulders, wearing her wedding dress, her hair ribbons waving in the winter wind. "I'm sorry. I never meant to disrupt the wedding."

"Nothing could make my wedding happier than catching the man who killed Danny."

"Up there!" A man pointed to the flat roof of the building. "They're on the roof!"

They could see glimpses of men running around the roof, and they heard them shouting.

Edna took Annie's hand then Iris's. "Father God, keep our good men safe. Help them capture the man who's perpetrated such evil. Settle this now, Lord. Bring about Your justice, and relieve this horrible man's victims of his wicked—"

A scream sliced through her words, and they watched as a man fell from the roof onto the street not twenty feet away.

Most of the women screamed and looked away, shielding their eyes from the sight. But Annie and Iris did not. They looked upon the broken victim, needing to see, needing to know.

"It's him!" Iris yelled. "It's Grasston!"

Annie stared at the bloodied body with no aversion. The way his limbs were askew, and the blood. . .

The curious ventured close, but most gave him a wide berth. A stream of men filed out of the building, looked at Grasston, and then joined their families on the church steps.

Last out were the officers then Thomas, Mr. Tuttle, and Sean.

Annie ran into his arms. "You got him! I was so afraid for you."

"He got himself," Sean said. He put a hand to his arm. His coat was slashed.

"You've been stabbed!" Annie said.

"He sliced at me, but the coat saved me. I don't think I'm even cut." He shook his head, turning their attention. "As I said, Grasston got himself."

"That he did." Thomas wrapped his arm around his bride. "We had him cornered on the roof, and an officer was talking to him, trying to get him to turn himself in."

Mr. Tuttle took over the story. "But then he turned toward the edge and dove over it."

Sean nodded. "He was standing there, a knife in his hands, ready to fight us all. But then he stood upright and got the oddest look in his eyes."

"As if he was being talked to. As if he wasn't quite *there*," Thomas said.

Sean finished it. "And then he jumped."

Edna drew in a breath. "We'd been praying for your protection, and for God's justice."

They all looked at Grasston. A light blanket of snow began to cover him, a pure blanket for a very impure man. The officers stood nearby talking among themselves.

"Danny finally has justice," Annie said.

"Indeed he does," Mrs. Tuttle said.

There was a moment of silence among the wedding guests, as all looked upon the scene, letting its gravity and significance settle.

But then Mr. Tuttle said, "Inside now. We have a wedding to celebrate. A new beginning for our bride and groom."

"And for you," Sean whispered to Annie.

Annie turned her face toward the sky and let the snowflakes fall upon her.

❧

Annie tied a bow around the vest she'd made Sean for Christmas. "What if it doesn't fit him?" she asked Edna.

"He'll love it anyway. Come help trim the tree before he gets here."

The fir tree was small and sat upon a table by the parlor fireplace, but it was more than Annie had ever had. "The Christmas tree at Crompton Hall was enormous and was always placed in the front hall in the crook of the sweeping stair. Each servant could put on one ornament, and I always chose a little silver bird with its wings outstretched. I just loved the shape of it. The glisten of it."

Edna looked through the box of ornaments. "Look what we have here." She held up a silver bird. "You may do the honors."

Annie placed it on the tree, her old and new lives merging.

"Did you have a tree when you were a child?" Edna asked.

"No. Christmas was just another day, with Ma complaining and Pa yelling about who and what had done him wrong."

"I'm so sorry for that. Every child should experience the magic of Christmas, even in the simplest of ways."

Annie nodded, knowing that what every child *should* experience and *did* experience were often widely disparate.

She chose to think of happier times. "The tree at the Hall used to be ablaze with candles."

"Not here," Edna said with a sharp shake to her head. "Not anymore."

"Did something happen?"

Edna draped a string of beads on the branches. "Steven was ten and thought it would be fun to light them in the middle of the night so St. Nicholas could see better. He knocked a lit candle over, and if I hadn't been awakened by his not-so-quiet boyish noises, the entire apartment would have gone up in flames." She walked to the candles on the pine-draped mantel. "Since then, these do."

"They do just fine."

There was a knock on the door, and Sean came in, smelling of winter winds. "Merry Christmas!"

"Merry Christmas Eve to you," Edna said, kissing him on both cheeks. She brushed snow off the shoulders of his coat. "I didn't realize it was snowing."

"Quite hard, I'm afraid. I was glad my only trip was across the street."

"Not too much snow, I hope. Tomorrow we're going to see your family in Brooklyn," Annie said.

"We shall see. If not tomorrow, we can see them on New Year's Day. Mother won't mind. She wouldn't want us venturing out in a blizzard."

Annie was disappointed yet also relieved. Meeting his parents made her nervous.

"The tree is lovely," Sean said, straightening the star on top.

The clock on the mantel struck six. "We have an hour until church begins. Would you like to open our presents?"

Annie saw that Sean hadn't brought anything. She didn't want him to feel bad. "That's not necessary," she said. "I am happy for the company."

He winked at her. "Fear not." He pulled a round tin from one coat pocket and a small box from the other. "I do bring gifts."

Annie was glad for it, for she was eager to distribute hers.

"Let me serve us a cup of wassail and we can commence."

Annie helped Sean remove his coat and, once again, noticed the slashed sleeve. "If we are snowed in tomorrow I will mend this for you—all the layers. How did your arm fare?"

"I was cut."

He hadn't said that yesterday. "Badly?"

"Hardly. Calm yourself. I am well."

Her thoughts strayed to yesterday's wedding and Grasston's death.

He pressed a finger on the space between her eyes. "There will be none of that. Tonight is a night of joy, celebrating Christ's birth and being together."

She loved how he could bring her back from darkness and into the light.

"Here we are," Edna said, carrying a tray with three mugs of spiced cider. When they each had one, she raised hers in a toast. "To us."

"To happiness," Annie added.

"To the God who brought us together."

They clinked their mugs and drank. The warm liquid was a balm.

"My presents first," Edna said as they took seats in the parlor. She handed a present to Annie, her face glowing with expectation.

It was nearly flat, the size of her lap. Edna had wrapped it in a bit of calico and tied it with a ribbon. Annie pulled the bow free and gasped.

Edna was quick to explain. "It's a pad of drawing paper, new pencils, an eraser, a sharpener and. . .guess what's in the skinny box."

The box had the words Faber-Castell in large letters. Then two more words. . . "Colored pencils?" She opened the end and couldn't help but say, "Oooh. So pretty!"

"Now you can colorize your designs."

Annie was truly moved and set the presents aside so she could give Edna a hug. "You are far too generous."

"Not at all." Edna handed Sean a small box with a ribbon.

Sean opened it. "A tie tack."

"The stone is a tiger's eye."

He unfurled his tie and set it in place. "I'm quite the dandy."

"You're quite the gentleman," Edna corrected.

He gave her a kiss on the cheek.

"Me next," Annie said. She gave a present to Edna and knew it needed some explanation. "It's a tea cozy. I quilted it myself—on the machine. It should keep your teapot warm."

"Very nice, girlie. Thank you."

Annie's heart beat a bit faster as she handed her wrapped bundle to Sean. "I hope you like it."

"I'm sure I will."

The brown tweed vest was revealed. It had a satin lining and back.

"I made it myself. It has a pocket for your watch."

Sean made note of that detail and immediately removed his suit coat and vest to try it on.

Please let it fit!

When he began buttoning it—and it was not too tight—Annie breathed freely. "I'm so relieved."

"A mirror?" he asked Edna.

"In my room."

He went into the bedroom and admired it. "It's very sharp, Annie. You do fine work."

"It matches the tie tack," Edna added. "A coordinated effort."

He flashed a pose as if for an advertisement, his chin high, a hand on his hip.

The women clapped and laughed. "Fit for the *Delineator*," Annie said. "For it is a Butterick pattern."

"Of course it is," he said.

They returned to the parlor, where Sean gave Edna the tin. Inside were assorted chocolates.

"You'll make me plumper than I already am."

"More of you to love," he said. Then he handed Annie the small box he'd had in his pocket. "For you, my sweet Annie-girl."

Inside the paper box was a royal-blue velvet box, flattish, with a hinged edge. "I love the box."

"I hope you love what's inside."

She cracked the hinge open and saw a gold cross necklace with intricate etching and a reddish stone in the middle.

"The stone is a piece of coral," he said.

She removed the necklace from the box, fighting back tears. "I've never had any jewelry of my own."

"Ever?"

She shook her head. "Would you clasp it for me?"

Sean moved behind her and clasped the gold chain around her neck. "My turn for the mirror," she said as she moved to Edna's room. Seeing her reflection, she pressed the cross against her chest. The length of the chain was perfect, allowing it to be showcased within her neckline. "It's lovely."

He stood behind her. "You're lovely."

She turned toward him and encased him in her arms. "Thank you."

For so many things.

∽⊗∾

God is here.

There was no other explanation for the fullness in Annie's heart as she sat between her two dearest friends for Christmas Eve services. The sanctuary was filled to capacity, with each person holding a lit candle. There was no other light. Yet the combined illumination created an undulating, heavenly glow. Surely God Himself was here among them.

A choir up front sang carols for the Christ child. Annie pressed a hand to the golden cross at her neck and let the music wrap her in a warm embrace. Some songs were new to her, some familiar.

But then the choir began a song she knew from her time at Crompton Hall—one the entire household sang together on this very evening.

"Silent night, holy night. . ."

The congregation began singing with the choir, standing one by one, and then in groups, their voices joined together as if they *had* to sing along. Sean held out his hand, and Annie stood with the rest. Then she let her voice join in, the music an offering of thanks to God for His beloved Son.

Sleep in heavenly peace. Sleep in heavenly peace.

CHAPTER TWENTY-FOUR

D on't be nervous."

"Nervous about walking across the Brooklyn Bridge, or nervous about meeting your family?"

"Both."

Annie held his arm tighter. "We're up so high over the river."

"The East River. And yes, we are."

"Until coming to New York I'd never been up high. Crompton Hall had three stories aboveground, and that was the extent of my experience."

"And now you work in a sixteen-story building, and even risked going on the roof."

She shook her head, in awe of her new experiences.

He pointed to the south. "Look there. The Statue of Liberty."

They stopped, and Annie was glad to grip the sturdy rail. "We saw her when we sailed into the harbor." The memory seemed distant and separate, as if it belonged to someone else. "It seems years ago when it was only a few months."

They began walking again. "A lot happened in 1911." He patted her gloved hand. "A lot will happen in this New Year. Your life has just begun, Annie-girl." He noticed her shiver and put an arm around her. "Are you cold?"

"A little. At least the sun is out and it's not snowing."

"The optimist."

"Hardly. The sun *is* out and it *isn't* snowing."

"You see what's there, don't you?"

She didn't understand. "Of course I see what's there."

"But you don't see what isn't there. You don't see what could be there, the larger scope of things."

"And you do?"

He stopped her, and they moved to the side to let other pedestrians pass. "Don't you ever dream of something that is beyond what you see in the moment?"

She was slightly offended. "Of course I do. I dreamt of being a lady's maid when I was a maid. When that didn't happen I dreamt of being a shopgirl."

"You got a job at Macy's because you needed a job, not because of any dream. The same with Butterick. Your job there is not the fulfillment of any long-held dream."

"Why are you harassing me?"

"I'm sorry. That was not my intent."

She looked at the ships cruising under the bridge. All going somewhere. Everyone on the bridge going somewhere.

Where was she going? "What do you dream of, Sean?"

"Fulfillment."

She shook her head. "That is far too vague. Everyone dreams of fulfillment."

"You're right." He set his arms on the chest-high railing, leaning against them. He peered out at the water, the ships, and the horizon.

She thought of talking then decided this was a time for silence. She *was* interested in his answer.

Finally he looked at her. "You put me on the spot."

"Tit for tat."

"But I do have an answer for you. I dream of knowing I made a difference. I dream of knowing there is a definite reason I was born, a reason I exist now—not a hundred years from now or a hundred years ago. I dream of knowing that a portion of God's greater plan gets fulfilled through me."

Annie felt shivers that had nothing to do with the cold. She put a hand on his arm. "You shame me."

"That also was not my intent." He pulled her hand around his arm, and she felt his warmth through her jacket. "I merely want you to see with a larger scope. Think beyond our jobs—which may or may not have much to do with our true purposes." He turned them around and nodded to the other walkers. "What do our lives have to do with *them*?"

"I. . .I don't know them."

"But our lives can touch them. Somehow. Some way."

She watched a Jewish family walk by, the men with long curls and beards, the women with their heads covered. "What we do at Butterick touches people we don't know."

"It does. And perhaps that is part of it. I don't know all the right answers, or even the right questions. But I want to know. And I want you to want to know. For you, for me, for us."

"I'm not used to thinking this way. I relate to facts. One plus one equaling two, not some number I can't fathom."

He touched her cheek. "God made us different, you and I. I fantasize and you organize."

"Perhaps together we make a whole?"

His eyebrows rose. "Is that a proposal, Annie Wood?"

She looked away.

"I wish it were."

She risked a glance at him. "You know I'm not ready."

"But you will be. One day."

"You sound so certain."

"I can dream, can't I?"

Annie snuggled close to Sean in the cab he'd hired to drive them from the bridge to the Culver home. "One last chance to tell me what your parents are like."

"I'd prefer not."

"Why?"

"You'll know who they are immediately."

"Their personalities are so obvious?" It didn't sound very inviting.

"Although my parents are as different as night is to day, they are fully committed to who they are."

"Are they. . .likable?"

He cocked his head. "Each in their own way." He pointed up ahead. "There. Just up there."

The cab stopped in front of a lovely three-story residence. "You live here?" Annie gazed at the beautiful tan-brick home with an iron gate, arched front door, and roofline edged with intricate molding.

"My parents live here."

"I thought you were poor."

"We started out poor, but the family's store is quite successful." He opened the wrought-iron gate for her then accompanied her up the stone steps to the front door.

Her heart began to pound. This was not a mansion near the size of the Sampsons', but it was a far step up from the rather ragged brownstones where she and Sean lived now.

"Ready?" he asked before he knocked.

The fact he even asked the question set her nerves on end. "I suppose."

His knock was answered by a butler, who smiled warmly. "Master Sean, how nice to see you."

"You, too, Baines."

They had barely entered when his mother swooped in. "Sean!" She embraced him warmly then smiled at Annie. "You must be Annie." She took Annie's gloved hands in her own. "Ooh, so cold."

"We walked across the bridge."

"Shame on you, Sean. You must promise to take a cab back."

"I enjoyed the walk," Annie said. "The view is incredible."

"That it is." She swept a hand toward the parlor. "Take off your wraps and come in by the fire."

A man stood by the fireplace, lighting a cigar. "Son," he said, with no emotion, as if simply declaring his existence. "Smoke?"

"No thank you, Father." He led Annie closer. "Father, I would like you to meet Annie Wood. Annie, my father."

Mr. Culver tossed the match away and gave her half a nod. "Miss Wood."

She'd heard it said that you only get to make a first impression once. So it was with meeting Sean's parents. Within those few seconds her impressions were set. Mr. Culver was proper, controlling, and a bit cold, while Mrs. Culver was friendly, warm, and generous. As Sean had said, each personality was immediately evident.

What do they immediately know about me? What do I want them to know?

Choices rushed forward. Should she be sweet and flattering? Confident? Nervous and meek?

The thoughts sped through her mind in seconds, yet three attributes stepped toward the front. Annie wanted the Culvers to know she was honest, grateful, and a bit unpredictable. "I'm very happy to meet the parents who raised such a remarkable son."

Mr. Culver stopped puffing on his cigar. "Really."

Mrs. Culver beamed and ran a hand across Sean's shoulders. "I happily take credit."

Sean blushed. "Mother. . ."

"Remarkable, you say?" Mr. Culver said amid a cloud of smoke.

"Absolutely," Annie said. "He discovered me."

Mrs. Culver raised her eyebrows. "Do have a seat and tell us all about this discovery."

Mr. Culver remained standing, but the other three sat upon maroon tufted chairs. "Now then," Mrs. Culver said. "How exactly did Sean discover you?"

Annie told them about working at Macy's and Sean seeing her sketch at Edna's. "I would not have the job at Butterick if not for him."

"What she isn't telling you," Sean said, "is that I had selfish motives." His smile was utterly sincere. "With both of us working there, I see her every day."

Mrs. Culver's eyes grew large. "So you are. . . ?"

"No," Annie said. "We aren't."

A shadow brushed over Sean's countenance then moved on. Sean slapped his hands on his thighs. "Today is the New Year, a new beginning."

"I do like New Year's," Mrs. Culver said, "when everything begins again, fresh." She looked to her husband.

"Hmm," was his only response.

There was a moment of silence then Mrs. Culver said, "So what do you do at Butterick, Annie?"

"I—"

"She's a pattern artist," Sean said.

"A designer?" his mother asked.

"To some extent," Annie said. "I work with others in taking an idea and turning it into a pattern for home sewers."

Mrs. Culver rose. "Well then, Annie, come with me. I have stacks and stacks of fashion magazines, and no female to share them with. You must give me your insight as to the new trends for 1912."

Annie was glad to leave the impenetrable wall that was Mr. Culver, but as she left the room, she saw a flash of panic on Sean's face.

"I'll return soon," she said.

"Do."

It was a cry to be rescued.

Annie followed Sean's mother into a room bright with sunshine. "I don't think we should be gone long," Annie said.

With a glance to the parlor Mrs. Culver said, "We won't be, but it's good to let them stew a bit in each other's presence."

"Does anything good come of it?"

"Not really. But I can only play the peacekeeper so long."

"Sean told me his father was angry that he wasn't working at the store."

Mrs. Culver moved some fringed pillows off a padded window seat. "I think if Mr. Butterick hadn't died on his own, Richard would have killed him."

"He blames Mr. Butterick—?"

"For stealing him away. Yes. Absolutely. And he blames himself for sending Sean for that first delivery instead of our usual runner."

"But it opened a new world for Sean. He's very good at what he does. He's a wonderful salesman."

"Which would have been of good use in the store."

"Of course."

"Enough of them," Mrs. Culver said, removing the long seat cushion. "Voila!" The window seat was hinged and, once opened, revealed stacks of magazines: *La Mode, Femina, Collier's, Young Ladies' Journal, The Designer, Vogue, The Delineator, McCall's*. . .

"I know," Mrs. Culver said. "There are a lot of them. That's why I keep them hidden. Richard would pitch a fit."

Annie laughed then put a hand on her mouth to stop it. "I'm sorry, but it just struck me as funny."

"It is funny in theory, but not so in reality." Her face was drawn.

"I'm sorry. I meant no offense."

Mrs. Culver negated the moment with a shake of her head. "None taken." She put her hands on her hips and nodded toward the stash. "You like?"

"Oh yes," Annie said.

"Then have a look. Enjoy."

Annie was surprised when Mrs. Culver sat on the floor and did the same. They pulled out magazine after magazine. When Annie chose a *La Mode* she said, "Lady Newley had this issue."

"Lady Newley?"

Annie renewed her choice of attributes: honesty, gratefulness, and being unpredictable. "I was a maid at an estate in England under the Viscount and Viscountess Newley. A housemaid."

"My, my."

"But I used to work on her ladyship's couture ensembles, making alterations."

Mrs. Culver clasped her hands beneath her chin. "You actually got to touch couture gowns?"

Annie was a taken aback by the sound of wonder in her voice. "I did. For both Lady Newley and her daughter. You see, Miss Henrietta's weight fluctuated, and it was my job to alter her dresses so they continued to fit."

"That doesn't sound like the job of a housemaid."

"It wasn't. But the two lady's maids at Crompton Hall weren't adept at alterations. They could repair an occasional seam or button, but ripping out and adjusting?" She shook her head. "They most certainly did not possess that talent."

"But you did. You do."

To hear it put so bluntly. . . "Yes, I do." Annie randomly turned the pages of a magazine in her lap. "I thought I would be asked to move up. I thought Lady Newley knew that I was the one doing the alterations."

"Ah. So the others took the credit?"

"That's why I left. Her ladyship and Miss Henrietta were here in New York visiting a relative when I finally realized what a dupe I had been." She shrugged. "I ran away, got a job at Macy's, met Sean, and am now at Butterick."

"You have ambition."

There was admiration in her voice. "Perhaps too much." Annie considered speaking of her relationship with Sean and how her ambition complicated things.

But Mrs. Culver did it for her. "Sean wants to marry you and you're not sure."

Annie suffered a laugh. "How did you figure all that out?"

"I saw the love in his eyes. He's never brought a girl home to meet us. But then you were quick to tell us you were *not* engaged."

"He hasn't actually proposed."

"He will. I guarantee it. And when he does, what will you say?"

Annie turned more pages, buying time. "I don't know. I think I love him, I do care for him tremendously, but marriage. . ."

Mrs. Culver shut Annie's magazine. "Don't do it."

"Excuse me?"

"Don't say yes—at least not yet. How old are you?"

"Nearly twenty."

"Still young. Very young."

"Don't you want us to marry? I know you just met me, but—"

Mrs. Culver put a hand on her arm. "I wanted to be a fashion designer when I was young."

It took Annie a moment to let her thoughts move from her engagement to Mrs. Culver's talent. "You did?"

She motioned toward the stash of magazines. "It's in my blood. Yet before I could do anything with my interest, Richard proposed marriage and I said yes, and then. . ." Her forehead tightened, and she cleared her throat before looking at Annie. "I love my husband and my children. I love my life. I have no real complaints."

"But. . . ?"

"But I never had the chance to even attempt making my dream a reality. That was twenty-five years ago, and women didn't have the choices they do now. Now, you have a career and a talent that needs to be nurtured so it can blossom. Sean will wait. Babies will wait—even though I am very eager to have grandchildren." She beamed. "Our daughter, Sybil, is expecting."

"Congratulations." Sean didn't mention having a sister. "Where does she live?"

"Chicago. We don't see her often enough. But when the baby comes, I'm going out to spend some time with them—with or without Richard."

It was clear this subject had been previously discussed.

Mrs. Culver continued, "I know it's important to support our husbands' careers and their dreams. For they are the breadwinners and the head of the household. I am very proud of our store and all Richard has accomplished. I simply advise you to think of the bigger picture of the future, rather than be confined to a future that involves the usual female choices, and *when* those choices are made."

"I merely want you to see with a larger scope." "Between the two of us, your son is the dreamer. He sees all the colors. I see things in black and white."

"Then you make the perfect pair." Mrs. Culver chose a new magazine for each of them. "Let him know your dreams and merge them with his own.

Then you—being the practical one—can help them both come to pass."

Annie's throat was tight. "That sounds rather perfect."

"Only because it is." Mrs. Culver opened a magazine and pointed at a hobble skirt. "What do you think of this silly fashion?"

❧

"So?" Sean said as they got in the cab to return home. "You and Mother seemed to get along well."

"She's wonderful," Annie said, adjusting the crate of fashion magazines on the seat beside her. "Did you know she wanted to be a fashion designer before she was married?"

"What?"

"She loved fashion and wanted to work in the field, but. . ."

Annie was relieved he filled in the blanks. "But then she got married and helped Father attain *his* dream."

"She loves her family very much, loves you very much."

"I know." He bumped her shoulder with his own. "Can you keep a secret?"

"Of course."

"She encouraged me to get a job at Butterick. If it weren't for her urging, I would still be working at the store."

Annie's respect for the woman grew. "I apologize for leaving you alone with your father so long, but your mother and I were having such a marvelous time."

Sean shrugged. "I suggested he show me the store and bring me up to date."

"How did it go?"

"He made constant digs about how all the improvements were done without me, and how I should have been there."

"So sorry that he holds a grudge."

"A wall of grudges, which he adds to every year I'm gone." He took her hand. "But enough of him. I'm so glad you had the chance to meet them, and they you. I've never brought anyone home."

Annie hesitated. "Your mother said as much."

He turned to her. "What else did she say about *us*?"

There was little about that subject Annie wanted to share—at least at this point. "She is happy we work together and have the same interest in business and fashion."

"That's all she said?"

"She likes me. She approves of me."

Sean drew her hand to his lips and kissed it. "Of course she does."

❧

"So?"

Back home, Annie laughed at Edna's simple question. "That's what Sean asked me after I'd spent time with his mother."

"And what did you say?"

Annie wasn't ready to share the conversation she'd had with Mrs. Culver, even though Edna would surely enjoy the details. Somehow that special time seemed almost sacred.

"She likes me and I like her." She moved to the box Sean had carried in from the cab. "Look at what she gave me."

Happily, the oohing and ahhing over the fashion magazines prevented any further questions.

CHAPTER TWENTY-FIVE

The New Year ignited a new passion in Annie for her work. Although she didn't say as much to Sean, his mother's encouragement had been instrumental in her zeal to excel.

The first day back at work after New Year's, she brought a stack of Mrs. Culver's fashion magazines to the workroom. "I come bearing gifts," she said.

The girls rushed forward as if they were starving and the magazines were a feast. Perhaps they were: a feast for the eyes and the imagination.

Dora chose a copy of *Femina*. "French. How fancy."

Annie opened a specific copy of *Vogue*. "Look at this...what if we changed this detail a little? Here, I'll show you." She retrieved a piece of tissue paper and spread it over the page. With a sweep of lines, she drew a revised version of the dress. "I think the side draping is too complicated for a home sewer, but if we simply add a few tucks instead..."

"Interesting."

Annie hadn't seen Mrs. Downs approach, but since she had her attention, she handed her the drawing. "Do you think it would work?"

Mrs. Downs looked at Annie's sketch a moment then at the design in the magazine. "If we showed it in a variety of fabrics I think the design could be made for many occasions."

"I agree," Annie said. "That's why I brought these magazines in. There are so many couture designs that could be adapted and simplified."

"Couture," Mrs. Downs said, tapping her bottom lip. "I do remember when you were hired that Mr. Burroughs mentioned you know something of couture, but I've forgotten the details."

The voices of Mrs. Culver and Mrs. Sampson combined. *"You have a career and a talent that needs to be nurtured so it can blossom. . . . Be who you are."*

"I used to be a maid for a viscountess whose clothes were all couture designed in Paris fashion houses."

"You were a maid?" one of the girls asked.

"I was. But I often made alterations and even improvements on her lady-ship's dresses, and those of her daughter. I'm familiar with couture construction and design. And since leaving that position, I've become familiar with the simpler construction and design preferred by the home sewer."

"Well la-di-da," Dora said.

Instead of being offended, Annie embraced the comment. "That's a fair description of those gowns."

Mrs. Downs paged through a few of the magazines. She closed the covers. "Get back to work, ladies."

Annie was disappointed at her response. She'd seemed so interested.

"Don't mind her," Maude said as they went back to their tables. "If the First Lady, Mrs. Taft, walked in, old Downs wouldn't be impressed."

"But she was—for a moment."

"That's more interest than I've ever gotten from her. Come help me piece out this bodice."

⊱◈⊰

Annie arched her back against the strain of bending over a worktable and cutting out muslin to shape the pattern pieces. She groaned at the excruciating, delectable stretch. "At times like this I wish I were shorter—or the tables higher."

"You're lucky to be tall," Suzanne said. "I often get mistaken for a twelve-year-old."

"That has nothing to do with your height," Maude teased.

Suzanne glanced down at her bodice and made herself useful elsewhere.

"You're nasty," Annie said.

"I tease. That's not the same thing."

Annie wasn't so sure and was about to get into a discussion about the difference when Mrs. Downs came in the workroom and walked over to her.

"Come with me, Miss Wood."

Her face was stern.

"Did I do something wrong?"

"Come."

Annie followed Mrs. Downs out to the corridor, sneaking glances at the girls she left behind. They looked curious, and Maude looked worried.

What could be wrong? This morning Mrs. Downs had seemed genuinely interested in her ideas. She couldn't imagine how she had offended her since then.

They took the elevator to the sales floor. Annie spotted Sean, but as he rose to greet her, she shook her head. *Not now.*

Mrs. Downs led Annie to a corner office. She knocked on the door and then entered. A striking middle-aged woman sat behind the desk. Her hair was pulled up in the loose fashion of the Gibson girl, yet looked modern with two ribbons woven through it in a haphazard yet determined way.

"Madame LeFleur," Mrs. Downs said. "I would like to introduce you to Annie Wood. Annie, this is our head of international sales and design, Madame LeFleur."

The woman made no attempt to rise or shake Annie's hand, so Annie nodded. "It's nice to meet you."

"So zis is the artiste."

Artist?

"Sit."

Annie let Mrs. Downs choose a chair first then sat beside her. With a glance she saw the walls were covered with beautiful fashion prints. On a table were stacks upon stacks of magazines, making Mrs. Culver's stash minuscule by comparison.

Madame LeFleur *was* fashion.

"So," the woman began. "You have ideas to adapt couture?"

"I. . .I do. I believe every woman deserves to wear beautiful fashion. If they can't afford couture, they still deserve to enjoy the essence of those designs—adapted to their specific financial and functional needs." Annie was rather surprised at her own eloquence.

Madame exchanged a look with Mrs. Downs. "As I explained," Mrs. Downs said.

Madame rose and beckoned Annie to the table where the magazines were stacked. She pulled one from the top and opened it at random. "There. Design." She handed her a piece of tissue and a pencil.

Put on the spot, Annie studied the dress on the page and quickly made adjustments. She placed the tissue on top and, with a few glances back to the original, made a sketch. "I think the key to most of these redesigns is removing the fussiness and simplifying the line. The spirit of the fashion remains, but the function and subsequent price is modified."

The two women held her drawing between them. Mrs. Downs traced a finger along the sleeve line. A silent decision was made, and the drawing was returned to the table. "How would you like to go to Paris with me in ze spring?"

Annie wasn't sure if there was anything Madame could have said that would be more shocking. "Me?"

Madame explained, "Each season a contingent from Butterick—led by myself—travels to ze Paris fashion shows to keep abreast of ze latest fashion. We return and adapt zat fashion to our patterns."

"Similar to what you just did," Mrs. Downs said.

"You are quick with ze ideas. Quickness is needed to study, remember, and adapt ze fashion we see."

Sean had mentioned such a process, but now to be asked? *Lord? What are You doing here? This is beyond anything I could have asked or imagined.*

Mrs. Downs straightened the magazines. "In the past I have gone on the trips, but I find that my time is better utilized here, keeping my department in line. And Maude has gone. She has an eye for the details others miss."

"Maude?"

Madame nodded. "And another woman, Mrs. Brown, has accompanied me, but she is off having ze baby."

Thank You, God, for Mrs. Brown's baby.

"So?" Madame said. "Would you like to go with us?"

There was no hesitation, no need for deliberation. "Yes. Very much so."

"*Très bien. Bon,*" Madame said.

"When do we leave?"

Madame laughed. "You are eager, yes?"

"I am eager, yes."

"We do not leave until ze mid of March."

Annie remembered Sean mentioning sales trips to Europe. Could it be? Could he? "Does anyone else go?"

"A few others perhaps," Madame said.

Annie only needed one other.

⤜∞⤛

Upon leaving Madame LeFleur's office, Annie desperately wanted to share the news with Sean. But his desk was empty. Telling Maude would be the next best thing.

But as she and Mrs. Downs reached their floor, Mrs. Downs said, "I would advise against sharing your news with the other ladies."

"Why?"

"Envy is a sin."

That is their problem.

"So is pride."

That is my problem.

"They will wonder where I've been, why you called me away."

Mrs. Downs plucked a scrap of muslin from the corridor. "I can only give the warning. Whether you heed it is your choice."

They entered the workroom, and the presence of Mrs. Downs was the only reason Annie's coworkers didn't swarm around her.

Maude sidled up close. "Well?"

Annie's excitement determined her choice—though shared in a whisper. "I'm going to Paris, to the fashion shows. With you."

Maude blinked. "I worked here four years before they invited me to go."

Annie was surprised. "I thought you'd be happy for me."

Maude's countenance changed from surprise to glee. "Of course I am. The two of us in Paris! Can you imagine?"

"What's going on?" Dora asked.

Before Annie could suggest to Maude they keep it to themselves, she told the entire group. "Annie and I are going to Paris in the spring!"

There were groans all around, and a few comments that were far from kind, but it was nothing Annie couldn't handle.

She was going to Paris!

❧

All day, Annie had but a single focus: she wanted to tell Sean about Paris, talk to Maude about Paris, and dream about Paris. But after the mixed reaction she received from the other girls in the workroom, she had to keep her excitement to herself—as best she could.

She was only partially successful.

"You need to stop smiling so much," Maude whispered as they sized out a waistline.

"I can't help it. I've never been offered something so exciting."

"I agree. But you're acting like the child who gets a pony on Christmas when all her siblings get a new pencil box."

Point taken. And yet, "Blast them if they find my excitement offensive. Maybe if they'd shown some initiative and had some talent they'd be going, too."

Maude's eyebrows rose. "Too much truth, Annie. Rein it in."

"I'm sorry. But surely you've felt it, too. After all, they also chose you."

Maude angled her back to the others as she pinned a dart in the waist. "My mother used to tell me that of those who are given much, much is demanded. For whatever reason, you and I have been given some talent the others don't have." She shrugged. "Mother always said it's my responsibility to use what I have." She gave a slight nod toward the others. "Use your talent boldly when possible and discreetly when necessary."

Annie laughed. "That may be the best advice I've ever received."

A young man in a uniform stepped into the workroom. All eyes turned toward him. "Telegram for a Miss Annie Wood?"

Annie raised her hand. "That's me."

The women gathered close. "Telegrams are always bad news," Dora said.

Suzanne nodded. "We heard my uncle Jed died with a telegram."

Annie immediately thought of her parents. Were they all right? Yet it couldn't be from them. They didn't know where she was.

Dora offered a snide opinion. "Maybe it's some fancy Paris designer inviting you to dinner."

"Very funny," Maude said. "Come on, Annie. Open it."

Annie removed the note from the envelope. She read it through and smiled. "It's from a friend who's traveling in Europe. Just wishing me a happy New Year."

The group of ladies deflated with disappointment. "That's all?" Suzanne asked.

"You'd rather my uncle had died?"

They straggled back to work. Annie slipped the note in a pocket.

Maude sidled close. "What's it really say?"

"Just what I said." She flipped a hand, shooing her away. "You're as bad as the others." Then she had a thought. "How do I send a response?"

"There's a telegraph office down the street. You just stop in, write it up, and pay."

"How much?"

"Not much. But you're charged by the word, so be brief. What do you want to say?"

Annie shook her head. "I'm just asking."

Annie desperately wanted to reread the telegram but made herself wait a half hour before she went to the ladies' and the privacy of a stall. Only then did she open the envelope a second time.

EUROPE LOVELY. OFFER STANDS. HAPPY NEW YEAR. MRS. S.

Lately Annie hadn't thought much about Mrs. Sampson's offer. Yet to know that it still stood added to her elation.

Mrs. Sampson is in Europe. I'm going to Europe. What if we could meet?

Annie fished a stub of a pencil from her pocket and wrote on the back of the envelope.

COMING TO PARIS MID-MARCH. FASHION SHOWS. TALK THEN?

She read it over, hoping to make it shorter, but there were no words to cut.

There were also no words to convey all she was feeling. Yet there *were* three she had to express: *Thank You, God!*

❧

After work Annie couldn't wait outside for Sean but instead met him at the stairwell, grabbing his arm.

"Well, hello."

"I have exciting news," she whispered as they headed outside.

They joined Maude. "She's been bursting at the seams all day."

Annie pulled him out of the stream of pedestrians, and Maude followed. Annie bounced on her toes. "I'm going to Paris in mid-March, to the fashion shows!"

His face brightened, and he lifted her off the ground and spun her around. "How did it happen? Who asked you to go?"

She told him the story of the magazines, Mrs. Downs, and Madame LeFleur. "They said there was another woman who usually goes, but she's having a child and—"

Sean looked at Maude. "Mrs. Brown?"

Maude nodded. "She's due around then. You're still going for your sales trip, aren't you, Sean?"

"I believe I'm going the first of March because I need to go to Berlin,

London, and Vienna as well as Paris, but I'm sure I can arrange to meet up with you, and perhaps take the same ship home." He held Annie's chin and kissed her once. "We can see Paris together."

They began to walk again. "It's like a dream."

"That it is," Sean said. "A dream come true."

CHAPTER TWENTY~SIX

"Y ou're what?"

Iris blushed. "I'm expecting. A baby."

Annie drew her into an embrace. "I'm so happy for you." She pushed her at arm's length and took a discreet look at her abdomen. She did not look pregnant. "When are you due?"

"In the fall. October."

Edna put an arm around Iris. "Plenty of time for Annie and I to sew up a proper layette."

The blast of the ocean liner's horn deafened them. "I think that means it's time to board." Annie looked toward her travel party. Madame LeFleur was instructing some porters as to their luggage.

Annie hugged Edna and Iris. "Take care of yourselves—and the baby."

"Have a marvelous time," Edna said.

"You will see Sean?" Iris asked.

"He's already been in Europe two weeks but will join us in Paris a few days after we arrive." She saw Maude motioning her over. "I have to go. Good-bye."

"Bon voyage," Edna said.

Annie rushed to join the others. With a shake of her head, Madame turned toward the gangway. "Come girls, *faites-vite! Plus vite!*"

As the girls scurried after Madame, Maude handed Annie two enormous hatboxes, keeping two for herself. "Madame doesn't trust porters with her beloved *chapeaux.*"

By the way Madame strode onto the ship, one would have thought she was a queen. The ship's attendants snapped to and gave her the attention she demanded.

"Do they know her?" Annie asked Maude.

"They know her type."

"But she's not wealthy."

"Madame acts as if she deserves deference, so she gets it."

A crewman walked alongside Madame, leading her to her stateroom. The men at the top of the gangway merely nodded to Annie and Maude. No one asked to take the hatboxes.

The two girls followed Madame and her guide up some stairs and then into a lush corridor. Annie was impressed that Butterick was letting them travel first-class.

The man opened a paneled walnut door. "For you, Madame LeFleur."

Madame perused the room with a glance to the *en suite* bath and water closet area.

"Does it meet your approval, madame?" he asked.

"I believe it suits." To Maude and Annie she said, "Go get settled. We shall meet later."

The hatboxes were relinquished and the girls left the room. "I just realized that I half expected her to ask me to do her unpacking," Annie whispered.

"You are not her maid."

"Last time I was on a ship, I *was* a maid." It seemed a lifetime ago, when she was a different Annie.

Maude looked at the papers that noted their cabin assignments then strode down the corridor and made a turn toward the center stairs. She descended the stairs.

"We're not on this level?"

Maude spoke over her shoulder. "You are not a maid, but neither are you first-class. We have second-class accommodations."

Annie couldn't help but be disappointed, yet when she saw the room they would share she was pleased. "It's much better than the third-class room I had before."

Maude plopped on the bed to the right of the porthole then removed hat pins securing her hat and tossed it on the low dresser in between. "Relax now. There will be plenty of commotion once we depart."

Annie couldn't remember any commotion from her trip over other than serving Miss Henrietta and her ladyship. "How do we spend our time on the voyage?"

"Eating, napping, reading, and strolling around the decks. Do you play cards?"

"No. The footmen used to play Whist, but I was never invited to join them."

"I'll teach you Pitch. But I warn you, I will win. I always win."

❦

They stood at the railing and waved good-bye to those on the pier. Annie scanned the crowd for Edna and Iris but couldn't see them. The ship slowly moved away from the harbor.

Will my life be different when I return?

Passengers gradually left the rail and began their promenade of the decks. Annie turned her back on the sea. "Now what?"

Maude laughed. "You need to be entertained already?"

"I am used to having something to do. I am used to schedules."

Maude pointed to a long row of deck chairs. "Sit."

Annie sat in one chair, and Maude sat next to her. They nodded at people walking by.

"You need to learn to put your feet up," Maude said, moving her feet to the chaise.

"It's not something I get to do very often."

"Suit yourself." Maude leaned her head back and closed her eyes.

Annie tried to do the same. The sun was warm and the sea breeze refreshing.

But then she sat upright with a startling realization. "I have never had leisure time! I have always worked."

"Everyone works, Annie. Even the wealthy have to work to make their money."

"But they have leisure time."

"More than us, that's for certain." Maude shielded her eyes from the sun. "You've never explained how you left servanthood behind."

"I ran away."

"Without telling them?"

"That's how running away works." Annie's past seemed like the skyline of the city, moving further and further away.

"You mentioned you'd run away but I didn't think you meant it so literally."

Annie told Maude about Lady Newley, the Friesens, Iris, and Danny.

At the mention of his name, a familiar lump formed in her throat. "Danny was killed by a footman named Grasston who worked at the Friesens'. He claimed I got him fired and was stalking me for months. He even attacked me."

"Meaning. . . ?"

"He tackled me to the ground and was on top of me, and. . ." She shuddered at the memory. "Some passersby saved me."

Maude hesitated. It seemed an odd reaction. But then she said, "How horrible for you."

"My pain was nothing compared to. . . Grasston killed Danny to hurt me. Danny died because of me."

Maude's feet found the deck, and she faced Annie. "Why don't I know any of this?"

"It's over now. Last December at Iris's wedding, the police were in the midst of arresting Grasston when he jumped off a roof and died rather than be arrested." She leaned back and closed her eyes.

"I'm so sorry you had to go through that."

"So am I." The stories she'd just shared about Iris and Danny came back to her, and with the stories came a conclusion. "Iris is where she should be—married and expecting a child. Perhaps I am where I should be."

Maude sat back in the lounger. "You're on a ship heading for Europe and the fashion shows in Paris. I'll take that over being married and having babies."

Annie glanced at her. "You don't want that?"

Maude shrugged. "Do you?"

The question loomed large, filling the expanse of sky and sea. "I like the idea of marriage, but the babies. . . I want to have a career. I just got started. I don't want it to end too soon."

"Then wait. Sean will wait for you."

"He hasn't asked yet." *I haven't let him ask.*

"Perhaps he doesn't want to ask until he knows you'll say yes."

"Perhaps." She thought back to her visit with Sean's mother. "His mother told me—almost warned me—to take my time in regard to marriage. She had dreams, too, but once she was married she had to give them up."

"I am determined not to give up my dreams for anyone." She put a hand on Annie's arm. "So. . .are you with me?"

It was a complicated issue. Annie loved Sean, but she also loved her work. All she could do was shrug.

Maude slapped the arm of her chair. "Enough of this serious talk. We're here to rest and relax. You are too tightly wound, Annie Wood."

She couldn't deny it.

❦

They walked out of the second-class dining room, and Annie put a hand to her stomach. "That was delicious. But far too much."

"And we can have as much as we want."

"Ugh," Annie said, feeling overly full. "It was like putting butter on bacon."

Maude laughed. "Let's go into the game room and see if we can gather two more for a card game."

"I told you I don't play."

"And I told you I'd teach you."

The girls found a deck of cards in the game room where others were playing billiards, checkers, and chess. Maude began shuffling the deck.

"It appears you've done this before."

"A few times." Maude looked around the room and raised a hand. "We need two more for Pitch."

Annie was a bit embarrassed when two young men came over. She couldn't imagine hawking for partners like Maude had done.

"Pitch, you say?" said the man with a dark black mustache.

"Ten-point. Women against men."

"You're on," the blond man said.

"I. . .I don't know how to play," Annie said.

"All the better," the first man said. He held out his hand and made introductions. "I am William and this is Stanley."

"Maude and Annie," Maude said, as she began to deal the cards.

❦

"Fifty-two!" Maude exclaimed. "We won!"

Stanley threw down his cards. "You two got the ace and the three nearly every time."

"You got the two a lot," Annie said.

"Small consolation," William said. "Let's play another."

Annie looked at the clock on the wall. It was nearly midnight. "I think not, gentlemen. I'm quite done in." As she pushed back her chair, Stanley rushed to pull it out for her.

"Until tomorrow, then?" he asked. "At two?"

"We'll see."

They bade the men good night and made their way back to their cabin. Only when they were inside, with the door shut and locked, did Annie feel the full measure of her weariness. "I had no idea it was so late."

"Time flies when you are having fun."

Annie sat on her bed and began to unlace her shoes. "It was fun. More fun than I've had in a long while."

"Stanley is interested in you."

"I know," Annie said, removing her shoes and enjoying the freedom. "I don't want him to be. I mentioned 'my beau.' I mentioned meeting Sean in Paris."

Once Maude's shoes were off she rolled down her stockings. "That doesn't matter to some men."

There was a slight edge to her voice. "William was nice to you."

"No, you don't," Maude said, setting her shoes near the wardrobe. "I do not want male attention. Ever."

Annie was shocked by this. "Whyever not? You're at ease with them, you're witty and pretty and—"

"I'm not saying I *can't* get their attention. I don't want their attention." She stopped all movement and kept her back to Annie. Her voice became soft. "I can't have their attention."

Something was wrong. Annie went to her and touched her shoulder. "Will you explain what you mean?"

They stood together like that for a full ten seconds. Annie heard Maude's breathing hasten.

"Maude?"

Maude turned around, gave Annie a glance, and then pointed to the beds. "Let's sit."

Annie took a seat on her bed, while Maude sat on hers, her head down, her arms crossed like a protective shield. What had the power to quash the vivacious, unflappable Maude?

Annie waited, wanting yet not wanting to hear what Maude had to say.

Finally, Maude drew in a deep breath. "Two years ago I was assaulted." It took another breath to get out the rest: "I was raped."

Annie gasped and stood to go to her, but Maude waved her back. "I was walking alone at night, not paying attention to my surroundings, when a man grabbed me, pulled me into an alley, beat me, and..." She shrugged. "He left me for dead. I thought I was dead. I wanted to die."

"Oh, Maude." Annie found herself at a loss for meaningful words. "I'm so sorry."

Maude lifted her gaze to the porthole. "I remember lying there, my cheek against the dirt of the alley, with the pain so intense that I wished for death to give me release. I opened the eye that wasn't swollen shut and saw a rat coming toward me, sniffing at me. Only the idea of him gnawing at my skin got me to move. Somehow I stood up and staggered to the street, where someone helped me."

Annie remembered Grasston's assault, and imagining what it *could* have been made her shudder. "I can see why that would put you off men."

Maude looked at her, shaking her head vehemently. "It's not that—though it certainly was at first. I was afraid of all men, but that eventually faded. It's not that I don't like men, or trust them, or even that I don't want one in my life, it's that...I can't ever marry."

"Why not?"

"I can't have children. I was...damaged."

Annie put the pieces together. "You don't want to encourage a man because he might want to marry you, and you don't want that because you can't give him children."

Maude touched the tip of her nose. "It wouldn't be fair."

Annie felt guilty for her previous talk about not wanting children at this point in her career. It was far different to face never having them.

"Not all men want children."

"Perhaps," Maude said. "But by the time a beau and I would have such a conversation, we would have feelings for each other. His finding out I couldn't...I don't want to inflict that sort of pain on anyone—nor experience it myself."

"If a man really loved you, he wouldn't care."

"I would care." She began taking hairpins from her hair, setting them in a pile on the bed. "For a long while I tried to play the part of a shy and reclusive sort in public, hoping men would ignore me. But for some reason many of them took my reticence as a challenge, and they tried to bring me out of my shell."

"You, shy?"

She ran her hands through her now freed hair, raking her scalp. "Being who I was *not* was too much work. And so I decided to go the opposite route. I decided to overwhelm them with wit and sarcasm—trying to be too much for them."

"Has that worked?"

"You don't see a man around, do you?" She covered a yawn with her hand. "If I do spot interest, I quickly nip it in the bud." She collected her hairpins then began getting undressed. "I've accepted my lot. Please don't feel sorry for me. My career is rewarding and I have many friends—like you. Those blessings save me from despair."

"You are the most courageous woman I know."

"It doesn't take courage to accept what is."

"But I think it does. You could resent it, fight it, and be bitter. You've chosen not to be any of those things."

"Don't make me a saint, Annie. I have plenty of bitter moments. Sometimes it's hard not to wallow in it." She stepped out of her skirt and moved to hang it up.

"Does my relationship with Sean make it more difficult? If it does, I won't talk about him and—"

Maude whipped around, making her petticoat swing. "Absolutely not," she said. "I am happy for the two of you. I want to hear the details of your courtship. I want you to be happy."

"Are you happy?"

Maude paused a moment then said, "I am. My mother always said, 'God is good, all the time.' I have to believe that. There's something good that will come out of my pain. It may be years down the road, but I truly believe that someday..."

Whether Maude wanted a hug or not, Annie embraced her.

CHAPTER TWENTY-SEVEN

Paris!

Madame LeFleur had so much luggage that she required her own carriage, leaving Maude and Annie on their own. Riding with Maude in the cab from the train station to the hotel reminded Annie of the same sort of ride she'd taken from the ship to the Friesens' home in New York City. "To think that a few months ago I was a maid at Crompton Hall, and had never traveled more than a few miles beyond Summerfield."

"Now you're a world traveler," Maude said. "And an expert Pitch player. We'll have to play on the ship going home."

"Sean will be with us then," Annie said. "I can't wait to—" She glanced at Maude. "Sorry."

"For what?"

"Being excited to see my beau."

Maude gave Annie a hard look. "There will be none of that. Remember how I said I want to share your joy? Don't take that away from me, too." She pointed out the window. "Look. You can see the Eiffel Tower."

❧

Annie and Maude stood at the check-in desk of Le Grand Hotel. Maude handled the paperwork, allowing Annie to fully take in the magnificent lobby. Fluted white columns, arches, and an enormous skylight in the center. A gorgeous spiral staircase made her want to climb it just to say she did. The entire area was bathed in the scent of fresh flowers, for a gigantic arrangement of white blooms graced a center table in the entrance, greeting the guests.

Annie could imagine Lady Newley staying in such a place, and Maude had told her that Napoleon's wife, Empress Eugenie, had inaugurated the hotel forty years earlier. Annie stepped beside a potted tree so she could watch the grand and the fashionable pass by.

Suddenly a man's voice sounded from behind her and asked, "What are you doing, mademoiselle?"

For a moment she feared she was in trouble. She turned around and saw. . . It was Sean! She flew into his arms.

"Now that's the kind of welcome I need."

They held each other until Annie noticed disapproving looks. She pulled away.

"I'm glad you've arrived," he said. "Was your voyage enjoyable?"

"I learned to play Pitch."

"Are you any good?"

"Maude thinks I am."

"Then you and I shall partner up on the trip home." He drew her to a duo of chairs, and they leaned forward so their knees touched. "I've missed you."

"I've missed you, too." She was glad to find it true. "How were the stores in Berlin, and London, and Vienna?"

"Thriving. I just have one more to visit here in Paris. I thought maybe you and Maude would like to join me."

"We'd love to." Maude strode forward holding two keys on large fobs. "Hello, Sean. Have you been here long?"

He stood to greet her. "Just a few hours. I thought I'd visit the Butterick shop this afternoon. Perhaps at three? That would give you ladies a chance to unpack and settle in."

It was a date.

❧

"You need to rest, Annie," Maude said as she unpacked the last of their suitcases.

Annie shook her head, enjoying the view from their small balcony. Not all the floors provided such a luxury, but theirs, near the top of the building, within the roof itself. . . She felt heady with gratitude. "I can't come inside. Not with this view. The opera house is across the street. I can nearly touch it."

Maude joined her on the balcony.

"Look at the opulent detail of it," Annie said.

"The French are an opulent sort."

Annie gazed across the square where carriages and pedestrians intersected as they made their way from here to there. "These buildings have such odd roofs, not harsh and angled, but narrow and swooped upward."

"They're called Mansard roofs. Again, very French."

She nodded, taking in the information. "This is vastly different from New York."

"Which is different from London, and different from Vienna. Each is unique."

"You have traveled to those places, too?"

"In my youth."

The information added another layer to Annie's view of Maude. "Did you grow up wealthy? I only ask, because to travel so much. . ."

"Yes. Very. My father was a British diplomat. We saw the world."

"You don't have an accent like I do."

"I've been in America a long while. Since I was twelve."

"What brought you there?"

"My father died, and Mother and I moved to New York to live with her sister."

"I didn't know you had family there."

Maude took in a deep breath. "We are estranged."

"May I ask why?"

Maude hesitated then sighed. "Mother wanted grandchildren. Since I am unable to give her what she wants. . ."

"Surely she didn't turn her back on you."

"I turned my back on her. She's suffered enough disappointment in her life." With a blink and a turn she changed the subject. "Come now. We have an hour to rest before we meet up with Sean."

<hr />

The trio stood across the street from the Butterick Pattern store on the Avenue of L'Opera, just a ten-minute stroll from their hotel.

Annie was in awe. "I can't believe there is a store dedicated to our patterns. In Paris. France."

"I told you about it, and the ones in the other cities. You knew I was making sales calls."

"I thought you were calling on sewing sections of department stores."

Maude adjusted a drawstring purse on her wrist. "The French love our patterns because we give them the essence of couture with simplified styles they can make at home." She swept a hand toward the storefront. "Shall we?"

They crossed the avenue, and Annie admired the mannequins in the windows wearing various dresses, blouses, and children's clothes, all made from Butterick patterns. Sean opened the door for the ladies. Inside was an elegant space—one room—with white fluted columns and tall wainscoting. Edging the room were tall tables and stools. Some women were perusing pattern catalogs as clerks helped them choose.

Another clerk approached. "*Puis-je vous aider, monsieur?*"

Annie was surprised when Sean answered in French. The two chatted back and forth, and then Sean turned to the girls. "Madame Seville, *Je peux vous présente* Mademoiselle Wood and Mademoiselle Nascato. Ladies, Madame Seville."

"*Bonjour,*" the woman said.

Annie knew that much. "Bonjour, madame."

Madame proceeded to show them how the shop worked. The customers chose patterns from catalogs then purchased them from a supply in the back.

"It's similar to the system we had at Macy's, but larger."

"And more prestigious," Maude said, "because it's a stand-alone store, a destination."

Sean commenced with his business, talking with Madame, taking notes. Annie moved to a stool and looked through a catalog. The garment descriptions were in French. She assumed the ones in Berlin and Vienna were in German. "I'm so impressed. I had no idea I worked for such an international company."

"We sell more of our patterns here than anywhere in the world. We've even earned praise from European royalty."

Annie was dumbstruck. "To think that something we design could be worn all over Europe, and receive royal praise."

"We have to design it first. We see the fashion houses tomorrow."

Annie could hardly wait.

❧

That evening Madame LeFleur gave each of her workers an envelope. "Here is your stipend for ze meals during our visit." She glanced at a mirror in the hotel lobby, adjusting the plume on her hat. "I have reservations at ze Café de la Paix, here at ze hotel, but you may choose as you wish. Ta-ta."

And she was off again.

Annie looked in her envelope. "There is a lot of money here. Though, since it's French money, I may be wrong."

"You're not wrong," Maude said. "It's a lot. Restaurants in this part of Paris are expensive."

Sean slipped his envelope in an inner coat pocket. "I have an idea. A brilliant idea." He took Annie's hand and Maude followed as they exited the hotel and ran across the square. He led them to a street vendor who offered long loaves of crusty bread and glass bottles of what looked like lemonade.

"Let's save our money, get some bread, and go sit on a hotel balcony and watch all the fancy people come to the opera."

"That sounds smashing," Annie said.

It turned out they could get ham on the bread. They gathered their street wares, and Sean led them into a pastry store where they bought berry tarts for dessert.

They returned to Maude and Annie's room. Their balcony was small, and not large enough for chairs, so they sat on its floor.

"It's a Parisian picnic," Maude said.

Annie took her first bite of the sandwich and moaned with delight. "The crust of the bread is perfect, and. . ." She opened the bread to see inside the sandwich. "There's so much butter."

"Of course there's so much butter," Maude said. "Parisians love their butter."

"As do I," Sean said, "love their butter. Love anyone's butter."

"Somehow it tastes better because it's Paris," Annie said. She looked across the street where the opera house was lit like a beacon for tonight's performance. She felt warm inside, as if *she* were glowing like a beacon from the inside out.

They had just finished their tarts when the carriages and automobiles began to arrive. Liveried footmen held the doors as beautiful people wearing beautiful clothing stepped out and made their way up the steps of the opera, disappearing inside.

Annie took hold of two rungs of the wrought-iron railing and peered through it, feeling very much like a child looking down on a parents' party. She'd seen Miss Henrietta do such a thing even as a young adult. It was surreal: the sights, the sounds of gaiety and movement, the smells of the café wafting up from below, the crisp air of the spring evening. She closed her eyes. *Thank You for this experience, God. I will never forget it.*

"You seem lost in thought," Sean said.

She opened her eyes and nodded, returning her attention to the spectacle before her. "How can this be real? How can I be here?"

Sean ran a hand along her arm. "You *are* here. With me. With Maude. We all have a purpose here."

"We all appreciate being here," Maude added. "It will never get old."

Annie looked at them in all seriousness. "Even when I am old, I will remember this night."

"Ah," Sean said, with a mischievous look on his face. "But the night is not over. Come with me."

After getting their wraps, once again Sean led the girls out of the hotel. But this time he turned to the left. They walked past the grand entrance of the opera house, past the grand people going inside, and skimmed the side of the building, heading toward the back.

"Where are we going?"

They came upon a back entrance. Sean looked both ways then opened the door. "Go! Inside."

The girls didn't have time to object. They came into a dark hallway but could hear voices calling to each other in French. Not genteel calls, but the calls of stagehands and actors backstage. They could hear the musicians warming up.

"Are we allowed in here?" Annie asked.

Even Maude looked apprehensive. "Sean, you go too far."

He stepped away as if scouting his next move. Apparently he found it, for he returned to them and said, "Not quite far enough. Not yet. Come with me."

He led them to a small space behind a curtain that was populated with extra music stands and stacked chairs. He freed three chairs. "Sit, mademoiselles."

The girls sat, and Sean sat with them. The space was small so they had to sit in a circle, with their knees touching. It was odd sitting in the dark, yet somehow the darkness heightened the experience. They could see a slit of light under the curtain.

Suddenly the cacophony of music stopped, and applause began. Some words were said, and then the orchestra began to play the most astonishing music Annie had ever heard. She'd never experienced any sort of orchestra. The sound was glorious, as if God Himself were directing His angels to play His own composition.

And then a new song began, and people began to sing with voices that soared and reached every corner of their hiding place, every corner of Annie's soul.

She began to cry.

Sean leaned toward her. "Are you all right?"

Since he couldn't see her nod, she answered by kissing him on his cheek and whispering, "Thank you. Thank you for letting me have a glimpse of heaven."

CHAPTER TWENTY-EIGHT

The House of Paquin was a short walk from the hotel, on the Rue de la Paix. Sean explained that *paix* meant "peace," though he pointed out that the Column Vendôme at the apex of the street was originally erected by Napoleon to commemorate some war victory.

No matter. Peace followed Annie up the street and interwove its strands with happiness, contentment, and excitement. Yesterday spent with Maude and Sean, eating on the balcony, hearing the heavenly music of the opera. . . Her heart was full of thanksgiving.

And excitement.

"There it is," Sean said. "The building with the peach-colored entrance."

The entrance was set apart from the gray stone on either side and had PAQUIN in gold letters above it. Faux fluted columns marked the door. Above the windows to the right and left were planters of spring flowers. There was a queue of women in front of the shop. "Are these ladies potential customers?"

"Hardly," Maude whispered as Madame presented her invitation to allow them entrance. "These are the women we design the patterns for—the ones inspired by what we see inside. They are here to see the wealthy patrons."

"But we're not wealthy and we are going inside."

"If not for Madame LeFleur we'd be out here with the rest of them."

Annie noticed a few of the women whispering behind closed hands as their gaze lingered on Annie and Maude. She imagined they were assessing the girls' lack of fashion and probably discussing why *they* were allowed entrance.

Annie was glad when Madame motioned them inside.

The space was elegant with paintings on the wall, gilded trim, and ornate chairs and settees. They let Madame take the lead, and once again Annie was impressed with her contacts and her way of fitting in as if she was one of the rich patrons, not just a pattern designer from New York.

Suddenly Annie heard her name. "Annie! Annie Wood!" She turned around and saw Mrs. Sampson coming forward to greet her.

"Mrs. Sampson," she said as the woman kissed her cheeks. "I didn't know you'd be here."

"Of course you did. You sent me a telegram saying you'd be in Paris in the spring. Harold and I always try to catch the fashion shows in Paris. The chance to see you again made it a must."

"*Galeries*," Madame said, coming to make her own greeting. "Zey prefer ze term 'galeries' razer zan 'shows.'"

"How French of them." Mrs. Sampson extended her greeting to Maude and Sean. "So then. What other houses have you seen?"

"This is our first," Annie said.

"See as many as you can. I do hope there are no hobble skirts in the mix." Mrs. Sampson lowered her voice. "But now is the time to gain the knowledge of what's being done so you can do your own designing. You *are* designing, yes?"

"I am here to adapt the designs for Butterick, yes."

Mrs. Sampson let out a dramatic sigh then leaned even closer for Annie's ears alone. "My offer stands. Harold and I will back you toward the creation of your own fashion company. In your telegram during the holiday, you mentioned speaking when we were both in Paris. We are here. It is time to talk."

When Annie had replied to Mrs. Sampson's telegram, she'd assumed she would have an answer for her. Unfortunately all she could say was, "I do appreciate all you are offering. But I'm not ready."

Mrs. Sampson shook her head. "Doors that open can be closed, Annie. Perhaps Harold and I were wrong in believing you were the one for our project?"

She didn't want them to think that! "I didn't say I'd never. . .just that I wasn't ready."

The woman's left eyebrow rose, and Annie feared she had delayed too long.

Yet Mrs. Sampson simply sighed and said, "Someday you will be. I am confident there is a 'someday' in your answer."

More confident than I.

"When are you heading back to New York?" she asked Annie, including

Sean and Maude in the conversation again.

"We take a train to Cherbourg April tenth to board the ship," Sean said.

Mrs. Sampson clapped her hands. "As are we! Which ship are you taking?"

Annie had to think a moment. "I believe it's called the *Titanic*."

Mrs. Sampson grabbed her arm. "As are we! How wonderful. We can enjoy the entire passage together. A few of our friends—John Jacob Astor, and Mrs. J. J. Brown—are also boarding in Cherbourg. I would love for you to meet them, especially Molly, for she is even more of a character than I am."

Annie had mixed feelings about sharing a ship with Mrs. Sampson. She enjoyed her company very much, yet she hoped the *Titanic* was as immense as its name so she would have some space. As she'd said, she wasn't ready to commit to the Sampsons' idea.

Then she thought of a way out. "Seeing each other on the *Titanic* might not be as easy as you hope, because I'm sure you are traveling first-class while the rest of us—" She stopped talking as she saw another woman she knew. Two women.

"What's wrong?" Mrs. Sampson asked, looking in the direction of Annie's gaze.

Annie glanced toward the door. Maybe she could avoid them if she slipped outside.

Maude took her arm. "Remove the look of panic if you please. And tell us what's wrong."

Annie turned her back on the women she'd seen then answered, "It's Lady Newley and Miss Henrietta."

Unfortunately, Maude, Sean, and Mrs. Sampson all looked in that direction.

"Don't look!"

"Too late," Sean whispered. "They're coming over."

"Turn around," Maude added.

"Smile," Mrs. Sampson said.

Give me strength. Annie turned around and braced herself for her mistress's anger. She managed a smile and bobbed a curtsy—feeling foolish for it in midbob. She was not a servant anymore.

Which was the issue at hand.

"Annie," Lady Newley said.

"My lady. Miss Henrietta. How nice to see you." *What a stupid thing to say!* The last time she'd seen them she was a housemaid—a housemaid who ran away with no notice other than leaving Miss Henrietta a note.

A few seconds passed and pulled on Annie's nerves. Then Lady Newley said, "It is nice to see you, too, Annie. How did you get"—she motioned around the room—"here?"

Annie looked at her friends. "Would you please give us a few minutes?"

They stepped away. At least Annie could endure her scolding in private. "I am so sorry for running out on you like I did."

"You mentioned 'no ladder to climb' in your note?" Henrietta said.

Annie didn't want to discredit the two lady's maids who'd betrayed her, for what did it matter now? "I have always loved fashion and. . ."

"You had a 'stirring,' I believe?" Lady Newley asked with a smile.

"You saw my note?"

"Henrietta shared it with me. There was much in it to remember," Lady Newley said. "Although it was perplexing at first, we soon discovered the reason for your departure."

Henrietta continued the explanation. "It seems Miss Dougard and Miss Miller have no talent for sewing without you doing the work for them."

Annie let out the breath she'd been saving for months. "You know."

"We found out quick enough. I do apologize for the two of them. If they'd given you the credit you deserved, you'd still be with us."

Annie's breath caught in her throat, and she took a fresh one. "But begging your ladyship's pardon, my place is not *there*, but here."

"You work for the House of Paquin?"

"No, no. I work for Butterick Pattern Company in New York. I help design patterns for home sewers. We are here to see the latest fashion and adapt it for the everyday woman."

Lady Newley's eyebrows rose. "My, my. Annie the housemaid is no more. Enter, Annie the pattern artist."

As if the words had the power of a strong wind, Annie felt knocked down with the truth of it. She was no longer the servant girl, Annie. She was the businesswoman, Annie Wood. "Thank you for saying that, my lady."

"I'm not your lady anymore. You have become an American entrepreneur."

Annie had to laugh. "I work for an American entrepreneur. I have much to learn."

"And you will learn it," Lady Newley said.

"I thank you for your encouragement. It means a lot to me."

"As your encouragement always meant a lot to me," Henrietta said.

With a nod, Lady Newley stepped away. "I'll leave you two to chat. Very nice seeing you doing so well, Annie. I wish you all the best."

"She's such a generous woman," Annie said.

"That she is. I am lucky to have her as a mother."

For the first time, Annie realized Miss Henrietta had lost quite a bit of weight. "I must say you are looking very fine, miss."

Miss Henrietta put her hands on her hips. "No more letting out seams for me. I've lost so much weight that we are here to order an entirely new wardrobe."

"How exciting."

"I plan on enjoying every moment. For I am not just ordering a wardrobe but a trousseau."

Annie gasped. "You are betrothed?"

"I am. He's an old family friend. He knew me when I was fat, and tells me he doesn't care how large or small I am. He loves me for me."

"He sounds like a true gentleman."

"Actually, now he says I'm too slim."

They shared a laugh.

"I have you to thank for my weight loss *and* my fiancé."

Annie was taken aback. "How did I . . . ?"

"When you ran away I was forced to stand on my own. Your courage to go after what you wanted made me think about what I wanted. I had been resigned to being a twenty-nine-year-old overweight spinster living with my parents. You gave me courage to think of what I *could* be. I finally gained the willpower to lose the weight, which gave me confidence enough to go after a man who truly loved me. Hank is that man. And I am a new woman."

"I'm so, so happy for you," Annie said. "Truly I am."

"As I am happy for you. Come. The show is beginning."

⁓⁓⁓

The three Butterick workers sat behind Madame for the fashion show. The models of the House of Paquin strolled by, pausing to pose and pirouette so the women could study the gowns and feel the fine fabrics and trims.

"I like that one," Annie whispered to Maude as a model approached. The girl wore a gown of ecru silk covered with delicate lace. The neckline crossed, forming a V, and the sleeves had no seam at the shoulder but were draped from the same piece of fabric as the bodice. The back bodice was the same as the front, but the back of the dress sported full-length pieces of blue silk embroidered at the bottom with mauve roses and green leaves. The blue was pulled around the sides at the empire waistline in the front and culminated in a pink rosette bow.

Annie quickly made a tiny sketch on the piece of paper they'd each been given to note the models and dresses they liked. Madame warned them to be discreet, and with just a few strokes, Annie simplified the dress into what could become a sewing pattern. The lace and silk were exquisite and out of the price range of home sewers, but the ensemble could be created in a cotton lace with a faille silk for evening. Or even a solid skirt with a contrasting color for the back piece, suitable for everyday use.

Model after model promenaded by, filling Annie's mind—and her card—to overflowing. She felt like a child in a candy store. She couldn't get enough.

But then it was over, and it was time to move on to the next galerie. The patrons who would order their own couture ensembles stayed behind to choose fabrics and have measurements taken. As her group was leaving, Annie caught the eye of Miss Henrietta, who pointed at a lovely dress of sage-green satin. Her nod asked a question, and Annie nodded back, giving her approval.

Annie walked a little taller as she left the House of Paquin.

❧

The time in Paris flew by. Over the next week the Butterick contingent visited the Houses of Louise Chéruit, Georges Doeuillet, Jacques Doucet, Paul Poiret, Redfern & Sons, and Worth.

Annie's stack of sketches grew. Back in their room, she arranged them, making changes and notes for each design. She held a sketch for Maude to see. "I think we can adapt this skirt easily if we—"

Maude snatched the page away. "Enough of this."

"Just a few more minutes."

With a sweep of her hands over the bed, Maude collected the pages and stuffed them in a drawer. "Tonight is our last night in Paris. We are *not* going to waste one more minute working."

"What did you have in mind?"

"It's not what I have in mind, but what Sean has in mind."

"Which is?"

"Dinner at Café de la Paix."

It was the restaurant in the hotel. "Isn't it expensive?"

Maude put her hands on her hips. "We've saved our meal money by eating simply. Don't we deserve one fabulous French meal?"

All hesitance left her. Work was done. Now was the time to celebrate.

⁂

Annie perused the tray of desserts that was presented by the waiter. "Mademoiselle?"

Annie moaned as she sat back in her seat. "*Non merci.* I couldn't eat a bite."

"But you must," Sean said. "Just a bite." He looked to the waiter, held up one finger, and ordered, "*Crème brûlée à la vanilla, trois cuillères, s'il vous plaît.*"

After enjoying an overabundance of exquisitely prepared French onion soup, *foie gras*, lamb, sole, and asparagus, Annie took one last look at the café, searing it into her mind forever. The ceilings and walls were detailed with ivory and gold embellishments; the chandeliers glistened in the deliberately dimmed light. Their table was set amid fluted columns with intricate scrolls like ram's horns at the tops. She ran a hand across the starched white tablecloth. The smells of food, both savory and sweet, combined with the perfumes of the fine ladies seated around them. It was like being in a palace—an eating palace.

"Annie? Are you still with us?" Maude asked.

She blinked and brought herself back to the moment. "Again I wonder at being here. Has all this really happened to me?"

Sean reached across the table and took her hand. "It has. And the evening is not over."

"I'm not sure my senses can absorb any more. I'm quite done in. With us leaving tomorrow, don't you think we should pack and—"

"No," Sean said. "Not yet." He exchanged a look with Maude.

"No," she agreed. "Absolutely not. We can sleep on the train, or on the ship."

Sean nodded. "There is only one last night in Paris."

The dessert arrived and was set in the middle, between them. The waiter brought three spoons.

"You first," Sean said. "As it is your first crème brûlée."

"I don't even know what it is."

"It's a custard with caramelized sugar on top. Go ahead. Break into it."

The term *break* seemed odd but was immediately appropriate as Annie's spoon broke through the sugar shell and reached the rich custard below. They awaited her reaction.

"Mmm. I would deem it perfect, yet 'perfect' is too small a word."

They laughed and joined in the perfection.

∽

Since she was tired, Annie was not keen on Sean's idea of a stroll along the Seine River. Yet not wanting to be a killjoy, she agreed to go.

The river flowed by them quietly, as befitted the late hour. The sky was deep navy, and the stars glittered and competed with the streetlamps.

"Worth the time?" Sean asked.

She squeezed his arm. "Mmm."

"That's what you said about the dessert."

"It still applies. This is delicious. And perfect."

"I think I'll sit here," Maude said as they passed a bench. You two go on. I will catch up."

As Annie and Sean continued talking, she glanced back. "Should we leave her alone? It's late, and it's a big city."

Sean stopped and suddenly faced her. "I needed to be alone with you, because. . ." He took both her hands in his. "I love you, Annie Wood. And more than that, I adore you."

Her heart flipped.

He knelt on one knee and took out a ring. "Annie, would you spend the rest of your life with me, as my wife?"

The knowledge that this was actually happening—and happening in Paris—collided with doubt and confusion.

Sean noticed the delay in her answer and stood. "You're supposed to gleefully answer yes and take me in your arms."

She felt horrible for causing him any sort of pain, yet there was no way around it. "I do say yes, but. . ."

He let out a sigh and rubbed the space between his eyes. "But?"

She looked to the river, to anywhere but the condemnation in his eyes. "But I am not sure I'm ready to be a wife."

"Is there training for it? If so, *I* am not ready to be a husband."

"There's more to it than that. With being a wife comes being. . .a mother."

He took her hands and smiled. "I would hope so. For part of my hopes for a future involve children. Don't you want children?"

"I do, but. . ."

His smile faded. "There is that awful word again."

"But I don't want to be a mother any time soon." She pointed back in the direction of the fashion houses. "I enjoy my job; I enjoy the challenge of it, the creativity of it, and the independence of it."

"You can do that and be a mother."

"Can I? None of our female coworkers have children. Few are married."

"But it's done. I know it is."

She thought of something else. "Mrs. Sampson is being persistent about their offer to back me. How could I ever start my own fashion design business *and* be a wife *and* be a proper mother?"

He dropped her hands. "You choose your career over me."

He made it sound dreadful and final. "I choose to get established in whatever path I'm supposed to be on, and then—"

He stepped back. "You assume I'll wait."

A wave of panic assailed her, nudging her to step close and take his hands once again. "I hope you will wait. I pray you will. For I do want to marry you, Sean. I love you, too. With all my heart."

She watched his clenched jaw relax. His eyes were plaintive. "You do?"

"I do. Immeasurably."

He began to lower himself once again to one knee, but she stopped him. "The next time you ask, I want to be able to gleefully answer yes and fall into your arms."

He nodded, but there was a mournfulness to his face. She slipped her hand around his arm and they turned toward the Seine flowing past them, in spite of them.

❧

They joined Maude, and the trio walked back to the hotel. She looked at each of them expectantly. "So?"

"You knew?" Annie asked.

"Why do you think I hung back?" Not getting the answer from Annie, she turned to Sean. "So?"

"She answered, 'yes, but.'"

"That's no answer."

"That's what I thought," he said.

Annie stopped their walking. "It *is* an answer. It's all the answer I can give right now. I thought you understood."

"Understanding and liking are two different things," Sean said. "Come now. We have packing to do."

They walked back amid silence. And regret.

⊗∽

"I can't believe you didn't say yes to him," Maude said as she and Annie finished their packing.

"I explained it to you." Annie thought of another point in her favor. "His family is wonderful, and mine is. . .negligible. I don't deserve him."

"No, you don't. But you will not give him up using those lame excuses."

Maude was right. Annie was trying to rationalize what couldn't be rationalized. "I don't know what else to say."

"I think you've said enough. Just keep in mind that Sean is a remarkable, handsome man. Don't delay so long that you lose him."

Annie dropped a blouse she'd been folding. "You think there's a chance of that?"

"He wants to marry you now. You're putting him off because of what might happen in the future. One is a known, and one is an unknown. Just be careful you don't lose both."

Annie sat on the bed, the blouse hanging from a hand. "So you're saying I'm wrong in wanting to wait for marriage?"

Maude sat beside her. "I'm saying that none of us know the extent of our days."

"That's a pleasant thought."

Maude shrugged. "Just think about it."

Annie knew she would think of little else.

CHAPTER TWENTY-NINE

Annie enjoyed being a world traveler, yet the logistics were daunting. A carriage from the hotel to the Gare Saint Lazare train station, a train to Cherbourg, and then the *Titanic* to New York City. She was glad the fashion shows were behind them. Yet the promise of shipboard discussions with Mrs. Sampson remained. She appreciated the attention yet didn't look forward to being mollycoddled. Annie fondly remembered her other voyage, when she and Maude whiled away their time playing cards, reading books, and gazing at the sea from deck chairs.

A porter transferred their luggage from a taxi to a rolling cart to take inside the enormous train station, with instructions to hurry because they hadn't given themselves enough time. Madame had insisted on taking the first taxi with her enormous collection of luggage, so Annie, Maude, and Sean had no time to spare. Yet on a whim Annie intervened. "I can carry my own on board, thank you."

"Why don't you let him take care of it?" Maude asked.

"I just have this one case. It has all my sketches and notes in it. I don't know what I'd do if it got lost."

"Lost between here and there," Maude said, pointing toward the platform. Annie shrugged.

Maude sighed dramatically. "I suppose now I'll have to do the same."

"Let me get yours and mine," Sean said.

Surprising them all, another carriage pulled up and Mr. and Mrs. Sampson emerged. They had no choice but to use a cart, for they had been in Europe all winter, with the luggage to prove it.

Mrs. Sampson swept toward them. "I wish I could get over the deplorable habit of being tardy, but here we are at the last minute." She took a breath. "I am ever so ready to go home. One can only be cosmopolitan so long. Let us proceed to the waiting hall."

Without meaning to, the young travelers were swept into her wake. They followed her through the arched doorways into the chaos that was the waiting area. Travelers of all sorts and sizes bumped against each other trying to get from here to there, all intent on the logistics of their journeys.

Sean checked the clock. "We only have five minutes until boarding."

"I despise cutting things so close," Maude said.

"You can thank Madame for—"

Annie cut off her sentence when she heard a child crying. She looked through the crowd and saw a boy of about six or seven, searching for someone. His cheeks were tear stained, his call of "*Maman? Maman!*" desperate. He looked like a younger Danny.

She rushed toward him. "What's wrong?"

The boy looked up at her, confused. Of course. He couldn't understand her. Since Sean could speak French, she called him over. "Shh. It will be all right, little one," she said, kneeling down to his level. To Sean she said, "Ask him what's wrong."

"*Quel est le problème?*" Sean asked.

The boy let out an agitated discourse, pointing this way and that.

Mrs. Sampson and Maude joined them. Mrs. Sampson listened intently. "His mother is missing? And she's expecting a baby?" she asked Sean.

"Seems so," Sean said. He put a hand on the boy's shoulder, trying to calm him. "*Il sera très bien. Ne vous inquiétez pas. Nous trouverons votre mère.*"

Suddenly there were shouts of, "*En voiture!*"

They all stood erect and looked toward the train. They were boarding.

"Go on ahead," Annie told the others. "I'll stay with the boy until he finds his mother."

"But you can't speak French," Sean said. "And I'm not leaving you alone."

"And I'm not going on the train without either of you," Maude said.

"Well, gracious sakes," Mrs. Sampson said. "You stay, we stay. Harold, go see if you can get our luggage off."

"What if I can't?"

"We'll catch up to it in Cherbourg."

Annie looked over the crowd and spotted Madame's face in the window of the train. She and Sean ran toward her. "Madame, we are staying behind to help a boy find his mother."

"What?"

Annie shook her head. "We need to help a boy."

"Zat is absurd. Let someone else help him."

Sean shook his head. "But no one else *was* helping him. He needs us—for a short while."

"Ze ship will not wait," Madame said.

Sean and Annie exchanged a look, and then Sean said, "Then we will board another ship."

Annie was ever so proud of him. "Go on, madame. We will see you in New York."

Madame looked past them. "Zis is ridiculous. You don't know ze boy. Let one of ze officials handle it."

That was an option, but Annie felt an intense nudge to stick with it to the end. "It will be all right. Let us do this. We must do this."

Madame rolled her eyes. "You are all ridiculous." The train began to move. She dismissed them with a flip of her hand.

Annie's heart beat wildly in her throat. What were they doing? It didn't make sense.

Sean took her arm. "We've made our choice. Let's see it through."

They returned to the boy, who was sitting next to Mrs. Sampson on a bench.

"Was Madame upset?" Maude asked.

"Confused," Annie said. "You realize we will probably miss the ship and have to take another."

"*C'est la vie*," Mrs. Sampson said. "It won't be the first time. Two years ago we missed a ship that was taking us from Naples to Lisbon because I wasn't feeling well. When we boarded another ship a week later we met the nicest couple from Barcelona. We still correspond."

Annie felt an odd comfort in the story. Whatever her feelings, what was done was done.

Mr. Sampson returned from the platform. "It's too late. Our luggage is going on without us."

"So be it," Mrs. Sampson said.

Suddenly Annie looked down at the luggage that she, Sean, and Maude had taken from the trolley. "It's good we have ours."

"Us staying behind. . .it's like it was meant to be," Maude said.

It was. But enough about luggage. "Have you learned any more about the boy's mother and where she might be?"

"His name is André," Mrs. Sampson said. "He and his mother were waiting for his father to arrive from Calais. His mother said she wasn't feeling well, and told the boy to wait for her. But she didn't come back."

"I checked the ladies'," Maude said. "No expectant mothers in there."

Mr. Sampson glanced at his pocket watch. "The father's train should arrive within the half hour."

"Good," Maude said. "Then he will take care of it."

Annie shook her head. Oddly, she felt an extreme sense of urgency. "But that may be too late."

"Too late for what?"

The baby? "We need to search for the mother. Get the porters to help. We stayed here for a reason. *She* needs us, too." They nodded in agreement, but just before they spread out, Annie felt a nudge to instigate something she'd never done before. "Stop a moment. We need to pray."

The contingent bowed their heads and each said a silent prayer. André crossed himself.

Mrs. Sampson stayed with the boy, and the rest of them fanned out over the enormous depot, gathering support from railway workers along the way. Even a gendarme became involved.

Annie looked again in the ladies', asking various women if they'd seen an expectant mother. Having no luck, she tried to imagine about how a very pregnant woman would react if she didn't feel well. Or if—even worse—she felt the baby coming.

She would seek a quiet place. A place to sit or lie down.

Annie walked the length of the waiting hall, peering through every archway. She was about to turn back when she heard a moan.

There she was! The woman was on the floor, her back to the wall, curled in pain, hidden from sight by a stack of crates. Annie knelt beside her. "Madame?"

The woman's eyes flashed with relief. She took hold of Annie's arm and pointed to her stomach. "*Le bébé s'en vient! Aide-moi!*"

"The baby. It's coming?"

"Le bébé!"

Annie stood. The woman grabbed at her, obviously afraid she would leave. Annie patted her hand. "I'll get help." She remembered a French word. "*Aide.*"

The woman nodded. "*Merci.*"

Annie stepped onto the platform and saw Sean talking to a couple in the crowd. "Sean! She's here! She's having the baby. Get help!"

Sean nodded and was off. Annie returned to the woman and sat beside her. She removed her jacket, rolled it up, and placed it under her head. She stroked her hair, which was matted with perspiration.

Suddenly the woman's eyes grew wide and panicked, and she looked out toward the platform. "*Où est mon fils? Mon fils!*"

Annie realized she must be asking about her son. "Your boy? *Garçon?*"

The woman nodded.

Annie pressed her hands down, trying to portray calm. "He's safe. He's all right. Très bien."

The woman nodded then without warning grabbed her stomach and moaned loudly. Her face contorted and her entire body tensed. She held Annie's hand so tightly it caused pain.

"Hold on, hold on!"

Please God, help mother and baby be all right.

⁂

A doctor who'd been waiting to board a train came to the rescue and delivered the baby girl right there on the floor where Annie had found her—found Maria.

Annie witnessed the entire birth because Maria insisted she stay with her. She'd never even been around a woman who was expecting, much less be there at the birth, but Maria and the doctor did the work. Annie held her hand, mopped her brow, and offered reassuring words that needed no translation.

The baby was born and took her first breath then wailed at being forced out of her warm and dark cocoon into the cold and light. Annie cried happy tears with Maria.

Accompanying the miracle were waves of gratitude and praise to God, not just for the new life and the health of the mother, but for the sacred experience Annie had been allowed to share.

Annie left Maria's side and helped the doctor with the baby. A blanket, towels, and a bucket of water had been procured from somewhere, and once the cord was cut, Annie set the baby on a crate to wash her. The little girl squirmed, her fingers and arms spread wide as if she were testing her new limits. Once the baby was clean, Annie wrapped her in warmth and held her close, bouncing to calm her. For a brief moment, the baby opened her eyes. "Hello there," Annie whispered. "Welcome."

Maria held out her hands, needing to hold what she had nurtured for nine months. Annie placed the baby in her arms. Maria cuddled and cooed at her, and Annie witnessed an instant love between mother and child. An everlasting love.

Suddenly a man came around the stack of crates that had offered the only privacy to the moment and ran to his wife and daughter. The doctor was also finished and washed his hands in the bucket. "You did well to help me, miss."

Annie could only nod. Her part was over. She moved to leave, but the husband called to her. "Mademoiselle, *attendez!*"

Annie turned back to them.

"*Comment vous appelez-vous?*" he asked, pointing at her. "*Le nom?*"

She pointed at herself. "Annie."

He nodded and exchanged a look with his wife. She pointed at the baby then said, "Annie."

They were naming the baby after her? Annie put a hand to her mouth and nodded. "*Merci.*"

He nodded his head and made a motion to include his whole family. "*Merci beaucoup.*" Then he added, "*Que Dieu vous bénisse*" and crossed himself.

She guessed at his words. "May God bless you, too."

Behind her André approached tentatively. His father motioned him over, and the family was fully united. Annie slipped into the crowd.

"A girl?" Mrs. Sampson asked.

"Her name is Annie."

"They named her after you?" Maude asked.

Suddenly Annie's emotions got the better of her, and she began to sob. Sean pulled her into his arms.

❧

While the baby was being born, Mr. Sampson made arrangements for passage on another ship and booked three rooms at a nearby hotel—at his expense. They enjoyed a light supper together, but Annie remembered little of it. She walked through the rest of the day and evening in a happy daze. The others respected her distance and talked around her, but their voices were vague, as though she were hearing them from the next room.

When it was time to retire, she went through the motions of her evening toilette by rote—and Maude had to help her out of her bodice when she forgot to unbutton the cuffs.

In her nightdress she sat upon the bed and found she could go no further without full release. "I witnessed a baby being born," she said.

Maude paused in the braiding of her hair. "I know."

"A new life, right there in the train station."

"Not ideal. Poor woman."

Annie blinked, bringing herself fully into the moment. "Fully ideal," she said with a shake of her head. "As if it was meant to be."

"The baby was meant to be born in a corner of a train station, on a dirty floor?"

Annie looked to the ceiling. It was hard to explain. "What if I hadn't heard André crying? What if we hadn't understood his mother was missing? What if we hadn't found her in time?"

"Someone else would have helped. Maybe."

"Maybe. But *they* didn't. We did."

"We missed our train and a chance to sail on the largest ship in the world. I was looking forward to being on the maiden voyage of the *Titanic*. It's been much talked about and is supposedly enormous and very lavish."

Maude was missing the point. Annie placed a fist at her stomach. "I feel very strongly that everything that happened today happened for a reason."

Maude got in her bed and pulled the covers up. "I guess we'll never know, will we?"

CHAPTER THIRTY

Finally!

The travelers stood at the rail as their ship left the dock at Cherbourg. They were only two days tardy from their previous schedule, but it seemed as though a lifetime had passed between April 10—and the birth of little Annie—and today.

And though they weren't experiencing the excitement of being on the luxurious *Titanic*, their accommodations were first-class. Literally. For Mr. Sampson had booked the young people two first-class cabins. Being pampered started out as a bit of a lark, but it soon revealed its lesser merits.

Looking around at the exquisite attire of the other passengers, Annie felt horribly underdressed. "We don't belong here, with these toffs."

Mrs. Sampson shooed the thought away. "As I know these 'toffs,' I also know that a little frippery and finery is not a measure of good character. You fit in with the best of them, Annie, and you overshadow the worst."

Annie laughed. "You do have a talent for making me feel right about myself."

Mrs. Sampson winked. "Ah, but I have ulterior motives, you know."

"I know."

"We'll talk at dinner." She turned to her husband. "Come, Harold. Let's take a stroll and leave these young people to wonder after us."

As soon as they left, Sean said, "She *is* eccentric."

"That she is," Maude said.

"But an eccentric woman of good character," Annie said. "They wouldn't have had to stay behind when we found André."

"I've thought about that," Maude said. "I do hope Madame is enjoying her voyage without us." There was sarcasm in her voice.

"We rarely saw her on the trip over," Annie pointed out. "She probably hasn't realized we're absent."

Maude faced away from the sea. "I for one don't miss her, either. What do you say we stir up some mischief in the game room?"

"Gaming parlor," Annie corrected. "We're first-class now."

Maude affected a haughty stance and flipped her hand. "Come on, then. Let us dally and dawdle with the other upper crusts."

❧

Their dinner in the first-class dining room rivaled their dinner at Café de la Paix. Six courses were served by white-gloved footmen. At first Annie thought it impossible that she would have the capacity to eat all the courses, but because of the refined pace of the service, she managed to enjoy each item—including Charlotte Russe for dessert. She'd seen the cook at Crompton Hall create the ladyfinger-and-fruit-cream delicacy but had never been allowed to taste it. Until now.

She savored every bite and tried not to close her eyes and moan at its scrumptiousness.

Tried and failed. "This is heavenly."

"Would you like another?" Mrs. Sampson asked. "It's fully within the concept of no limits stated in the first-class rule book."

"There's a rule book?" Mr. Sampson asked.

"Unwritten, dear one, but valid just the same."

"This one helping is plenty," Annie said. "It will more than suffice."

Mrs. Sampson laughed. "Well, then." She waved to the waiter to remove her plate. "We have tippy-toed through conversations involving all things but the conversation I've been longing to have regarding your future."

Her husband shook his head. "Subtlety is not my wife's strong suit."

"I see no need," she said. "Annie knows the plans we have for her. We only need her yes and the world will fall at her feet."

"My," Maude said. "All that for a yes? But may I ask what the question is?"

Mrs. Sampson looked confused. "You haven't shared with your best friend?"

Annie shook her head, feeling guilty for it.

"Shared what?" Maude asked.

Mrs. Sampson did the honors. "Harold and I have offered financial backing and support for Annie to start her own fashion house, focusing on function over fad."

Maude blinked, and Annie could almost see her mind whirling. "I'll set aside my disappointment that you've kept me in the dark to advise you to say yes, Annie. If you don't, I will."

Mrs. Sampson got an odd look on her face then said, "Actually, I think that would be a fine idea. Why don't both you and Sean join Annie in her new venture?"

The notion beamed upon the table like a ray of sunlight sent from God. What had seemed gray and cloudy now glowed with promise. "You'd do that?" Annie asked. "You'd let all three of us work together and open a design shop?"

"'Shop' is too meager a word, but yes," Mrs. Sampson said with a glance to her husband. "I think that would be a capital idea. Don't you, my dear?"

Mr. Sampson nodded and turned his coffee spoon over and over against the tablecloth. "I don't see why not. From what I've heard, you all have different talents to bring to the venture."

Sean raised a hand. "It's true that I have sales experience, and Maude—"

Maude interrupted. "I know dress construction better than anyone on the planet."

Mrs. Sampson laughed. "Confidence. I like that."

Mr. Sampson set the spoon aside and leaned forward. "So with the two of you we have sales and construction, and Annie brings design and illustration talent. With our financial backing and connections, it sounds like the makings of a strong and vibrant company."

"Hear, hear!" Mrs. Sampson said.

Sean looked at Annie. "Seeing the idea in this new light, as a larger whole. . . I never thought I'd say this, but it *would* be exciting to be a part of something totally new."

Annie couldn't believe what she was hearing. She'd never imagined the Sampsons would consider including Sean and Maude, but she now realized she couldn't imagine the venture without them. Yet to draw them into something that would pluck them out of the positions they'd held for years. . . "Are you sure?" she asked her friends. "It's an enormous risk. I am still new to this business. You two have far more experience, and your careers are well established. You'd be giving up much more than I." She looked directly at Sean. "When I previously mentioned this offer you seemed against it."

He bit his lip. "I wanted us to be together at Butterick. I didn't want to lose you."

Mrs. Sampson touched his arm. "And now you will be together." She turned her attention back to Annie. "You have intrinsic talent, my dear. It's a gift recently discovered, but a gift nonetheless."

Annie felt herself blush at the flattery and the opportunity. "This newest discussion has flipped the world on its axis."

"Because it's showing its full form, it's falling into place," Mrs. Sampson said. "Seeing you at the fashion show and having this special time on the ship together are blessings from God. I do not believe in coincidence."

"Nor do I," said her husband. "Things happen for a reason."

"That's what you said last night, Annie," Maude said. "All this is happening for a reason. Maybe this is the reason."

Mrs. Sampson extended her hands, palms up, presenting Annie the world. Her face was expectant.

Annie looked to Sean. "Are you truly for this?"

He let out a long sigh. "Oddly, I think I am. But it all hangs on you, Annie. The seed was planted with you."

"Indeed," Mrs. Sampson said. "You are the seed."

"Which makes you the sun?" she asked.

Mrs. Sampson chuckled. "I'll let Harold be the sun. I'll be the rain." She raised her right hand. "We promise to give you just enough sun and rain to thrive. No more, no less."

Annie was overwhelmed. She was in front of yet another door, being offered the chance to open it and step through, or back away. Had all the doors in her life been gifts from God, a series of chances to exercise the free will He championed?

"I've had so many doors," she said to herself.

"Doors?" Mrs. Sampson asked.

Annie pulled her thoughts together. "Since I've come to America I've been offered one door after another: leaving service, finding a job at Macy's, moving to Edna's, getting the job at Butterick, and traveling to Paris. And now this." Mrs. Sampson started to speak, but Annie stopped her with a hand. "It's not just a matter of the doors being opened for me, but the fact that every door that opened seemed to shut once I was through it."

"There's no going back," Sean said softly.

"I don't think there is—which is why this decision is so important, and why I haven't taken it lightly." *And why I'm waiting for Your direction, Lord.*

Everyone at the table nodded.

"It's your choice," Sean said. "I go where you go."

"Me, too," Maude said.

Annie looked into the eyes of her friends. It *was* up to her. Yet the stakes were far higher than they were when she was deciding only for herself. Her dearest friends were offering themselves to her, depending on her to take this leap together.

She drew in a long breath, and held it a moment. *Lord? Yes?*

As she exhaled she found herself saying, "Yes. I say yes."

⁂

Not a single card game was played.

There was no time. After agreeing to start their own design company, the five partners put their heads together to make a plan. To start something from nothing was daunting. Where would they begin?

Mrs. Sampson offered an idea to gather regular women together and get their opinions as to how they would like their clothes to look and function. The idea was a good one, for if they were going to design for the masses, they needed to *ask* the masses.

The third day into their voyage they sat around a table in the ship's first-class lounge, and Maude took notes. "Who is our customer? Working women? The wives of merchants and middle-class families? Or your set?" She looked to the Sampsons.

Mrs. Sampson tapped her finger on the table. "We're not sure. We want to set women free of frivolous fashion, yet we need to make it affordable."

"But couture clothing is not affordable," Annie said. "Far from it."

Sean nodded. "To keep costs down it will have to be manufactured, not hand sewn."

Annie's mind swam. "Will stores like Macy's take it on?"

Mrs. Sampson nodded. "That's where Sean's expertise will come in as our salesman. Plus, we can sell to other department stores like Gimbel's, Henri Bendel, Bergdorf Goodman, Lord and Taylor—"

Suddenly the captain of the ship entered the room along with a large gathering of passengers, each noisily vying for his attention.

"What's going on?" Maude asked.

"Let's find out." Mrs. Sampson pushed back her chair.

"Please, ladies and gentlemen," the captain said from the middle of the lounge. "I assure you there is nothing to worry about."

Annie asked a woman nearby, "What are we not to worry about?"

"Last night another ship on the White Star line hit an iceberg and—"

"Which ship?"

"The *Titanic*."

Annie's entire body gasped. "We were supposed to be on that ship!" She spread the news to the others in her party, and they all moved closer to the captain to get details.

"Is the ship being repaired?" Mr. Sampson asked.

"Her wireless installation enabled her to call for help. With this means of communication, the terrible isolation of her mid-ocean position was negated. Every ship within range hurried to her assistance, and all risk of graver loss of life was averted."

"'Graver loss of life'?" someone asked.

"I assure you, all is well," he said.

"It doesn't sound well," Mrs. Sampson said.

The captain pressed his hands downward, trying to calm them. "A smaller ship than the *Titanic* might well have succumbed to the concussion caused by striking the iceberg. I believe this is proof that the increased size of our modern ships is a vital achievement."

"Big or not, it still struck an iceberg."

"But"—the captain said, raising a finger—"the *Titanic* is still afloat and has escaped without any loss of life."

This last didn't make sense. "You mentioned 'graver loss of life,'" Annie pointed out. "That means there were fatalities."

By now the crowd had grown to many dozen.

"Now, now. Do not jump to conclusions, ladies and gentlemen. I assure you the most violent collision means the crumpling of her bow and perhaps the filling of her forward compartments, at the worst. But with her gigantic size and the system of watertight doors in her bulkheads—that can be closed from the bridge—there is nothing to worry about. Modern methods of ship construction have been put to the most crucial test that can possibly be imagined, and they have triumphed. The *Titanic*'s situation is fresh proof of the safety of the modern steam vessel, a free illustration of the dominance that man has established over the most treacherous forces of nature. Now go back to your enjoyment of this fine vessel. I assure you we shall keep you informed of further news."

He left, but the crowd did not.

"I wonder how Madame is handling this," Maude asked.

"She would not appreciate any alteration to her entertainments," Annie said.

"Or meals," Maude added.

They laughed—though softly. For there *was* the chance their levity was misplaced. They returned to their table, but all thoughts of planning a new business were forgotten.

⚬⚬

The moon shone brightly as Annie stood with Sean and Maude at the railing. They gazed out to sea. Somewhere to the west, the *Titanic* had hit an iceberg.

"We're all so quiet," Sean said.

"I can't get it out of my head," Annie said. "I can't imagine such a terrifying event. There must have been utter chaos."

"And fear," Maude added. "I'm sure the passengers had no idea what was going on at first."

"Madame doesn't like not knowing what's going on," Annie said.

Her comment sparked another round of silence. Then Sean said, "I wonder if all the passengers have been taken to New York by now."

"Madame will have such a story to tell once we get back."

"But for a little boy in a train station, it could have been our story," Maude said.

Sean leaned his back against the railing. "Speaking of, how are we going to tell Butterick we're quitting? Do we do it all in one day?"

Annie looked down at the water below. "I feel dreadful quitting the job just months after I started."

"*Are* we quitting immediately?" Maude asked. "Or are we going to wait until our plans are more firmly set in place?"

"I choose the latter," Sean said.

Annie was a bit put off. "Don't you believe it will happen? Don't you trust the Sampsons?"

"Yes, to both questions," Sean said. "But there are a lot of details to sort through."

Annie agreed. "I do want to finalize the sketches we're bringing back from Paris for Butterick. The company paid our way there. We need to make sure the work is completed well. We owe them that."

"I agree," Maude said. "One step at a time."

As if on cue, they all stepped away from the railing. "Good night, then," Maude said.

When Maude left them alone, Sean drew Annie into his arms, and she heard the beating of his heart. "I hope we're doing the right thing," she said against his chest.

She felt him nod. "We need to pray, to make sure we're doing what God wants us to do."

Annie pulled back to see his face in the moonlight. "I prayed during that dinner when we all agreed. I never imagined you would be a part of it, and then suddenly, you were. All that was left was for me to give the nod."

"I never expected any of it," Sean said. "And then the opportunity was suddenly set before me."

Annie suffered a moment of doubt. "Were we all drawn into the excitement of the idea? Is it the right thing to do, or are the Sampsons merely skilled in the art of persuasion?"

"That's what we need to figure out." He put his finger beneath her chin. "God will guide us if we ask."

"Ask for guidance and pray for the passengers on the *Titanic*."

"Agreed. Now, let us try to get some sleep."

Annie guessed the latter would be the harder task.

CHAPTER THIRTY-ONE

Annie, you must eat," Mrs. Sampson said at breakfast.

"If you don't like the eggs, request something else," Mr. Sampson said. "Toast? Porridge?"

To appease them, Annie ordered some toast. She simply wasn't hungry. The toast was quickly brought, and Annie nibbled at a corner.

Mrs. Sampson put down her fork. "Really, Annie. What is the matter this morning?"

A list of possibilities streamed through her mind. She landed on one. "Logistics."

"Of the business?"

She nodded. "It's so complicated. Starting from nothing, resigning our positions... It's such a gamble."

"That it is," Mr. Sampson said. "But to gain much you must risk much. The Bible tells us that whoever is given much shall be asked to do much." He spread his hands, allowing the words to speak volumes.

"You're right. Forgive my doubt and my jumbled thoughts. What with the close call of us being on the *Titanic*—"

"Such a blessing we weren't," Mrs. Sampson pointed out.

"Such a blessing," Annie agreed.

"The captain said that everyone on the ship was rescued. All is well," Maude said.

Annie was being silly—and ungrateful. "I'm sorry to put a damper on the day. I promise to be all joy and anticipation from now—"

She was interrupted by a shriek coming from the hall.

Mr. Sampson and Sean rose. But before they could check on it, a man burst into the dining room and shouted for all to hear, "The *Titanic* sank! Hundreds are dead! They are compiling a list of the victims!"

Those in the dining room stood, and spatterings of disbelieving, panicked conversation intertwined.

"The *Titanic* was unsinkable. It can't sink."

"Victims! Hundreds?"

"I know people on that ship!"

"The captain said there were no fatalities!"

"Could this happen to us?"

The comments were universal, the questions frightening.

"Madame," Annie said.

"And our friends," Mrs. Sampson said. "Astor, Molly, the Strauses. Guggenheim."

"Mr. and Mrs. Straus?" Annie asked. "From Macy's?"

She nodded. "We ran into them in Nice and they said they were going back on our ship."

"Our ship," Sean said. "That was supposed to be our ship."

Maude put a hand to her mouth. Mrs. Sampson sat down. Annie couldn't move, frozen by the knowledge that their ship had gone down into the dark depths of the endless sea. "Would we have survived?" she asked aloud.

Mr. Sampson held Annie's chair for her to be seated. "Let's not jump to conclusions. The first news from the captain said everything was under control. This one says the opposite. One of them is wrong."

"But which one?" Maude asked.

"Let me see what I can find out. Return to your breakfast."

"Surely you jest, Harold," his wife said.

With a shrug he left them. All thoughts of food were forgotten.

Sean held out his hands. "Let us pray, ladies. Pray."

⁜

The food was taken away, but the dining room was full. People stood in small groups, comparing fears, astonishment, and disbelief instead of their usual stories of villas, museums, and European soirees. There was a desperate need for facts yet an oppressive dread. Each minute that passed without Mr. Sampson's return added to the burden.

Finally he returned with a group of men who had left to gather news. Everyone stopped talking. All eyes fell on them.

Mr. Sampson stepped forward to speak for the group. His face was ashen, his forehead tight. Annie felt a wave of shivers course through her body.

"Yesterday's information was horribly false. The latest news is that the

Titanic sank to the bottom of the ocean, and of the 2,358 souls on board over 1,500 people are missing."

There was a gasp, and many fell upon chairs for support. Some began to wail.

Another man stepped forward to add, "There were only enough lifeboats for 970 people, so even if. . ." He stepped back and muttered, "It's a travesty. The passengers were doomed from the start."

Mr. Sampson moved to their table, taking his wife in his arms.

"Our friends, Harold. Are they saved or not?" she asked.

"There are lists coming out, but none available over the wireless. We won't know until we land in New York."

"Poor Madame," Maude said.

"If she's alive," Sean said.

"Sean!" Maude said. "Don't say that."

"How can I not say that?"

Mr. Sampson had other news. "I sent a telegram to my office, asking after your Madame LeFleur, Mrs. Brown, Astor, Guggenheim, and the Strauses."

"Thank you, dear," his wife said. "I'm not sure I want to know the truth, yet not knowing is its own torture."

Annie heard the voices of the room rise and fade like the waves of the ocean around them. Their speculation was futile. There was no praying for the safety of those on board. Their fates were already decided.

As are yours.

She startled at the thought. "We were saved," she said softly.

"What?" Sean asked.

She looked at each one. "We were saved. If we had not missed our train we would be on that ship. We might have been among the missing. The dead."

Sean took her hand. "If you had not heard André's cries. If you had not helped him. . ."

"Helped his mother," Mrs. Sampson said.

"We owe our lives to you, Annie," Maude said.

Annie shook her head vehemently. "Don't place that on me."

"It's a compliment."

"But it doesn't belong to me. God did it. He gave us the opportunity to help the boy."

"But we wouldn't have had to accept it," Mr. Sampson said. "You could have ignored him. We could have felt sorry for him but left him to someone else because we had a train to catch."

"A ship to catch," Maude said.

The what-ifs assailed them. Then Annie remembered something else. "Madame LeFleur told Sean and me to leave the boy's problem to others."

"What if we'd followed her direction?" Sean said.

"What if I hadn't heard him in the first place? After all, it was a busy, noisy train station."

"What if we hadn't understood what he said about his mother?"

"What if we hadn't chosen to hunt for her?"

"What if we'd given up, and boarded that train?"

"What if Madame had gotten off the train with us?"

"What if little Annie hadn't been born right then, delaying us just long enough?"

This last comment stopped the questions. The timing of the events at the train station solidified the sobering conclusion that they had unknowingly been offered a way to be saved. Plus, they reached the equally sobering conclusion that if they hadn't said yes, they might all be dead in the cold, black water of the Atlantic.

The captain entered the dining room with a man wearing a clerical collar. "Reverend Benson would like to lead us in prayer before he visits the other areas of the ship to do the same."

The reverend nodded. "Let us pray."

What more could they do?

<hr>

The friends moved onto the decks, strolling without seeing, simply needing to walk lest the news sink too deeply into their consciousness if they remained still. Perhaps the fresh air would awaken them from their awful nightmare.

A steward approached Mr. Sampson. "A telegram, sir."

Mrs. Sampson put her hands on her heart. "Oh dear. An answer to your query?"

Her husband rubbed a hand roughly over his mouth then expelled a breath. He opened the envelope, read the news, and then reread it out loud in a voice that quavered with emotion. "Astor, Guggenheim, LeFleur, and Strauses gone. Brown saved."

Annie grabbed the telegram away from him, needing to see the words. Unfortunately, they could not be denied.

Maude gripped Sean's arm. "Madame is dead? It can't be."

Annie's memories rushed back to the times she'd spoken with Mr. Straus during her time at Macy's. "Mr. Straus was the kindest of men. He took an interest in me. He showed compassion when Danny was killed. He can't be dead." She looked at the list. "His wife, too?"

Mrs. Sampson cried against her husband's chest. "A finer couple you could never know," Mr. Sampson said.

Annie couldn't take anymore. She ran away, along the promenade, bumping into people as she passed.

"Annie!" Sean ran after her.

She let him catch up to her and fell into his arms. "Why? Why?"

He stroked her head. "I don't know why they died. There is no sense to it."

She pulled away from him. "Not why did they die, but why did we live? If good people like Madame and Mr. Straus can die, and important people like Mr. Astor and Mr. Guggenheim, then why were we saved? Sean, tell me! Why were we saved when important people—and good people—died?"

He led her inside where it was warm and sat beside her on a settee. He kept his arm wrapped around her, and she leaned against him, feeling as if she would fully falter without his presence.

"I have no answers for you, Annie."

She sat erect to fully see him. "Why did God let this happen? What purpose could it serve?"

Sean didn't answer but shook his head back and forth, back and forth. Finally he said, "Only He knows."

Annie burst from her seat. "Why should we worship God if He causes such tragedy to so many people?"

"I'm not sure He caused it. Perhaps there were choices other people made that caused the accident. Not having enough lifeboats was a choice someone made."

"He created the iceberg."

"But did the ship sail carelessly? There are a myriad of factors and choices that were made." Sean pulled her down beside him again. "Just as we made the choice to help André, so others made their own choices."

"You're making it too simple."

"The truth remains: it simply *is*. What happened to them, happened to them. What happened to us, happened to us. The biggest choice we have now is deciding what we do with our second chance."

Annie looked up and saw Maude and the Sampsons coming toward them. "Are you all right?" Mrs. Sampson asked.

"Silly question, my sweet," Mr. Sampson said. "None of us are all right. Lives were lost."

"And we were supposed to be on that ship," Maude said.

Annie's mind cleared. "Actually, no we weren't. Beyond our grief, *that* is what we must deal with."

Maude sat in a nearby chair. "Annie, do you remember what I said about not knowing the extent of our days?"

"I do remember."

"That is the gist of it, isn't it?" Maude said. "We don't know how long we have."

"We are alive now," Mrs. Sampson added.

Suddenly Annie heard Danny's voice inside her head. *"Make the most of today!"* She closed her eyes and could see him smiling at her with his impish grin. How wise he'd been for one so young. What a joy he'd been. What a gift.

She stood and faced the others. "My friend Danny had more life in him at the age of thirteen than people five times his age. He always told me to live for today. Don't waste a moment. *That* is why we were saved. To live. To grab hold of life and live it to its fullest each and every day."

"A commendable idea," Mrs. Sampson said.

"For what more can we do?" her husband said.

With a sudden clarity Annie knew exactly what could be done—what should be done. All that had happened since her arrival in America gathered together like a crowd of events and people and conversations. The murmurings of the others faded into a dull hum as her mind attended the gathering.

She remembered the Kidds who gave her a job and rescued her from a family where she was told she had no worth. They brought her to the United States—which was the start of everything. Without that trip, none of the rest would have happened. She thought about the lady's maids who'd been inept at sewing. If they hadn't been lacking that talent, Annie would never have been given the opportunity to step up and learn. And their betrayal, though hurtful, had been the impetus needed to move her out of a life as a servant into the streets of New York City. Into the American dream.

With a start she remembered how *her* dream had been to be a lady's maid. How meager that dream seemed now. And how thankful she was that God had closed that door and forced her out into the new and frightening world of New York City.

Without that door closing I would still be a housemaid. How cocky she'd been, thinking she knew best. How ignorant she'd been about life and God.

A wave of gratitude swept over her. *Thank You, Lord, for propelling me into the world and giving me a new dream—Your dream for my life. Thank You for getting my attention and showing me how Your way is the best way.*

She thought of Danny and Iris, her dear friends who'd had dreams of their own. And the kind Tuttles who had taken them in and eventually provided Iris the family and purpose she longed for and so desperately needed.

But what of Danny's dream? Annie thought of Danny's exuberance and love of adventure. His words would stay with her the rest of her life. She would always be thankful for his friendship and wisdom. There was no explaining his life being cut short, but she took comfort in knowing he was fully exploring the adventures of heaven.

Her thoughts clouded with dark memories of the torment, assault, and murder caused by Grasston. Where Danny elicited all things good, Grasston was the epitome of evil. There was satisfaction in his death in that he would not bother anyone ever again. She pushed all thoughts of him into a far corner of her mind. He didn't deserve her time. Yet even his presence had been important, for he had helped her leave her girlhood behind and become a woman.

She returned to the thoughts that stood at the forefront. Sunny memories of Mr. Straus and working at Macy's where she met friends she would have forever: Mrs. MacDonald, Edna, and even Mildred. She smiled when she thought of Edna, whom she loved as a mother. She would have so much to tell her about this trip *and* the business opportunity that was in the future.

Annie had a sudden thought. Surely there was a place for Edna in the new business. . . .

During Annie's time at Macy's she'd learned how to sew and had met Sean, who'd brought her to Butterick where she'd learned about fashion, design, and pattern making. There, she'd met Madame, Maude, and the

Sampsons, and had been given the chance to go to Paris to see couture fashion in person. Her. Annie Wood. In Paris!

The details of the drama at the train station shot by in a flash: André, his mother, little Annie. . . And then the news of the *Titanic*, and the realization that they had been saved from death by the cry of a little boy.

"By Me. You were saved by Me, Annie."

Annie bowed her head in gratitude and humility. *You saved us. A thank-You is not enough.* A promise rose in her heart, and she voiced it to the One who deserved everything—her everything. *I give my life to You. Show me what to do.*

"You know what to do. Just do it."

With the blink of an eye, the moments and people that had sped through her thoughts stepped aside—but for one. And with the recognition of that one person, she knew what God wanted her to do.

During her mental discourse, the others had been talking, and she had no idea how long she had been caught in her reverie. But the nudge to "do it" was strong and could not be ignored a moment longer. She came back to the present and interrupted them. "Sean." She stood and held out her hand to him. "Come with me."

Annie led him down a corridor and out to the deck. She found a private place at the railing and faced him. Her heart pumped with a determined vigor. Her mind was clearer than it had been in months. "My darling Sean. We are alive."

"That we are," he said, leaning forward to kiss her.

She pulled back. "Let me finish."

He stood erect.

"We are alive. We are together when many couples on the *Titanic* have been ripped apart. No matter what happens with our careers, we are a pair, you and I." She glanced out over the sea. "What lasts beyond death is love. No matter what tragedy befalls us, love remains." She took his hands in hers. "I love you, Sean."

"I love you, too, Annie-girl. More than I can say."

"God brought us together. And saved us to be together."

He nodded, and his voice caught in his throat. "I know it with my entire being."

Annie took a deep breath, recognizing this as the pivot point of her life, the point from which she would measure the before and the after. "Ask me."

"Ask you?"

"The question."

His face lit up, as if God's light shone down upon the moment. Then he knelt before her on one knee. "My darling, dear Annie. Would you marry me?"

She kissed him, saying yes to Sean, yes to God, and yes to their future together.

Dear Reader,

Thank you for entering Annie's world! It was a delight to write about her eventful life. Even though she didn't come to New York City to find the American dream, *it* found *her*. We probably all have such stories to tell regarding our ancestors first coming to America.

I have sewn all my life. I didn't have a store-bought dress until I was nearly in college. My mother made all my prom dresses and even the wedding dresses for me and my two sisters. My first job was in a fabric store where I saved up enough money to buy a Pfaff sewing machine. Just this year (after over forty years) it conked out on me! It was like saying good-bye to a friend.

I grew up making garments from multiple patterns and improvising. The true perk of home sewing is being able to create something unique. In many ways, all home seamstresses are pattern artists.

It was fun to incorporate moments of history into Annie's story. I hadn't planned on having her work at Macy's, but when I discovered an old book (1943) called *History of Macy's of New York* by Ralph M. Hower I was hooked. The book painstakingly details the store (including charts of operating data and photos). Discovering that the store she would have worked in on Thirty-Fourth Street was the store that still exists—and is the store in one of my favorite movies, *Miracle on 34th Street*, it was a done deal.

When I discovered that the New York Giants were playing in the World Series in 1911, and that crowds gathered across the street at the *Herald* offices to hear news of the games, it was an added bonus—and games four and five *were* delayed due to rain. I love when history falls at my feet and begs to be used in the story.

I hadn't planned on the *Titanic* being a part of the story, either, but when the dates worked out, and when I discovered that Mr. and Mrs. Straus (he was the owner of Macy's) lost their lives on the ship when she declined to get into a lifeboat, I had to share that bittersweet fact. There are memorials to the love of Isidor and Ida Straus. If you watch the James Cameron movie *Titanic*, they are portrayed as the older couple embracing each other in bed as the ship sinks. I urge you to do an Internet search for them, where you'll find many stories about their amazing love. Brett Gladstone, their great-great-grandson, says, "I have their letters. They spent only ten days apart from each other during their marriage, and then they wrote each other every day." The couple even gets a duet in the musical version of *Titanic*—which leaves the audience weeping. I tear up just thinking of them.

The initial words of the captain of Annie's ship, describing the *Titanic*'s accident, are taken from actual newspaper accounts—that obviously gave false information, and false hope.

The address of the Sampsons (451 Madison Avenue) still exists and is called the Villard House. In 1978 it was altered into Helmsley Palace (remember the notorious Leona Helmsley?).

I also slipped in a reference to some characters from my Manor House series. The love story of Lady Newley (Lila) is shown in *Love of the Summerfields* and *Bride of the Summerfields*, and Henrietta shows up in *Rise of the Summerfields*. I like to intertwine story lines when I can, as it makes the characters seem more real, as if life goes on after the last page. I hope you agree.

So if I didn't plan on Macy's, the World Series, or the *Titanic* being a part of the story, what *was* my story supposed to be about? In a single word: patterns. Ebenezer Butterick changed the world by developing sized patterns. Before his invention, women would have to buy a one-size-does-not-fit-all pattern and try to adapt it. What started out as a home-based business became one of the largest companies in the world. Again, the American dream triumphs! I wouldn't be a home seamstress if not for his invention. Butterick *did* have special pattern shops in Paris, London, Vienna, and Berlin. The Paris shop sold more Butterick patterns than anywhere in the world. There are a few old photos of this shop and the one in London on the Internet and on my Pinterest board for this book.

I stretched for the sake of story in having Annie and her contingent go to the fashion shows in Paris. From what I could determine, usually the fashion representatives from the couture houses came to New York to show their wares, which were then copied. Forgive me for my creative license. It *could* have happened the way I wrote it. It *might* have happened that way.

The Le Grand Hotel in Paris, across from the opera? My husband and I stayed there in the nineties (it's now InterContinental Paris Le Grand Hotel), and the Café de la Paix is still serving fabulous meals. It's interesting how life experiences can sometimes be resurrected and used. Actually, *all* life experiences are fair game to a writer.

I hope you enjoyed *The Pattern Artist*. Please let me hear from you!

Nancy Moser
www.nancymoser.com

Annie's Borrowed Dinner Dress

Chapter 19: "It was created from a peach-colored dupioni silk with a high waist and a daring scooped bodice that gained modesty with a dark brown chiffon covering the upper chest. The neckline was adorned with a wide flat collar of brown satin, with matching cuffs on the three-quarter sleeves. The shorter overskirt was edged in the brown satin that curved from the center front to the back, ending in a short train. Annie had never worn anything so beautiful. To go from wearing the uniform of a housemaid to this?" *The Delineator*, March 1911

Iris's Wedding Dress

Chapter 20: "The high-waisted dress of gray-blue moss cloth had straight three-quarter sleeves, a scooped neckline, and a straight overskirt with a diagonal hem, edged with a twelve-inch band of satin. The overskirt was short enough to reveal the soft drapery of the crepe underskirt. There was little trim, just some braid at the cuff of the sleeve and neckline." *The Delineator*, May 1911; Butterick Pattern #4639

House of Paquin

Chapter 28: "The girl wore a gown of ecru silk covered with delicate lace. The neckline crossed, forming a V, and the sleeves had no seam at the shoulder but were draped from the same piece of fabric as the bodice. The back bodice was the same as the front, but the back of the dress sported full-length pieces of blue silk embroidered at the bottom with mauve roses and green leaves. The blue was pulled around the sides at the empire waistline in the front, and culminated in a pink rosette bow." House of Paquin, 1912

Discussion Questions for *The Pattern Artist*

1. What do you think about Annie's decision to leave her job as a house-maid? What would have happened if she'd stayed?

2. Grasston becomes a threat to Annie and all who know her. Annie stealing his gloves does not seem to be enough to get him sacked. Why do you think he was sacked?

3. Danny's death in Chapter 12, defending Annie from a bully, is a blow to all who knew him. How does his death change Annie and Iris?

4. Chapter 13: Edna talks to Annie about her newly discovered gift to draw. "A talent uncovered is a talent recovered…it's always been there. You just didn't know it was there. It's a known fact that God's gifts can't be returned." What talent have you recovered unexpectedly?

5. Chapter 13: God tries to get Annie's attention, flooding her mind with promises of love and care if only she will choose Him. But she does not. Why do you think Annie hesitates about surrendering to God?

6. Chapter 15: Annie talks about her parents being negative people, bringing everyone around them down. Do you know anyone like that? How do you deal with them?

7. Chapter 15: Sean suggests that Annie doesn't take compliments well, because, "To accept compliments means someone else has seen into your world and has judged it." How is this statement true?

8. Chapter 16: Before Annie calls Butterick to interview for the job she realizes if she *doesn't* call, the answer is automatically a no. She has to risk it. What time in your life did you accept a "no" rather than take a

risk? If you could do it over again, would you handle it differently?

9. Chapter 16: Sean tells Annie: "The old Annie is dead and a new Annie has risen in her place." Name a time in your life when you closed the door on the past and started fresh. Did the new life live up to your expectations? If you haven't done this yet, should you?

10. Chapter 17: Annie took a leap of faith in staying in NYC and not catching the ship back to England with the Kidds. Hebrews 11: 1 says that "faith is confidence in what we hope for and assurance about what we do not see." What leap of faith have you taken, a no-turning-back leap?

11. Should Annie have borrowed the dress? Do you think she got the punishment she deserved?

12. At her dinner party in Chapter 19, Mrs. Sampson tells Annie, "Just be who you are, Annie. Who you are is enough." Is that good advice, or bad? Explain.

13. In Chapter 20, Edna and Annie are stronger from forming a three-strand cord with God. Who in your life creates your cord of strength?

14. Chapter 24: On the Brooklyn Bridge Annie and Sean talk about their dreams. Sean explains his this way: "I dream of knowing I made a difference. I dream of knowing there is a definite reason I was born, a reason I exist now—not a hundred years from now. I dream of knowing that a portion of God's greater plan gets fulfilled through me." Do you have an inkling about why you were born—your purpose? Have you asked God to show you His purpose for you?

15. Chapter 24: Sean's mother encourages Annie to go after her dreams and her career goals. As we know, opportunities for women were lacking in 1911. What woman do you know who gave up their dreams or a career for the sake of getting married? What would you have done in a similar situation? Was it worth the sacrifice?

16. Chapter 25: Maude and Annie discuss their talents and how best to use them. Maude says, "Use your talent discreetly when necessary and boldly when possible." Share examples of people who have done this—and those who have not. How did others react?

17. Chapter 29: Annie and her friends are saved from harm because God gave them a choice. They were not forced to help the little boy at the train station, but because of their kindness, they missed the horrors of the Titanic. Have you ever had such a "save" in your life? Share the details.

18. Chapter 30: Given the choice to take the job offer from the Sampsons, Annie realizes that her life has been full of doors—but more than that: "It's not just a matter of the doors being opened for me, but the fact that every door that opened seemed to shut once I was through it." What doors have you gone through, where the door was shut behind you?

19. Even though Annie didn't come to America to find the American Dream, *it* found *her*. Discuss some of your ancestors who immigrated here. Why did they leave their homes? Did they discover the American Dream?

20. Chapter 32: Annie realized that her old dream was to be a lady's maid. If the door to that dream hadn't been closed, she never would have been propelled into New York City to find a better dream. Name a dream from your past that was exchanged for a larger, better dream.

ABOUT THE AUTHOR

Nancy Moser is an award-winning author of more than twenty-five novels that share a common message: we each have a unique purpose—the trick is to find out what it is. Her genres include contemporary and historical novels including *Love of the Summerfields*, *Mozart's Sister*, *The Invitation*, and the Christy Award–winning *Time Lottery*. She is a fan of anything antique—humans included. www.nancymoser.com.

More Historical Fiction that You'll Love

The Captive Heart by **Michelle Griep**
Paperback / 978-1-63409-783-3 / $14.99

The American wilderness is no place for an elegant English governess on the run from a brutish aristocratic employer, yet Eleanor Morgan escapes from England to America, the land of the free, for the opportunity to serve an upstanding Charles Town family. But freedom is hard to come by as an indentured servant, and downright impossible when she's forced to agree to an even harsher contract—marriage to a man she's never met.

Backwoodsman Samuel Heath doesn't care what others think of him—but his young daughter's upbringing matters very much. The life of a trapper in the Carolina backcountry is no life for a small girl, but neither is abandoning his child to another family. He decides it's time to marry again, but that proves to be an impossible task. Who wants to wed a murderer?

Both Samuel and Eleanor are survivors, facing down the threat of war, betrayal, and divided loyalties that could cost them everything, but this time they must face their biggest challenge ever. . .Love.

Michelle Griep's been writing since she first discovered blank wall space and Crayolas. She seeks to glorify God in all that she writes—except for that graffiti phase she went through as a teenager. She resides in the frozen tundra of Minnesota, where she teaches history and writing classes for a local high school co-op. An Anglophile at heart, she runs away to England every chance she gets, under the guise of research. Really, though, she's eating excessive amounts of scones while rambling around a castle. Michelle is a member of ACFW (American Christian Fiction Writers) and MCWG (Minnesota Christian Writers Guild).